My Enemy's Cradle

MY ENEMY'S CRADLE

SARA YOUNG

THORNDIKE
WINDSOR
PARAGON

This Large Print edition is published by Thorndike Press, Waterville, Maine, USA and by BBC Audiobooks Ltd, Bath, England.
Thorndike Press, a part of Gale, Cengage Learning.
Copyright © 2008 by Sara Young.
The moral right of the author has been asserted.

LIBRARY OF CONGRESS CATALOGING-IN-PUBLICATION DATA

Young, Sara, 1951–
  My enemy's cradle / by Sara Young.
    p. cm. — (Thorndike Press large print reviewers' choice)
    ISBN-13: 978-1-4104-0651-4 (hardcover : alk. paper)
    ISBN-10: 1-4104-0651-2 (hardcover : alk. paper)
    1. Jewish women — Fiction. 2. Pregnant women — Fiction.
  3. Netherlands — History — German occupation, 1940–1945 —
Fiction. 4. World War, 1939–1945 — Netherlands — Fiction. 5.
Large type books. I. Title.
  PS3625.O973M9 2008b
  813'.6—dc22   2008000923

BRITISH LIBRARY CATALOGUING-IN-PUBLICATION DATA AVAILABLE

Published in 2008 in the U.S. by arrangement with Harcourt, Inc.
Published in 2008 in the U.K. by arrangement with HarperCollins Publishers.

U.K. Hardcover: 978 1 405 64947 6 (Windsor Large Print)
U.K. Softcover: 978 1 405 64948 3 (Paragon Large Print)

Printed in the United States of America
1 2 3 4 5 6 7 12 11 10 09 08

*To the mothers and children who were
lost to each other*

ONE

September 1941

"Not here, too! *Nee!*"

From the doorway, I saw soup splash from my aunt's ladle onto the tablecloth. These days, there was no fat in the broth to set a stain; still, my heart dropped when she made no move to blot the spill. Since the Germans had come, she had retreated further into herself, fading away in front of me so that sometimes it was like losing my mother all over again.

"Of course here, Mies," my uncle scoffed. His pale face pinked with the easy flush of red-haired men, and he leaned back and took off his glasses to polish them on his napkin. "Did you think the Germans would annex us as a refuge for Jews? The question is only why it took so long."

I brought the bread to the table and took my seat. "What's happened?"

"They posted a set of restrictions for Jews

today," my uncle said. "They'll scarcely be able to leave their homes." He inspected his glasses, put them back on. And then he turned to look at me directly.

I froze, my fingertips whitening around my spoon, suddenly reminded of something I'd witnessed in childhood.

Walking home from school, a group of us had come upon a man beating his dog. All of us shouted at him to stop — our numbers made us brave — and some of the bigger boys even tried to pull him off the poor animal. A boy beside me caught my attention; this boy, I knew, was himself often beaten by the older boys. He was crying, *"Stop! Stop it!"* along with the rest of us. But something in his expression chilled me: satisfaction. When my uncle turned to look at me, I saw that boy's face again.

"Things will be different now, Cyrla."

I dropped my gaze to my plate, but I felt my heart begin to pound. Was he weighing the risk of having me in his home?

His home. I stared down at the white tablecloth. Beneath it, a table rug was edged with gold silk fringe. When I had first arrived it had seemed strange to cover a table this way, but now I knew every color and pattern of its design. I lifted my eyes to take in the room I had come to love: the tall

8

windows painted crisp white overlooking our small courtyard; the three watercolors of the Rijksmuseum hanging in a column on their braided cord; the glimpse into the parlor beyond the burgundy velvet drapes, where the piano stood in the corner, necklaced with framed photographs of our family. My heart began to beat even faster — where did I belong if not here?

I glanced at my cousin — Anneke was my safe passage through the treacherous landscape of my uncle's world. But she had been distracted all day, drifting away whenever I'd tried to talk to her, as if she was harboring a secret. She hadn't even heard her father's threat.

"What?" I kept my voice calm. "What will be different here?"

He was cutting the bread. He didn't stop, but I saw the warning look he gave my aunt. "Everything." He cut three slices from the loaf and then laid the knife down carefully. "Everything will be different."

I drew the loaf toward me, picked up the knife as deliberately as a chess piece, and cut a fourth slice. I laid the knife back on the board, then placed my hands on my lap so he wouldn't see them trembling. I lifted my chin and leveled my eyes at him. "You counted wrong, Uncle," I said. He looked away, but his face was dark as a bruise.

At last the meal was over. My uncle returned to his shop to take care of his bookkeeping, and my aunt and Anneke and I cleared the table and went into the kitchen to wash the dishes. We worked in silence; I in my fear, my aunt in her sadness, Anneke deep in her secret.

Suddenly Anneke cried out. The bread knife clattered to the floor and she held up her hand; blood streamed into the basin of suds, tingeing the bubbles pink. I grabbed a dishcloth and pressed it around Anneke's hand, then led her to the window seat. She sank down and stared at the blood seeping through the dishcloth as though it was a curiosity. I grew afraid, then. Anneke was vain about her hands, would go without her ration of milk sometimes to soak them in it instead, and she could still find nail polish when it seemed no one in Holland had such a luxury. If she didn't carry on about a cut deep enough to scar, then her secret was very big.

My aunt knelt to examine the wound, chiding her for her carelessness. Anneke closed her eyes and tipped her head back; with her free hand she stroked the hollow at the base of her throat with a contented smile. It was the look she wore when she crept back into our room in the middle of the night . . . flushed and deepened, re-arranged.

I did not like Karl.

And then I knew.

"What have you done?" I whispered to her when my aunt left to fetch the disinfectant and muslin.

"Later," she whispered back. "When everyone is asleep."

There was ironing and darning to do, and that night it seemed to take forever. We listened to Hugo Wolf's music on the pho-nograph while we did these chores, and I wished for silence again because for the first time I could hear how the tragedy of Wolf's life flowed through his music. The beauty itself was doomed. When my aunt said good night, Anneke and I exchanged looks and went upstairs as well.

We washed quickly and put on our night-clothes. I couldn't wait another moment. "Tell me now."

My cousin turned to me, and I'd never seen her smile so beautifully.

"A wonderful thing, Cyrla," she said, reaching down to stroke her belly.

The cut on her finger had begun to bleed again; the bandage was soaked through. As she stood in front of me smiling and caress-

11

ing her belly, a smear of blood bloomed across the pale blue cotton of her night-gown.

Two

"I'm leaving. I'm leaving here!" Now Anneke could hardly stop talking. "We'll get married here, at the town hall I suppose. Karl's family lives outside Hamburg — maybe we'll get a place there when the war is over, with a garden for children, near a park, maybe. . . . Hamburg, Cyrla!"

"Shhhhhh!" I quieted her. "She'll hear." It wasn't my aunt we were careful of, but Mrs. Bakker in the next house, which shared a wall with ours. She was old and had nothing better to do with her days than spy on people and gossip about what she'd learned. She sat in her front parlor all morning long and watched the goings-on of Tielman Oemstraat through the two mirrors attached to her windows. We knew from her coughing that her bedroom was next to ours, and we didn't think it would be beneath her to hold a glass to the wall. But I didn't really care about Mrs. Bakker at all. I wanted to stop Anneke's words.

I unwrapped her finger and cleaned it with water from the wash pitcher. "Change your nightgown. I'll go downstairs for more bandages." Out in the hall, I made myself breathe calmly again. I gathered the muslin strips, and also a cup of milk and a plate of *spekulaas* — Anneke had hardly eaten at supper, but she loved the little spice cookies she smuggled home from the bakery. If I distracted her, I wouldn't have to hear her plans. And if she saw how much she needed me, she might understand that it was a mistake to leave. It was always a mistake to leave.

We sat on her bed and I dressed her finger; I couldn't look into her face although I felt her studying mine. "Are you sure? And how did this even . . . weren't you careful . . . ?"

Anneke looked away. "These things happen." Then she broke into her brilliant smile, the one that always disarmed me. "A baby . . . think of it!"

I wrapped my arms around her and laid my head on her chest, breathing in the scent she brought home to us from the bakery each day — baked sugar, sweet and warm, so perfectly suited to her. What scent clung to me, I wondered. Vinegar from the pickling

14

I'd been doing all week? Lye from the upholstery shop?

Anneke stroked the tears from my cheeks. "I'm sorry, Cyrla," she said. "I'll miss you so much. More than anyone else."

That was my cousin's way. Sometimes she was careless with my feelings — not in cruelty, but in the innocent way that beautiful girls sometimes have, as if being thoughtful were a skill they had never needed to learn. But when she did think of me, her sweetness, completely unmeasured, would fill me with shame.

"But I'm so happy!" she cried, as if her face weren't already telling me this. "And he's so handsome!" She fell back onto the bed, clutching her heart. "He looks just like Rhett Butler, don't you think?"

I sighed in mock exasperation. "He looks nothing like Rhett Butler, for heaven's sakes. For one thing, he's blond."

Anneke waved this detail away with her bandaged hand.

"And he has blue eyes. And no mustache." I rose and brought the glass of milk from the dresser over to her night table. "All right. He's handsome. But frankly, my dear, I don't give a damn."

Anneke laughed and sat up. "You'll be an aunt! And the war will be over soon, and

15

then you can visit."

I knew she believed it would be that easy. Everything in Anneke's life was easy; her very name meant grace, and sometimes it seemed as if grace poured over her from the skies, so abundantly she could scoop it up in her pretty hands and let it sluice through her fingers.

She never acknowledged that my situation was different. When I had first come, she seemed to have decided that I had simply left my Jewish half in Poland, exactly as I had left my childhood there. *Oh, yes,* she might have thought if she ever questioned it, *Cyrla was a little girl in Poland, and she was Jewish, but look: She's not a little girl anymore!* Here in Holland, I lived as everyone around me did, and since I looked enough like her that we were often mistaken for sisters, she viewed me as just that.

In Poland, I had lived with my father, his second wife, and my two little half-brothers. With his remarriage, my father had become more observant, and we began to celebrate Jewish traditions. After a while, I seemed to bear nothing of my Dutch mother except her blond hair.

In fact, Anneke's view was the very argument my father had used when the idea of fleeing to Holland seemed to me a betrayal.

"You are not denying half of yourself by accepting the other half. You are correcting something that has been unbalanced. Go to your mother's world. Learn to fit inside her life, and you will find how she fits in yours."

The first Friday after I'd arrived in Holland, I'd stood in the center of the parlor as the sun went down, feeling lost without my stepmother lighting the candles to mark the beginning of the Sabbath. My aunt had noticed; she shook her head and then came over and held me tight. "No," she had whispered. Five years later, Friday evening was just another evening. I kept track of the holy days in my head, but I'd learned to sweep aside any feelings of guilt about not celebrating them. Any day now, I told myself, it will be safe again to go home. To become again who I used to be.

Poland was a very long time ago.

But Anneke should have known how devastating her choice of husband would be to me. Instead, she denied the other half of the issue as completely as she denied the Jewish half of me.

"He's a boatbuilder," she argued in the beginning when my aunt and I tried to persuade her not to see Karl. "He's not a Nazi. He was conscripted. He didn't have a choice."

No one else felt this way about the German soldiers. Anneke's friends sometimes bragged that they were going out with them and were going to get them drunk and push them into a canal, although I never heard of any dying that way. We all passed along jokes about the soldiers — ridiculing them made the Occupation more bearable. And everyone did their part to foil the Nazis when they could: switching road signs, pretending not to understand German when asked for directions, or painting *OZO* — Orange Will Conquer — wherever we could in our forbidden national color.

Anneke was different though. I should have seen right away how she was with this one. I should have stopped it.

Because I wouldn't have liked Karl any better if he had been a soldier in the Dutch army. I had met him only once, a week before. Anneke had arranged for us to meet at the bakery, when he picked her up, as though by accident, so I could get a look at him, see how handsome he was. And he was. Although the only way a man could be attractive to me was Isaak's way: dark, with serious, concerned eyes. Karl was fair and tall, and there was something closed about his face. When Anneke introduced us, his eyes slid past me. If he had been anxious to gaze at Anneke, I would have understood, would have liked him for that, but I remember instead he was scanning the shop, as if looking for an escape. I did not tell Anneke this.

"Well, his eyes," I told her instead, "the clear blue of them against the white, remind me of hyacinths blooming against a late snowfall." This pleased her and in fact it was true. But now I wished I had told her what I had sensed — what kind of man he was.

So much was wrong, but that first night all I could think of was that Anneke was leaving me. My throat was so swollen with all I wanted to say that I could say nothing at all. I turned out the light and rolled over to face away from her, but I couldn't sleep.

Around midnight, I needed to use the toilet. I crept out into the hall quietly, so as not to wake anyone, and as I passed my aunt and uncle's room I heard their voices.

". . . if it means putting our family in danger," my uncle said.

"She *is* our family, Pieter," my aunt replied, angry with him.

"She's *your* family," my uncle corrected her. "Not *our* family, *yours.*"

In the morning, I watched Anneke as she

19

got ready for work. I could tell by the care she took dressing that she was going to see Karl afterward.

"When will you tell your parents?" I asked from my bed.

"Well, I'll tell Mama tonight, I think." She chose a lipstick the color of ripe cherries and stained her mouth. "First I want to tell Karl."

I sat up. *"Anneke!"*

She laughed and flicked her fingers at me in the mirror in that way she always did — as if worries were merely little gnats she had to chase away. "He'll be happy; he wants a large family. He has a new niece he adores."

"But all the plans?"

"You're too serious, *katje!*" She hadn't called me Kitten for a long time. It was the name she'd given me when I had first arrived, when I was only fourteen and she was sixteen. She came over and sat beside me on the bed. "Give me your hand. I'll read your fortune."

I held out my hand and she kissed it, leaving a heart-shaped lipstick stain on my palm. "Look at that," she said. "That's a very good sign — it means you're going to fall in love soon. And you'll get married, too, and you'll live happily ever after and we'll both have ten children and they'll all have ten children and you and I are going to grow old together and always be happy."

I curled my fingers over the mark on my palm. "Are you sure about this, Anneke? Do you even love him?"

Anneke went back to her bureau and pulled her clips from her hair and combed out her waves before she answered. "I'm *in* love with him. I want to get married . . . and there aren't as many men around, now that they're diving under. Have you noticed that?" She sighed and turned from the mirror. "He loves me. I want to get out of here. And now I'm pregnant. I think that's enough." She came over to me and sat on the bed. "Here, let me brush your hair. You ought to let me cut it before I go. No one wears it this way anymore, and you'd be so beautiful."

I would never be beautiful. Anneke and I shared the same features — our mothers' features — but fine breads and coarse loaves are made from the same ingredients. And I would never cut my hair; I wore it braided and pinned up, as my mother had. I let Anneke brush it out loose, and when she left, I didn't go downstairs right away. I folded her nightgown, placed it under her pillow, and put the cover back on her lipstick. I straightened the pictures she had cut from magazines and tucked along the mirror's frame: Princess Elizabeth and Princess Margaret, Gary Cooper, Carole Lombard. What would this room be like empty of her things? Empty of *her?*

After my mother died, my father had paced through the house gathering up her things without looking at them, his face set in angry lines. Everything she had touched, packed in dark boxes. It had hurt him too much to see them. But it had hurt me more not to. I sank down on Anneke's bed, suddenly stung with tears.

Later that day, as I set the brushes and pail out on the front steps to scrub them, Mrs. Bakker called to me from her doorway.

"Have you heard the news? The Nuremberg Laws are to be implemented here."

"Ja," I agreed carefully, pouring the water over the steps. I had heard, although I didn't think my uncle had said so exactly. I bent over the bricks and began to work.

"It will be very bad for Jews here, I think," she continued, and something in her voice made me wary. "For anyone with Jewish blood."

I forced my arms to continue scrubbing, but suddenly I didn't have enough air, and the sounds of the street spun together into a whine. I kept my head down, focusing on the pattern of blue and gray tiles that bordered the threshold, so she wouldn't see my reaction. Never since I'd arrived had anyone asked me about my father or my life in Poland. Never, as far as I knew, had my aunt or uncle explained why I had come, except to refer vaguely to my mother's death. It was a subject we didn't even discuss among ourselves.

"Well," said Mrs. Bakker, "take care of yourself, Cyrla." She closed her door.

I finished the steps as quickly as I could. Inside, my aunt was peeling pears — she had been stewing and canning fruit for weeks.

"I'll do the shopping now," I told her, taking the ration coupons from the shelf. I didn't wait for a reply; I grabbed my bicycle and set out.

But not to the market square.

THREE

I took the bicycle path along the Burgemeester Knappertlaan, which I usually
avoided in favor of smaller streets that
didn't border the canal. Despite the years
I'd lived in the Netherlands, I'd never
grown comfortable with so much water,
waiting deep and black behind the hunched
shoulders of the banks. Nearly a year and a
half since the bombings in Rotterdam, I
imagined I could still smell the smoke on
the canals, and in fact they still carried
cinders and chunks of rubble washing down
from the seaport. I couldn't help but wonder
how long bits of charred human flesh or
bones floated in that sour brine also —
nearly a thousand people died that day,
burned in the hot oven of our ruined city
— and so I took pains to stay away. Today
the fog rose up from the water like cold
breath, but I needed to see Isaak, and the
route along the canal was the shortest to

the Jewish Council.

A board nailed to the trunk of a willow caught my attention. I pulled over and read the words lettered on it. *Park — No Admittance to Jews.* Another sign was on the gate to the Promenade. I looked ahead; every clump of trees had apparently been declared a park: *No Admittance to Jews.* I began to pedal again and tried to see only the flaming scarlet and gold of the chrysanthemums that burned along the banks.

The Council was located in the first floor of a worn brick building, which had once housed a bank, a fish market, and an ice-cream parlor, all of which had closed after the yellow "J"s had been painted on their windows. I had been here many times before with Isaak as he picked up papers or stopped in to speak with someone. Always it had been a simple matter of walking through the doors. But this day was different. Two Gestapo leaned against the gate in their long green coats and black boots, smoking and looking bored. A third stood by the door nailing up a notice. The new restrictions. I stood behind him to read them.

He turned. "This is no business of yours."

I moved to pass into the building, but he blocked me. "Nothing here is any of your business."

"I'm looking for a friend."

"You should know better than to have friends inside here." By the way he looked at me, I could tell it amused him to think a Dutch girl would want to enter this place.

"I need to go inside," I tried again. "I want to find someone."

Now he wasn't so pleasant. "You should be more careful choosing your friends."

One of the other agents stubbed out his cigarette and raised his eyes to us.

I got back on my bicycle and rode the few blocks to the synagogue. Rabbi Geron was in his office; yes, Isaak had been called to a meeting in Delft the night before, he said, although, no, he didn't know when to expect him back. I asked him to take me to Isaak's room. If he was surprised, he didn't show it, and this thrilled me somehow, as if I had stolen an intimacy. I found myself smiling as we crossed the stone courtyard that separated the synagogue from the small outbuilding where Isaak lived.

Before the Occupation, this building had housed offices and storage rooms. Now, anyone who needed shelter could stay here. Isaak told me a lawyer had come, and a man who had lost his position as a professor and was now alone after sending his wife and daughter to relatives in America. The old man who cared for the grounds slept here as well, and a fifteen-year-old boy, recently orphaned.

"Do you make a family for yourselves?" I had asked Isaak once. "The boy, is he a brother? Is the professor a father to you?" He had just looked at me, puzzled.

In all the time I'd known Isaak I'd never been inside. As in everything else, he kept what was most private to himself. But when Rabbi Geron opened the door to Isaak's room, I would have known it among a thousand as his.

A single cot in the corner was made neatly with a gray-and-blue–striped blanket. The goosenecked lamp beside his bed was the only curved line in the room. Books were everywhere, but in orderly stacks. Two prints of da Vinci drawings and half a dozen maps hung on the walls, all perfectly aligned.

A cracked white china mug on the desk held a stick of charcoal and three pencils. I lifted each one for the pleasure of touching something Isaak had touched. Beside the mug were two drawing pads. The smaller, I knew, was full of his bird drawings — he loved to draw birds, although he seldom took the time now. I picked up the larger pad and opened to a sketch of the castle ruins at the edge of town. I remembered walking there with him the previous spring and sitting a distance away working on a poem while he sketched, feeling hurt that he wouldn't show me his drawing later or ask to see what I'd written.

Isaak had captured the sense of abiding strength in the old bricks and stone, solid yet softened. But there were no people in the scene, none of the picnickers or lovers reading to each other on their blankets whom I had watched in jealousy, none of the small children running with their dogs. And he had drawn the branches of the chestnut tree rising above the ruins bare of their leaves, like blackened bones. I felt a small chill: Isaak had drawn this scene only a few weeks before the Germans had come with their bombs.

For a few moments more I stood there, breathing in Isaak's air. Tomorrow I would come back with a pot of geraniums for his windowsill. And a basket of apples, and I would take the curtains from my own bedroom window and hang them here for him. Pleased, I took off my shoes and slipped into his bed. Lying there with the scent of him on his sheets, it was easy to imagine Isaak beside me. I slipped my hand

28

into my dress and stroked my breast softly, and felt it swell.

When I awoke, Isaak was sitting beside me. I could tell by the light it was late in the afternoon. "So you heard," he said.

I was confused; how did he know about Anneke?

"But you shouldn't have come here."

"Anneke's leaving," I said, reaching for him. "She's pregnant."

Isaak rose and looked down at me. I couldn't tell if it was worry or anger in his eyes, but as always I thrilled to have them on me alone. "You shouldn't have come here," he repeated. "What were you thinking?" He glanced at my neck.

The new decrees. I pulled out my legitimization card, which I wore around my neck on a thin cord. "I'm wearing it, Isaak. I was careful! Did you hear me? Anneke's getting married. I can't bear it if she leaves!"

"If she's pregnant, that's her own stupidity."

Isaak was always short of compassion when it came to Anneke. "She's spoiled," he often said. "She has to wear lisle stockings instead of silk now, coffee is too expensive to drink every day, and she can't see the newest films. Well, too bad. All over

29

Europe people are losing their homes, their freedoms. Their lives."

"*Ja,* I know," I would always agree. What I never admitted, though, was how much I loved this about Anneke. Just a week before the invasion, she and I had seen *Ninotchka.* When I was with her, it was possible to believe that any day now we would be able to go to Greta Garbo's next film, or enjoy the feel of silk on our legs, or drink coffee in the middle of the day and gossip about fashion. We could think about entering the university again. And Isaak might allow himself to fall in love. *His* luxury.

"*Verdamt!*" Isaak swore softly. He ran his long fingers through his curls, in the way that always made me want to reach out and do the same. "That German soldier? This is bad. Has she told him?"

I stared at him, not understanding.

"Cyrla, it's going to come out, who you really are."

"Anneke would never do that."

"You can't walk around blind just because you don't want to see. Anneke won't care. She'll do whatever suits her."

"Why are you always so hard on her?"

"Because she's too easy on herself!"

Isaak said it as though he knew Anneke, but he didn't. Not the way I did. It was an old argument.

He sat beside me again. I tried to wrap my arms around him, but he held me away. "You're not safe anymore. It's time for you to leave. I'll start the arrangements."

"Don't. Nothing's changed."

"Everything will change. You heard about the restrictions yesterday."

"They don't affect me. And Anneke won't . . . Isaak, all these years — how many times have you told me I'm not even Jewish because of my mother? Now, suddenly you're deciding I am?"

"To the Germans you are."

"I have papers. I'm perfectly safe. And I can't leave — this is where my father wants me to be."

Isaak looked away. "Don't. You know where this leads."

I did. I hadn't heard from my father in nearly five months. In his last letter, he reported that the Lodz ghetto was to be sealed. A few months before, he said, girls my age were forced to clean latrines with their blouses. When they were finished, the German overseers wrapped the filthy blouses around their heads. I'd gone to school with some of these girls. *I am grateful you are not here,* my father wrote.

If my family was in Lodz when they sealed

the ghetto, Isaak said, then they couldn't have left afterward. Unless they had been relocated. "Relocated" meant something too terrible to be possible. His logic was harsh. He read me transcripts from his intelligence.

"Not my family," I would remind him. "They're working in a factory. That will keep them safe, my father told me."

Isaak shook his head. "Not for long. We think they're emptying the ghetto. They're taking them to the camps." He didn't stop even when I wept. I had to accept it, to know that my family might be lost; I had to know the danger. Most of all, I had to learn to be strong.

I hated Isaak when he did this, but I forgave him, because it was just his nature to see the worst, to see demons where none existed. He relied too much on logic, but I knew logic was not always the clearest lens. He should have understood; after all, he told me often enough that drawings told more truth than photographs — it took a human being to find the essence in things. But he'd been orphaned at birth, without a family. He couldn't know what I knew.

I knew how much life was in my father. I knew his passion for music and how much he loved his children; I had seen him dance with my mother. People with that much life couldn't disappear. My family's spirit was strong. Not hearing from my father only meant it was dangerous for him to write. His silence was keeping my brothers safe. Isaak and I had stopped arguing about this months ago.

"Last week we got two families out on a fishing boat from Noordwijk. They made it to England. There are still ways. You have papers; it won't be that difficult."

"I'm not leaving," I replied calmly.

"You have to. Anneke's marriage puts you at greater risk."

I was glad I hadn't mentioned Mrs. Bakker's words, or what I had overheard my uncle say. I got out of the bed and stepped into my shoes without looking at Isaak. If I looked at him, I would see the way his hair curled behind his ears, or the gold flecks in his brown eyes, or the crease in his cheek where he wore his rare smile, and I wouldn't be able to walk out of his room. If I didn't walk out of his room, I knew what I would say next: that I couldn't leave because I loved him, and because I had done enough leaving and he had had enough leaving done to him. And I couldn't bear to hear his answer. I crossed to the door.

Isaak followed and reached out to hold

the door shut. His sudden nearness made my breath catch. "You can't go now. Wait until it's dark. Phone your aunt if you need to." He opened the door. "There's a telephone in the hall. I'll take you."

"I can find it," I told him coolly. How could he even think of sending me away? If you send people away, they can be lost forever. But it didn't matter. I was nineteen; no one could make me do anything I didn't want to do.

I called my aunt, suddenly hungry for her voice. From her tone, I could tell she hadn't heard Anneke's news yet — she wouldn't be able to keep this from me. I asked to speak to her.

"She's not here," Tante Mies said. "I thought she might be with you. She was to work until three, so I thought you had met. I suppose she's with that man. And where are you, Cyrla? You're not with . . . your uncle says that now with the new restrictions . . ."

"I'll be home soon." I hung up and walked back to Isaak's room. Inside, the space between us loomed huge, silent. Isaak took a thick book from the shelf, *Birds of Europe*, and placed it on his desk. From the window sash he drew out a fine wire I hadn't noticed before. I watched over his shoulder as he

34

opened the book. Inside, fitted into a hollowed-out rectangle, was a radio. The *Birds of Europe* were songbirds.

He fitted the wires together and made adjustments, and in a moment I heard the radio crackle. The broadcast was from the BBC, and as my English was poor and there was a lot of static, I could catch only a few words.

"The news is bad today," Isaak said, after he had disassembled the radio. "Eighteen thousand Jews murdered in the Ukraine, at Berdichev. Nearly twenty-five thousand in Kamenets-Podolski last week. Hitler is stepping things up there. But Churchill didn't address it. He talked only of the *Einsatzgruppen* in Russia, as if the killings were a military defense instead of murders."

"Then maybe it's not true," I tried.

"It's true. I think he can't say it publicly because then the Nazis would know he's getting this information. I hope that's it. But he knows. And Roosevelt knows. What we heard from Berdichev was confirmed by the London underground. Also that the numbers are high in Lithuania. It's getting very bad in the east, especially in the Baltic countries."

"But not in Lodz."

"Not in Lodz."

"And not here." I regretted it immediately.

"What does it matter? Eighteen thousand, twenty-five thousand!" Isaak frowned and rubbed his forehead. "No, not here. Yet. But it's only a matter of time. After the restrictions, we'll be forced to wear the stars. After the stars, the ghettos; and after the ghettos, the deportations. It's the same pattern in every country. There are 140,000 Jews in the Netherlands. Maybe not enough to make us a priority right now. But soon, I think. If Anneke is marrying a German soldier, you have to leave."

"Anneke loves me."

"She'll be careless. She doesn't understand the danger . . . she doesn't need to. You need to, and you won't understand. That's worse. Sometimes, Cyrla. . . ."

"This isn't your decision to make," I said quietly, and gathered my things to go home.

FOUR

My aunt was sitting on the window seat in the kitchen. An issue of *Libelle* and a cup of tea were beside her, untouched. I put the ration coupons back. She didn't notice.

"You know how she is," I said, unbuttoning my cardigan. "It's not even eight o'clock." I moved to take my aunt's cup, to put fresh tea in it if it were cold. "She's fine," I added, irritated with Anneke. It was just like her to forget about everyone else if she were having a good time.

My aunt caught my wrist. "There were soldiers everywhere today . . . new checkpoints. . . ."

I put her cup down and pulled away. "What would they want with Anneke?" *What about me?* I wanted to ask. *I'm the one you should worry about with those new checkpoints.*

Then I froze.

The scent of baked sugar.

"Wait here." I ran up the stairs to the attic and threw open the door to the bedroom there, unused since Anneke's grandmother had died. She lay on the bed on her side, facing the wall. The light from the hall curved along the silhouette of her hip. She looked diminished and vulnerable. I knelt beside her, my arm around her shoulder.

"Tell me."

Anneke turned her face to me.

"He's stupid," I whispered. I peeled a little moonstone earring from her jaw; a lacy pattern was pressed into her wet skin from the gold filigree. She had been weeping for hours. "He doesn't deserve you." Suddenly I felt guilty, as if my not wanting her to leave had caused this. I was sorry for everything I had wanted to steal from my cousin. "You don't have to keep the baby. Or you can, and I'll help you."

Anneke found my hand. New tears pooled, but she still didn't speak.

"Your mother's worried. You need to tell her. Can you . . . ? Never mind." I kissed her cheek. "I won't be long."

My aunt's face crumpled when I told her about Anneke's pregnancy. She pressed her hands over her mouth and looked as if I were striking her. It had never occurred to me that she had held secret dreams for her daughter, but now they lay exposed in her eyes, and it was terrible to watch them shatter and die. She didn't say anything to blame Anneke, or even Karl, but I could see her tighten her lips against the words.

We brought Anneke down to her own bed and for an hour we simply cared for her. We brushed her hair and put on a fresh nightgown. I put a clean bandage on her finger — the wound was not healing well. Anneke allowed us to do these things, but she stared past us to the window as if she could see through the blackout paper. I made her cocoa and toast with the last of the gooseberry jam, her favorite, then brought up the blue-and-white Delft vase of yellow tea roses from the kitchen windowsill. My aunt asked no questions, only murmured, *"Lieveling, lieveling."* I wondered how much it cost her to swallow every "How could you?" and "If only." The branching nature of consequences was so easy to see when it was too late.

At last Anneke sat up and began to talk. It wasn't that Karl didn't love her. But he had to leave. He was being sent back to Germany. Worse, he had a fiancée in Hamburg; they would marry when he got there. Anneke broke down again. "She doesn't mean anything to him," she managed. "But he has no choice. He's promised her."

I was filled with indignation — at Anneke, for defending this man, and at Karl, too: How foolish, to marry someone he didn't love, and leave Anneke alone with his child. Keeping his promise had nothing to do with real honor. I would find him in the morning and make him see.

Anneke suddenly remembered her father. "He's in Amsterdam," Tante Mies told her. "He went this afternoon for a shipment of wool. It was held up and he's spending the night." Anneke slumped in relief. "But he'll be home tomorrow on the evening train," Tante Mies warned her. "And you know we can't keep this from him."

Anneke's eyes pleaded for more time. "It will be all right," my aunt assured her, stroking her forehead. "I'll tell him, and it will be all right."

My aunt gave Anneke a sleeping pill and asked me to stay and read to her until it took effect. I looked around the room for the right book. A new collection by Verwey was by my bed. Also Rilke's *Poems from the Book of Hours,* its pages thickened from my constant fingering. I loved Rilke. It seemed to me he had fired his poems through time like arrows directly into my heart. But those poems would wound Anneke tonight.

I asked my aunt to bring up the copy of *Libelle* I had seen in the kitchen. It was a women's magazine, full of foolish articles that Anneke and I swore we were too worldly for, but devoured every month. It was a good choice, and soon Anneke fell asleep.

I couldn't, though. I went back up to the attic room and pushed the bed under the skylight, climbed up, and opened it to look out. Before the Germans attacked, Anneke and I used to love to do this; from this vantage point we could see the whole skyline of Rotterdam and the harbor at the mouth of the River Maas. No matter the time, the city was always bright with life. The night of May 14, the whole family had stared in disbelief at the charred silhouette of our lost city, black against the flames, until we could not breathe the sooty proof any longer. A snowstorm of ash covered our town for days as Rotterdam burned — the Germans shot anyone who tried to put out a fire as a warning to the rest of us. We hadn't looked out again after that night.

Now I needed to look. Light from a waning quarter moon — since the blackout restrictions, we had all become experts in the phases of the moon — spilled over the dark city, which still looked ragged and

41

scorched after a year and a half. There were a few dull lights to the east, where the docks were; probably the Germans working their sleek gray boats. I planned the things I would say to Karl in the morning. Whatever it took, I would say.

Then I closed the skylight and sat on the bed — I had things to say to Isaak as well. I went over the conversations we had had earlier. He wanted me to leave because he loved me. Isaak would never tell me this; it wasn't his nature to talk about how he felt. It was for me to wring the softer meaning from his hard words.

But I was safe now. There would be no German husband for Anneke to tell, and as long as no one knew I was half-Jewish, the new decrees had no effect on me. Besides, they were only decrees. Insulting and inconvenient, but not threatening. Isaak worried too much about things that might never happen. If it ever came that he was in danger, then we would leave. We would leave together. I would make him see this.

I awoke at dawn, left a note, and cycled into town.

My aunt was right: There were more soldiers now. Pairs of them stood at each entrance to the park across the street; others were nailing up notices. More were at each tram stop, checking ID cards. One of them glanced at me as I rode by; even when he touched his helmet and smiled, my heart skidded. Karl's unit was billeted in several of the houses on Ruyterstraat — Anneke had shown me which one last week. By the time I got to it I wasn't sure my legs would hold me. But I knew a trick to make myself do things when I was afraid: I told myself I just had to take the first step.

Today, for example, I merely had to knock on a door. After that, I could leave.

A grandmotherly woman, short and fat, with an old-fashioned white cap and a long apron answered the door. *"Goedemorgen!"* She smiled up at me and I wished her good morning back, and that was that. In another moment, I had asked to see the German soldier named Karl. And then I was in her kitchen, which was rose-colored and smelled of cloves and bleach and normalcy, and she was offering me coffee. "Ersatz, phhht!" She grimaced and rolled her eyes as if to say, *What are we going to do about it, eh?*

She led me to the back door. "There they are; they take their exercises in the garden. Last week they stomped all over my jasmine. Go on out."

Two soldiers. They had their backs to me

43

but I could tell neither was Karl. My chest began to squeeze again, but I had no choice now. They turned at the sound of my footsteps, and I was shocked to see how young they were.

I asked for Karl Getz.

"He's gone," the taller one said. This boy had brown hair and a round face, and didn't even look as if he shaved yet.

"When will he be back?"

The soldier narrowed his eyes for a second, then seemed to decide I was no threat. "No, he's gone. Munich. You missed him by an hour."

My German was good, but I was sure I had misunderstood. "Munich? He wasn't ordered back to Hamburg?"

No, both of them assured me, Karl wasn't going to Hamburg. They exchanged looks, and then the other boy, the quieter one, whose hair was lighter and curly, took a step toward me and asked if I were Karl's girlfriend.

I ignored the question. "What about his fiancée? Will they still be married?"

The soldiers looked at each other again, smirked. "I guess he's been keeping a secret from us."

And then I understood. "Never mind."

"Wait," the shorter one said. "What's your name?"

I saw he was nothing more than lonely, so eager to talk for a minute that I felt sorry for him. "No, I . . . I'm sorry I bothered you." I turned to leave, but he tried again.

"I just wondered if . . ." He stopped and looked away, then brushed at his hair as though it had fallen over his forehead. I heard him take a sharp breath and then he looked back at me. "I wondered if you wanted to do something tonight . . . go to a café? It's only that you look very much like my sister, and I haven't seen her for so long."

I mumbled an excuse about having to work at night, and fled.

I pedaled over the cobbled streets as fast as I could. The world was cracking in two. One world held boy soldiers who missed their sisters and longed to sit in cafés with girls. The other held men who wrapped girls' heads in latrine filth, and sliced my family from me, and who would not let me pass into a park or a tram if they knew who I was.

The world was cracking in two, and I was falling into the void.

FIVE

All that day before my uncle arrived, we waited as if for a storm. Even the air was heavy. I phoned the bakery and said Anneke had sprained her ankle. We made ourselves busy; we washed windows, made apple dumplings and pea soup. We cleaned out the hearth and took blankets from chests and aired them in preparation for winter. We never once mentioned Anneke's condition or speculated on my uncle's reaction to it, but every time I stole a glance at my aunt's face, it was folded in worry. My cousin's face was blank, and this was worse. I wanted to smash something, or scream.

Finally I couldn't bear it anymore. "Anneke and I are leaving now," I said, in the middle of the afternoon. We had planned to go out in the evening, just before my uncle's train was due, to eat our dinner at a café while my aunt was to eat with him at home. She had bought him his favorite pickled ham and would speak to him after the meal. This wouldn't have been my way. I would have simply said to him: Here's what's happened. Now accept it and support your daughter. I wouldn't have fed him delicacies to make the news more palatable.

Anneke was content to follow my lead. We took the train into Scheveningen. The afternoon was warm, so we took off our shoes and stockings and strolled along the strand, and then walked out to the end of the pier, hanging out over the pilings to watch the fishing boats unload in the sunset. We hadn't seen a single German soldier since getting off the train, and miraculously there was nothing to remind us of the Occupation except some bunkers built on the dunes — the kind that always made us laugh, painted to look like Dutch houses with silly windows and geraniums. Did the Germans really hope they would fool anyone?

We found a bistro and drank beer and ate fried flounder, and then a cake with cherries. We talked about nothing troubling, as if we had laid our problems beside us like shopping parcels: Anneke told me about Kees, the baker's son, who had just gotten his first bicycle, and I told her about Mrs. Schaap's little red and white chickens, who were refusing to lay. After dinner, we lingered over coffee. I think both of us knew that night might be the last for such things.

Finally Anneke began to talk about Karl. He was more passionate, more mature than the boys she had dated before. A man. If he hadn't been sent away, she said, they might have worked this out. Because he loved her. But he had to keep his promise.

I felt so grieved for her, knowing the truth, and feared this would show. "I need to tell you something," I said. "I went to speak to Karl this morning."

Anneke froze, startled.

"He wasn't there," I said quickly. "But I spoke to two of his friends. He was gone already. The orders to leave came earlier than he'd thought. He was very upset; he didn't want to leave you. He told them that." I would have said anything to ease her pain.

She looked at me, her expression unreadable, and turned toward the window. "Well."

And then it was time to go home, both of us knew. As we left the bistro, a soldier stopped us on the pretext of asking if we had a light. Of course he was really just drawn to Anneke. All men were. She ignored him, keeping her eyes on the street, but he was reluctant to let us go. He was Austrian, he said. He had been a teacher. He played the piano. "Do you know where I could find music here at night?" he wanted to know. *Will you come listen to music with me?* his eyes ached to ask Anneke.

Anneke turned her head away and stepped past him to leave, but I could see that tears gleamed.

She was quiet on the train back, but I could tell she wasn't afraid. The worst had already happened. My uncle's reaction would be meaningless in the face of what she already had to carry.

He was waiting for us in the hall.

I'd expected him to be furious; his temper flew to extremes. But his face was cool, and when he saw Anneke, his eyes filled with something worse than anger.

She took a step toward him. *"Vader?"* It was the smallest of voices.

He threw up his arms to ward off her embrace and twisted his head away. "Stupid whore!" he spat. "You are not my daughter."

My uncle delivered each word as deliberately as a blow, and each one found its mark. Anneke wrapped her arms around her belly — how quickly the body knows where it's most vulnerable.

"You are not my daughter!" he repeated. Then he took his coat from its peg and stormed out.

My aunt stood by and let him go. She only put her arms around Anneke. "It's all right. He's just upset now."

It was not all right. I opened the door and called to him from the step, enraged. "What kind of a father would call his daughter a whore? What kind of a father would walk out on her?"

Even under the thin moonlight, I saw his face darken in rage. "You are not my daughter, either. Remember that."

"I'm glad of it!" I cried. "You're worse than no father at all!"

"Cyrla, no!" My aunt pulled me inside.

I hated my uncle for the look I saw on Anneke's face. I followed her up to our room and watched her carefully, wishing I could think of something to erase it. Something to make her look proud again. We pulled our nightgowns out from under our pillows and undressed without a word.

Finally, when we were in our beds, I broke the silence. "Tell me how it feels. Tell me how to do it."

"How what feels? Oh!" She laughed. "You won't need instructions, *katje!* Your body will know what to do, and your heart."

"I know what to do, Anneke . . . I want you to tell me *how* to do it."

"Really, you'll know." Anneke paused and stroked her curls from her forehead. I knew instantly that Karl had done this. "It will feel as if your body has always known how to make love, was born to do it, but didn't realize it until you met him."

I frowned at her.

"Oh, all right," she sighed. "But really, it's natural, and you only have to do what your body's urging you to do. Have you felt it, that urge?"

Yes, I said, I had felt the urge to make love.

"No. I mean have you touched each other, stroked each other and kissed until you felt it in your body, between your legs, like electricity. The urge to pull him inside you — a heat."

No, I admitted, not yet.

"Well, that's the first, then. Once you feel that, you can let go."

I raised my eyebrows at her, waiting.

"Cyrla, honestly, don't you know?" She paused again, remembering, I supposed, that I hadn't gone to school for a long time. Since the days of Napoleon, all the cities in the Netherlands had recorded each birth, death, and marriage in their registers, with duplicates at The Hague. Though I had papers, I wouldn't be in those civil registers,

51

so my aunt had decided that until the Germans left I shouldn't risk going to school. For the same reason, I worked only in my uncle's shop. My closest friend had moved from Schiedam after the bombings, and so I'd had almost no contact at all with other girls for a year and a half.

"All right," she said. "Here it is. Kiss him. His tongue is his soul. Pull it into you, give yourself into his mouth. Breathe his breath. Hold him, touch him. Learn his face, his chest, his belly . . . lower. Be gentle when you stroke him; it will make him want to be in you. And that's it. Truly. The rest will be natural, as if you couldn't possibly do anything else. It will feel as if . . . it will feel as if with every movement you're saying to yourselves, 'I know you! I know you!' And afterward . . . afterward, the world will be singing in your ears."

"Thank you, Anneke." This was what Isaak never saw in my cousin, and what I often forgot: how generous she was. Once I had confided in her my dream to become a poet. "Well, but you already are," she'd said. "It's in the way you choose your words, in the way you see things and the way you show them to me."

Until then, I had only read poetry, and never written it. Lines had come to me —

often senseless — and I would find myself jotting them down, but I had never followed them deeper to shape them into form and meaning. That night I had found the courage to write my first poem: four lines about gracc.

I was the selfish one, so glad she wasn't leaving me now.

"So? Aren't you going to tell me who it is? I'm sorry — I was so wrapped up in Karl, I guess I wasn't asking about you."

"It's Isaak, of course!"

"Isaak? Oh."

"Oh, what?"

"Nothing. I just didn't know. That's wonderful. For both of you." She turned out the lamp between our beds. "Wait," she said in the darkness. "There's something. You should prepare yourself before. Otherwise it might be difficult and hurt and you won't enjoy it the first time."

I waited for her to explain.

"Your hymen. You can break it yourself; it's not hard. Gera told me; her aunt told her, and she knows these things. Use something smooth and rounded, not too big. Gera's aunt says some cultures carved little goddesses from stone or wood to do it, and it was a sacred ritual. But anything will do; a spoon is fine. Clean."

"What did you use?" I asked.

Anneke laughed and even in the darkness I could sense her rolling her eyes — for just that second she was back, her old self. "Jan Wegerif!"

I sat up. "Jan Wegerif? I didn't know you ever went out with him!"

"I didn't. We just sneaked onto his grandfather's houseboat one time. It was terrible. That's why I'm telling you to use something first. And Cyrla, one more thing."

"Yes?"

"Don't get pregnant."

Six

My uncle didn't soften. For the next two days, he glared his disgust at Anneke and ignored me. He was hardly ever there though — either he was too angry to come home for lunch, or he was too busy. The shipment of wool he had received was for an order from the German army for six hundred blankets.

This made me uneasy. My uncle was as upset by the Occupation and its discomforts as anyone I knew, and was especially outraged to hear the constant trains rumbling eastward, loaded with plundered Dutch goods — each container stamped with the insulting lie: *A gift from the people of Holland to their German brothers.* I'd always assumed his anti-German stance was based on principle — certainly he had many friends among the Jewish merchants who sold him supplies on Breedstraat in Amsterdam. But lately, although I never heard him express sympathy with the Nazis, I'd begun to wonder if he was entirely unsympathetic.

Lately he had been doing a lot of work mending uniforms for the German soldiers billeted in our town. At first, Tante Mies had begged him not to accept this work. "Close the shop," she pleaded, more than once. "Do not be part of this."

My uncle always answered that he feared for our welfare if he didn't do the work. If he closed the shop he'd have to register for the labor conscription. How would we manage then? There was no reason to disbelieve him — all the men in town were making these compromises. But when I helped him in the shop, cutting cloth in the back room, I could hear him talking with the Germans, and I was shocked at how friendly he sounded. How accommodating.

In the past few months, my aunt had given up the argument. Each piece of war news had extinguished a piece of her spirit until she was a shadow drifting through the days, leaving my uncle more and more the force of our family. At his core he seemed to carry a constant bitterness that leaked out through everything he did or said and hung over us, sullen as smoke. If it hadn't been for Anneke's good spirits, the house would have been unbearable. But now suddenly, with the absence of my uncle, my aunt was back.

Anneke and I awoke to the sound of hammering the first day. We found my aunt in the cellar, fitting boards between two posts to make a hidden shelf. "Gather all the nonperishable food," she ordered. "Hide it here." We did: raisins, boxes of dried peas and beans, the fruit my aunt had canned over the summer, the remainders of the week's sugar and flour rations, bouillon cubes, and even the sad cupful of noodles at the bottom of its jar.

Later that morning, as we went through the newspaper for the week's rationing instructions, she informed us of some new plans. "Each week, we'll take part of our dairy rations as tinned milk. And we'll begin trading. We don't need the cigarette or sweets rations — we'll trade those for extra flour or milk. We'll start using the textile coupons for things we can use for the baby later."

Anneke and I looked at each other. I could tell she wasn't able to picture the time when she would have a child; it was too difficult to even think about being pregnant.

She had chores for us all day. Anneke and I were so amazed at the sudden return of my aunt that we did what she asked without questions. It was good to lose ourselves in this work, a relief to be doing things instead of having things done to us. But there was a trace of desperation in my aunt's frenzy, and it struck me that in these preparations she was seeking some sort of atonement. I wondered where she felt she had failed. Did she think she could have prevented Anneke's situation by being more prepared, more alert?

I always imagined the mother-child bond as a constant river of love and support, and I'd been so absorbed in grieving its absence that I'd never considered the possibility the river might loop back around to its source. That children might sustain their mothers as well. I resolved to watch my aunt more closely, and Anneke, too, after the baby came.

At the sound of my uncle's arrival that evening, my aunt glanced up at Anneke and me and nodded toward the back door. While she greeted him in the living room, we hurried into our sweaters and went outside. We sat together on the brick steps, eating the last of the tomatoes from the yellowing plants and watching a narrow moon rise. The breeze picked up and rustled the drying leaves of the walnut overhead, so we could hear only shredded murmurs drifting from the dining room. But we could tell the conversation was spare and grim.

Anneke pulled a packet of cigarettes and a lighter from the pocket of her trousers. She lit one and offered the packet to me.

I shook my head. "Your father." Anneke had taken up cigarettes when she'd met Karl, but my uncle hated the sight of women smoking in public, so she never smoked at home. Sometimes in the afternoons we would walk to the big warehouse where the barges were unloaded and we would sit on the dock, listening to the men talk as they tossed barrels of nails and tobacco and salted herring. She would share her cigarettes with me, the smoke mingling with the heavy scent of spices and tar.

Now she shrugged and gave a wry smile. I could see her point. I reached over and took a cigarette, and we sat smoking, shoulders hunched against the chilly night, until we heard my uncle leave to return to his shop. I wondered how long we could all go on living in the same house.

The next day a bitter rain sliced down all morning. Anneke didn't go to work again, and with the extra pair of hands the housework was done quickly. She and I put on a record and took out the backgammon set. My aunt walked through the living room carrying the linens the laundryman had just delivered. "We may need to trade them for food when the baby comes," she said, nodding at the ivory playing pieces. "Wrap them and hide them, in case the Germans come again to requisition things. They've had the last they're ever going to get from this house. Oh, and the chess pieces, too. Put them behind the coal bin. And those figurines, and the fireplace tongs. . . ." She looked at the gramophone and frowned, considering. I felt a tiny prick of worry then about my aunt's behavior, and I think Anneke did, too.

"They wouldn't want it," she assured her mother. "Besides, it's too big to hide."

"Of course." My aunt smiled. But the faint scent of anxiety that had entered the house did not dissipate, and by the time the rain stopped in the afternoon, both Anneke and I were desperate to go outside.

We cycled to the park beside the canal. It was cool, but the sun was brilliant after the rain and I worried that the sky, so fiercely blue against the white clouds, would remind Anneke of Karl's eyes. I wanted her to have one afternoon free of thinking about her problem, but of course this wasn't possible. We passed a couple leaning into each other on a bench, and I saw her think, *Karl deserted me.* Children too young for school were out in the fine weather with their mothers, playing marbles and hopscotch, running and tripping in front of us, and the thought stabbed her, *I'm pregnant and he deserted me.* The smallest things stung: two pigeons fighting over a crust of bread, an old woman trying to keep her skirt from blowing up in the breeze, a flock of geese arrowing through slanted bars of sunlight — these made us smile, but each time Anneke caught herself, and I knew she was thinking, *Wait, no. I'm not happy.*

I watched her face cloud and her lower lip begin to tremble for the hundredth time. "Do you want to keep the baby?"

We had reached a bridge. Anneke stared down at the canal glinting green and peaceful, but reflecting her own truth back at her. You couldn't escape yourself for very long with so many mirrors snaking through the land. Holland was cruel that way. I picked up a stone and tossed it in, breaking the surface, and Anneke turned.

"I wish I weren't pregnant. Since I am, I wish Karl were with me. But that's as far as I can think. I know I'll have to make some choices soon. I know I don't have to keep the baby. I know I don't even have to *have* the baby; Gera's aunt says there are ways. . . . But when I try to think past that, I just can't." She lifted her hands, then clasped them across her belly in a gesture that was already becoming familiar.

"What if we moved away, got a place together? Leisje and Frannie went to Amsterdam last year, remember? They both got jobs in a bank. Diet de Jonge moved to Utrecht by herself. It would be a fresh start. I probably have to leave soon, anyway — your father doesn't want me here. . . ."

Anneke waved her fingers in that way she had, as if my problems were only words she had to brush away. "I wish I weren't pregnant . . . but I am. Who knows how long I can work? And if I have a baby, what . . . you'll support all three of us?" She leaned her head on my shoulder. "I'd be so lonely now without you, *katje*."

I stepped away and took her by the elbows — carefully, because I suddenly wanted to shake her, hard. "Then you will be lonely if you don't leave with me," I told her. "Because I don't think your father's going to let me stay. Can't you see how it is now?"

"You should talk to him. It's your home, too."

"No, it isn't. I understand that now. When I came here, he allowed me into your house. That's all. Not into your home, not into your family. And I certainly didn't walk into your easy life, where all you have to do is pout and someone will come running over to make you happy again."

"My easy life?" Anneke shrank away from me, stung. But I didn't take my words back. "My easy life?" She spread her hands over her belly and stared at me. "Would you like to walk into my easy life now, Cyrla?"

I pressed my lips together and looked away. Because my answer was *Yes*.

From the east came a familiar droning buzz and three planes appeared above the trees. Silence fell and all of us in the park raised our heads. We still did this every time, although we no longer ran like mice fleeing a circling hawk. The shadow of the closest plane rippled over the canal, darkened the grass, and swept over Anneke and me. I shivered and Anneke straightened and nodded to herself. "Well," she said. "It's getting late. We can't hide from Father forever."

But we should have.

SEVEN

He was already home when we got there, setting up a new stove in the parlor. He didn't look at us when we walked past him into the kitchen to help my aunt with supper.

"New fuel restrictions," she explained, frowning. "We'll be tending that thing every hour. And the dust!" She handed me four potatoes and an apron.

I took a paring knife from the drawer, sat at the table, and began to peel. A few minutes later, my uncle came into the kitchen, a newspaper tucked under his elbow.

"You'll be at dinner tonight," he informed Anneke. I could read nothing at all in his face, and nothing at all in hers.

He crossed to the table, dropped his newspaper in front of me, and reached over to wipe his hands on a dish towel. Then he left the room.

On the page facing me was a large notice: a "short summary" of all the places Jews were not allowed. The paring knife fell from my hand. *Joden Verboden.* All restaurants, all shops, all cinemas. Schools. Parks. Public beaches, public transportation. It would have been shorter, I thought, to list the places they *were* allowed.

The places *I* was allowed. There was no mistaking my uncle's message — it had just come sooner than I'd expected.

I folded the paper and tried to slip it under the pail of potato peelings, but Anneke saw. She took it and read it, not understanding. And then understanding.

She passed the notice to my aunt. My aunt came over and put her arm around my shoulder. "Oom Pieter . . . this has been a difficult time. He doesn't mean —"

"He does." I got up and closed the kitchen door. "Do *you* worry about this?" I asked quietly so my uncle wouldn't hear, looking from my aunt to my cousin. "About me?"

"No," Anneke said, "I never do. Cyrla, do you want me to?"

"I don't know."

It was a good question. In the spring, when the signs had first gone up in the shops and restaurants, the words didn't actually bar Jews. *JODEN NIET GEWENST,*

JEWS NOT WELCOME, they said, in harsh black against white. I was in the greengrocer with my aunt the first time we saw one.

My aunt had been incredulous, outraged. "What does this mean?" she demanded of Mr. Kuyper, whom she'd known all her life. "You have customers who are Jewish! Friends!"

My fingers tightened around the apples I was holding. Part of me wanted her to say, "This is my niece, she's half-Jewish. Is she no longer welcome here?" But if she did, what would happen? In that instant, I saw that my life was built on sand, and that a single wave would wash everything away.

"Mrs. Abraham? Mrs. Levie?" my aunt asked. "Suddenly, after all these years, you don't want their business?"

I was washed in relief that my aunt took no offense for me at these signs. I was ashamed of my relief. I was angry also; indignant for my father and brothers, for Isaak. But mostly relieved at this settling of things; with this exchange my aunt told me clearly what I had sensed since I had arrived: Here in the Netherlands, I wasn't Jewish. She must know best.

"I don't know," I repeated. I began to slice the potatoes into even wedges. "I never want to think about it. But Isaak says —" I paused, imagining what Isaak might say about what my uncle had just done, then quickly pushing him from my mind. "As long as no one knows, it doesn't matter."

I turned to my aunt. "Did you ever say anything to Mrs. Bakker?" I explained what had happened the other morning.

"No, of course not. It's just her way. She's harmless. We've never told anyone — it was what your father asked when he sent you here."

I hadn't known this. I was only fourteen when I had come, and it hadn't occurred to me to question anything. Or perhaps it had frightened me too much.

"Well, then. Good. No one knows, and maybe you're right — maybe Oom Pieter is only upset." And maybe I wouldn't have to mention any of this to Isaak.

I went to the stove and slid the potato slices into the hot skillet. Anneke put down the spoon she was stirring the gravy with and touched my arm.

"Cyrla," she said. "Karl knows."

"Anneke!" my aunt cried.

I was speechless.

"It's all right," Anneke said quickly. "He hates the Nazis. You would like Karl; you would trust him."

You trusted him and look what happened! I

wanted to shout. Did she still think she knew him? But I could see she was already asking herself this.

"Never mind," I said. "He's gone, so it doesn't matter."

But of course it did. Here was the wave I had been dreading, come from the direction Isaak had told me to watch. Everything would collapse soon, was already starting to crumble. I knew it, but I couldn't take it in right now. Not with Anneke and Tante Mies watching me. Not with Oom Pieter waiting for Anneke at the table. I made my face firm with resolve as we finished preparing the food and brought it out to the dining room. There was meat tonight; not just bits flavoring a soup, but a whole piece of beef — a week's worth — roasted in a covered pot with onions. My aunt was trying to soothe my uncle again.

We sat in our usual seats, but because Anneke and I hadn't been there for two nights, everything felt strange.

My uncle blessed the food, began to eat. He looked up. "Eat."

We took up our forks and tried to swallow.

My uncle talked about the weather, the coming winter, the new way we would heat our house. "Half anthracite and half coke," he mused. "That's the best we can hope for, I suppose." As if anyone at the table were interested in coal.

He told us one of his machines had broken down and needed a part. Such bad timing with the big blanket order. And he needed to hire two seamstresses; this shouldn't be difficult with so many people out of work

A vein rose at Anneke's temple. Her skin was stretched brittle as glass, and I thought she might shatter at the slightest tremor. I wished I could think of something to say that would hurry my uncle along without angering him. The meal took hours. Hours. Finally he put down his fork and looked at each of us to see that he had our attention.

"I have found a solution," he said. "A maternity home."

"Anneke doesn't need a maternity home," my aunt said reasonably. "She'll be here, with us."

"No, not here with us. That I won't have." He cut a piece of meat and ate it, drank some beer, and didn't look at us. We waited.

"It's a decent thing they're doing. Very progressive. She'll be treated well. They're not all evil, you know."

"Who're not all evil?" my aunt asked.

"The Germans. They've set up these homes wherever their soldiers are. They're very modern. All the best facilities. They're taking care of this problem all over."

We stared at my uncle. Only my aunt could form the questions.

"What problem? What do the Germans have to do with us?"

"Anneke's not the only one. They're taking care of the girls who've gotten in trouble this way. They're taking responsibility, even if their soldiers aren't."

"How did you learn about this?" I asked. I saw my uncle's jaw stiffen, but I had to go on. "Who told you? Who did you tell about Anneke?"

He didn't answer. But he didn't need to.

"You told them?" Anneke whispered. "You told the Germans in the shop?"

"You shamed me." My uncle's voice rose. "I have found a solution."

"Pieter, what have you done?" My aunt's eyes were fierce.

"Anneke has an appointment tomorrow. An interview and some tests. I'll take her. I can't work anyway, until I get that part."

"What kind of tests?" I asked.

My uncle looked at me for a moment, his eyes narrowed behind the steel rims of his glasses. I couldn't tell if he was considering his answer, or deciding whether or not to speak to me.

"A formality," he said at last. "Medical records, documents." He was lying.

"*Nee.* I do not allow this," my aunt said.

She had never before defied my uncle directly. All of us at the table knew that some axis had shifted, and everything from now on would need to find a new balance.

My uncle's face flushed and his scalp showed dark red through his light hair. "Our daughter shamed us. I've found a way to take some honor from this shame."

"What honor, Pieter?" my aunt cried. "What honor?"

I got up and stood behind Anneke, my hands on her shoulders. "What shame?" I asked. "She loved a man. Love is the opposite of shame. Don't send her away!"

My uncle shoved his chair back and rose. "Anneke, be ready to travel in the morning. We will be back Sunday."

My aunt rose also. "*Nee,*" she repeated. "I will not allow it."

Anneke fell limp under my hands. "Stop," she said. "Please stop. I'll go."

Afterward, she hadn't wanted to talk about her decision. As we got ready for bed, she would only say, "Have you thought about what it would be like for me here?"

I hadn't. When I did, I could see it would be difficult. Everyone would hold it against her that Karl was a German soldier.

They would be wrong. I thought about Isaak. His citizenship had nothing to do with the way my heart caught whenever he came into view, as if it were too stunned to beat. His politics had nothing to do with the way my thigh burned if it brushed against his. It didn't matter that Karl was German. Goethe was German, and Schiller, who wrote about freedom. Rilke. Beethoven, Bach, Brahms. Bakers and teachers and painters and nurses; men and women who loved their families and led good lives. It was the Nazis we hated, and I believed Anneke that Karl was not a Nazi. That she loved him in spite of the army that had conscripted him only showed how large her heart was. She had misjudged his character, but she hadn't violated any standard of behavior by loving him — she had risen above one.

But I could hardly hope to convince a town of this. Anneke was right. She could not stay here. So we would move.

EIGHT

That night I dreamed of my parents, the same image I'd seen often in my sleep. They were lying in their bed; my father on his back, my mother on her side, folded against him with her head over his heart, tucked under his left arm. My mother's hair was loose and it cascaded in an arc of rippling amber up over my father's shoulder and into his beard and hair, where it gleamed gold against the black. My father's other arm crossed his chest just below his ribs, and his fingers rested entwined with my mother's at the small of her waist. A composition of perfect peace. The linking arc of hair and the linking arc of arms formed a circle, beautiful in its completion, terrible in its exclusion.

For this was the dream: I approach my parents, desperate to be inside their circle, but they don't break open for me. They can't; their hands are melded together —

they show me by lifting their arms helplessly — and their hair is woven into one rope. Sorry, sorry.

I awoke with it fresh in my mind, sore as a bruise, and found Anneke gone.

It was just for the day, I reminded myself. Just this one appointment and she would be home tomorrow. And then I would tell her the new plan, the one I'd made before I fell asleep.

At breakfast, my aunt didn't want to talk about what had happened last night. We talked instead about the work we would do that morning, and as it was not much, we lingered at the kitchen table with coffee and sunlight warming us.

I plucked a dead leaf from a geranium. "Tante Mies," I said. "Tell me about my parents."

My aunt looked up sharply. I didn't ask about them often. "What do you want to know?"

"Well, how they were when they met. How they were before I remember them."

My aunt leaned over and tucked a strand of hair behind my ear. "How do you remember them, Cyrla?"

"Close together." I hadn't known I would say this. "I always remember them standing or sitting very close to each other, touching.

When I think of them, I always think of them together." I rested my chin on my fists and considered this. "Except, I remember my mother alone with me in the kitchen. She spoke Dutch then. I thought people spoke Dutch when they cooked." For a second I was lost in that kitchen, my mother's arms white up to the elbows with flour, her face bright with reflecting me.

"*Ja,* from the beginning, it was as though they had always been together. And as though they were two parts of some whole. Although they were so different! You're a lot like your mother, you know that? Sometimes I see so much of her in you; so much of her spirit. She loved your father very much. And you're right, they were always close together, always touching."

I realized that I never saw my aunt and uncle touching. I never saw my uncle touch anyone, in fact. I knew by her face that my aunt was thinking this also.

"Your uncle loves us," she said. "His way is just different. He likes rules. And what Anneke did . . . well . . ."

What did Anneke do? I wondered. Were there rules for love? I was sure if I were ever lucky enough to be part of a whole with someone that would be enough. I would never ask love to follow rules.

75

"And with that paper last night . . . he's only worried."

I lifted my palms to her. It didn't matter anymore. But she wanted to explain.

"It's complicated. He's not a sympathizer — you know that. Cyrla, listen to me. Try to understand. Your uncle's family was rich. But they'd invested in czarist bonds; a lot of Dutch had. When the Bolsheviks canceled all their foreign debts, they lost much of their wealth. Your uncle had to leave the university and learn a trade. I don't think he ever got over it."

I thought of my uncle, putting up new drapes in our parlor each spring. Only in the parlor — the one room which over-looked the street. The first spring I was there, I remember my aunt scolding him for lining them with the same russet satin as the drapes themselves. "Who are these for, Pieter?" she'd asked. "Us? Or the people passing by?"

"It's good for business," he'd answered.

But I could tell from his face that my aunt's words had opened an old wound. And when she made things from the still-usable fabric of the drapes he took down — coverlets for our bed from the gray-striped damask; capes for Anneke and me from the bottle-green velvet — he scowled.

"So in the beginning," my aunt was saying, "before you arrived, Hitler's anti-Bolshevism appealed to him. But not now."

"Then what is he telling me?" I crossed my arms and braced myself.

My aunt pushed her coffee away and steepled her hands to her lips. "Jews are supposed to register. It's a terrible rule. We don't want any of the Germans' rules. But he's worried about that one. About breaking it. And now with the new restrictions . . . I can talk to him, though."

"No, don't," I said.

As soon as the housework was done, I telephoned Isaak at work. "Meet me. I need to talk with you."

"Cyrla, I can't. Where would we meet?"

"The park on Burgemeester Knappertlaan," I suggested. It was a beautiful day; we would walk.

I heard Isaak sigh and then I remembered: There was no place Isaak could go without breaking the new restrictions, except within the Jewish quarter. And he didn't want me to go there. But he couldn't keep me away.

"I'll come to the Council now," I told him.

"No, that's not good, you know it. We can talk on the telephone."

"Isaak, wait. My uncle's shop is closed

today. Meet me there in an hour."

"Cyrla, no. I put a lot of people in danger if I get caught. . . ."

"The back door," I said. "Just this once."

As I dropped the receiver into the cradle, I was struck by something: I always needed a reason to see Isaak, a problem for him to solve. I presented my problems to him like coins to pay for my admittance to him.

Isaak was irritated, I could tell when I opened the door for him. He walked in, and just as he did I realized what he would see: counters covered with bolts of brown wool. It would be so easy for him to ask what such a big order was for.

"The roof. It's safer." I took his hand and led him to the stairs, and for an instant I felt him stiffen. Isaak didn't understand touch. How much having no family had cost him. He'd been raised by good men, he told me; he'd spent the first few years of his life in an orphanage, but then the elders in the synagogue of his town had seen to him. No one had held him at night, though, to explain to him through his skin how he was loved. Isaak never pulled away when I touched him. But he never returned the touch.

He relaxed on the roof. We walked to the

edge and gazed out. The brick houses with their stepped roofs glowed ocher in the afternoon sun, the canal was a cool ivy green, and the trees were turning gold as far as we could see. It was quiet and peaceful above the sounds of the street, and when I looked at Isaak, I could tell he was wishing he had brought his sketch pad.

"Listen, Cyrla," Isaak said. He crossed to the other side of the roof. "An oriole. I think he must be in those pear trees. But that's his mating song. I've never heard it so late in the season."

"He has no mate yet?" I thought of Rilke's poem about the coming of autumn, the one that haunted me. I recited the lines to Isaak.

He who has no house now, will no longer build.
He who is alone now, will remain alone.

"Like your oriole," I said. Like us.

"Well, not exactly. It's more likely he had a mate and she died. And if she died their babies most likely didn't live. If she even had a chance to lay eggs."

I saw Isaak's face close, and knew we had stopped talking about birds. We settled ourselves on the sun-warmed gravel, our backs against the short wall.

I told him about my uncle's threat and what Mrs. Bakker had said. That Anneke had told Karl about me. There was no point in hiding it anymore. "You're right," I said. "It's time to leave." I stole a secret glance at his face, to see if he felt pain at the thought of my leaving. But of course he was careful to hide his feelings.

"I'll start making arrangements. The *Verzet* are good at this. I trust them."

"No. I'm going to move, but not too far. Not out of the Netherlands. There's no need."

I told him my plan, about how I would move to Amsterdam or Rotterdam and take a new identity. He could help me with that, I said. He only listened, nodded. Until I mentioned that Anneke would be moving with me. He lifted an eyebrow. I told him where she was and what my uncle had done.

"I've heard of those places," he said, gathering a handful of gravel and shaking it in his palm. "Lebensborns. You know what they are, don't you?"

"Places for girls to have their babies safely and not be ostracized."

"Not exactly." Isaak sieved the gravel through his fingers. "Not exactly a humanitarian service. Do you know why they do it?"

"She's pregnant by one of them. They're taking responsibility; they want her to be healthy and safe."

"Yes, but why? Think of what the word 'lebensborn' means. Wellspring of life. Source of life."

I felt Isaak studying me, waiting. He always said I should question things to their end. I wanted to please him now, so I thought about it through his mind. And there was the answer: "No."

"Yes," Isaak insisted. "Those are dark cradles. *'Have one baby for the Führer'* is the slogan. All German women, whether they're married or not, are expected to have children. Every place they take over, they will want to fill with their own. And they'll always want troops. Do you know what really frightens me about them? How far ahead they think. Babies aren't babies to the Nazis, Cyrla. They're resources. And now they're taking them from occupied countries."

I pictured the child Anneke was carrying. A little boy, a little girl. The Germans wanted to take Dutch babies the same way they were taking our fuel, our food, and our textiles. A blessing ran through my head, one we had spoken at the naming of my youngest brother, Benjamin: *May you live to see your world fulfilled, may your destiny be for worlds still to come, and may you trust in generations past and yet to be.*

I could almost smell Benjamin's soaped neck, could almost feel his rich damp weight on my hip, sleeping with his fingers twined through a loop of my braid so with every step I took, I felt the smallest of tugs. "I'll make her understand," I told Isaak. "She'll come with me."

"She'll do what she wants to do," Isaak said. Bitterly, I thought. "But wait and see. She probably won't be accepted. Most girls aren't. Do you know about the tests?"

I nodded yes, then shook my head.

"They have to prove their lineage. Have to have acceptable hair color, eye color. Aryans, they call them. Desirables."

Somewhere — I didn't know where — they were doing this to my cousin now. Could they measure her sweetness? Would the light she spilled over our family be acceptable? There was nothing more to be said. I was suddenly exhausted, as if I had been holding myself rigid for days. I leaned my head against Isaak's shoulder and felt him tense.

Anneke had said that once two people began to touch each other, they would know how to make love. But Isaak needed to learn the language of touch first. And it would be up to me to teach him. Who else did he have?

I lifted my hand to the base of his neck, where his shirt collar opened, and very gently stroked my fingertips against his throat, warm and smooth and summer-brown over the corded muscle. In an instant the world narrowed, and then poured into this deliberate questioning of skin. I held my breath for his answer.

He took my hand and held it tight, and then pushed it away.

"Cyrla, no. It isn't . . . I have to get back." He got to his feet and looked away.

I wanted to reach out and pull his eyes back onto me. I understood, though. He needed time to become comfortable with this new language. But we didn't have time.

That night, when I washed the dishes after supper, I pulled a teaspoon from the hot suds and slipped it into my pocket.

NINE

The person who came home Sunday evening was not my cousin.

When I came up to her, she flinched. She went straight to our room although it wasn't even nine o'clock, and when my aunt and I followed, at first she wouldn't answer our questions, wouldn't look at us with her wounded eyes. Or couldn't.

"All right," my aunt said. She kissed Anneke. "We'll talk tomorrow." She left and I knew she was going to go find out from my uncle what had happened.

Anneke stepped out of her dress and hung it up, something I had never seen her do. Thin crescents of white tipped her fingernails where the polish had worn off — I had never seen that, either. She put on her nightgown and pulled the blankets over her, all of her motions small and careful.

I suddenly felt guilty, as if I had let her down. "I've thought this through. If you left,

I'd leave, too. I don't want to be here without you — even if your father let me stay. So why don't you and I move away together? We'll get a place in Amsterdam, and jobs, and no one will know us. We'll tell people whatever you want."

"I'm so tired, Cyrla" was all she said.

"No, wait," I said. "Isaak told me about the Lebensborn. Where did you go? Tell me what happened."

Anneke cringed, inched deeper under her blankets.

I got up and sat on her bed and put my hand on her shoulder. She was cold under her nightgown, but she wasn't shivering. "No," I said again. "Please talk with me. I'm not going to sleep until you do. You're not going into that place, and they're not going to take the baby. Are you all right?"

Anneke sighed and looked at me. "You don't understand." Her eyes were still far away, older and slow; something at her core had vanished. "I'm fine. It was nothing. I saw some doctors . . . at the headquarters . . . just some tests. They measured . . . they measured everything. They asked about our family. That's all. I want to go to sleep now."

"Anneke, do you hear me? You don't have to go." I suddenly had a wonderful idea.

"Your mother's to go to Amsterdam tomorrow, to pick up that part your father needs for the order. Let's go with her. We'll see Frannie and Leisje. We'll ask them to help us find a place to live. We'll have fun."

Anneke slipped farther away. "Leave me alone, Cyrla." She rolled over. I grew angry with her for a moment, that she had gotten herself into this situation, and now wouldn't let me show her a way out. Later, when I heard her crying, I was ashamed.

The next morning, she was up when I awoke.

"Well," I said immediately, "Amsterdam?"

"I'm going back to work today. But you go with Mama, Cyrla. It's a good idea. See what you can learn." She put on a gray woolen skirt and a wine sweater, and I thought she seemed better, stronger. "Will you go today?" she asked me a few minutes later, and she waited until I promised. I was pleased — my idea had given her hope.

She talked with me while I dressed, and asked questions about Isaak and me. How did I feel when I was with him? How did he act? Was I sure? A hundred questions.

"Is anyone ever sure?" I asked her. And then she gave me more advice, about how I'd know if he were the right one, what I might feel. I stopped listening. Isaak had

86

been the one for me since the day I'd met him, the day I'd arrived in Holland. There was no question. What mattered was that Anneke seemed to be herself again. But she didn't check herself in the mirror before she went downstairs, and she didn't fix her nail polish.

I should never have let her out of my sight.

The train was crowded — they were always crowded now. The Germans had requisitioned our modern electric engines and left us with only older coal-burning ones, which broke down all the time, and the worst of the carriages. By the time we reached Amsterdam, there were hundreds of people on board, crushed shoulder to shoulder in the aisles so that if anyone fainted, he probably wouldn't hit the floor, while the last two carriages were empty — NUR FÜR WEHRMACHT, the signs said, although there were no soldiers in them that day. I thought it was a good omen — all these people traveling to Amsterdam must mean there was work.

The air was sooty and stale, but as Schiedam was early on the route, we had seats, so we felt lucky. On the way, my aunt told me what she'd learned last night. There was a home in Nijmegen, barely a hundred kilometers away, called the Gelderland. Anneke had passed all the tests and she was welcome to have her baby there. Most girls waited until they began to show to enter, but my uncle had pressed for her to go in right away. She was due there next Friday.

"They have food. Fresh vegetables and fruits every day. Plenty of milk. All the finest quality. And it's not that far away —"

"Tante Mies!" I interrupted her. "You're not thinking of letting her go?" But of course she was. I'd heard the words that swayed her — plenty of food, the best quality — words as nourishing to my aunt as the meals she could no longer make for us. Anneke and I had lost weight in the past year. Since meeting Karl, Anneke had grown even thinner, as if she had been burning hotter and faster at her core. Sometimes my aunt would reach out to pull at the loose waist of a skirt, visibly pained by the accusing fabric.

"*Ja,* I am. We can't provide this for her here. I can't even feed her properly. They have doctors and nurses, she'll get the best medical attention —"

"No!" I cried. Several people standing near glanced down at us, but I didn't care. "It's not what you think at all. Isaak told me: It's a Lebensborn. Do you know what that means? Did you ask what the tests were? Did you ask Oom Pieter what will happen to the baby? Where he'll go?"

I told my aunt everything I had learned; then I told her what I wanted to do. There was no reason not to. We were at the end of all choices.

My aunt listened carefully, listened to me for the first time as an adult. She didn't disagree with anything; even when I said Oom Pieter couldn't be told, she only turned toward the smudged window to look at the countryside rolling by and nodded.

"I'll help," she said when I finished.

I felt hopeful suddenly. Anneke and I could make a life in Amsterdam until the war was over. It wouldn't be the one we'd imagined for ourselves, but who in Europe could say any different? The wheels of the train sang against the track.

I had an address for Leisje and Frannie, and I boarded a tram for their district. The tram was crowded also — with men and women dressed for business, with university students, with people of many nationalities, something we didn't see in Schiedam. Amsterdam was always a tolerant and welcoming city, and very modern; sometimes when I visited, I came home thinking Schiedam was living twenty years in the past. The girls especially had a different look here — a look that excited me. I wondered how long it would be before I wore that look, and if I'd notice it on myself.

I felt anonymous and free — as if I'd already taken a new identity and were starting my life over. I'd have to choose a new name. I had always liked Kalie, the name of the girl who had been my first friend in Holland, or maybe I would call myself Alie, or Johanna after my mother. No, not Johanna.

I got off on Konigsstraat and began to walk toward Leisje and Frannie's address. Their flat was above a shoe-repair shop. This was a good omen, too, I thought — in Schiedam the shoe-repair shop had been out of business for months. There was a cheese shop next door, full of customers.

The door to the flats upstairs was in an alcove between the two shops. Tubs of sun-colored dahlias flanked the entrances, and above these, each shop door displayed one of the new signs — *JODEN VERBODEN*, in letters larger than the old signs, and blacker.

"Do you see that sign?" I jumped at the voice behind me.

"What kind of a world are we living in that we're told who can come into our shops? It makes me not want to bring my business here. But what can we do? They're everywhere now." The man shook his head and passed by me into the cheese shop.

I climbed the stairs to the flats quickly and willed my heart to slow down, not allowing myself to question why it had raced.

No one answered my knock, but of course Leisje and Frannie would be at work by now. I went back down to the street and started to walk. I didn't know which bank they worked in, so whenever I passed one, I stopped and asked. No one had heard of our friends, but at each I saw the new signs. At each I asked if there were any jobs. Two of the banks said, no, sorry, and the third said perhaps in a week or so; come back. Well, so I would tell Anneke I was sure we could find work.

I walked for several hours, gathering things to tell Anneke about Amsterdam, to present to her like gifts: I heard someone practicing a clarinet; a young man was painting at an easel in front of a canal house; a group of students was handing out leaflets for a play. There were German soldiers everywhere I looked, but here they seemed to belong to the city, not the other way around. We could do well here, make a new life.

It was almost time to meet my aunt. I stopped into a pastry shop and to buy some *taartjes* for the train. The sign was there on the shop door, once again: JODEN VER- BODEN. I wasn't hungry anymore. Just as I turned in the doorway to leave, three elderly women stepped up to come in.

I flattened myself against the door in politeness, smiled, and wished them *"Goedemiddag,"* and as they made their arthritic way past me I slipped my right hand between my back and the glass door, found the insulting notice, then ripped it off and dropped it crumpled to the tiles below. "It's a beautiful day!" I added, and walked out, smiling even more widely. Yes, Anneke and I might do well here.

It was dark when my aunt and I walked up to our house, and the telephone was ringing. I hurried ahead, unlocked the door, and ran inside to answer it.

It was Mr. Eman, from the bakery. He wanted to know if Anneke was ready to come back yet. "My wife's been covering the extra shifts, but if Anneke's going to be gone any longer . . ."

Ten

My aunt understood before I did. As I stood with the telephone to my ear, she came into the hall and called for Anneke. Then she reeled backward as if she'd been struck: The news hung in the air, in the crushing languid smell of so much blood, finished with its lifetime of coursing. She dropped her coat and bag and flew upstairs. The smell was so heavy, it coated my tongue and made me gag; still, even as the receiver fell from my hand, even as I watched my aunt run up the stairs, I refused to acknowledge its meaning.

My aunt screamed. I followed the cry. There were a hundred steps on the stairway that night, and then a hundred more. I climbed with legs of stone.

Anneke.

A lake of blood, drying to crust at its shore and pooling under her mattress, drenched the rag rug between our two beds and made

93

four mahogany islands of the night table's legs. My aunt knelt in the blood beside the bed howling, her head buried next to her daughter's. Anneke's face was white — white as her pillowcase, white as her slip above her waist. Below, her slip was clotted red and black, its lace hem swollen dark, slick as seaweed, knotted up between her legs at the blood source.

"No. Oh, please no," I begged. I climbed onto the bed next to Anneke's still body and begged her not to have left me, not to have miscarried, not to have been pregnant at all. "No," to everything. Too late. My aunt held her, wailing.

My uncle appeared in the doorway. He roared and flew across the room, bent over Anneke, and lifted her out of our dark well and crushed her body to his. He crouched with her beside my bed, reached for my blanket and wrapped it around her. I thought, *No! Don't take her away!* and then I thought, *Yes! Warm her, make everything all right again. Bring her back! Bring her back!* I climbed from Anneke's bed and knelt beside him and cradled my cousin with him, and my aunt followed.

We sat on the floor holding her, six arms touching the lost center of our wheel. I didn't know how long — half an hour, or all night — because time lost its meaning. One by one we would spin off from each other, jolted by a fresh stab of pain, then fight our way back. Worst of all was to watch my uncle lose his battle. I could see the blow land each time, like a cannonball to his chest. He crumpled with a single gulping sob and clutched his big head in his big hands.

My aunt's pain was sharp and terrible to see. But sometime during the night she disappeared into it. She left in her place a woman with eyes that burned brightly but didn't cry. She rose from our circle, breaking its power, and began to fit the day together.

"Who saw her last? What time did she leave?" She stood in front of us, kneading the flesh around her heart, as if she could dig out what was hurting.

"We had breakfast together after you left," my uncle said, his eyes never leaving his daughter's face. He seemed to be unable to look away, as if he felt she had only gone deeper into it and he might find her again if he searched hard enough. I couldn't look at Anneke's face because she was gone from it. Worse to look at, though, were her limp arms: Her fingers were stuck together in the dark red glue of her blood, her hands covered to the wrists in it, as if she were wearing wine-colored gloves on her pale arms.

"I left first. She said she was leaving soon, too. She asked how late I'd be." Oom Pieter brushed Anneke's hair from her forehead and repeated softly, "She asked how late I'd be."

"But why didn't she call someone? Why didn't she go to a neighbor for help?" my aunt asked over and over, her eyes darting between my uncle's face and mine, but not quite focusing on either of us.

Anneke had asked me twice if I would go to Amsterdam with her mother. Had she known then something was wrong? Had she wanted me to stay? It had felt exactly the opposite, as if she had been eager for us to leave. I considered telling my aunt this, but didn't. What good would it do?

I tried to remember our last words, but I couldn't. This seemed to be the most important thing in the world to know. The only thing that was of any importance at all, because if I could remember what Anneke had said last, I could have changed my answer to her. I could have stopped whatever was going to happen.

My aunt grew desperate to do something, to take any kind of action. I understood her urge, but it frightened me. It reminded me of her frenzy to strip the house of anything the Germans might come for. The connection was too grim. The Germans had wanted what Anneke carried within her. They wouldn't get it.

"Go downstairs," she ordered. "Fill a pail with soapy water, very hot, and bleach. Get rags and a scrub brush. Lots of rags."

I stumbled down the stairs and pulled aside the parlor drapes. Outside there were no lights at all, not even moonlight, and it seemed possible the real world didn't exist anymore. My legs buckled and I vomited.

When I came back with the pail, my uncle was bent over Anneke's bureau, lifting her brush, her lipstick, her perfume awkwardly, as if his hands were too large and clumsy. My aunt was washing Anneke's hands. She wrung a flannel cloth in a bowl of soapy water. Lavender, Anneke's favorite.

"Strip the bed first," my aunt said, as if this were an ordinary washday morning. I crossed to the bed, grateful for a task, but unable to look at the dark proof of Anneke's death in the center. I lifted the pillow to loosen the sheet from underneath, where it was unstained, keeping my eyes away from the rest. Under the pillow was a steel knitting needle, smeared with dried brown streaks. I held it up.

"What's this?" I asked.

What was left of the world fell apart.

ELEVEN

"Gera's aunt says there are ways. . . ."

The stupid waste of it! For a second I could almost feel myself shaking her to make her see. But then I saw her limp arm, clean and white now, trailing onto the floor from my aunt's embrace, and my heart seized.

The knitting needle fell from my hand. If I had run it through their hearts, I couldn't have caused my aunt and uncle more pain. My aunt hugged Anneke's body tighter with each image that occurred to her. My uncle sobbed into Anneke's sweater, slumped over her bureau, her things. Their daughter had done this herself.

She had been alone, she had not wanted me here. But something didn't make sense: I had seen the way she had stroked her belly.

I saw the answer first, and my hands flew to my mouth as if I were afraid it would spill from me. I would have given anything

99

in the world to be able to shield my aunt and uncle from it. My uncle saw it next, gasped, and collapsed over the bureau under the weight of his guilt: She hadn't stabbed her womb to rid herself of her child, but to avoid going to that place. She had taken her baby herself rather than give him away.

My aunt rose from the bed and began to beat on my uncle's back, her small fists smashing down as if this would spend her grief. I jumped up, knocking over the pail of suds, and pulled her off him. I held her tight, but she was strong in her fury. She struggled toward him. Her body shook and she swallowed her sobs to pull a voice from them.

"You and your rules!"

"Mies —" His voice bled and he lifted his doomed hands to her. One of the lenses in his glasses was shattered.

"Are you satisfied now? Is there enough honor here now?"

"Tante Mies, please," I begged. There was already so much damage in this room.

But she wasn't finished. "She shamed us? *She* shamed us? Get out of here." Her voice was so low and cold that I didn't recognize it. *"Leave this house."*

My uncle caught the accusation in her

eyes and absorbed it. He seemed almost relieved to reach the bottom of his fall; anything was better than to keep falling. And perhaps relieved to accept blame, to be given a measure of punishment. Mercy would have been unbearable. He crashed out of the room, still clutching Anneke's sweater along with a lifetime of guilt. On the floor, Anneke's blood drifted through the soapy water in slow curls, tingeing the bubbles pink.

TWELVE

The sky was gray now, not black. Or maybe I was getting used to the dark. I wanted daylight, as though daylight would bring back normalcy. I wanted daylight because I wanted more people in this house; neighbors, friends, Isaak. Isaak, mostly. He would make sense of this, know what to do. But my aunt wouldn't let me phone anyone.

She had bathed Anneke herself. After my uncle left, she hadn't let me back into the bedroom. I was grateful. I would never go back there. But I could hear her washing the floor, and the slow, steady sloshing of the water made my throat hurt. I curled up on the floor of the hall, lost in sorrow and shock.

Then she remembered me. She came out and knelt down. "You should get some sleep, *kleintje*," she said, stroking my hair, which had come undone. "There's nothing for you to do now. Go into my bed." She helped me peel off my clothes, sticky with drying blood, and then she washed the blood off my skin. I felt ashamed of my body's warmth, knowing she had just washed this same blood off her child's cold skin.

Then she gave me a sleeping draught and one of her nightgowns. I didn't argue. I wanted to be unconscious.

I awoke to a different world. The late-afternoon sunlight was bright and brittle, and it hurt my sore eyes. Instead of clearing away all that had happened in the dark, it seemed an assault. What right did sunshine have here? I found my aunt in the kitchen, washing a window. Her fingers were white and swollen, and there were moons of perspiration under her arms. The harsh scent of vinegar hung in the air; without looking, I knew she had washed all the windows downstairs. We had cleaned them only three days before. A lifetime ago.

My aunt sensed my presence and turned. Her face was drawn impossibly tight, the color of ashes. A blood vessel in one of her eyes had broken, the bright red shocking against her gray face. She looked as if she had been crying blood.

She put down her rag and I wrapped my

arms around her. "Anneke —" I began.

Her head jerked and she took a step away from me.

"Tante Mies —"

She opened her mouth, then bit the side of her lip. She took a card from her pocket and handed it to me. A notice. I recognized it at once as the one Isaak had showed me in January that had been tacked to his door. They had been everywhere then.

JEWS MUST REGISTER WITH THE
AUTHORITIES.
FAILURE TO COMPLY WILL RESULT
IN SERIOUS PENALTIES.

"Where was this?" I asked in a voice so calm it couldn't have been my own. Last night had wrung me dry.

"I found it this morning, slipped under the door."

While we were upstairs losing everything, someone had been here, taking even more. In that one moment I lost all hope. But in its place poured relief. I'd been dreading this unspoken threat for too long and it was better to have it face me. I crumpled the notice and threw it onto the table. "Anneke —" I tried again.

My aunt reached for the notice and flat-

104

tened it out. "Not the *Wehrmacht;* they would have posted it on the door last winter, when the orders came. Mrs. Bakker, do you think?" she asked. She looked twenty years older than she had yesterday. "Maybe another neighbor, maybe she told someone else. Or maybe Karl."

We searched each other's faces, neither of us able to speak my uncle's name.

"Well. It doesn't matter today," I said.

"You're right." My aunt's voice held a strange urgency. She left the kitchen and came back with another piece of paper.

I felt the breath leave my body: CERTIFI-CATE OF DEATH.

"She's gone? They came already?"

My aunt pushed the certificate into my hand. "I've taken care of it." The way her eyes jumped warned me something was wrong. But of course everything was wrong.

I looked at the certificate again and I reeled: my name.

She led me to the window seat, still staring at the paper, and sat down next to me. "Yes. You died last night, not . . . You're safe now — no one will know."

I almost laughed, but I caught myself in time. My aunt's bloodshot eyes were too desperate. "You didn't really do this, did you? Tante Mies, did you sleep at all? You'd feel better — you'd see that this is wrong."

"The Schaaps were just here." She nodded to a bouquet of asters and a loaf of
bread on the table. "They saw the funeral
cart. I'm sure they're telling the other
neighbors now. People will be here soon.
Go upstairs. You'll have to hide, just until I
can take you to Nijmegen. No one will look
for you there. It will give us time to —"

I held up my hands. "Tante Mies, you're
not making any sense. This is just wrong.
When the others come we'll tell them
there's been a mistake. But you need to
sleep. I'm worried about you."

My aunt leaned over and dug her fingers
into my shoulders. "I've lost one child. I
will not lose another." Her voice was steel
wire, beginning to snap. I grew a little
afraid. I understood she was frantic and had
lost her reason. Where did reason fit when
you have lost a child?

"We'll talk about this later," I said gently.
"After you've slept."

The doorbell rang. My aunt rose and I
followed her. She looked out the parlor
window to see who it was.

"Mrs. Bakker," she whispered. "Go upstairs now."

"No, Tante Mies, let me help you . . .
please listen. You're not thinking right;

you're so upset. But you can't say it again, that it was me, not Anneke. I'm going to get Mrs. Sietsma, we'll tell her everything, and then she'll help us. All right? I'll get her now."

"Cyrla, go upstairs now! Let me handle this. I will *not* lose another child!"

What could anyone say to those words? It seemed dangerous to argue with her now — like taking a hammer to glass. I didn't have the strength to face Mrs. Bakker yet, anyway. Another few minutes wouldn't matter.

I hurried up the stairs and hid behind the door to my aunt and uncle's bedroom.

My aunt opened the door and Mrs. Bakker invited herself in, filling the hall with her bustle. "My God, Mies! I've just heard. So terrible. Come, let's make you a cup of tea, such a sad thing! Such a young girl!"

They went into the kitchen. I crept halfway down the stairs.

"A miscarriage. Cyrla was . . . we hadn't known. . . ."

I listened, stunned. There was a moment's silence, or perhaps I couldn't hear Mrs. Bakker's response. But I could almost see her take in this piece of news, the way she always did when she heard something she could tell others: head cocked and eyes glittering like a magpie who's found a shiny coin.

"And dear Anneke?" she asked next. "They were so close."

My aunt hesitated for only a second. "Yes, it's terrible for her. She's gone to Apeldoorn with her father to tell Cyrla's relatives in person. She wanted to do that. For her cousin."

I couldn't imagine what that lie must have cost my aunt. How much she must have wanted to tell someone — even Mrs. Bakker — her daughter was dead. To spill some of her grief. But then I understood. My aunt wanted to believe this — that Anneke wasn't dead after all, that it was only Cyrla who was lost. A niece only, not a daughter.

"She had relatives in Apeldoorn? I didn't know that."

"Very distant. A cousin of her father's. He's much older. Pieter thought he should be told in person."

"Of course, of course. But Mies, you shouldn't be alone. I'll tell the neighbors; I'll help you make the arrangements. And I'll bring you some supper; you must eat. There'll be a service, of course."

Mrs. Bakker was planning to stay for a while. She ignored us all these years, but now we interested her. When the doorbell

108

rang again she answered it and led in two more families from our street. She told them in reverent tones what had happened, and I loathed her for how she took on what wasn't hers to tell, for how self-important she sounded, for the false display of sympathy. Just for a second I thought that maybe it was a good thing if she thought I were dead: If she were the one behind the notice last night, I was glad to take that satisfaction from her. Then I realized how crazy that was.

I needed to see Isaak. I looked out the window; the evening was settling in, the sky the deep blue of dusk. He would be irritated with me for coming to him before it was totally dark, but he would understand.

I could hear Mrs. Bakker in the dining room with the neighbors, setting teacups on the table, making a fuss about things. I smelled something baked with cinnamon and apples. As long as everyone stayed at the table, I wouldn't be seen. I couldn't face going into the bedroom where Anneke wasn't anymore, so I buttoned one of my aunt's sweaters over her nightgown and slipped down the stairs, carrying a pair of her shoes, and opened the door as quietly as I could.

THIRTEEN

I took the back ways and regretted it. This close to the harbor, the water carried the hard odor of metal from the Germans' constant welding. It was too close to the smell of blood. The thought of Karl slammed into me — his lie and the blood Anneke had spilled over it. If I had seen him at that moment I would have torn his throat out with my teeth. Twice, I dropped from my bicycle and pressed my hands to my chest, it hurt so much to breathe.

Although it wasn't yet dark, Isaak didn't say a word of reproach when I collapsed into the doorway. In his work he had learned to recognize the look of ravaged humans. He led me to the bed and eased me down, then sat beside me.

"What?"

I crawled onto his lap, curled up in his arms, and sobbed into his chest. "I want her back, I want her back, I want her back!"

Isaak waited. "She was so beautiful," I whispered finally, my throat raw. "I used to feel she pulled the sunlight from the air. I was so jealous. Now I'm so sorry, I'm so sorry —"

"What's happened?"

It was so hard to put words to the horror we'd found, to make it that real and that final. Almost impossible to speak the violence Anneke had committed on herself. Each word tore my heart open and I ached for Isaak to tell me I was wrong, this couldn't have happened.

But instead, he only listened to what Anneke had done with a frown. "Stupid." He muttered it under his breath when I was finished, but I heard it. "Stupid and selfish."

I pulled away, wiped my eyes and stared at him. "Isaak, are you . . . blaming her?"

"She took a life. It was inconvenient and —"

I jumped up to face him. "How can you say something like that? Think of how upset she must have been, how desperate to . . . to take that risk. She didn't deserve any of this. This is Karl's fault, not hers. She died, Isaak! She was beautiful and full of life and kind and generous. She made everyone smile; everyone she met! And oh, Isaak . . .

111

I loved her and she didn't tell me. She didn't trust me."

I began to cry again and Isaak softened. But all he said was "I'm sorry. I know you loved her."

Until that moment I hadn't realized how much it had damaged Isaak to be raised without a family. How much distance he kept from people. It wasn't his fault, I reminded myself. But I would keep my grief from him now.

I gathered myself and sat beside him again. "There's more. I need your help." I told him about the notice that had been slipped under my door. "My aunt's out of her mind. She made Oom Pieter leave — she blames him for all of it. And Isaak, she won't talk about Anneke's death. She told the funeral home that it was me who died, not Anneke. She thinks this will protect me; she actually thinks she can keep this a secret and I can go away and use her papers and that whoever left that notice will give up. I don't know what to do. Will you come back with me?"

Isaak got up, went to the window, and pulled the blackout shade aside to look into the night. Then he turned.

"Cyrla, what if . . . look, you wanted to stay in Holland, you were planning to dive under, right? But it's much safer to live with papers, an identity —"

"Did you hear what I said?"

He picked up the chair from his desk, placed it in front of the bed, and sat facing me. He braced his elbows on the arms and rested his chin on his clasped hands — the reassuring position I imagined him in when he met with people at the Council. Relief melted over me: He was going to hear me and find a solution, logical and sound.

I was wrong.

"Let me finish. Real papers are much better than false ones. But they're almost impossible to come by. Someone near your age and description has to die or disappear, and that person's family has to arrange for the exchange — it doesn't just happen. Now here you have what every Jew in Europe wants: legal papers from someone who looks enough like you she could be your twin, and a family willing to go along with it."

I couldn't believe what I was hearing. I was standing at the edge of a cliff, and the people I trusted most were trying to push me off. "I can't even talk about this. Anneke's dead, and I can't imagine my life without her! I can't remember the last thing I said to her. I want her back. I just want her back!" I felt hysteria rising, but I swallowed it. "My aunt's out of her mind. Could you come back with me and help with her?"

He ignored me, still working through her idea, I could see.

"Isaak, it would never work. I don't even look that much like her."

"Of course you do. You could be twins. You even have the same . . ."

Isaak's hand lifted, as if to touch the nape of my neck where my braid was pinned up. I had a mole there. Anneke did, too, but hers was hidden by her curls — Isaak couldn't know about it. "Hair," he said. "You have the same color hair. But never mind. That's not the point. The point is that someone knows — that notice was a threat. You need to leave. There are legal papers available to you. If you don't take them, I'll ask your aunt to release them for someone else. This is what I do. I know fifty women who would take them today and be grateful. A hundred and fifty. They wouldn't look anything like Anneke, but they'd take them for the chance to survive. Things are going to get worse here, Cyrla. No matter how much you want to deny it, it's true. And you're going to need papers now. I could get you a set from the Free Netherlands, but it would take a week and they'd be forged."

"Isaak," I interrupted, grabbing his hands. I took a breath and felt it cut through me, as though I were made of nothing more substantial than ash. I tried to hide my panic. "Please listen. It's not the papers. My aunt is in shock. She wants me to step into Anneke's life. She's planning to take me to that maternity home — it's in Nijmegen — next week, in her place! That's the part that's so . . . if I did take Anneke's papers, if by some miracle my aunt could convince everyone it was me who died, couldn't I just disappear in Amsterdam? Would you help me do that?"

Isaak got up and went back to the window. "I forgot about the Lebensborn. There's one in Nijmegen? I didn't know that. She passed the tests, then? Yes, you could go to Amsterdam, but it would be dangerous. Because if the Germans are expecting Anneke next week, they'll investigate when she doesn't show up. Each baby is that valuable to them. If you didn't take those papers, if I could get them for another woman, yes, that's what I'd tell her to do: Disappear into a city with them and just hope to buy some time. Because no one else would look enough like her to pass in the maternity home. But Cyrla, think about this: Of all the places to hide, perhaps this is the best.

Living right in the midst of them, with them caring for you. Surrounded by nurses and doctors and other Dutch girls —"

I jumped up and turned away from him so he wouldn't see me force back tears. "Stop it! How could you possibly consider my going to a place like that? We're not going to talk about this anymore."

Isaak came up behind me, but he didn't touch me. I yearned for him to fold me into him and tell me of course he wouldn't let me go there.

"It would only be for a little while — until I could arrange something permanent. I still think a passage to England is best, especially now. Until then, the maternity home sounds safe. I can't imagine the Germans hunting for Jews in a place like that. In fact it may be the only place in the whole country they would never look. There are *doctors* there, not the Gestapo. Think about it: Anneke's papers say not only that she's Dutch, but that she's passed every test of Aryan heritage they require for entrance. You would be safe there, I think. And remember, it's only for a few weeks. A month at most."

I spun to face him. "A *month?* Isaak, are you asking me to try to pass as Anneke in that place for a month?" I bit down on my lip but it was no use. I began to cry.

Isaak wiped my cheeks with his fingers. Even then I was aware: This was the first time he had ever reached out to touch me. It had taken my tears. "I am telling you I don't have a better solution right now. And it might be longer," he said. "No one can predict these days. It's best to be prepared."

Anneke was gone. My uncle was gone. My aunt was gone, too, in her way. Isaak wasn't going to help me. I had only myself to get out of this. And then I saw I was all I needed.

I began to laugh, still crying. I couldn't stop. I fell back on the bed weeping and laughing. The answer had been there all along, so obvious we had missed it.

"What?" Isaak asked. "What?"

"Oh, Isaak!" I wiped my cheeks with my own hands, the way I was used to. The way I would have to my whole life. "I'm not pregnant!"

And then I stopped laughing.

FOURTEEN

Isaak and I looked at each other without speaking. I saw everything pass through his mind. I saw him reject the idea. I saw him search for a better place to hide me than the home. I saw him consider the risk of having me stay in that place without being pregnant. And I saw him come back to the obvious.

I hoped Isaak didn't see my thoughts: Once more, I was leaving my home, but this time I had a choice: I could create a family for myself before I left, or I could go alone. There was no choice.

"Your child," I whispered. "I would take your child to safety in England." A promise of flesh and blood to a man who had never known it.

I saw him fall into my promise.

FIFTEEN

I had loved Isaak from the day I met him, the day I arrived in the Netherlands.

Three weeks earlier, my father had told me the plan: "The new regime," he'd begun. I'd hated those words already: He'd lost his teaching position because of the new regime; we'd had to move to Lodz because of it. And now, the *numerous clausus* — the closed-numbers law to limit the number of Jews who could attend the universities. "You'll be better off in Holland. You can get an education. Your brothers might not be able to."

"But I'm only fourteen, Papa," I'd protested.

"Just until things change," he'd promised. And then he'd closed the argument. No matter how I'd begged, he'd remained firm.

I hadn't understood any of it. And then, as I boarded the train, I remembered: My father had packed away everything my mother had loved. I pressed my face to the train window, the dirty glass wet with my tears, and watched him on the platform. His arms were clenched over his chest, his face set in angry lines. I was the last thing my mother had loved, the last thing to remind him of her. I'd ridden for two days frozen rigid in that thought.

When I stepped off the train, I saw my aunt. She looked so much like my mother that for a moment I felt as if I'd been given her back. In my exhaustion, and in the shock of seeing my mother's face, I began to cry again.

When I lifted my head from her shoulder, I saw Isaak standing behind her, watching. For the first time in my life I was aware of how I might look to a boy. I knew my face was streaked with tears and two days' worth of train grime, and my hair was a tangle escaping my hat.

Isaak smiled. "Welcome to Holland. I like your name. I have never heard it before."

I wiped my face with my mittens and stared at him dumbly. He nodded at the package he held. On the brown paper was my name in my father's script. "Cyrla," he said. I told him how to pronounce my name the correct way — with the Y sounding as if it were a U — and then wished I hadn't. I suddenly felt I would like my name to sound different coming from his lips than from all others.

"Cyrla," he repeated, then he handed me the package. "Your father sent it ahead. He didn't think it would be wise for you to cross through Germany with it."

I opened it. A framed photograph of my mother and father with me at four, reaching up to hold their hands. My mother's jewelry. The silver Sabbath candlesticks my father's father had given him.

"My father worries too much," I heard myself say.

Isaak shook his head. "I don't think so. I think people should worry more." He handed me a card. "When you write to your family, bring the letter to this address. The people there will post it. It's what your father asked."

I went the next day, and we took a walk. We fell into this habit. I would bring letters — more often, I admit, than I might have otherwise — and we would walk and Isaak would show me some area of Schiedam, although in a few months I think I knew the town as well as he did.

For the first couple of years, it was as if my new family had adopted Isaak, too — he came almost every night for dinner, and then afterward he and Anneke and I would listen to music, talk, visit friends. The closeness the three of us shared eased the pain of leaving my family, and in fact Isaak's height and dark curls reminded me so much of my father that it was a comfort. But then war became more and more the topic of Isaak's conversation and Anneke did or said something that irritated him — neither of them ever said what it was — and he abruptly stopped coming.

He and I stayed friends. He was an orphan and in a way, I was too. It was natural we would feel that bond. But there was more — it felt to me as if something had ignited between us on the train platform, and I still felt the heat every time he was near.

In the five years I knew Isaak, I was certain he never lied to me or failed to put my welfare first. Until that day after Anneke died, he could have said the same about me.

Isaak and I didn't talk about what we had just decided. I didn't want to — it was dangerous to talk about miracles, to hold them up to the light. And this was a miracle. I was about to receive everything I'd ever wanted after losing everything I'd ever had. My loss, in fact, had brought about my gain: a terrible twist I couldn't bear to face.

At last Isaak spoke. "When was Anneke due there?"

"Two weeks from the day she went for the interviews. So next Friday."

"Well. Ten — no, eleven — days, then," Isaak said.

"Eleven days," I agreed.

"And is it possible? I mean . . . is it your time?"

"I don't know. It was over a week ago that . . . yes, I think it's possible."

"And do you want to . . . should we try . . ."

"No." I picked up my coat. "Tante Mies will be wondering where I am." I needed to go home first, although I didn't know why. Isaak seemed relieved, so perhaps he needed this pause also.

We rode back to my house. For once I was glad of the blackout, although it disturbed me to have become someone who needed the cover of darkness. We slipped around to the back garden and he waited while I pulled the key from under its flowerpot. He had never waited before, but of course everything was different now.

Suddenly I didn't want to say good-bye. My house was dark and so was Mrs. Bakker's, but I felt exposed on our back step. I wondered if this was how I would feel now wherever I went. I pulled Isaak into the narrow space between our shed and the high wooden fence.

"Tomorrow," I whispered. I put my arms around his waist, and after a second Isaak put his arms around mine.

"I have to go to Rotterdam tomorrow. I'll be back in the afternoon. Where shall we . . . meet?"

"My uncle's shop. He won't come back. Go to the back door."

I leaned my head against his chest, then raised it to kiss his neck. I waited for him to find my mouth; I wanted that much to be from him. He didn't. I pressed my body closer. I had never felt him this way, the hardness of his hips igniting a sudden thrill deep in my belly. I thought of his warm skin beneath his clothes, imagined it sliding against mine, and shivered. I slid my hand down the small of his back and urged him closer.

I raised my lips to his and we kissed. I opened my mouth and pulled him into me and poured myself into him, as Anneke had said. I was overwhelmed with yearning, with an ache to be filled.

Eleven days was so little time.

The moment Isaak and I made our decision, Anneke disappeared from my thoughts. But once I stepped into my home, nothing but her death existed. It was as if both things filled me so completely I could hold only one or the other.

Inside, Anneke's absence was everywhere, enormous and total. Her hand was missing from the coffee grinder, the teacups, the wooden spoons. Her face was missing from the reflections of the hanging pans, the blacked-out windows. The air itself seemed empty without her fragrance and her voice, and everything, everything was wrong.

My aunt heard the kitchen door and came down. She looked worse than when I left, only a few hours before — on top of her grief, she had been worried about me. Hot and still breathless from Isaak's kiss, I felt ashamed. So I told her right away what she wanted to hear: Isaak agreed with her plan and would help us, and I wouldn't oppose it.

She nodded in relief. "I've moved your things into the attic bedroom. You can stay there. No one can know you're here."

"I understand," I told her. "Tante Mies, are there . . . have you made arrangements?"

She turned to the sink and braced herself, her fingers whitening around the porcelain edge. It hurt that she didn't want me to see her cry. She turned back to me and wiped her face. The skin under her eyes was chafed raw, as if she had been trying to scrub away something deeper than tears. She pressed her lips together and took a breath.

"I'll call the funeral home tomorrow and arrange for the burial to be in Apeldoorn. I've told everyone you had relatives there, and that Pieter and Anneke are there already, so . . . What else can I do? If I bury her here, everyone will come. They'll expect to see Anneke."

"But no! She'll be so far away! I'm sorry, I'm so sorry, Tante Mies. Don't do this. It's not too late, we'll just explain —"

"No. No, that would be worse. I will see you safe. If I can't do that . . ." She straightened and smiled, but it was just her lips stretched tight. "I know a woman in Apeldoorn. A childhood friend. Your mother knew her, too. I'll look her up, and perhaps I can stay with her. I don't think I'll want to come back here for a while."

The thought of her house empty was the one that undid her.

Anneke was our home.

SIXTEEN

The next morning, I awoke with Isaak already in my mind, as if he'd lain beside me through the night. He would not have been welcomed here, though, I thought as I looked around the room Anneke's grandmother had lived in. She'd been my grandmother, too, but I had never known her because she had disowned my mother for marrying my Jewish father. I didn't exist for her.

When I went downstairs, I wondered if my aunt had slept at all: The kitchen curtains were hanging on the line bleaching in the sun and apple syrup was simmering on the stove, which gleamed as if she had just pulled it apart and cleaned it. She was holding a blue bowl, and when I walked in, she turned away and began to beat a batter fiercely. In grim silence she cracked eggs into a skillet and made my favorite pancakes with plum jam. I knew not to argue. I hadn't

127

eaten for two days, and it was as if I'd never tasted before: The yolk was hot and runny in my mouth, the butter rich and smooth, and the jam so sweet it stung my cheeks. It was all an assault, though, and it hurt to swallow in the silent kitchen: Anneke would never taste food again.

She was dead. Each time, this fact stunned me, slammed into me like a kick to the chest. Each time, I had to remind myself to breathe again. When my aunt leaned over to pour my tea, she rested her trembling hand on my shoulder, and I felt lonelier than before. She was trying to fill an empty space with her busyness. I had Isaak to fill mine. I wondered what my uncle had.

After breakfast I ran a bath and poured in the gardenia-scented salts I saved for special occasions. My throat closed when I slipped into the fragrant water: Anneke had given me the salts on my last birthday. I fell into silent sobs, until I felt I was floating in my hot tears. Had I ever cried this much?

But I didn't want to stop. I wanted to keep Anneke with me always, to think of her every day, even if it meant opening the wound over and over again. I forced myself to imagine what she might say if she were here right now, if she knew what Isaak and I were about to do. The answer made me smile a little: She would have told me to do just this, to use the gardenia-scented bath salts. She always prepared like this before she was going to see Karl, as though her body were a gift and she wanted even its wrapping to give him pleasure.

Although it felt like betraying Anneke, I allowed myself to think of Isaak's hands as I soaped my body, how they might feel on my breasts, on my belly. How I might feel to him. Everywhere I touched, I felt the heat rise. I imagined the thrill he might feel entering me. Imagining him filling me nearly made me faint.

I washed my hair and was rinsing it under the tap when my aunt knocked.

"Cyrla!" she whispered, coming in. She looked wild, with her one bloodshot eye. "Mrs. Bakker is at the door again!" The bathroom was in the hall underneath the stairs. She wrapped a towel around my hair. "I'll try to get her to leave. But go upstairs. Hurry."

I ran up and hid again in the bedroom. My aunt opened the door and tried to send our neighbor away. "I was just going out," she said. "So many things to do."

But Mrs. Bakker entered anyway. "Perhaps I can help?"

"No, well . . . it's very kind of you. But I

should leave now."

There was a pause and I held my breath. I could almost see Mrs. Bakker sniffing the gardenia steam, eyes narrowed like a prowling cat. Then I heard her voice again, and in it was the sly tone that had frightened me on the steps a few mornings ago. "Your floor is wet, Mies. You've spilled something."

"Oh . . . I was running a bath. I was just about to step into the bath. That's all." She was a poor liar.

"I thought you were going out?"

"Well, yes. I mean, I was going out after my bath. Really, I'll be very late if I don't hurry now, so I'm afraid I'll have to ask you to —"

Mrs. Bakker left, but I knew she'd be back. It would be difficult living in my own home without anyone knowing.

I stood at the open window drying my hair in the sun. The rain had washed down so many leaves that I could see the horse chestnuts gleaming in buttery pools of light on the cobbled streets. The air itself seemed rinsed clean. The thought struck me that I would never again walk along Tielman Oemstraat and greet my neighbors, stop to chat with them. The telephone rang three or four times, and I heard my aunt tell the lie about what had happened in our family.

130

With each repetition, I felt less solid, as if I had really died.

A pair of crows landed on the elm branch nearest the window and looked in at me with their bad-omen eyes. I rushed at them, waving my arms, but because I couldn't make a noise, they ignored me, shifting their wings lazily. My hair still damp, I turned and went up to the attic room.

My aunt had brought everything I owned up there, and I saw how easily all traces of my life could be packed away. Had I made any mark at all? But today, I reminded myself, I wanted to leave this house. I dressed carefully, the way Anneke would have. I chose a champagne satin slip she'd insisted I buy a few years ago — Jean Harlow had worn one just like it. It was the only truly beautiful thing I owned, and I'd never worn it. The satin poured over my shoulders like cream. Then I put on an ivory blouse with pearl buttons and tiny darts all along the waist, and a black skirt, flared through the hips and slit in the back. It had been Anneke's, but she had given it to me; she said it fit me better because my hips were wider than hers, although my waist was narrower.

My cousin was everywhere, and everything made me wince. I could almost see her sitting on the bed, tilting her head to gravely consider each piece of my outfit. "It doesn't matter," I would tell her if she were really here. "Isaak never notices what I wear."

"It *does* matter," I heard her reply. "*You'll* know what you're wearing. Now, put on some lipstick," she surely would have encouraged me next. "And leave your hair down."

No, that I wouldn't do. I wasn't a girl who wore lipstick and loose hair.

Although maybe that was who I was about to become.

Then I remembered something Anneke and I had talked about before I left for Amsterdam: how I might be changed after making love. She'd told me I would begin to live through my body more, and learn to trust the things it told me. And she had talked about courage: "You have to be brave to be in love," she'd said. I still couldn't remember our last words, though.

Downstairs, my aunt was still in the kitchen, ironing dish towels that already looked stiff with starch. She looked up when she heard me, and for an instant I saw hope bloom on her face and then wither. It was only me.

"Where are you going? You can't go anywhere."

I raised my hands helplessly. "I'm going to Isaak."

Somehow she understood. "Oh . . . oh." I could see she wanted to object, or at least felt that she should. But the effort was too great. She sank to the window seat and then straightened herself and drew in a breath through clenched teeth. She'd probably done that a hundred times already today. It was the cost of not drowning in the river of loss. "Be careful," she said. "Be careful."

"We're meeting at the shop. I'll wear your coat and hat and bring the lunch basket. The neighbors are used to seeing that."

She nodded and I went over to hug her, but she stiffened and pulled away.

When I came back down at noon, my aunt seemed better. She had packed a basket with tomato sandwiches on rye bread, pears, and cheese. I put a book of poetry in the basket to read while I waited for Isaak.

She sat beside me and began to braid my hair. "You look so much like your mother when she was your age. That's when she met your father, you know."

My spine arched at the mention of my mother. Sometimes I could think of her, but sometimes not. I relaxed and asked my aunt to tell me the story, although I knew it well. My parents were both studying music in Vienna, both lonely from having left their homes in other countries. My father heard my mother playing a Mozart sonata in a practice room one day, and fell in love with the pianist inside.

"He knew only her name, which was posted outside the door on the schedule," my aunt said. Remembering her sister seemed to bring her pleasure and only a little sadness; would we ever feel this way about Anneke? "He went every day at that hour, even if it meant missing his own classes. But he was too shy to stay and introduce himself. Finally, he slipped a note under the door one day and asked her to meet him later. She did, and I don't think they spent a day apart after that. And Cyrla . . ."

There was a look on her face I didn't understand. She patted my cheek and smiled. "Cyrla. Your parents were married in July. You were born in December. I think your mother would have told you this to-day."

I stared at her for the moment it took to understand. I hugged her for the generosity of her gift, then set out.

My heart raced, but at my center I felt a calm. I had changed already.

SEVENTEEN

I clutched my aunt's hat to my head as if the wind were trying to blow it away, and hurried to the shop. No one saw me. At least no one I noticed.

The shop was empty, the air thick with the stale damp smell of boiled wool. It was the wrong place for Isaak and me to be together. I remembered the roof and ran up. Yes, here. But there was only gravel to lie on.

I went back downstairs to find something. But except for the Germans' brown wool, the shelves were nearly empty; my uncle hadn't been able to buy new material for months. There were odds and ends of old orders, and some useless scraps in boxes on the floor.

I almost missed it. Behind the piles of brown wool was half a bolt of heavy velvet, blue so dark it was nearly indigo. The yardage left over from an order of a year ago:

The wife of a hotel owner in Scheveningen had ordered drapes for her dining room, but had been unable to pay for them after the Nazis confiscated the hotel for their headquarters.

"Were they for the hotel dining room?" my uncle had asked when she came to explain.

"No. They were for our home. But now there's no work. No money."

"As long as the Germans won't use them, take them anyway," my uncle insisted. "What am I going to do with them, after all?"

First I brought two bolts of the Germans' fabric to the rooftop. I walked around to find which corner caught the warmest sunspill, and there I arranged the thick wool to make a nest. Then I went back down for the velvet. I spread the blue plush over the blanket fabric, tucking it in so none of the wool showed, so nothing with a Nazi taint would touch our skin. For the same reason, I took off my legitimization card and hid it in my basket. Then I stood back to see what I had made and I smiled at the way the sun lit the velvet to the color of sapphires. Anneke had told me to listen to my senses. She would have approved.

Anneke. A rush of tears besieged me —

how much I wanted her! I wiped them away and walked to the edge of the roof and took a deep breath. The scent of windfall apples hung in the air. There was train smoke, as always, and faintly, the earthy smell of bricks baking in the sun. The noon sunlight sparkled on the canal and burnished the September landscape below — this world looked so peaceful. As if it weren't going to collapse on me in a week.

Then I took the poetry book from the basket and sat with it to wait, beside the bed, not on it. The bed would be for the two of us only. I searched for just the right poem, and found a title by Boutens I had never read: "Kissing."

After last night, but not before, I could have written that poem.

I wanted to kiss Isaak again. But I grew nervous thinking about what would happen after that. I wasn't ready. What had I been thinking? But Rilke's "Autumn Day" ran through my head, and wouldn't leave. *"He who is alone now, will remain alone."* I had been alone long enough. Terrible things happened to people who were alone. So when Isaak knocked below I told myself I was ready enough.

I let him in and we climbed to the roof. We searched each other's eyes, and then looked away.

"Well," I said.

"Well."

We were the closest of friends, yet we stood beside each other awkwardly and gazed out at the roofs of our city, our closeness between us now. There was nothing to say, as if we were finished speaking through words. I took his hand and led him to the bed I had made, and then I lay down.

My heart beat so hard I thought Isaak would see it jump through my skin. I remembered my trick for being brave: Take only the first small step. I lifted my fingers to my throat and unbuttoned a single button.

Isaak fell to his knees beside me.

Carefully, deliberately, as he did everything, he unbuttoned my blouse. I took his hand and led it under my slip, onto the bare skin of my breast. I gasped at the touch and Isaak pulled away, as if he had hurt me. He pulled the velvet over us, and then he lay down beside me and worked my clothes off under my skirt. My skin chilled in the surprise of cool air, but burned where it met his. He spread my legs apart and rolled between them and began to push against me.

Anneke had been wrong, that our bodies

would know what to do. Then I remembered. "Wait, wait . . ." I whispered. I found his mouth and kissed him. I could have done that forever. But he broke away and buried his face in my neck and began to press against me again.

I stopped him. I took off my slip and opened his shirt, ran my palms down his chest, then pulled him to me to feel our hearts beat together. But when I reached lower, he pushed my hand away and grunted. And then I felt him inside me and I cried out at the deep, sweet shock of it.

And then, finally, it was the way Anneke had promised. We pressed our bodies closer because we couldn't pull them apart. We moved in a rhythm that was the only one that had ever existed. It had always been inside us. But suddenly Isaak shuddered and cried out, then crumpled and fell beside me.

He rolled away and reached for his shirt. I tried to pull him back. "Stay."

He tensed and raised his head.

"Listen!"

It took me a moment, as if I were struggling to the surface after a deep dive. The blood rushing in my own head was all I heard at first. Isaak rose and crept along the wall. I took my blouse to cover myself, and followed. The words were German, and angry.

I crouched beside Isaak and peered over the edge down upon the shoulders of two men. Soldiers.

"The second day," I caught, and murmured curses.

And then: "Break it down."

Eighteen

I gathered my things.

"Stay calm," Isaak said. But he was dressing quickly also. "Maybe they won't look here."

But maybe they would. The door to the stairwell was in the back room, and I couldn't remember if I had closed it, or left anything out that might lead them up here.

Glass shattered on the pavement.

"I'm going down," I said.

Isaak held my arm. "No! We'll stay still up here until they leave."

I heard more glass — the splintering of wood. "You stay. I'll send them away." I twisted away from him, grabbed my blouse, and ran down the stairs, buttoning as I went.

They were inside already. I tried to sound angry as I walked out of the storeroom. "What do you want?"

They were SS, not *Wehrmacht,* and their uniforms told me they were a *Kapitan* and a

141

trooper, an *Oberschütze.* They had smashed the window beside the door and the trooper was behind the counter, pulling papers from a drawer.

"We have business with Pieter Van der Berg. Where is he?" The officer tried to enter the storeroom, but I stepped in front of him. My uncle kept money back there, hidden in an empty sewing-machine housing.

"He's not here. He's away."

Too late I realized how I was dressed — my blouse half-undone, no slip, and no stockings. I crossed my arms over my chest, but the *Oberschütze* was staring. He was wide-shouldered and powerful looking, with bristly hair so short it looked almost shaved and a face flat and red as a cut of meat. His look frightened me, as if I were a prostitute sitting in a window in Amsterdam. I took a step away.

"When will he be back?" the captain asked.

"Oh, tomorrow," I lied.

And then the worst thing happened. I felt a wetness between my legs. Hot at first, then sliding down between my bare thighs and cooling. When I realized what it was tears sprang to my eyes, but I bit them back.

"Come back tomorrow," I urged him.

"We have an order here for six hundred blankets. Are they ready?"

The wetness slid farther down my legs. How much did a man leave inside a woman? Enough to give Isaak away? "He's gone to get a part for the machine. For your order. I'll tell him you were here."

The officer pushed past me and the trooper followed. I didn't try to stop them now. They suspected my uncle had taken their fabric to sell on the black market, and I thought if they saw it was still here, they would be satisfied.

The officer came back into the doorway carrying a bolt of wool. "Take the rest of it and pack it onto the truck," he ordered the other one as he left.

I was worrying whether they would notice two bolts were missing, and planning what I would say to explain it, and so wasn't prepared for what happened next.

The *Oberschütze* stood beside me and let the officer pass out of the shop. Then he dropped the wool he was holding and shoved his hand against my back, pinning me over the cutting table. His other hand pushed my skirt up and grabbed at my hip. He laughed when he found I had nothing on underneath, and began to grind himself against me.

143

I tried to twist away, terrified he would find the evidence I had just been with a man, and struggled to climb over the table — a pair of shears hung from a hook in the cupboard below. His hand dug into my neck and I smelled motor oil. I heard the clink of his belt buckle, the rip of his buttons.

I bit my lips so I wouldn't make a sound that might bring Isaak down and I dug harder and found the shears. I wrenched backward and jammed the open blade as hard as I could toward his throat.

"Bitch!" He knocked the shears away, drew back, and raised his hand over me.

Suddenly the officer was back. "Off her!" he yelled, pulling the trooper from me. "Animal! This one's pregnant. She's going to the Lebensborn."

The trooper released his grip and glared at me, his face sweating, red as a ham, pulling his uniform together. Then he picked up the bolts of wool he had dropped.

I backed up against the counter, not sure my legs would hold me. The officer leaned over and reached for me. "Are you all right?"

I pushed his hand away. He looked as though he expected me to thank him. He had told his soldier to respect me because I was carrying a German child, as if that were the only reason I shouldn't be raped. I would not thank him for that.

"Tell your father we'll be back tomorrow. He had better have that part." The officer straightened and motioned to the other one to leave.

"Wait," the trooper said. "Let's see her identification."

He reached for my neck. He saw me look down with disgust at his fingers, black with grease, and he smiled, then slowly wiped them down the front of my blouse, over my breast. I slapped his hand away and spat in his face. He reared back and raised his arm again, and again the officer stopped him, this time with his hand to his gun.

"Nein," said the captain. "I know this one, I've seen her picture. She's Van der Berg's daughter."

They left, the trooper hesitating at the door long enough to throw me a look of pure hatred. As if everything in the world were my fault. I sank to the floor.

Isaak came down — he had watched the men go — and found me there. He crouched beside me. "What happened?"

I looked away so I could lie. "They took the wool."

He motioned to the mess of papers on the floor, the shears, everything that had been thrown to the floor in my struggle. "You fought them? For some material?"

His eyes fell to the streak of grease over my breast and I turned away again, trying not to cry.

"That was stupid, Cyrla!" He shook his head. "You have no idea what they're capable of. They make up their own rules, and there's no one to stop them. Think of what could have happened here."

"Nothing happened, Isaak. They're gone. They wanted their blankets; they wanted my uncle."

Isaak looked out the window, thinking. "They'll come back here tomorrow, and if your uncle isn't here, they'll go to your home. And your uncle . . . it would be better if you weren't there. When it's dark, you'd better come home with me. I'll tell your aunt."

I nodded, grateful for his calm and his logic and that he had stopped questioning me. He wrapped his coat around me and helped me back to the roof where we sat down on the bed of velvet again to wait for dark. Every time the memory of what the trooper had tried to do forced its way in, I pushed it away. But once I wasn't quick enough, and I thought about what might have happened: What if I had gotten pregnant with his child? I cried out. Isaak asked what was wrong. "Nothing," I said, and felt foolish allowing something I only imagined to wound me. Somehow I would have to erase his attack from my memory of this day. Isaak and I made love today . . . that's what happened today, I told myself.

Later, we watched the sun set over the Schiedam gate and ate the meal my aunt had packed. I read Isaak the poem about kissing, and as I read it I was suddenly struck with the certain knowledge that today had not been Isaak's first time. I didn't know how I knew, but I did: He had been with a woman before. I'd been his closest friend since he was sixteen, and I'd never guessed. I tried to keep my voice steady as I finished the poem, but my throat hurt, as if it had been cut. I'd have to erase this from the memory of the day, too.

Before we left, I bit two notches into the corner of the velvet we had lain upon and ripped off a square to save. I tucked it into the bottom of my basket, and then pulled out my legitimization card and hung it around my neck, my back to Isaak. I realized joy was not something that fell randomly, something to hope for. Joy was something to steal.

NINETEEN

I felt calm and safe in Isaak's room. It was Wednesday evening, and I wouldn't leave until the next Friday morning. I thought that here the world would stop for nine days.

I was wrong.

I sat on the bed and watched Isaak while he worked. *This is how it will be when we are married. And there will be a child asleep in the next room.*

I realized with pleasure that from now on, when I thought of my life, it would fall cleanly into two parts — before and after this day. I went up to Isaak and put my hand on his neck, thrilled that this gesture was now mine to make. "What shall we name him?"

"Who?"

"Our child. What shall we name him? Or her?"

He turned in his chair to face me. I could tell he didn't like my question.

"This isn't . . . You shouldn't count on anything . . ."

"You're right," I said, eager to erase his frown. "First I have to be pregnant."

While I unbuttoned his shirt and kissed his chest, he watched my face in that careful way he had, as if he were considering what to do. This time I tried to think about making a baby because I knew that was what Isaak was thinking about. But my arms around his shoulders looked like someone else's, and I couldn't help seeing the way those shoulders were ridged with neat, hard muscles that lifted in a cadence as he worked his way into me. I couldn't help stroking these muscles down to the small of his back and, although I was sore, kneading him to bring him deeper into me, trying to fill the new place that was so hungry. When I cried his name, he hushed me. I had to bite my lip to keep from crying it out louder. And when he made the sound, stifled into my neck, that meant he was spent, when I should have been satisfied because he had given me what I asked for, I wasn't.

I couldn't help it. I wanted something more.

I squeezed my legs around him, to show

him I wanted him to stay. "Say my name," I asked.

He raised his head to look into my eyes. "No. When you go to Nijmegen, your life might depend on responding to Anneke's name. I won't call you by yours again."

Nijmegen. I had forgotten. "Please, Isaak. Just once more."

"No."

He lifted himself away from me then. He got up and lay down on the mattress he had put on the floor. His bed was too narrow for us both to sleep in, I understood. Still, I felt abandoned. When I could tell from his breathing he was asleep, I slipped down to the floor beside him.

I lifted his arm and curled myself up against his side. I laid my head on his chest and matched my breathing to his. Careful with my movements so as not to wake him, I unbound my hair and spread it up over his shoulder and twisted my curls into his. Then I pulled his arm across his chest, and wound his fingers through my own. When he awoke, I hoped he would understand this circle, the one I dreamed of so often. I fell asleep glowing, as if I had swallowed peace.

TWENTY

Thursday. Isaak told me he would be gone until late afternoon. I asked if I could come with him to his meetings, since they were only in the synagogue.

"No," he said right away. He averted his eyes, as if he were embarrassed by my nakedness, as if we didn't know each other's bodies now. "It would be noticed. I don't want anyone to know you're here. Not even the people I trust. The fewer who know, the better. That's always the way."

When Isaak left, I put on one of his shirts and then his overcoat, and took the clothes I had been wearing for two days to the bathroom to wash them. I scrubbed at the grease stain the trooper had left on my blouse, but it left a shadow.

In that one day, I grew absorbed with the sensations of skin, like a woman born blind who can suddenly see and is unable to sleep for the looking she must do to catch up. I lay on the bed trying to read, but was distracted by the touch of his shirt and the miracle of air on my body. I sat on the floor to work on a poem but could only write about the feel of my back pressed against the brick wall and of the sunlight streaming over my bare thighs. I craved the heat of Isaak's skin against my own. Anneke hadn't told me how hot blood was when it rose in two bodies.

When he returned, I was again lying on the bed. This time he didn't look away.

"Don't move." He came over to the bed and loosened my hair, which I had twisted into a soft roll to keep out of my book. "It's like honey," he said, sifting it through his fingers and arranging it over my shoulder. "It flows like honey."

His hand brushed my breast, and I caught it and held it there. I let the book fall.

"No, I want to draw you." He pulled away. "You're beautiful."

"I'm not. Anneke is."

Was.

"No, Anneke was pretty. What's pretty can never be beautiful. *You* are beautiful. I'll show you. Get up, I need to move the bed for the light."

Isaak moved his desk aside and pushed the bed underneath the window.

"There, lie down," he said.

Holding his gaze, trembling, I took off his shirt. Isaak watched, then nodded. I let him arrange me as I had been before, lying on my side, one arm propping my head, the other draping my waist to lift a page of my book. I couldn't breathe when he touched me. He poured my hair over my neck, my shoulder. When he tilted my hip back into the sunlight I shivered. *See me, Isaak. Want me.*

He picked up a pad and a pencil and brought the chair to the side of the bed. He sat still for a long time, just looking at me, moving two fingers softly over his lips. I pretended to read, but whenever I could I watched him studying my body, appraising it with his artist's eyes. I traveled into them to see myself as he began to draw. I wanted to be found a prize.

A stream of hair fell and parted over my breast; I watched his hand shape my swell and then the half-moon shadow beneath. He traced the curve of my belly with long, smooth gestures, and I saw that it was graceful. When he swept the rise of my hip, his hand moved as if he were stroking a melon.

I could see that I pleased him — had I ever pleased Isaak before? For the first time,

I felt desirable.

But I didn't want him to draw me anymore.

I rolled over onto my back and let my fingers drift along my belly and my hips, everywhere I wanted him to be. I closed my eyes so he could watch. And when he dropped his pad, I felt I had won. But if I had won, what was it he had lost?

Afterward, Isaak dressed and took his coat from its peg. I lifted my head from the pillow to ask where he was going.

"Your house." He tied his shoes. "I'll get your things. It's dark enough."

Once again I wasn't full the way Isaak seemed to be when we finished making love. If anything, I was hungrier than before. I wondered if there were any amount of lovemaking that would be enough. I wondered if something was wrong with me. I reached out and tried to pull him back into the bed.

"Go tomorrow night. I don't need anything."

"No. Your aunt's leaving for Apeldoorn in the morning. I need to get everything you'll take with you next Friday. Anneke's papers. Her clothes."

Next Friday. I got out of bed and began to dress.

"You're not going," Isaak said. "It's too dangerous. And it's not necessary; I'll get everything."

"Yes, I am going. I have to see her again." I suddenly felt guilty for how much pleasure I'd taken the last day and night while she had been alone in our empty home.

Isaak studied me for a moment, then nodded.

I wore his clothes and borrowed the lawyer's bicycle. Once more we set out across the town in the dark, with me in disguise. Like a criminal. At first the dry leaves of the plane trees overhead rustled softly like paper, but as we rode the wind picked up and they began to sound menacing, like breaking glass. A storm was coming. I wanted to be back in the safety of Isaak's room.

I could be pregnant now.

TWENTY-ONE

"Cyrla!" My aunt pulled me into the kitchen and for a second I thought how good it was to hear my name again, how it made me feel whole again. "You shouldn't be here."

It was a mistake to have come to this place that was no longer my home.

And it was difficult to look at my aunt, shrunken like an old woman, her face pouched and colorless. I looked away, but everything in the kitchen pulsed with memories, each a stiletto. My apron hung on its peg beside Anneke's, from a time when my most unpleasant chore was to chop onions. There were the Delft blue-and-white sugar and flour containers, each side painted with a different scene Anneke and I used to make up stories about. The pretty beaded milk cap we borrowed to drape over our dolls' heads. Even though the blackout shades were down, my aunt was anxious someone might be able to see me here;

when she turned off the kitchen light and lit a candle, I was relieved.

"I'm so sorry about —" Isaak began.

My aunt threw up her palms in fierce warning, then left the room. She came back in a few minutes, her face closed, with my suitcase. "Take her now," she said, handing it to Isaak. "Hurry. I saw Mrs. Bakker this morning — she said she heard voices here yesterday. I told her I must have been talking to myself, but . . . And two soldiers were here this afternoon — just as you predicted. I told them Pieter had been delayed and would be back tomorrow, but I don't think they believed me. What if they're watching the house now?"

I felt ashamed hearing this, as if I'd done something wrong. I hated being someone for whom lies must be told.

"I don't think that's likely," Isaak replied. "It's only some blankets. But we'll leave. Do you have the papers?"

My aunt pulled a packet tied with string from behind the meat safe. "There's money in here, too. I didn't know what she'd need. But it's only for a few weeks, and then . . ." She turned to me and her face crumpled. "Oh, *kleintje*. How did we get to this?"

I embraced her without answering. The war couldn't go on much longer; everyone

157

except for Isaak said this. When it was over, I would have my own home. With Isaak. With our children. I would never ask anyone to leave it.

My aunt stepped away and crossed her arms over her chest, her fingers digging into her arms as if to keep them from reaching for me again. "Take her," she said, not looking at me. "See her safe. Go now."

Isaak took my hand and pulled me to the door.

My aunt watched, then suddenly called out, "Wait!" For an instant I thought, *See? She couldn't send me away after all.* But that wasn't it.

She turned the light on again, pulled a pair of scissors from the shelf, and lifted them up to me. I stared, not understanding.

Isaak put my suitcase by the door. "Sit down," he said. "Undo your hair."

My hands flew to my head. "No, not that! I'll keep it pinned up. No one will know. It's the way my mother —"

They were right, though. I took the scissors from my aunt — I would cut my hair myself. And I wouldn't cry. But I turned away just in case.

I unbraided my hair and cut a handful quickly, so I couldn't change my mind. It was so thick it was like cutting rope, and I

158

could do only a small section at a time. The room was silent except for the slicing of the steel blades and the sighs of my hair hitting the linoleum. It took so long.

I turned to face them, my head higher, freed from the weight. My aunt's hands flew to her mouth and she ran from the kitchen, but not before I'd seen her eyes. In Isaak's eyes, for just a second, I thought I saw anger — perhaps for the loss of my hair. He set his mouth and took the scissors from me and snipped at a few places. "Does it look right?" I asked.

He didn't answer. Nothing was right about this. We just stood together for a moment, not knowing what to say. My aunt came back. She kept her eyes averted, but held out a mirror.

My hand shot out and knocked the mirror from her hand; it shattered against the tiled wall. I hadn't meant to do it, but how could I have borne the sight of myself stealing my cousin's life? I bent quickly to pick up the pieces of glass, glittering in my fallen hair, but Anneke's face looked up at me from each shard.

TWENTY-TWO

Friday. For the first time, Isaak had fallen asleep beside me in the narrow bed, his long, hard thigh between my two soft ones. I thought I could stay like this forever, lying skin-to-skin with him, my breath softly feathering the hairs of his chest, the rain beating against the window hard as hurled nails. But Isaak woke and rolled to sit at the edge of the bed.

"Don't leave," I said. "Don't go to work. There's so little time."

Isaak rubbed his face awake. "I'll be back after services. We have a week."

He left, and the storm made the wait until he returned worse.

I sat at his desk to write to my father. I tried twice and tore up both letters. What of all this could I tell him? I tried a third time and made my letter short so he wouldn't read between the lines or sense where I was lying.

Dearest Papa,

I have news to tell you, but you must promise not to be sad or worried. I am leaving Schiedam. It is just a precaution, and only for a short while. Possibly you have heard that there are more restrictions here now. Isaak and I feel it would be wise for me to go away for a while, and we have found a safe place. As always, I am hopeful you will meet each other soon. How you will like him, and how Mama would have loved him!

In a way, I feel better because of this, knowing that if you are hiding and sacrificing to be safe, then so am I. I have been living so comfortably these past years that I have begun to feel guilty.

Please write and tell me how you are — I haven't heard from you for so long, and it is difficult to not know. You can still reach me through the same address — Tante Mies will know how to get your letter to me. Everyone here is well and sends you their love. Kisses to my brothers, who must be fine big boys by now — Levi will be almost nine; how I wish I could see him. And I cannot even imagine that little Benjamin is seven. The war is almost over, and when it is I will be with you.

All my love, your daughter,
Cyrla

I put the pen down and my hands found my belly, flat and empty, and yet perhaps so full. I was no longer the last link in my family's chain, but rather I might be carrying it already, curled inside me. Safe. I tore up the letter.

That afternoon I slept and paced and read and ate the food Isaak had left for me. I ached for Anneke, as though I had just awakened to the understanding that she was gone. I cried until I couldn't possibly cry any more, and then I cried more. If only I hadn't left her. I'd taken her for granted, had left her alone, and she'd fallen away.

I walked around the room, suddenly anxious to mark it as mine somehow. Could I move the gooseneck lamp? Rearrange Isaak's books? Finally I took down the da Vinci prints and hung them back up in a different order. I thought about where I would be when he noticed and grew ill with fear.

When Isaak returned I told him I wasn't going. "I'll stay here until you arrange my passage. Or until you get me a set of false papers so I can live somewhere nearby."

Isaak sat at his desk. He riffled through a pile of papers, pulled a pair of glasses from his pocket, put them on, and then took them off again and rubbed his eyes. He glanced up at the da Vinci prints and his mouth narrowed for a second, but he didn't say anything. He looked terribly tired.

"Isaak?"

"In the first place, you can't stay here. It is too obviously where you might be."

"But no one knows I'm missing. I died, remember?"

"Your uncle. A man doesn't walk away from his home. I have someone watching the shop and the house. The Germans are watching the shop, too. He hasn't returned, but he will. And he'll look for you here."

I climbed onto Isaak's bed and wedged myself into the corner, my back against the walls. Where I couldn't be bent. "He won't look for me. He'll be glad I've gone. Isaak, this is my life. My choice."

Isaak looked down at his hands on his knees, and spread his fingers. "We've been over this. You don't have a choice. If Anneke doesn't show up, there'll be too much interest."

I didn't like the tone in his voice. As if I were a willful child. "Isaak, it won't work. They'll see right away I'm not Anneke . . .

my eyes! Tante Mies always said they were the blue of winter seas, while Anneke's were light, like summer seas! You said they measured her eye color. . . ."

Isaak bent over the wastebasket, pulled out my torn letters. His face fell when he saw my father's name. "You didn't."

"No. I saw it wasn't safe. Besides, I don't know where to post them anymore."

"You refuse to see —"

"Don't!"

"I have to! You think you can simply not show up there? That it will be fine if the Nazis find out Anneke's dead but her cousin's using her papers and by the way, she's Jewish? There were roundups in Twenthe and Enschede last week! Did you know that?"

"Isaak, stop."

"They took them to the labor camp at Westerbork. But they won't stay there long — they'll ship them to Auschwitz. And do you know what happens then? We've just gotten a report — they're gassing people."

"That's not true. That *can't* be true."

"It's not confirmed. But you can't be blind anymore . . . we know they're killing people at the camps! Do you want to take that chance? Are you going to take that chance with your baby? With *my* baby?"

I glared at him.

Isaak retreated and sat still for a moment. "You're right, that was unfair. But you've got to understand that the risk is too big if you *don't* go. And there are other people involved."

I crossed my arms over my chest and leaned back into the corner. "It's just all out of my control."

We sat with this quietly for a moment, then Isaak pulled the packet my aunt had given him from beneath a stack of books and brought it over to the bed and sat beside me. "Let's look at this. It's time we talked about it." His voice was conciliatory and I softened. This was the way Isaak showed his love — by worrying about the worst that could happen and by taking care of things.

He unwrapped the documents, chose an envelope from the packet, and put the other things aside. Anneke's Lebensborn agreement. He held it for me to read, as if he knew I wouldn't be able to touch it.

"You see," he said, "there's nothing here about your eye color, or your description. Those things are filed. The names at the bottom here are important for you to learn. There is a woman's name here; I expect she did the paperwork to admit Anneke. Avoid

165

her if you can. And see this name? Inge Vi-
ermetz? She's the head of all the Lebensborns outside Germany. But see? It's just a
stamp. I don't think she'll be there."

"How do you know all this?"

"I asked a contact in Germany for information on how things are done at Lebensborn homes. The information I got yesterday
came from the home in Klosterheide, near
Berlin, but I'd be surprised if it didn't apply
to all of them. The Nazis are like that, very
standardized. Anyway, it's the best we have.
Now, listen. I have a lot to tell you.

"When a girl applies to enter, they put her
through a lot of tests. Anneke had them all
— we know that. There's the doctor's name
— you'll have to stay away from him, too.
But listen — at least in the Klosterheide
home, the girls aren't examined again until
the sixth month. You're not going to be
there then."

"But what if someone sees that I'm not
the person they met last week?"

"People see what they expect to see. The
staff will expect to see Anneke on Friday,
and all you have to do is allow them to see
her."

"My accent, Isaak —"

"I know. I've thought of that. But the staff
is all German, and you'll be speaking Ger-

166

man in the home. You learned it here, didn't you? It should be all right."

"How are you going to get me out?"

"I'll send a letter. It will be from Anneke's mother saying that the apple tree blew down. Whatever day and time it blew down — Monday at noon, say — that's when you'll leave. Whatever direction the wind was from, that's the direction you'll head in. You'll take a walk off the grounds and someone will meet you. Do you understand?"

I took the papers and lay them down. "I know what happens if you leave people."

"If you were my own sister, I would ask you to do this. And I swear I will come for you in a matter of weeks . . . a month, I can almost promise it will be no more than a month. But just in case, did we . . . do you think you're pregnant?"

I was angry with him for being able to compare me to a sister.

"It's too early to know. But Isaak —" I tried to hold his eyes as I slipped my hand down, but he closed them.

"Wait," he said, "there's more to talk about. I want to finish this."

"Isaak, I am not your sister."

TWENTY-THREE

The week passed. In the middle of it, Isaak left for two days of meetings in Amsterdam. I thought I would go mad from loneliness, and I couldn't wait for him to return. But when he did, it was as if only part of him had come back. He answered when I asked him questions, but he never spoke to me otherwise. Each night, we came together in the cot and that was silent, too. I bit my lip against the urge to cry.

And then somehow it was Wednesday, the day before our last. I awoke frantic with a longing for him that was a hunger. Suddenly I understood: I was pregnant. I had to be: I'd felt a shift in my core, as if I'd grown a second heart, deeper. Once more Isaak had meetings to attend. In forty-eight hours I would be on a train to Nijmegen and I wouldn't see him for weeks. The idea made me ravenous. I dropped to his mattress and lifted his blanket, and found him with my mouth.

Isaak woke and pushed me off him. He rolled away and looked at me as if he didn't know me. Well, how could he . . . I didn't recognize myself. Or, no; it was the person I had been before this week who was a stranger. A person who knew nothing at all. Who wasn't carrying a child. I lay down on his chest and pulled the blanket around us, still overwhelmed with my need for him. "Isaak." There was no other word to say. Surely he must say my name now. He didn't, but I felt his body stiffen.

"It's all right." I lifted my head to smile at him. "I'm pregnant."

Isaak studied me for a moment. "How do you know?"

"I just do. I know."

"Well . . . good. I'm glad." But he didn't return my smile. He slipped out from under me and rose to sit on his bed. He held his forehead in his palms, his elbows on his knees — his position of worry. "What do you want?" he asked. "What do you want?"

I stood up and started to sit beside him, but I suddenly saw that I was always moving toward him and he was always moving away. I wrapped myself in his blanket and crossed to the window instead. "You."

169

I prayed for him to stand up and walk over to me. When he turned away, a tight, cold bud of fear unfurled in my chest.

"That's not what this has been for."

My face burned. I flew across the room and knelt in front of him. "Isaak, I love you. What's so difficult? You love me, too."

I took his face in my hands; still I could see it falling away from me in regret.

"No." He took my hands away and sighed. "For God's sake, Cyrla, don't make this — if I could love anyone, it would be you. It *should* be you. But I can't. Not now."

The fear now swelled to fill my chest, a pressure against my ribs so it was difficult to take a breath. Years ago, I had gone out with a friend on her father's fishing boat. A gale had blown up, and she and I had spent the afternoon seasick and terrified below-decks, pitched about in the dark hold. I felt this way again now, battered by blows I couldn't see coming and unable to find a lifeline.

But then Isaak himself threw one.

"The war," he said. "It's too dangerous to have any ties. Any complications."

"Complications? Oh, Isaak. It's too dangerous *not* to love anyone now." I took his hand and sat beside him. "Loving someone gives you a reason. And what else is it for, all the work you do? Why are you helping people escape, if not so they can live their lives? That means loving people."

"I did this so you could take Anneke's place. That's all." Isaak turned away from my eyes and what they were accusing him of. "All right. Yes. I wanted a child. In case —"

"But who will raise this child, Isaak? When the war is over, you'll come for me in England, won't you?" The fear was now huge and tight in my throat, but I had to ask these things. "We'll come back here to live as a family. Isn't that what you're planning?"

"Why do you never see how things are now? Why can't you open your eyes and see it?" Isaak said, rising, suddenly harsh. "Planning anything these days is dangerous. Hope for a future is a liability; it makes you vulnerable. I plan nothing."

"You have it all backward! Hope makes you strong. When the war is over —"

Isaak was pulling his clothes on in a hurry. "When the war is over, you'll be safe. And the child will be safe, too. That's what I'm doing. If I'm still here, I'll do whatever you and our child need. But you don't really think I'll still be here, do you? I'm a Jew and I'm visible. I'll be the first to go."

"You're on the Council."

He shook his head. "In Dubossary, two weeks ago, men who refused to serve on the Council were hanged in public. But a few days later, in Piortków, eleven members of the Council were executed for cooperating with the Underground. It doesn't matter — either way, we're simply more visible."

"Then stop what you're doing. You can't help people if you're dead, Isaak. Come with me to England, now. Arrange it — I need you!"

"You don't need me as much as the others need me. This is my place."

"This is your place, too." I stood and let the blanket drop, and placed Isaak's hand on my belly. He tried to pull it away, but I held it firm. "No. Look at us. We need you. Our whole government is in England — you could work from there."

"This is my place," he repeated. "These are my people. I won't abandon them."

But you'll abandon me? And our baby? I didn't say the words, but I knew Isaak heard them. "You said if you could love anyone, it would be me. Anneke said you have to be brave to love someone. I think you're being heroic to avoid being brave. Isaak, be brave now."

In that moment, with Isaak's hand pressed

172

to my belly, I felt our family being born. Then he pulled his hand away and turned to put on his shoes.

"You're right," he said without meeting my eyes. "I'm not brave. But you are. And that's exactly why it will never be right for us, even if the war were over tomorrow. Don't you see this?"

The room spun, my life collapsing into it. "See what, Isaak? *See what?*"

He walked to the door and turned. "See this: I draw birds. You fly."

Isaak was gone from me all that day and night, even when he was in the room. It was as if someone else was living behind his eyes. He didn't touch me and he hardly spoke. He watched me return the prints to their proper places in silence.

When he left at two for a meeting, he warned me as usual not to leave the room, but the words seemed cool and hard, tossed at me like stones. I didn't answer.

When he returned, he brought a jar of soup and a loaf of dark, sour bread. We ate in silence. Once, our fingers met as we reached at the same time to tear a piece of bread, and we both jumped back as if burned. Anneke had said that when we made love it would be as if our bodies were saying, "I know you; I know you." She had been wrong.

After we ate, Isaak told me some news from his afternoon, the kind of things he might have told a stranger. Only unimportant words. But then finally, just before we got ready to sleep, he suddenly said, "Anneke."

I smiled at him, glad he wanted to talk and that he was thinking about my cousin. "Yes," I said, "I've been thinking about her so much. I miss her so much."

"Anneke!" he called again.

When I realized what he was doing, I slapped his face. I slapped Isaak's face, which I loved more than any. "Don't call me that!"

"You'll have to get used to it. You can't make a mistake."

"I'll be fine. I'll answer to it. But don't you ever call me that again, Isaak."

I felt free then, as if I no longer cared what happened. Not as if I had risen above caring, but that I had fallen below. Having lost Isaak, and all the others I had left, I had nothing else of value to lose.

TWENTY-FOUR

Thursday, my last day. Isaak left me alone
— he would be gone until late — and I was
glad. I sat at his desk, his bible open in front
of me, trying to read the Hebrew. But I had
been gone from it too long. I paced. I stared
out the window. I tried to pray, but couldn't
remember any words that would fit. God
hadn't foreseen this.

When night fell, I dressed in Isaak's big
overcoat, found the lawyer's bicycle, and
rode into the moonless streets. In the past
year, since food had been rationed, some
people had released their dogs to fend for
themselves. These hungry-eyed animals for-
aged the streets, their flanks hollowing in
like spoons. Three of them followed me,
darting and retreating. I wondered if they
recognized the look of abandonment in me.

The darkness around my home was solid
and still, as if it had been knitting itself into
a shroud over the past week. I let myself

175

into the kitchen and lit a candle. The darkness seemed to press around the flame as I made my way up the stairs to my room. Anneke's room.

The house was cold, but in this room the cold was deeper. This room would never be warm again. I stood in the doorway for a long time, drawing the cold air into my lungs. It was like breathing knives. The scent of blood was still in this room, and once again I was filled with a sudden rage against Karl — for what he had stolen from all of us, for what he had set into motion.

Then, without allowing the halo of candlelight to fall upon Anneke's bed bare of its mattress, I crossed the room. On my shelf, my few books. I chose my worn copy of Rilke's *Letters to a Young Poet* and pushed it down into my pocket. I opened the drawers of my dresser before I remembered: My aunt had already removed the proof of my life here. No, not all of it. I lifted my mattress and pulled out the flat cigar box I'd kept hidden there. From it, I took the photograph of my family and the tiny box that held my mother's wedding ring, her ruby earrings, and ivory barrette, and slipped them into the deep pocket of Isaak's coat. The silver Sabbath candlesticks my father had sent so long ago; I pressed them

176

to my chest for a moment, wishing I could bring them with me. I set them on the shelf behind me instead and took the last thing from the box: a packet of all the letters my father had sent since I'd come to Holland.

Eleven in all. Only eleven. On top was the last he had written, when the ghetto was being sealed. I knew it by heart, but sometimes only holding it in my hand and reading my father's script brought me peace: *We are safe, all of us. It brings me great comfort to know that you are safe, too.* The letters were too dangerous to bring, so I left them with the candlesticks; my aunt would know how to dispose of them.

Then I turned to Anneke's dresser and opened the inlaid wooden box that held her jewelry. I fingered the gold and silver pieces that had ceased to gleam without the light of her skin and chose a pair of tiny moonstone teardrop earrings, the ones I had seen her wear most recently. "I'm sorry," I whispered as I closed the jewelry box. Then I took a handkerchief and her bottle of scarlet nail polish. These things would have to sustain me.

At the door, I turned for my last look at this room, empty of me except for a couple of books, the candlesticks and . . . I ran back and pulled the top letter from the pile and stuffed it into my pocket, then left quickly in the dark, like a thief.

But I wasn't ready to go back to Isaak's room. I rode down the back alley to my uncle's shop, pulled over, and got off my bicycle for a minute. I cupped my hands around my eyes and peered through the window. The darkness inside was deep and still here also, as if it had been pooling all week; my uncle hadn't been back either. As I drew away to leave, I caught a movement reflected in the darkened glass. Then a gloved hand over my mouth; an arm across my neck; the scent of motor oil, familiar too late, now mixed with stale beer and cigars.

"You bitch!" the *Oberschütze* hissed into my ear. The time that had passed had only fed his fury. I screamed and tried to twist away, but he grabbed my hair and jerked my head around to him, then he back-handed my jaw. I felt my lip split.

He dragged me into the alley beside the shop, shoved me to the ground, and pinned me there with a knee to my chest and one hand on my throat. For a second, I thought only of the letter in my pocket, but then I thought of the baby I might be carrying. I fought. But he ignored my screams and fists, and with his teeth, he tore the heavy leather glove from his other hand. The hatred in his

178

eyes terrified me.

I clawed his face. He struck like a viper, jammed the glove into my mouth. I struggled harder, but he shoved the glove down my throat until I gagged. He grabbed my jaw in the vise of his fist and he held me that way, with his knuckles and the glove in my mouth and his thumb digging into the skin beneath my chin, while he ripped open his trousers. In a second he was between my legs, a knee crushing my thigh now, his weight on his knuckles in my throat. I beat at his chest and clenched myself closed, but he cleaved me open as if I weren't resisting at all, like an ax to a peach. He drove himself into me fiercely, as if the object of his rage was at my core.

He wants to kill me from inside, I thought.

And then all I thought was . . . air.

I heard myself wheezing, gasping for gulps of air but barely drawing in a thread. With each breath I couldn't take, the world narrowed. The trooper's battering grew more distant as my heart hammered harder and harder, like a fist. The sounds of his attack and even the sounds of my own suffocation grew fainter until all I heard was the roar of my blood pounding in outrage through my head. I panicked and the night turned red, as if my eyes had burst. Then the red world blackened and I felt myself sink away, slack. It felt like mercy washing over me.

At first, all I was aware of was the miracle of cool air filling my sore throat, my aching chest. I drew it into my lungs in great waves, tides, of breath. I tasted blood and leather and I spat it out and then I remembered. I froze. The thud of his boots on the street rang in the darkness. He was leaving. It was over.

But it wasn't. He came back and bent over me with an anger that seethed like heat. He grabbed his glove from beside my neck, wiped it against his thigh, and pulled it on, snapping it hard over his wrist, all the while glaring down at me with the purest hatred I had ever seen. He leaned closer, curled his lips back, and spat in my face.

Then he left. He walked into the street and stopped there to light a cigarette. Then he crossed and disappeared between two buildings. I heard a door open and then close and still I lay there, frozen. I waited until the night was silent again before I wiped the spit off my cheek and crawled to my knees.

I felt in my pocket. There were the two photographs, the small box with my mother's wedding ring and barrette. An earring

— but one of Anneke's earrings was missing. Also gone was my father's letter. I crawled around in the dirty alleyway, sweeping the ground with shaking hands, and I found first the earring and then, against the wall, the letter.

It brings me great comfort to know that you are safe, too.

TWENTY-FIVE

"Where have you been? Someone could have seen you! Do you know how foolish —"

Isaak looked at my face. The anger in his eyes softened with worry, but only a shade. He reached out for my mouth. I put my hand over the place where my lip had split, and when Isaak pulled it away there was a small heart of blood on my palm.

The warmth and the brightness of the room made me dizzy. I sank to the cot and stared at the mark, confused. I felt Anneke beside me, kissing my palm with her dark lipstick. What had she said? That we would each have ten children and live to be a hundred and be happy forever? I had a sudden image of her buried deep under the earth — dirt in her pretty hair, dirt in her pretty teeth, even and white as sugar cubes. Dirt filling her nostrils so she couldn't catch a breath. Anneke had stopped struggling, too. I looked up at Isaak and he seemed to be trembling in front of me, but it was just that tears had welled.

"What? What happened to you?"

"I couldn't breathe," I heard myself say. I turned away.

"What do you mean? When?" He reached out to my chin to turn my face to him. I winced. "What happened?" he asked again. He lifted my jaw. "You have a mark here. And on your neck." He bent and brushed the grit from my knees. "Did you fall off the bicycle?"

I held my hands up to him, saw they were shaking, and dropped them. "I need to wash." I couldn't tell Isaak what had happened; I was afraid, yes, that he would go after the soldier. But I was more afraid that he wouldn't. I shrank away from him. "I need to wash."

There was a knock at the door. Isaak started for it, but it opened before he could get there. Rabbi Geron stood in the doorway. He didn't say anything about my being there, only looked at me for a moment, questioning, then told Isaak he had a phone call.

Isaak followed him out and I took Isaak's towels to the bathroom. I turned the tap on as hot as it could go, and while the tub

183

filled, I wet a towel and began to scrub the soldier out of me. Away from my baby. Out of us.

I got in and sank below the surface until the weight of the water was a gloved hand over my face and I couldn't breathe and then I burst up into the air again, gasping. I scrubbed myself with the rough washcloth and the gritty soap until my cuts stung and my bruises throbbed and all the parts of my body the soldier had touched were scoured raw.

But it was no use.

When I came back into the room, I knew by his face that Isaak knew.

"That was the man I had watching the shop."

I shut the door behind me and leaned against it. "He saw?"

"He saw."

"But he didn't —"

"What could he do? You should never have —"

"Stop! Don't. Don't you dare!"

Isaak stared at me for a long time. I saw him work through the things he wanted to say. The things he couldn't.

"Do you need a doctor?" he asked at last.

"No." And I realized: It was not the day on the roof that would divide my life in two, into before and after. It was this day. Starting tomorrow, though, it was not my own life I would be living. And what happened to me tonight did not happen to the person whose life I was about to steal. "What I want is a needle."

"Are you all right —"

I warned him away with my palms. "Just get one."

He looked puzzled, but he left and came back a few moments later with a needle and some black thread. I put the thread down on the bed and gave the needle back to him, then I reached into my pocket and handed him Anneke's earrings.

"It will hurt," he warned.

"I want it to."

Isaak lit a match and held the needle to its flame, and then the earrings. "This one's broken," he said. "I think it's ruined."

I lifted the little earring he held to me. The stone was missing and the gold filigree around the setting had been crushed. "It's broken. It's *not* ruined." I gave it back to him and when Isaak plunged the hot needle into my earlobe I didn't feel anything.

I barely slept. Over and over I reminded myself I was already pregnant. I had known it. When dawn lightened the room, I crept out of bed and sat on the windowsill with the square of velvet I had saved from the rooftop. That day seemed years behind me. I stitched the velvet into a crude bag and made a drawstring from the twine Anneke's papers had been tied with. I took out everything from the coat pocket: Anneke's nail polish and handkerchief, my mother's jewelry and barrette, my father's letter. The envelope was creased and marked now with a heavy boot tread; I tore it up and threw it away, then folded the letter into quarters and put everything into the bag. I took a drawing pencil from Isaak's desk and slipped that in, too, and then I hung the bag around my neck and dressed. After almost twenty years, these were all the things of value I had.

Isaak awoke and came over to me.

"Are you all right?"

I looked at him, too bitter to answer.

"I mean . . . can you travel?"

I nodded and pressed the backs of my fists to my eyes. Then I turned away, splashed water from the pitcher on my face and burning earlobes, and packed my night-clothes into the suitcase my aunt had prepared for me. Isaak tried to talk with me about little things, details I must remember, how the day would go. I stopped him.

Whatever would happen now was out of my control, or his. "Just come for me," I said.

I left before it was fully light and walked to the tram stop, then rode into Scheveningen. There were soldiers on the tram, and whenever I caught sight of one, I smelled motor oil and I couldn't fill my lungs. I rode with my eyes closed and my hands clenching the velvet bag against my chest.

Isaak was at the station with my suitcase. We didn't acknowledge each other. Just before the train to Nijmegen was due to leave, he walked up to me casually and dropped the bag at my feet.

"Go with God," he said. "I will come for you soon. Remember: You'll get a letter, and then I'll meet you."

I didn't answer because my lips suddenly longed to kiss him, and I didn't move because my arms wanted to pull him to me forever.

"I'll come for you soon. I promise," he repeated.

I picked up my bag and boarded, choosing a seat on the far side of the train so I couldn't look back to see if Isaak stayed to watch. I leaned against the window and stared ahead. Gray clouds sagged along the horizon, aching with rain.

TWENTY-SIX

It rained the whole way. Beside the tracks, ditches and bomb craters filled with brown water — a muddy Morse code of dots and dashes slipping by the grimy train windows. In the station, I sat on a bench looking out at the flooded fields, thinking there was nothing sadder than rain at a train station. But I sat dry-eyed. What was the use of tears?

When two German soldiers arrived, my hand flew to my cut lower lip and I went rigid. But of course it wouldn't be that one. I would never see that one — the *Oberschütze* — again. These were sergeants. They spotted me and came over — a good sign, at least: I had passed this first test.

"Anneke Van der Berg?" one asked.

"Yes," I said, finding the lie a relief.

He looked at my waist doubtfully, but he took my papers and the other one, taller with a narrow face, picked up my bag. I followed them out to their car and sat in the back with my suitcase; in front of me the soldiers talked of new tires coming. Or rather the driver talked — the other one, the taller one, just nodded or agreed with him, although they were the same rank. I listened to them, still wary, trying to tell myself that I was Anneke now: Grace surrounded me now, not danger.

But I didn't believe it.

The trees passed by in a blur of browning leaves, sheeting with pewter rain. Winter was coming. But I would be safely away by then; this was only for a few weeks. Still, my breathing grew shallower. After about fifteen minutes, I noticed a sign for the border.

"Excuse me," I interrupted the soldiers. They looked at me as if surprised to find me still with them. "We've left Nijmegen."

The driver glanced at me in the mirror then shrugged.

"We've left Nijmegen! Where are you going?"

"Steinhöring. Outside Munich." He said it as if he expected me to know this.

"No. There's been a mistake. I'm entering the home in Nijmegen."

The other one turned to me. "What home in Nijmegen?"

189

"The home in Nijmegen! I'm due there today."

He shook his head and laughed. "There's no home there. There's one planned, but there's nothing there now. Who told you this?"

"My . . . my father. Please turn around. There's been a mistake."

The soldier picked up a packet of papers from the seat beside him and waved it at me. "Steinhöring. No mistake."

My heart began to pound so hard I was sure it could be heard if it weren't for the rumble of the engine. "But it's so far. I can't leave Holland," I said and heard the desperate illogic. "My family," I tried again. "No one will know where I am. . . ."

"You can write," he said.

But we had all agreed: no letters. Isaak's address wasn't safe, and my aunt didn't know how long she'd be gone or when my uncle might return.

"No, turn back! I've changed my mind!"

The taller soldier twisted around again. He laid his arm along the back window beside me, so close I could see the hairs on the back of his hand and a thin white scar across his thumb. I shrank away.

"We have orders to deliver you to Steinhöring. That's what we're going to do." The warning in his voice alerted the driver. They exchanged looks.

"We'll be driving straight through," the driver said. "There's a basket in the back. It's better food than we get." Then he sped up. For a second I thought about opening the door — throwing myself out and taking my chances — but we were on a main road now.

Why had my uncle told Anneke she would go to Nijmegen? Had the Germans lied to him? Or . . . could a father really be so angry with his daughter that he would banish her from her own country?

My questions rushed by with the landscape.

Too quickly, we reached the border. We stopped for only a moment, while a guard in a mud-brown uniform leaned into the car, said a few words, and checked our papers. I wished I had picked up something from Schiedam — a stone, a twig, anything. I would press it into my palm now as an amulet until it disappeared into my flesh.

I was in Germany. And Isaak didn't know.

We headed south, faster and faster. The land rose up from the soggy fields that were my last sight of Holland, but as we climbed, I felt I was plummeting. Everywhere on the roads were convoys of trucks and jeeps, lines of slow-moving tanks. No civilians were out, not even on bicycles, not even on foot. Only military — a country of soldiers. I could only watch as I hurtled into my enemy's heart, frozen and helpless.

No. I fingered the little moonstone earring in my sore earlobe.

"It was a good idea." I leaned forward between the two men and forced a smile, my voice contrite. "I could write to my family. Would you have a pen and some paper? I'd like to do it now, so I can post it as soon as possible."

The driver handed a pen back to me. The other one reached under his seat and pulled out a pad of paper, ripped off a sheet. "You can use the back."

I thanked them and pulled my suitcase over beside me to use as a desk. *Dear Mother and Father,* I wrote, in letters big enough for the soldiers to read if they glanced back. *There has been a change of plans.* And then, in tiny lettering underneath: *Checkpoint at Beek. E, SE, then E. Through Essen. To the Rhine.*

I ate some of the food from the basket, wrapped the rest, and tucked it into my pocket. We pulled off the highway once, so the soldiers could relieve themselves. "Get out if you'd like. There are some hedges," they offered. I considered running, but beyond the hedges stretched open fields on all sides, and I had seen a gun flash at the driver's hip. Besides, even if I could get away, where would I go with only a few guilders in my pocket? I shook my head and we got back on the highway.

We followed the Rhine. The mountains folded along both sides grew steeper and the sun came out, lighting the snowcapped peaks in the distance. The landscape was beautiful, more stunning than any of my geography books had conveyed, but harsh, not soft like Holland. The river was soft though, its rising mist hazing the vineyards and villages that tumbled down to its banks. The Rhine flowed through the Netherlands, too, and so its presence comforted me a little each time it curled into view below, like a silver thread from my home. Except once, when the river widened and an island appeared, parting its current. From its center, like an illustration from a fairy tale, rose a stone castle. I stared as we passed along beside it, the feeling of comfort suddenly a terrible dread. Fairy tales always held great evil. Great danger.

Bonn, due East. Koblenz. Gretel dropping her bread crumbs.

Toward the middle of the afternoon, the

soldiers talked of stopping. There was to be a new Lebensborn home in Wiesbaden; they'd been there before to do some preliminary work, they knew of a restaurant.

We parked in front of a tavern but before we went in the driver pointed across the street to a tobacco store. They would get some cigarettes first. We stepped into the street, me between my guardians, and that was when I saw them.

Blooming on the left sides of coats with the suddenness of daffodils — at first that's what I thought they were: daffodils tucked jauntily into breast pockets. A sign of hope or defiance against the realities of war. But as we approached an elderly couple, I saw the cheap shine of the material, the color too garish for nature, and then the chunky Gothic letters, JUDE, in the center. Isaak had told me about the stars — people would be wearing them in Schiedam soon. The couple huddled against a doorway as we passed by, their eyes cast down, and the left side of my chest began to burn.

"What is it?" the taller soldier asked. He had stopped and was staring at me and I realized I was clutching my heart.

"Nothing, nothing." I forced my hands to my side, amazed that the fabric of my coat did not burst into flame.

In the restaurant, I left to use the wash-room. I drank cold water from my hand, then I bent over, gripping the sink, staring at my face in the mirror. My half-Jewish face. "No one knows. No one knows." I stood there, shaking, until I was startled by a knock on the door.

The driver. "Are you all right? The meal is here."

They had ordered sausages and soup and bread, but I couldn't eat. I couldn't even pick up my cup of tea because my hands would not stop shaking.

TWENTY-SEVEN

It began to rain again. I leaned my head against the glass and from nowhere came a memory: my mother coming to find me at the window, looking out at the rain, disconsolate, wanting to go out. "The rain that falls today doesn't fall tomorrow," she said, patting my shoulder. Later, I learned what the saying meant, but that day I remember pushing her hand off and telling her tomorrow would be too late.

The soldiers hadn't said anything, but as we approached I knew. A granite wall, grown over with ivy, hid the grounds, but the stylized SS initials molded into the iron gates of the entryway left no doubt. From the first time I'd seen them, those double-S runes looked to me like gashes, like the teeth marks wolves might leave in their victims' throats. A tall white watchtower rose up beside the gates; towers like this held girls prisoner in fairy tales. And in the wet dusk, I saw fields sliding away in all directions. Beyond them, to the east and north, mountains rose. There would be no walking into the woods here.

The driver pulled to a stop at a hut and flashed his lights. A guard left the station buttoning his raincoat and came to the driver's door. His muddy boots, rain-slick in the lights, seemed covered in blood — like the butcher's boots back home in Poland when I was a little girl. He leaned in when the driver rolled down the window and spoke to the soldiers for a moment, confirming their orders. Then he pulled a black leather ledger from under his coat and opened it, read something. In the glow of the dashboard instruments, his eyes shone, ice-colored like a wolf's.

He turned them on me. "Anneke Van der Berg?"

"Ja." The lie was not so easy now.

"Date of birth?"

"Eight July, 1920." Had I hesitated?

He nodded, then motioned for us to pass up the drive and followed on foot.

When I stepped out, I was afraid my legs would give way. "Do you feel faint?" the guard asked, reaching for my elbow.

I jerked my arm away. No one in that uniform would ever touch me again.

There was a large desk immediately inside, imposing as another wall. Behind it hung a photograph of Hitler; underneath that sat a middle-aged woman with steel-colored hair piled on top of her head in a braid so tight it reminded me of the cables coiled around the pilings where the canal barges unloaded. She rose and saluted the driver and the guard; standing, she was as tall as they were. The Nazi eagle flashed on her lapel. I stepped away.

"Frau Klaus," the men greeted her. *"Heil Hitler."*

The driver handed her the file from my envelope, which she checked against some papers of her own. I turned my back to them, my fraud of a face turned away.

Along one wall were more photographs of Hitler — accepting flowers from a girl in a white dress; raising his arm in salute to a vast sea of troops; riding in an open car past crowds of Germans waving handkerchiefs. There were also several of Heinrich Himmler — Isaak had told me he was in charge of the Lebensborns. On the opposite wall were posters of mothers and their children. EVERY MOTHER OF GOOD BLOOD MUST BE SACRED TO US! declared one. THE PRAM IS MIGHTIER THAN THE TANK! read another. My uncle had sent his daughter here.

I shuddered and lowered my eyes.

Marble tiles in a black-and-white diamond pattern gleamed in the light of a chandelier. I was unused to seeing lights lit at night anymore. Beside me a mahogany credenza smelled of lemon oil, which was a familiar scent from home, and over that floated the rich aroma of roasting pork, which was not. I smelled bread baking, and also something sweet, with vanilla. Anneke's scent. But *I* was Anneke now. On the credenza was a huge bouquet of pink roses and white chrysanthemums and in front of that a platter of fruit: crab apples, shiny red pears, and plump grapes so dark they looked black. Fruit used as a welcoming decoration — how long since I'd seen such extravagance?

"Follow me," Frau Klaus said, and in her voice it was an order. Women speaking like men — another thing to get used to. She rose and started down the hall. I had the sudden urge to call out, *Wait, wait!* But for what? I followed her tall form, her heels clacking on the marble tiles, up a stairway and down a long corridor with rounded corners. She rapped on an open door numbered 12B, startling a girl lying on a bed with her legs propped up on pillows. The girl looked as if she wanted to jump up, but the mound of her belly was so big it seemed to be sitting on her, pinning her down.

"Leona, this is Anneke, your new roommate. Show her how things are done here."

And then Frau Klaus was gone.

"I'm sorry, I can't get up." Leona crossed her eyes and groaned. "I don't think I'll ever be able to sit up again. But welcome. Make yourself at home." She waved to the far side of the room. "That's your bed . . . well, of course . . . and the bureau in the corner with nothing on it. I hope you brought magazines. . . ."

I couldn't move. Just this way, five years before, I'd stood in the doorway of my new home in Schiedam, my grip tightening around the handle of my suitcase, afraid if I stepped inside I would shatter.

Leona struggled to get up and came over and took my suitcase, set it down. "I've been here so long, I forgot how it can seem. Come in. Sit down." She sat on my bed and patted the space beside her. "I haven't had a roommate for weeks."

I sat and found my voice. "There aren't many girls here?" I asked it mostly to keep her talking, for the sweet comfort of hearing Dutch words in a girl's voice — it felt like a lifetime since I'd heard that. Since Anneke.

"There aren't many *Dutch* girls here. They

like to keep us together, you know. But actually, it's almost full. Where are you from? You sound —"

A moment of panic surged and passed. "I was born in Poland. How many girls are here?"

"About a hundred and twenty, a hundred and thirty." I must have looked alarmed because she told me not to worry. "It won't seem like that many. For one thing, a lot of them are in the mothers' wing. You never see them except in the gardens, pushing their prams with their noses in the air like it's some sort of divine miracle to give birth to a German baby. They've gotten themselves knocked up, is all. Just like the rest of us." She lay back and then heaved herself over to her side to look at me. "Where are you from?"

"Schiedam. You?"

"Amsterdam."

I was glad. Girls from the country kept to themselves. Leona would probably be more open and more generous with information. And she looked open and generous — her face was round and deeply dimpled, as if she was trying to hold back a laugh. She wore her hair waved and pinned up on either side, like the American movie stars.

"So how many girls here are still pregnant?"

"Oh, maybe seventy now. But some of them are the married ones. They keep to themselves because they're so much better than we are . . . oh, maybe you're married? No, why would any of us . . . well, they have husbands, you see. Except most of the babies have nothing to do with those husbands — they're out on the Volga somewhere. That's why the *Frauen* come here, and why we're not supposed to use last names . . . very secret."

"How many other girls are from the Netherlands?"

"Six others. Counting you and me, that's eight. But Resi will be leaving soon; she's overdue. And there are three girls from Belgium, and two from France. You have to speak German in here — how's your German? — except for in the rooms."

"Good."

"Mine wasn't. It's gotten better since I've been here." She propped herself up on her elbow and pointed to my middle. "You're not even showing!"

Isaak had prepared me for this. "No, but you don't have to be, you know. Things aren't very friendly at home."

Leona's glance darted to my split lip and

I saw her decide against asking me about it. "Not for me, either. My parents stopped speaking to me when they found out. But . . . why did you tell them so soon?"

"I thought" — a sharp stab, seeing Anneke's face so radiant — "I thought we'd get married."

"So he was your first? I've had a few. Not that they're such good lovers — Germans are the worst, all business, don't you think? How far along are you?"

"Oh, a couple of months." I relaxed my stomach and rubbed my back. As if that would fool her.

"Well, some of the German girls come in right away. They usually work here for a while first. I've just never seen one of us do it, is all. Watch out for the German girls, by the way. They hold it against us that their men lowered themselves to sleep with us. Anyway, you should unpack. Dinner's soon."

I got up and opened my suitcase. I put Anneke's nightgowns and underthings in the bureau, then her sweaters. Then I went to the wardrobe to hang up her dress and skirts.

"You didn't bring much," Leona said. "Nothing for later? Well, it's fine. There's always a lot of clothing left here by the girls who leave. I'll leave you my things when I go — I'll never want to see them again."

"How long do you have?"

"Five more weeks, can you believe it? I'll never make it. I swear it's twins, but the doctor says no."

I had come to the bottom of my bag. My back still turned, I slipped the velvet bag from my neck and tucked it into a yellow layette that had been Anneke's when she was a baby, and put that back into the suitcase.

"Cyrla," Leona said. "That's an interesting name."

I froze, then closed my suitcase carefully and turned.

Leona held up *Letters to a Young Poet.* "I never heard it before."

"It's Polish. She's my cousin. She loaned me the book."

Leona waved to her night table. "I have some romances. I've read them all. You can borrow them if you get bored. It's easy to get bored in here."

I opened my suitcase again. "Is there an extra key for me? For the wardrobe?" I asked, trying not to sound concerned.

"No, you can't lock it. I heard you used to be able to. But then last spring, the *Reichsführer* made a surprise visit to the Klosterheide home, and apparently he was appalled by how messy the girls were keeping their things. He ordered all the keys to be confiscated so the staff can do spot checks anytime. Himmler is such an old woman. He's got his nose into everything here —"

"And do they? Are the rooms searched?"

"I don't know. I suppose so. I've only been here two months. I've never noticed anything disturbed."

I hid the bundle beneath my coat at the bottom of the wardrobe.

". . . and what we eat, for God's sake," Leona was saying. "He was a chicken breeder, you know that? He acts as if we're a bunch of brood hens and he's experimenting with the feed to see how big he can get the eggs. Well, you'll see. It's almost time — let's go down and get in line for the first sitting. Here, help me up."

I gave Leona my hand and she grunted as I pulled her up. I glanced back at the wardrobe — I would find a better hiding place later, when I was alone.

TWENTY-EIGHT

Dozens of girls chattered softly by the closed glass doors leading to the dining room, their hands fluttering up from their round bellies like rising doves, then settling back down protectively. "This is Anneke," Leona told the girls we joined. "She's going to be here for a while, so let's be nice and not scare her too much her first night."

I could see right away what Leona had warned me about. The French and Belgian girls were clustered with the girls from Holland, and the German girls were pointedly ignoring us. In the dining room, we sat together, but we filled only one end of the table; there were German girls at the other end, separated from us by several empty seats, and the air from them was icy.

"Where are the older ones, the ones who are married?" I asked Leona.

"Oh, the *Frauen* . . . never at first sitting . . . that's why we come early. They're

206

over in the crèche. They bring their other children here for the food. They'll put them to bed and then they'll come over and talk about their husbands, like old cows chewing their cuds. Would you pass the bread basket?"

I handed it to her and she pointed into it. "See? Just last week . . . that Himmler. Oh, those lovely white dinner rolls we used to get. Now it's only wholemeal bread."

Servers were at our table now, setting down platters of food. A groan went up at the bowls of shredded cabbage.

"This is the worst," Leona explained. "Two-thirds of our vegetables have to be eaten raw — that's the new rule — and that includes sauerkraut. Can you imagine? Nobody eats it, of course."

I hadn't seen so much food in a year. Bowls brimming with vegetables, roasted potatoes, onion pies. Pitchers of milk, the heavy cream stirred down, waiting to be poured into tall glasses. There was real butter for the bread. The kitchen girls served everyone a single portion of the roast pork, but you could help yourself to seconds of everything else. I ate until I was ready to burst, and then when an *Obsttorte* was offered, I ate that, too, and still I wanted to eat and to fill my arms with the food, stuff

207

my pockets. All that food made me careless.

Another girl from the Netherlands, Resi, the one who was overdue, was asking me questions about Schiedam. She had gone to university with a girl from there — Juul Kuyper — did I know her? I didn't.

"Maybe she was ahead of you in school. How old are you?"

"Nineteen," I answered, then realized my mistake.

"Oh, well, she would be twenty-one by now, like me," Resi said. Then she went on to describe her friend, but I couldn't really listen.

When an announcement was made that there would be a film shown in the dayroom after the second dinner sitting, I was still shaken. Leona told me she was too tired to stay up and I told her I was, too, after my long day of travel.

Up in our room, Leona pulled her clothes off. I had never seen a pregnant woman's body before and I couldn't help staring at her swollen belly, shot through with purple stretch marks, her heavy breasts resting on it. I tried to picture my own body swelling up, ready to burst. With Isaak's child. Isaak's.

"Awful, isn't it?" she laughed, patting her

huge roundness. "I'm a victim of my own lust!"

"Did you love him?"

Leona struggled to pull her nightgown over her middle and fell into bed with a huge sigh, like an old woman. "That night I did. He was a wonderful kisser, I'll give him that much. God, I miss kissing, don't you? He took his time with it. He had chocolate and cinema passes. I had too much beer. And I loved him that night." She sighed, then shook herself. "Well. Just look where it's got me."

"You're almost through it."

"I am. And I'll go home as soon as I can. As soon as they cut that cord." Leona read my glance. "If I let myself hold him or feed him, it'll be worse."

"You're afraid he'll feel like he's yours, then? How do you think of him now?"

"Like a medical condition. Something to get over. Don't look at me that way — you don't know yet."

"You're right. I'm sorry."

"I know how it sounds. But my first roommate gave me that advice — you can't think of it as a baby. Otherwise you could go mad from the pain. Some of them do."

"Go mad?"

"You can hear them. Screaming when they

take the babies away. You never hear a sound from the labor ward, and you know that's got to be as loud. But you hear their screams afterward — the one's who've made the mistake of holding them. You'd think someone's tearing off parts of their bodies." Leona eased herself up on her elbows. "Well, tell me about your soldier."

The word brought him back to me for a split second: that one, the *Oberschütze,* with his pale bristly hair and his ham-red face and his rage. My heart kicked. "My soldier." I pictured Anneke's boyfriend instead, turning his blue eyes away from me in the bakery, with that strange look of worry, it had seemed. Or despair. "His name was Karl. He's gone. Transferred."

"Is he going to take the baby?"

"What? It'll be adopted."

"Well, of course it will be adopted; they certainly won't let you keep it. But the Germans will pressure him to take the baby home to his wife — can you imagine those wives, taking their husband's little souvenirs into their families and raising them? — that's the first option. If he's married, that is. Is he?"

"No." I felt the sweat begin to form on my back — all these details.

"Then they'll give your baby to a good

Nazi family." She laughed bitterly. "A good Nazi family. I hate thinking about that part. Well. What did you think of your first night?"

"It was all right," I said. "I liked the girls we sat with, anyway."

"Be careful," Leona said. "You'd be surprised how fast things can go bad around here. A hundred women locked up together, none of us virgins and no men — that's bad enough. Then add a bunch of patriotic German girls — Hitler's whores. Just be careful."

She turned off the lamp and instantly the dark brought me back to that alley, to those knuckles in my mouth.

"I like the *rolladen* up," Leona said. "It's not allowed, but if the lights are out they don't know. I like to see the stars. But you can leave them closed, if you'd rather."

"No, open. Open." I rolled the wooden slats into their casing and looked out. The sky was familiar, at least — these same stars glittered over Holland tonight. These were my stars, and I really wasn't that far from home. I lay back and closed my eyes. Immediately I saw the other stars, the yellow ones. They were mine, too. And I was very far from home.

TWENTY-NINE

I awoke screaming. Leona was beside me, squeezing my hands. "A bad dream," she said. "Are you all right now?"

I shivered; my nightgown was wet, clinging to me. Leona pulled my coverlet up to my neck. "Can you go back to sleep?"

I couldn't. When I closed my eyes, I couldn't breathe — the stench of motor oil covered my face like a blanket. When I opened them, I saw the mountains outside my window — immense, the tops white and jagged as broken teeth, glowing in the moonlight.

I wanted Isaak, wanted his body next to me. I saw his face, so pained: "I can't love anyone." A sob built like a wave in my chest and I got up quietly and found his drawing pencil on my bureau. Clutching it, I got back into bed and tried to think about him coming for me. It wouldn't be for at least a week or two; until then, I would have to get through these nights. The days would be easier — I would only have to stay out of the staff's way, try to talk to as few of the girls as possible, and take advantage of the resources here.

For one thing, the babies. I lay in bed, calmer, imagining it: There were babies in this building, dozens of them, a richness of pleasure. As soon as I could, I would find out if I could visit the nursery to see them. Perhaps even to hold one.

I watched the sunrise — so normal, as though the sun wasn't shocked to find itself in Germany. A bell rang. Leona stirred and opened her eyes. She looked as though it was a surprise to see me in the next bed but then she smiled, as though it was a nice surprise. She reached over to her night table and found her watch. "We'd better go down."

We dressed; Leona in her vast shift and me in the skirt I'd worn yesterday. This morning the waistband seemed tighter — was that possible already? Or was it just that enormous meal?

Downstairs, a line of girls stretched along the hall, more than had been there the evening before.

"What time do they open the dining room?" I asked.

"Oh, it's open," Leona said. She was still buttoning her sweater. "It's just weigh-in day."

"Weigh-in day?"

"Every Saturday morning. They set up the scales at the dining-room doors . . . ruins your appetite, I can tell you that."

The girls chatted and the line moved forward steadily. My mouth tasted of metal, and a bloom of perspiration shivered down my spine.

"Frau Klaus. Try not to make eye contact," Leona advised me in a low voice as we got near. "Don't even smile at her. Once I . . . if she singles you out for anything . . ."

Leona got on the scale and groaned at her weight.

And then it was my turn.

"Name?"

I told her.

"Step out of your shoes. Hurry up, there are girls waiting."

"Fifty-nine kilos," Frau Klaus announced and then noted it. I stepped off the scale and moved next to Leona.

"My belly alone weighs fifty-nine kilos!" she sighed.

Please call the next girl, I willed.

"Wait."

I turned slowly, pretending not to know

214

who she was calling.

She frowned and lifted a paper accusingly. "Fifty-three and a half kilos on your last weighing." She looked back down at the form. "Eleven days ago."

I tried to look amazed. "I've been eating everything in sight," I said, as agreeably as I could. The chatter of the other girls had disappeared entirely.

"Five and a half kilos. That's impossible, of course."

And then I thought of something. "Wait," I said. "Are you sure it says fifty-three? Because the nurse who weighed me said fifty-eight and a half last week. I remember, because it was more than I'd thought."

Frau Klaus stood, my chart in her hand.

"Couldn't that three really be an eight?"

Frau Klaus shook her head, pinched her mouth down into a thin white line. "Where were you weighed?"

I realized that I didn't know. Where had Anneke gone that day? "In the Netherlands," I said.

She looked at me hard for another moment.

"They seemed to be very careless there," I confided. "Not organized, like here."

She nodded, satisfied. "Incompetent." She sat back down and changed the three into an eight with her pen. "Next girl. Name?"

In the dining room, Leona handed me a plate and I took it with both hands so it wouldn't shake. Once again, I was struck by the sheer abundance of food — in a year and a half, I had forgotten that food could be offered as choices. Platters of fresh fruit, real eggs, muesli, cheeses. Three kinds of jam. Again I had the urge to take everything, to fill myself. At either end of the buffet table sat a large tureen of porridge.

"Porridge at every breakfast," Leona muttered. "And if you don't eat it, you'll hear about it."

"They keep track of what you eat here?"

"Just the damned porridge . . . Himmler's got an obsession. The rumor is he has to eat it because he suffers from terrible stomachaches, which I hope is true. So I guess he feels everyone else should eat it, too."

"I don't mind it," said Aimée, behind us in line. She was Belgian, and seemed as sweet as her name. "Back home in my village, people would be grateful for it."

Next to her was the other girl from Belgium. "Me, too," she agreed. "I don't mind anything here. It was much worse at the home in Liège."

We took seats at the table — I was between Leona and Aimée. "What was wrong there?"

I asked her, low enough that the serving girls pouring tea at the end of the table couldn't overhear.

"For one thing, the doctor there was only a dentist!" Aimée pointed at her belly. "Does this look like a tooth to you?"

"None of the staff was professional," the other girl agreed. "And it was filthy. They found bits of wire in the babies' broth once, and I heard they'd let the chamber pots in the nursery overflow before they'd empty them."

"And you couldn't keep anything valuable," Aimée added. "Everything was stolen. The nurses just took whatever they wanted — we were always running out of soap and linens — and they'd steal half the food. No, say what you want about the Germans — at least they run the homes right over here."

"Oh, there's plenty of stealing here, too," Leona said. "My last roommate came here with a fur coat — God knows why in the summer — and it disappeared right out of our room. She didn't even trust *me* after that . . . slept with her things under her pillow."

I thought of my father's letter and the photograph at the bottom of the wardrobe. Maybe I could bury them outside.

Suddenly Greetje, sitting across from us,

threw down her spoon and stood. "I've had it!" she cried. She dumped her bowl of porridge onto the tablecloth. "I can't look at another bowl of this shit again. I say we boycott it and send a message to Himmler."

There was a second of shocked silence, as if the other girls were thinking what I was thinking. But Greetje's face said, *Well, what are they going to do about it?* She was right: We were geese about to lay golden eggs, safe at least until we gave birth. Then the other girls laughed, and a few others dumped their porridge onto the table, the gray clumps spattering over the white linen and the silver sugar bowls.

"You can give him the message in person in two weeks," Aimée said, and the table went quiet again.

"I'd almost forgotten," Leona said. "On the seventh."

I'd been trying not to talk — to just listen — but I wanted to know about this.

"What happens on the seventh?"

"It's his birthday — the *Reichsführer* himself, the great porridge-eater. We're being graced . . . a naming ceremony . . . I'm planning to have a headache. And if I go into labor that day, someone chain my legs together."

Resi came in then and eased herself into

218

Greetje's empty chair. "I wish I could wait that long." Her belly rode so high and enormous, it was hard for her to reach the table.

"Why?" I asked, lost.

"If your baby is born on the seventh, he gets special presents. Not just the bank-book."

I was about to ask what she meant, but I felt Leona tap my thigh under the table. She broke in and changed the subject.

Later, in our room, she explained: "Resi's boyfriend is a Dutchman who joined the Waffen SS. That's the worst, as far as I'm concerned — traitors. She's going to marry him, and they'll keep the baby. So there'll be another little collaborator in the Nether-lands soon. I just thought you should know. Be careful how you talk around her."

I suddenly remembered a picture I'd seen in a schoolbook once. A beekeeper. Bees covered his face, his head, his neck. Covered him. He wasn't wearing a shirt, the caption said, although it was impossible to tell this from the photo — his chest and arms were black with bees. "The bees are harmful only if disturbed," the caption assured the reader. The photograph had haunted me for weeks.

I thought again of those bees, trembling against my skin.

"Leona, why do they room us by country?"

"Divide and conquer, that's what I think. I don't think they want a dozen girls from enemy countries getting together any more than they have to. Not that there's anything we could do . . . what do they think, anyway? Of course, they certainly don't want us rooming with German girls, either."

"Too many fights?"

"*Ja,* that. But it's more . . . I wasn't here when this happened, but my first roommate told me about it: Three or four months ago there was a huge blowup here, had everyone in a . . . Seems one of the older women was always bragging about her work with the Gestapo — in Smolensk, I think — about how they were murdering Jews. Once she told about how they were killing the babies, too. Bullets to the back of the neck . . . can you imagine?"

"Babies?"

"They shut her up, of course. Told the girls she was crazy. And she must have been, to make up something like that: Everyone here is pregnant, for God's sake! And there are a lot of prisoners from the camps working here — the cleaning women and the men who work on the grounds. By the way, don't ever talk to them."

"Leona, do you believe it? What she said?"

"About the babies? No, of course not. Although . . . no, she was only trying to horrify us. It worked — some of the girls from Holland and Belgium tried to leave. Since then, they've had this policy of rooming the German girls separately and keeping girls together by nationality if they possibly can. I like it."

"Me, too," I said. "Leona?"

"Yes?"

"Where is she now?"

"Who?"

"The woman who worked for the Gestapo. Is she still here?"

"Well . . . I don't know. I doubt it. Most of the older ones go home immediately. But I don't know. Why?"

I didn't answer.

Bullets to the back of the neck.

THIRTY

It was difficult being surrounded by so many people, feeling wary all the time. But it was worse to be alone — thoughts of the soldier were always waiting. I filled my time by studying the layout of the home and the schedules — the two things that would be most important to know when the time came for my escape. The information was not encouraging.

The building had originally been owned by the Catholic Church and used as a hostel for retiring priests. It was completely surrounded by walls: granite and brick in the front, and then on the sides and the back, where the hostel had needed only hedges, the Germans had erected well-lit steel-mesh fences. The perimeters were guarded, by dogs as well as armed men. The first time I saw the patrol, I was disoriented — the guards were on the outside of the fence. Then I realized: I was probably the only one inside who wanted to leave. These walls were to keep people out.

The year before, Leona told me, the townspeople had staged a violent demonstration when it was learned that a shipment of chocolates and oranges had been delivered for the girls at Christmastime. The townspeople were hungry. They kept away now, afraid of the dogs and the guns. Isaak, or whoever he sent, would have to walk up the front entryway, past those guns and those dogs, and be admitted to get me.

Because I couldn't leave. This was a new development, and I worried about how Isaak could learn about it. Just a few months ago, some of the girls who had been working outside the home in Baden had contracted tuberculosis and there had been an epidemic. After that, the girls needed official permission to leave the grounds and when they returned they were quarantined for two weeks. Then in August, a group of girls from the Austrian home had been set upon by a group of villagers angry at the "horizontal collaborators" — beaten and stoned — and one of the girls had lost her baby. So just three weeks before I'd come, Himmler sent down the new order: No girl could leave a Lebensborn home for any reason, except in the company of an SS guard or the soldier who had fathered her baby. Only the German girls complained about this.

In that first week I stayed to myself as much as I could, only braided myself into the constant lines and knots of girls at meals, classes, and lectures, and tried to avoid conversation. Leona had been right about the German girls, and in some ways we felt like their prisoners of war. The staff never allowed any open hostility toward us — their job was to deliver healthy babies — but it seeped through as an undercurrent nevertheless.

I stayed away from the staff as well. Frau Klaus especially — she had never had any children and she seemed to take every rising belly as a personal attack.

"If you need anything, go to the little nurse with the dark curly hair . . . in charge of the delivery ward." Leona leaned in to study herself in the mirror. "Do you think I should get a permanent? When I . . . in Amsterdam, they're doing a new wave . . ."

By now I was used to Leona's rambling conversation, the way her thoughts flitted like fireflies. "Sister Ilse? But I've met her. She's German."

"But she's not a Nazi like all the others. And she likes us better than the German girls — you can tell."

I stored this bit of information, but I reminded myself that my situation was different and I could never allow myself to trust anyone in here. What worried me most, of course, were the letter and the photograph I foolishly had brought with me. I knew I should burn them, but whenever I even thought of lighting the match, my chest hitched, breathless.

At the end of that first week, I found a solution.

The girls on my floor used the laundry on Tuesdays and Fridays. I took my time in there. The big washing machines growled too loudly for conversation, and the other girls left as soon as they could, so I could be alone in the hot room — a luxury to not hear German. And it was a comfort to iron and fold Anneke's clothes, although I hated wearing them. Except, strangely, for a pair of pearl-gray trousers. Anneke had loved wearing trousers — she said they made her feel different: modern, stronger, freer. I'd just laughed at her, but now I understood.

On my second trip to the laundry, I noticed three large rolls of tape on a shelf. The instant I was alone, I took one of them and hid it in my basket of clean laundry.

Back in my room, I pulled out my accusing belongings in the velvet bag and knelt down to find a piece of furniture with enough clearance. The base of the wardrobe, too heavy to be moved casually, stood about fifteen centimeters from the floor — perfect. Just as I was finishing taping the bundle to the bottom, I heard the door open. I rolled out and raised my head, prepared to tell Leona I had dropped an earring.

But it wasn't Leona.

For a second, I was shaken — the woman standing in my room could have been any of the shopkeepers in my hometown in Poland, any of my friends' grandmothers. She was not as plump, though, and her dress and kerchief were the color of concrete — when the women in my town gathered, they always reminded me of a collection of stuffed rabbits, dressed in gaily colored dolls' clothes.

"Sorry, sorry!" she said. She lifted a mop and pail as if in offering for some offense. "I will come back."

We cleaned our rooms ourselves, but on Fridays the floors were mopped. I had forgotten. "No, I was just leaving."

I realized my safety could depend on knowing exactly how things were done here, down to the smallest detail. By the end of the week, I knew where the sun fell in each room, what day we ate herring, what nights we heard lectures on nutrition. I found out what time the post was delivered and what days the food shipments came in. I learned how long it took the staff to set up for meals and how long it took them to clean up afterward. I learned the hierarchy: Dr. Ebner was the chief of the medical staff, but like the other doctors, he was rarely seen, and Frau Klaus was in charge of the nurses. All the nurses were called Sisters, from the head nurses down to the student nurses, or Little Brown Sisters, none of whom seemed old enough to have had any medical training. I knew that in addition to the delivery ward, Sister Ilse was in charge of the newborns' nursery, and she didn't mind if I went down there to gaze at the tiny babies in the neat rows of white iron cribs.

Another week passed. I began to watch for Isaak.

THIRTY-ONE

I became used to responding to Anneke's name more quickly than I would have guessed. But hearing it could sometimes completely undo me — like cutting the strings of a marionette — and I could never tell when it might happen.

"What were you studying, Anneke?" Leona asked one morning, walking back from breakfast. "Before this happened?"

A sudden image: Anneke curled over her books beside me, tapping her red fingernails on the table, frowning and then pushing the books aside. "Come on, Cyrla! We can study later. I want to see a film!" The image was so vivid and the wish to see her again so sharp that I gasped.

"What?" Leona asked.

"Nothing." I tried to gather myself, but the tears were too close. I touched my stomach and motioned to the washroom ahead. "Maybe something I ate. Don't wait."

There was no one inside; still, I shut myself into a stall before I fell against the green-tiled wall, shaking. It was so hard to be alone in this place. I pressed my fists to my eyes and calmed my breathing; after a few minutes, just as I was ready to leave, I heard the door open. Then the sound of a bucket being set down and water sloshing. It brought back the sound of my aunt washing away Anneke's blood. I fell back against the wall again, my hands to my mouth to stifle a cry.

I heard the door open again, then close. The mopping stopped.

Voices — a young woman and an older one — whispered so quietly I could only make out a few words. The younger woman asked something about children and grandchildren. "Who can know, who can know?" the older woman sighed. I didn't want to hear any more. I pulled the chain and walked out.

Sister Ilse's hands flew behind her back and the cleaning woman — the same one who had startled me in my room the week before — fumbled at her pocket with something. She looked so frightened, I wanted to reach out and comfort her. But at that instant the door opened again, and Frau Klaus swept inside.

Sister Ilse and the cleaning woman froze. An apple fell from the old woman's skirt and rolled under the sink. In the silence, the sound filled the room.

Frau Klaus bent and picked up the apple. She held it up to Ilse's face with an ugly smile. "You've been warned before. I'll have to report you this time."

Sister Ilse flushed. "It isn't right," she began.

Fear flickered across the cleaning woman's face.

I stepped forward. "I'm sorry! I took the apple at breakfast, but then I didn't want it after all. Sister Ilse was just explaining that I shouldn't have given it to her."

Frau Klaus narrowed her eyes, trying to pry out my lie, or the reason for it. She looked between Sister Ilse and the cleaning woman. No one spoke. No one breathed. She dropped the apple into the dirty mop water. Gray suds splashed over the old woman's apron.

"Don't let this happen again." It was unclear to whom she was speaking. "Now get back to work."

The cleaning woman hurried to the far corner of the washroom. Sister Ilse turned for the door. As she passed, she flashed me a look. I had made an ally.

Of course, I had made an enemy, too.

THIRTY-TWO

The third week began. No letter came for me, but I didn't panic. Things might take a little longer, depending on when Isaak learned I was in Germany. Every day, I merely wished that it would be my last in this place and I could finally draw a peaceful breath. When I thought about leaving, I never thought about making the passage to England or even about arriving there safely. Only of Isaak coming for me and bringing me back to Holland. Everything would start over then. The things we had said that last day, well, that was the beginning of the discussion, not the end. Maybe he didn't love me, but we could make a home. And after living together with the miracle of a child as our reality, well, who knew?

One morning, Leona asked me to sweep her side of the room while I was doing mine, and I snapped at her. Just because she was pregnant, did that mean I was her slave?

My response surprised us both, and I suddenly realized something: It was my time of the month. It was always a clear sign — the day before I was moody and impatient. Anneke usually noticed it first: "Let's talk about this again in a few days," she'd tease, "when you're not such a witch."

I hadn't considered that I might not be pregnant. I'd been so sure on that last day . . . before that last night. Before.

I watched myself all that day for more signs of irritability, going out of my way to be sweet and patient. Because it was unthinkable that I would bleed in here. It was the next day I really worried. A dozen times that morning I excused myself to go to the bathroom to check; each time I would be relieved, but my relief would melt half an hour later — didn't I feel something? — and I'd have no peace until I went and checked again.

I was a little calmer by bedtime, when I still had no show of blood or cramps, but it wasn't until a few more days had passed that I relaxed. And began to understand that I was carrying a child.

The thought would startle me, like a burst of sunlight, warming me and lighting everything with a flash of radiance. But like the sun, it was too bright, too powerful to look at for more than a second at a time. I might think, *there's life inside me!* but the thought would melt before I could grasp it. *It will grow, a separate thing!* might flash through my mind, but then a second later it would be gone, too stunning to hold. The only image I could keep was of me, handing Isaak his baby. I had to laugh at myself, the image was so self-indulgent — in it I looked as beatific as Mary herself — but what satisfied me more was the look on Isaak's face.

But like sunlight, the thought could be wiped out by a cloud. By the memory of that uniform, or the smell of motor oil.

By the end of the third week, Isaak still hadn't written. He might come without a letter, might be here any day now, but on October 7, I prayed he would stay away. Himmler was coming. Of course Isaak knew about this. Of course he did.

We had been preparing for days. The sisters had polished everything that would take a shine, and when I walked down a hallway my reflection — in the mirrors, the candlesticks, the furniture, the floor tiles — was constantly startling me. China rattled and pots banged all morning. Whole chrysanthemum plants lined the lobby, garlanded with green ribbon — green was the

Reichsführer's favorite color — the scent spicy and dangerous. Frau Klaus snapped at the nurses, the nurses snapped at the Little Brown Sisters, and the Little Brown Sisters snapped at us.

We had cleaned our rooms early in the morning in case Himmler decided to inspect them, and I checked the tape on my bundle every time Leona stepped out. He was to arrive at lunchtime and address us in the dining hall about the importance of proper nutrition. Then he would eat with Dr. Ebner and Frau Klaus in the parlor, which had been set up with the best linens and china, and precisely at 1:30, the naming ceremony was to be held. Notes had been issued to all the mothers instructing them to arrange their babies' naptime so neither their fussing nor their sleeping would insult the *Reichsführer.* It had been impossible to get into the laundry for days, with the mothers busy washing and ironing their children's best outfits.

By noon we were all in our assigned places. No girl was to be found in the halls when he entered; the women who had already presented Germany with children were given the honor of greeting him in the front lobby, while the rest of us were to be already standing at our places at the table.

But as the dining room looked out over the drive, of course all of us were crowded around the windows.

A few moments before twelve, a trio of black Mercedes-Benzes, all flying the SS death's-head flags, spun into the gravel. Four SS officers stepped out of each of the first two cars, and came to attention along the drive, their tall black boots gleaming. The third car was longer and bore the license plate SS1. Two more officers exited that car and opened the doors in back. Three civilians got out: two women and a man. And then Himmler.

There was no mistaking him. He was a small man, made smaller still by the large presence of his uniform and the height of the men surrounding him, but every person was turned toward him, moving with him like a wave as he passed up the walk.

The procession entered the building quickly, and we lost sight of him. We hurried to our places, our hands behind our backs like schoolchildren. Well, pregnant schoolchildren — I suddenly felt flat next to all these rounding bellies. And very dark among these fair women. The chicken breeder would see my heritage.

And then Himmler was in the room. Flanked by a dozen uniformed men and the three civilians we had seen leave the cars, he wasn't visible to us at first. He was the shortest man in the group — smaller even than the women. But the group parted in a practiced deference, and as he walked to the podium at the front of the dining room, every eye was upon him as though pulled by strings.

My first thought was that without the uniform, without the cortege, you would have mistaken this mild-looking man for a clerk. He held his hat at his chest now; his forehead was very high — dark thinning hair swept across the crown of his head. He wore perfectly round glasses which gave him an expression of bewildered surprise, as if he weren't sure how he'd gotten here, and had a tiny clipped mustache — a weak imitation of his *Führer*'s. His face was soft and baby-ish, with a small double chin. The second most powerful man in Germany showed no strength in his face anywhere, and when he spoke, no strength in his voice.

Power that sprang from weakness was to be feared the most — my father had told me that.

"Ladies," he addressed us. "You carry within you our nation's greatest wealth, Germany's future strength. Please sit down." He waited through the bustle of fifty pregnant bodies seating themselves, and then he began flattering them again. "Every war involves a tremendous letting of blood. It is the highest duty of German women and girls of good blood to become mothers, inside or outside the boundaries of marriage, and not irresponsibly, but in a spirit of deep moral seriousness, of children of soldiers going on active service of whom fate alone knows whether they will come back again or die for Germany. . . ."

He didn't seem to know that there were non-German women in the room. Or, more likely, he didn't care. I couldn't listen. And I couldn't look at him, either — it felt too dangerous. I dropped my gaze to his hat instead. It lay in front of him on the podium: the golden eagle perched on the sweeping crest; a death's-head medallion below it rode a black velvet band — plush and evil.

"And not just one or two!" he was exulting. "Supposing Bach's mother, after her fifth or sixth or even twelfth child, had said, 'That'll do, enough is enough'? The works of Bach would never have been written."

And then he talked about porridge. Porridge!

"You must abandon the absurd belief that eating porridge will rob you of your figures! Besides, one need only look to the English

238

to see that the eating of oatmeal flakes has nothing to do with the weight of persons of quality. Look no further than Lord Halifax, whose slender form is a result of eating those oatmeal flakes called porridge every day . . ."

I clamped my hands over my mouth and ran from the dining room, through the empty kitchen, and out to the back garden.

THIRTY-THREE

I only just made it, vomiting behind a low brick wall. Then I sank to the wall and clutched at my stomach, shaking.

"He has that effect on me, too," came a voice. Then a laugh. Then cigarette smoke, which made me feel ill again.

Sister Ilse, the short dark-haired nurse, stuck her head out from behind a granite buttress beside me, smiling as if we were in on a secret. She drew on her cigarette, then noticed my face. "Sorry," she said, grinding it out with her heel. "Would you like some water?"

I shook my head. "I don't know what happened, I suddenly —"

"Do you feel all right now?"

"Yes. I'll go back in." I stood up, but I swayed.

"No. Just sit down again." She came over and eased me back down, then sat beside me. "You're pale. See this uniform? I'm a nurse, so you must listen to me." From the pocket of her apron, she pulled a handful of wrapped candies and offered me one.

"Thank you." I unwrapped it and put it in my mouth to let the licorice clear the taste of rust. "But I ran out in the middle of the speech —"

"Don't worry. If anyone asks, I'll say I was tending you and wouldn't let you go back in. Besides, morning sickness is perfectly normal, and anything to do with being pregnant is fine around here."

I stared blankly for a moment. Of course.

"Is this your first time?"

I nodded.

Now it was her turn to stare. "How far along are you?"

"Not very," I admitted. "I just thought I'd eaten something bad last night."

"Perhaps you did. But it's more likely morning sickness. You might have it for a week, you might have it all the way through. Water crackers are good. Do you want me to get you some?"

I groaned.

"I know," she said. "But they can help. The thing is to listen to your own body — try different things to find out what helps. Don't let anyone tell you things should be a certain way, or you must do a certain thing.

Some of the doctors here forget that having a baby is a perfectly natural thing. Wait here. I'm going to make you some tea."

I leaned back against the white stucco wall and sat with the sun on my face, too weak to go inside even if I'd wanted to. Morning sickness. I smiled a little — *so you're making yourself known already.*

Sister Ilse came back with a cup cradled in her hands and passed it to me. Bits of bark were floating in the tea and I looked back at her, suspicious.

"Dried ginger root. Try it, it usually helps. I keep a package in my room. Ask me for it anytime. Apple-peel tea is good, too."

She sat beside me and offered her hand. "I'm Ilse. I've been trying to run into you so I could thank you for last week, in the washroom."

"Anneke." For the first time I wished I could have said my real name.

"You're from the Netherlands. How awful for you in there, listening to that ass go on about precious German blood. And I know how hard it must be to hand your children over to them. Everyone here — the girls, the staff — you must hate us all sometimes."

I looked straight ahead and sipped my tea. It tasted sharp and clean, and it cut through the nausea.

Ilse read my mind. "Don't worry. Everybody's eating by now. Then they'll be in the dayroom with the new mothers. They'll hand out the candlesticks and make a big fuss about the bankbooks, and pretend the babies are the most beautiful they've ever seen." She looked at her watch. "Nobody will come out for at least another hour. Things like this, this ceremony. It must be terrible. I just want you to know that's how I feel sometimes, too."

I edged away.

She turned and measured me, her green eyes pleading for understanding. "You can trust me, Anneke. You won't, though. No one trusts anyone these days. So instead, I'll trust you.

"My father lost his job because he spoke out against the Nazi party. He was a professor of languages at the University in Munich, and he'd traveled all over Europe and the United States lecturing, and was very well respected. Suddenly, about two years ago, his position was no longer needed. The week after, it apparently was needed again, because it was filled. By a good Nazi, of course.

"So my father, my brilliant, decent father, with his two doctorates, is stocking the shelves at a tobacco store at night. And he got that job only because the owner is a friend. And I had to leave the university."

The connection startled me badly. I saw so clearly my father's face just a few months before he sent me away, the night he came home after losing his position at the university, telling us not to worry — he could still teach at a Jewish school — but looking so worried himself. Even picturing him felt dangerous, as if this woman could look into my eyes and see him there. I looked away, making sure there was no one to overhear, then I asked her what she'd been studying.

"Medicine. I was going to be an obstetrician. I was halfway there."

"Ilse, how do you know it's safe to talk to me this way?" I whispered.

"You're Dutch. I'd never talk to the German girls this way. And I'd know if you were a sympathizer. Non-German Nazis are the worst, the most fanatic. It's as if they have to prove themselves or something. I've been here two years and I've met only a few girls from your country who are sympathizers. And you know what? They're just girls in love with their boyfriends, who happened to be Nazis."

We sat for a moment in the quiet sunshine. I finished my tea, then stood up.

"Do you feel better now?"

"I do. The tea helped, thanks."

"Well, I'm not going back in until this whole business is over. You're welcome to sit with me if you'd like."

There was something comforting about this woman. I sat down again. Ilse reached into her pocket and then seemed to change her mind.

"I feel a lot better. It won't bother me now."

She smiled in relief and lit up a cigarette, then offered me her packet. I shook my head — I didn't feel *that* well. She leaned back and inhaled deeply. "My father," she said, her voice lower now. She took another deep pull on the cigarette, then flicked her ash and watched it fall and melt into the grass. "My father hates that man in there. He knew from the beginning, and he was right."

I waited beside her while she stared out over the garden hedge. "Back in '35, he used to say, 'Watch that man. That man is dangerous.' He used to make a joke about it in the very beginning. Himmler was a fertilizer salesman once, did you know that? My father used to say, 'That man is still trying to sell us a load of shit.' But then he stopped joking about it. Because right away, Himmler stopped trying to sell anything. He once said, early on, something like 'We know there are people in Germany who feel ill when they see our black tunics, and that's fine. We don't expect to be liked.' That's the thing, you know. They have no feelings, just this religion of blood."

We sat together, neither of us talking, while she finished her cigarette. Then she stubbed it out with her white nurse's shoe. "Do you know what I hope?"

I shook my head. "What?"

"I hope we lose the war. If we win, we're doomed."

The sound of a window opening not five meters away made us both jump. Then two more a little farther down.

"He's filling the dayroom with his hot air." Ilse laughed.

But it wasn't a laugh.

That evening, Leona asked me where I'd disappeared to.

I put my hand over my stomach and groaned. "I sat outside all afternoon, getting air. Morning sickness."

She nodded. "Me, too, for the first couple of months. It'll pass. I wish I'd spent the afternoon outside. I watched the naming ceremony — have you heard about them?"

I shook my head.

"I won't go to another one. They laid the babies on a pillow in front of a big swastika. 'Variations on the German Anthem' was blaring, and they placed a sword across its little belly . . . the sword was bigger than the baby itself! It looked so evil there. Imagine it: a sword blade across a tiny baby's belly. Who would think of doing that?"

Thirty-Four

Isaak didn't come. A month, he'd said. At the most. But he didn't come. On the thirty-first day, I convinced myself that he was on his way.

That morning, I awoke feeling nauseated as usual, went down to breakfast with Leona as usual, and had only tea and dry toast as usual. The day was brilliant and mild after two days of a chill drizzle, and I decided to spend as much of it outdoors as I could. Partly to be able to watch for Isaak's arrival, but also because when I was outdoors, it was possible to imagine I was in a park in the Netherlands — there were tall firs, boxwood hedges, clipped lawns, and gravel pathways — all these things could have been at home as well. Late asters and chrysanthemums, browning and spindly, still bloomed along some of the walks. And if I stayed at the far edges of the grounds, looking over the peaceful lake toward the distant mountains, I could almost forget entirely where I was. The land itself refused to acknowledge the politics of war, even when it bore its scars.

On that day, my thirty-first day, the shouts from the children's playground drew me. I walked to one of the stone benches that flanked the small grassy play-yard where mothers took their babies to crawl and practice their first steps. Directly across from me was a life-sized statue of a nursing mother and child. The mother's hair was tied in a demure bun; I ran my fingers through my clipped waves and shook my free hair.

I settled down on the bench with my feet tucked up under me and took out the handwork I had brought out — a white receiving blanket I was crocheting with a scalloped blue border. We were encouraged to practice the domestic arts, especially to knit or crochet layette items either for our own babies or to donate to the crèche. Crocheting reminded me of my aunt, and that gave me pleasure.

Sitting there in the sunshine, feeling that Isaak was near, I felt almost peaceful. I smiled watching a sturdy boy stomping around a birdbath with big exaggerated steps, with a little girl following him, laughing so hard she kept falling down. A young mother came to sit beside me, carrying a baby who looked to be about two months old. "May I see him?" I asked, leaning over the sleeping bundle.

Some new mothers were delighted to show me their babies and some would glare daggers if I dared to steal a peek. This one didn't seem to care either way. She pulled the blanket from the baby's head and held him toward me. I smiled to see his plump mouth purse and open, dreaming his milk dreams, and touched the silky fringe of his hair with one finger.

"What's his name?"

The girl shrugged. "He hasn't been named. There's another ceremony next week." She wore her light brown hair plaited into two long braids, and her skirt was the kind a schoolgirl might wear.

"What do you call him to yourself?"

She shrugged again. "He hasn't been named," she repeated, as though I hadn't understood.

"Well, he's beautiful."

She frowned a little and cocked her head, assessing the child on her lap as if he were a piece of fruit she was deciding whether or not to buy. She nodded. "He's perfect. Do you want to hold him?"

"Of course," I said, and lifted him from her. The girl stood and walked across the lawn to join a group of friends. She didn't look back.

It was the first time since becoming pregnant that I had held a baby. I drank in the scent of his neck, nuzzled his soft cheeks, pressed him close, and thrilled at the rightness of his solid weight against my heart. I worked my fingertip into his fist, and when he squeezed, I felt it pull deep in my belly.

Too soon he stirred, his mouth working in hunger, his face nudging more and more urgently into my breast. His forehead creased in consternation when he opened his eyes and found my stranger's face above him, and he began to wail his distress.

His mother came over when she heard him, almost reluctantly, it seemed to me, lifted him from my arms, and sat down to nurse him, without wiping away his tears. Without even looking down at them.

"How old are you?" I asked, before I could even think about my rudeness.

"Almost sixteen." The girl saw my shock and lifted her jaw to me. "Young mothers are healthy mothers. And the earlier you start, the more children you can bear." Her answer sounded practiced.

I couldn't help myself. "You're already

planning on having *more?*"

"Of course! It's a woman's highest duty and her privilege. The future of the Third Reich will be glorious and vast. Millions of Germans of good blood will be needed."

Her speech was just general propaganda, I knew, but the look in her eyes was aimed more personally. *Who did you think was going to run your country once we've won the war?* it mocked.

"And what does your boyfriend have to say about all this?"

She looked at me with disdain. "The father isn't my boyfriend. That's an outdated idea. And he's very pleased. His wife was only able to give him three children."

I felt myself gaping, but I didn't care. "Your boyfriend is married and his wife knows about this? And she's going to take the baby?"

"I told you he's not my boyfriend. He's an officer; he taught sports at my youth group. I asked him to help me present the state with a child. And he agreed, as he wanted more children."

"You made love with a man so that —"

"We had *relations,*" she corrected me. The sophistication she was trying for made her seem only younger.

"How old is this man?"

"Thirty-two. He's young enough he should have more children. They're taking this one next month, and then as soon as I can, we'll have another."

"You're fifteen years old, and when you leave this place you're going to have relations with a man of thirty-two, and then hand over the baby to his wife? For the second time?"

She nodded, defiant.

"And then? You'll keep doing it?"

"I'll keep having children, of course. As many as I can. But I might get married next year. I'll be old enough."

Sister Ilse came up from behind us and leaned over, cooing at the baby. "A kiss without a beard is like an egg without salt, you know."

"My aunt used to say that," I said, glad for the interruption. "I thought it was Dutch."

"It's German, too, I guess."

The girl looked annoyed. "What's it supposed to mean?"

Ilse and I answered at the same time: "Don't marry too soon."

The girl rolled her eyes and let out a sigh — she probably meant for it to sound world-weary, but it just sounded petulant. She pulled her baby from her breast roughly and buttoned herself up, then slung him over her shoulder. She left us without saying good-bye.

"That one," Ilse sighed, settling down beside me.

"You know her?"

"I attended the birth. She's one of the faithful. Refused all pain medicine and stared at her portrait of the *Führer* instead. Even at the end, even when her pelvis cracked. That's the badge of honor, to do that. If you ask me, it's the sign of insanity. Brainwashed out of all common sense."

"Wait." I put my hand on her arm. "Her pelvis cracked?"

"Don't worry!" she assured me. "Your hips look fine. Hers hadn't widened yet. And the baby was over four kilos, I remember that —"

"Could you hear it?" I interrupted.

Ilse reached over to pat my arm. It was the first time someone had touched me in thirty-one days. No, thirty-two. "Please forget I said that. It wasn't very professional of me. Her body was immature. You'll be fine. Besides, you'll be smart enough to take the ether if you need it. Promise me you'll stop thinking about this."

I couldn't. I didn't want to, but I could picture the girl's delivery. Her thin child's legs splayed wide, knees knobby as a colt's. Her narrow child's pelvis cracking under the increasing thrusts of the baby's descent. The doctors splitting her open to pull him out. She bit her lips so hard they poured blood — somehow I knew that was true. And all the while she stared at Adolf Hitler, her God. I shivered.

"Anneke?"

"I'm sorry. It's just that she's so young. Fifteen!"

"Girls grow up fast these days. Children always lose the most in wartime."

"And she's so cold, completely without romance — that seems very sad."

"It *is* sad. When I was her age, we were so excited about our possibilities. It felt like the world was opening up to us. To women. My mother was very modern — she told me I could be whatever I wanted to be, and there was no shame if I didn't choose motherhood. What a difference now."

"What does she say now?"

"She would have been . . . she's dead. She died in childbirth with my sister."

"I'm so sorry." I suddenly ached to tell her that we shared the sad bond of motherlessness, but instead I asked her if that was why she'd gone into obstetrics.

"It is." Ilse gave a wry laugh. "This isn't

exactly what my mother would have chosen for me, though. Or my sister. She's just like that girl. Except that she hasn't yet been asked to give a baby to the *Führer.* She's dark and short like me, so she's not being recruited. But she's brainwashed all the same. I don't even try to talk to her about it — I don't dare. I swear she'd turn me in if she thought it would get her into the Little Brown Sisters."

Ilse stopped herself then and looked around. The young mother was standing across the path beside the statue with two other girls; all had their babies slung on their hips as if they were nothing more than sacks of grain. Ilse flicked her fingers at them in a quick wave, then she stood up. "Let's take a walk."

We walked along the edges of the property. There was no one else around, but Ilse didn't speak about her family again, or about the girls here. I was glad enough to leave those subjects. I looked out over the meadows stretching out to the east. "These back fences. They're patrolled all the time, or just at night?"

Ilse looked at me sharply. "Are you going somewhere?"

"No. I just wondered, you know, how safe everything is here. That's all."

Ilse stopped. "Anneke, why did you come here so early? You can't be more than three months along, and Holland isn't so bad off that you need the food."

I gave her my lie about my parents being so angry they kicked me out. Ilse didn't believe me — I could see it in her face. And she looked hurt that I had lied to her.

"Can I ask you something?"

"Of course."

"What would it feel like. . . ." I caught a breath, suddenly dizzy. "What would it feel like to bleed to death? Would it . . . hurt?"

Sister Ilse stared at me.

"A friend of mine died. Please. I want to know. Did she feel pain?"

"Well . . . no. If you bled to death, you would just feel weak. Weaker. Until . . ."

"She wasn't in pain?"

"No. She would have felt cold, but no pain. But what caused the bleeding?"

I pictured it, streaked with blood, lying under that white pillow. I saw my uncle's face. My aunt's. "A knitting needle," I said quietly.

"A knitting needle? How . . . ? Oh." Ilse's face fell. "Oh, how terrible! Abortion is illegal here, but the real crime is what it forces girls to turn to."

I clenched my jaw, close to tears now. I

257

saw her gaze drop to my bag, where the crochet needle lay on top. She pulled her head back to look at me harder. "Anneke, are we really talking about something someone else did?"

"Yes, really. Someone I knew. Did it hurt?"

Ilse looked at me for a long moment, her eyes sad. "Yes. There would have been pelvic pain from that. But she wouldn't have felt it for long. She would have slipped under. Anneke, are you sure —"

I raised my hands and took a step back.

"Anneke," she said again. "If you ever want to talk . . ."

THIRTY-FIVE

I had never felt the need to talk more in my life — to tell someone about Anneke's death; how frightened I was here; my pregnancy; all the things that needed to be made right between Isaak and myself. Everything I needed to make him see.

I couldn't talk, so I began to write instead. Not about these things, though. I began to write poetry. Or, rather, it began to write me.

Lines would come to me, challenging me to make sense of them, to chase them down to their meaning. I would bend over the paper, forcing words into couplets, couplets into stanzas, stanzas into completeness. I would finish a poem and feel one measure of calm, and then I would feel the need to start again.

The problem was paper. Sheets of stationery were available, but if I took paper to write letters on, wouldn't someone expect me to have letters to mail? And to whom could I possibly write? I became the oddest of thieves. Everywhere in the home I kept watch for things that wouldn't be missed: the wrappings from deliveries, drawer liners, and once a windfall — a full sheet of discarded gift-wrapping paper. I wrote as small as I could, tiny cramped words, crossed out and written over dozens of times.

I became equally clever at hiding these orphan sheets, lining the bottoms of my drawer with them, sandwiching them between my mattress and box spring, slipping the smaller ones inside my few books.

But once I was careless.

Leona had thrown away an envelope and I'd retrieved it from the wastebasket and had been working a poem on it for a week. I had just slipped it beneath a book on my bedside table when she walked into the room.

Maybe she recognized the address or the handwriting on the corner sticking out. Before I could do anything, she pulled out the envelope.

She read the poem, turning the envelope around and over, squinting to read my tiny notes, my scratched changes. She read it a second time. Then she held it up toward me, raising her eyebrows.

"I was only . . . it's nothing."

"It's not nothing." She chided me as though I'd said something that hurt her. "I didn't know you were a poet."

I reached for the envelope, but she lifted it away. Then she held it out again. "Read it to me. Read it the way it's supposed to sound."

I hesitated for a moment, then nodded, and Leona gave me my poem. She sat on her bed with her feet up and leaned back against the headboard, closing her eyes.

Dusk is endless here, and you would love
These indefinite walks inside its long red
     bottle.
I sing alone
Past black branches and white picket
     fences
To the corral that says No Trespassing.
The brown horse has heard me singing
     from down the road
So he brings the lightning on his face
Over and nudges it under my hand.
Sometimes I know why I am not dead yet.
I still haven't brought a human to the edge
     of the fence.

Leona opened her eyes and looked at me

thoughtfully. "Tell me what made you write that."

Maybe I trusted Leona. Maybe poetry felt like a safe subject. Or maybe there was a quota: After a hundred lies, or a thousand, a person simply must tell the truth. Whatever it was, for the first time since I'd come to this place, I told the barest truth.

"I was trying to understand what was missing between us — the father and me. That seemed a good way to explain it — that in the end, I never brought him to the edge of the fence."

"Maybe you shouldn't have to bring a man there. Maybe he should go that far himself."

I shrugged. "Maybe I should have given him more reason to." But Isaak would never go to the edge of the fence for any single human being. Only for an ideal. Ideals can't abandon you, can't hurt. Ideals can't let you down.

"Is that why you write poetry — to understand your life?"

I thought about it and then nodded. "That's part of it. Sometimes, though, I think I'm trying to write myself out of my life. To escape myself."

"You're lucky, then." Leona sounded more serious than I had ever heard her. "I escape myself by sleeping with men." She looked down and stroked her huge belly. "At least no one else has to pay the price for your escape."

The envelope suddenly began to burn in my hand. I slid it inside the book and stood up.

"Wait." Leona shook her head and gave me her funny smile — the one where her lips didn't curve upward, but the dimples at the corner of her mouth deepened. Then she got up and went to her bureau. She opened a drawer and pulled out a box of stationery — large creamy sheets with deckled edges and a bunch of lavender tulips in each corner.

"My mother gave me this before I left. To write to her. I tried once, but I couldn't do it. It was as if I didn't want to make this real for her. When I get home, I just want to pretend none of this happened. So take it. For heaven's sake, at least write the finished ones down on decent paper."

All that next week — the sixth week I was in that place — I wrote every day.

I wrote and Isaak didn't send word and he didn't come.

Every day of that week, I woke up thinking, *This is the day.* As soon as I got up, I searched the horizon for signs of good or bad weather and tried to decide which would be better. Each day, my eyes strayed to the door of whatever room I was in more and more often, until finally one afternoon, Leona asked me what on earth I was always watching for.

"Nothing," I answered with a laugh. But I was shaken and I learned to watch doors from the corners of my eyes.

Leona grew larger that week and her belly seemed to rise higher and tighter. Then one morning she looked down as she was dressing and gave a little cry. "Look, Anneke! I've dropped! I didn't know I'd really be able to see it. But it feels different, heavier. I feel even heavier. Can you tell?"

Our eyes met. She kept a pamphlet by her bedside — *Signs Your Baby Is About to Be Born* — and each evening she read it to me. "Do you think my ankles are bigger?" she'd ask, anxiously. "Do I seem more restless to you, more emotional?" Number four was "As the baby prepares to be born, he will often begin the descent toward the birth canal, and your whole belly may actually drop."

"You *are* lower. Today, do you think?"

"I don't know. Anneke, what if I can't do this?"

"You can do this. You're going to be fine."

All that day, I would often catch her staring at nothing, concentrating as if she were
struggling to hear something and then melting into a dreamy smile, as if the thing she
had heard was secret music. I felt very
lonely then. And worried for her — she no
longer seemed like a girl who wanted to be
rid of a medical condition.

The day after that, I awoke to find her
already up, although not dressed. She was
standing by the window, her suitcase beside
her, and she turned as soon as I stirred, as
if she'd been waiting.

She gave me a little smile — worried but
resigned. "It started a few hours ago."

"You should have gotten me up."

"No, it was too soon. It's mild right now,
like a squeezing, that's all. And it was nice
to be alone with it. It felt sort of . . . I don't
know . . . mysterious, I guess, to be awake
with it in the dark. And then we watched
the sun rise together." She laughed. "That
sounds strange, doesn't it? But that's what
it felt like — like my baby and I were watching this new day, his birth day, being born."

I got up and joined her at the window.
"Are you changing your mind?"

She waited too long to answer. "No. No.
What would I do with a baby, anyway? And
can you imagine how my family would treat

him? Or my neighbors? It's just that . . . well, now I wish things were different and I could keep him. I wish there weren't a war on and I wish I had a father for him and a family that would welcome him. It's just going to be harder to give him up than I thought."

I took her hand and squeezed it.

"You should go down," she said when the bell rang. "I can't eat."

"No, I'll stay with you."

"Oh, don't. This is going to take a while. I'll still be here when you get back."

I was gone only an hour — there were announcements and a number of new regulations were read — and when I got back to the room, it was empty. The silence was deep — different from the quiet Leona left when she was out of the room for a minute. I realized that the girl I knew really was gone — the next time I saw her she would be a different person. If I ever saw her again. I missed her already.

The day dragged on. Whenever I saw a sister in the hall, I asked if there was any word yet. "I don't think so. I haven't heard of any babies being born today," they said. I spent the hours after dinner standing by the doors that led to the labor ward. Finally

Sister Ilse came on duty and took pity on me.

"She's fine," she assured me. "First babies take their time. Go to bed, she's still got hours to go."

So I did. But I didn't sleep well — in my dreams, I heard screaming. I watched the dawn come up and couldn't wait any longer — I went down to the delivery wing. Sister Ilse was coming down the hall.

"Did she have it?"

"She did. Around midnight. A boy."

"How is she? Was everything all right? I know it's early, but may I see her?"

"She's fine. But no. No visitors."

"But I'm her roommate."

"She's fine, really. It's just that . . . well, sometimes they get upset at the end. Giving birth is a stressful time. The policy is not to let the pregnant ones talk to the new mothers."

"Please let me see her. If she's upset, I could help."

She looked worried, but I could tell she was considering it. I stood my ground until she sighed and gestured to the door on the right. "One minute," she warned.

They'd given her drugs, more than ether. Her eyes were heavy, swollen, and red.

"Mistake" was all she managed before her

face folded in grief. Her eyes, wept dry, pleaded with me as if I could change anything. "My baby." Her words came out slow and thick, as if pulled from tar. "Mine. Mistake."

"I don't think so." I took her hand. "I think you were brave and wise, and you did the right thing."

She shook her head. "Saw him. Mine. I let him go."

"Leona, no," I tried. "You'll see. This is a hard time . . . you'll see."

Sister Ilse came to the door and I was relieved. "I'll come back later and we'll talk."

Leona shook her head again.

"I'll look you up when the war is over. Give me your address."

Leona rolled over to the wall and closed her eyes.

THIRTY-SIX

"I can't sleep next to a window." Those were her first words.

I had taken Leona's bed when she left because it was warmer away from the window's draft, but I didn't really care which was mine for the short time I had left.

"We'll switch," I said. "That's fine. My name's Anneke."

"Neve."

I pulled the bedding off and we remade the beds. Then I sat on mine to watch her unpack. She'd brought only one small suitcase, but it took a while because she folded and refolded each article until it was crisp and flat and perfect. Neve was interesting looking — different from most Dutch girls — tall and sharp and narrow-boned. Her round belly looked out of place, as if it had been stuck on against all those angles. Her hair was pale blonde — straight and cut short. Her brows and lashes were almost white, her face fragile except for her chin, which was square and defiant, as if daring you to want to protect her.

Besides her few clothes, she'd brought nothing except a brush and nail scissors, which she lined up precisely on top of the bureau, and a lighter and three packets of cigarettes, which she placed in her top drawer. No mementos, no family photos. No ties.

I looked at the jumble on my bureau — Isaak's pencil, my cousin's earrings, and the things my aunt had packed: Anneke's combs and barrette, the photograph of Anneke and me taken when I'd first come to Holland, in matching blue cardigans, a china figurine of a prancing horse I'd won at a fair. They were a fraud — I had no ties, either.

Neve followed my gaze to my bureau. She pointed her chin at the scarf I'd draped over the mirror. "You can't see yourself," she said.

I stood up. "I'll show you around. At dinner you'll want to get downstairs in time for the first sitting — it's when most of the single girls eat, and it's best to stay away from the married *Frauen.* They can be —"

"Fine," Neve cut me off, her voice as sharp as the collarbones jutting from her ill-fitting shift.

Fine, yourself, I thought. Ask someone else if you want some help. But she didn't ask a single question.

From the bottom of her bag, she withdrew two books and placed them beside her lamp. *Basics of Aeronautic Engineering* and a slimmer book whose title was so worn I couldn't read it. Neve meant "unknown." I picked up the second book. *Amelia Earhart, a Biography.* "She crashed," I began.

"No," my new roommate corrected me, almost fiercely. She snatched the book from me and replaced it, sliding it next to the other volume so the spines were perfectly aligned. "She *flew.*"

When the first bell rang, she snapped her suitcase closed and left without another word. I got up and crossed to my mirror, leaned in. The scar on my lip was still there, although it was now only a thin stitch, neat and white but jagged as lightning. A single S rune, taunting me as usual: Where was its mate? Had the *Oberschütze* left the rest of his mark deeper inside me? I draped the scarf over the mirror again and went down for the meal.

Neve sat beside me at dinner, but she spoke only to ask me to pass something. I saw her assessing the other girls coolly. I wondered if this were her first time at one

271

of these homes, she seemed so comfortable here. Or maybe she was just that confident. After dinner, she stayed downstairs to watch the evening's film. She came upstairs around nine-thirty; I was in bed, reading, and when I said hello, she only nodded.

In the weeks I had been here I had become an expert in guessing the stages of pregnant girls. Neve looked to be about six months along. I was glad I would be leaving soon — who could put up with three months of this girl?

"I need to sleep," she said when she'd gotten into bed. "So . . . the lights."

"All right." I marked my page and turned off the lamp, then rolled up the blinds. There was no point in entering a battle with this girl — I didn't need an enemy in here. Obviously we wouldn't be friends, but I would try at least to be friendly. "Where are you from?"

"And the blinds. I can't sleep with them open."

I closed the *rolladen* and then rolled over to sleep. But in the middle of the night, I awoke to darkness so deep it seemed to press on my chest. I had been dreaming of being buried alive, of how the earth would feel pressing down on me as I struggled. I sat up, gasping, and lifted the blind beside me, staring out until I could make out the stars, just a few pricking the black night. More stars appeared; they'd been there all along. I wished I knew the names of the constellations — the same ones stood watch over the Netherlands as well. And then I raised the blinds all the way, quietly, and lay down again.

I had entered the battle after all.

November brought worse weather. Each morning, I awoke to find the mountaintops shrouded in dense clouds — as if the ragged teeth were now covered by a cold gray lip, and somehow more ominous than bared. I still went outside as much as I could, but now the decaying leaves clumped together beside the paths in rotting mats made me uneasy, and the smell of them turned my stomach. There was a long stretch with only a few bright days — several times the gray sky furrowed and darkened and began to spit snow, but there was never a storm. It was as if the weather was gathering itself, waiting for something. As *I* was. Growing more tense. As *I* was. No letter came, and each day it became harder to convince myself that Isaak was on the way. Or that anyone even knew where I was.

I decided to risk a letter. Not to Isaak

directly. I needed to route the letter through a safe address. Someone I trusted, who would forward a note without asking questions. The problem was that everyone who might do this for me probably had been told I was dead. Finally I settled on Jet Haughwout, one of Anneke's oldest friends; I would just have to have faith that my aunt kept up the deception and Jet wouldn't be surprised to hear from my cousin in this place. I printed the note, trying for Anneke's round, short letters, and as I formed them I thought, *I am a thief. There is nothing of my cousin's I wouldn't steal.*

I kept the note brief; I told Jet I was fine and would write more later, but for now could she do me a favor? *Please see that this note is posted,* I wrote. *It is to my cousin's friend. He is still very grieved over her death, and I wanted to write some things to comfort him.* I didn't explain why I couldn't send the note myself — she would come up with some explanation.

And then I wrote to Isaak.

I wrote three times. The first two letters were filled with my fears and questions, my hurt that he could have abandoned me for so long. I crumpled them up. I went down to the front desk for one of the postcards of the home — they made it look like an

274

exclusive hotel. On the back I wrote a single word: *Hurry.* I sealed the postcard into an envelope, addressed it to the synagogue, and tucked it into Jet's letter. I sealed that one and drew a deep breath.

Then I saw the problem.

Neve kept a lighter in her top drawer. I checked the hall to be sure she wasn't coming, then closed the door and went to her dresser. As I lifted the lighter, I noticed something — the drawer was filled with food: apples and crackers, a few hardened rolls, a piece of cheese, darkening at the edges, wrapped in waxed paper. I shut the drawer.

I held the first two letters with their damning words over the empty washbasin and burned them. I shook the ashes out the window and then took the basin to the bathroom across the hall to rinse it. When I returned, Neve was standing in the center of the room. She held the lighter to me, her eyebrows lifted.

"I borrowed it — I'm sorry. I wanted a cigarette."

Neve smirked — the open window and the smell of burned paper made my lie absurd. But then she sat back on her bed and looked at me as if she found me interesting for the first time. "Why are you here so early?" she asked.

"I had nowhere else. My family kicked me out."

She nodded. "Mine would have, too, if I'd told them. I went to live with a friend when I started to show."

"I can't blame them, I guess. They hate the Germans so much."

"Mine don't. Mine hate *me*." She shrugged off my expression of sympathy. "I learned a long time ago to take care of myself. Isn't that what we're all doing here?"

"Taking care of ourselves? How?"

"Three or four months before the baby's born, fourteen after. A year and a half with food and heat and no one looking at you like you're dirt."

"You're staying the whole time? You're going to nurse the baby?"

"Of course. Fourteen months of not worrying where you're going to sleep — in return for taking care of a baby? Of course." Neve's face closed and she got up. She lifted my letter from my dresser and studied the address. "Schiedam? Is that where you live?"

I nodded.

"We were practically neighbors." She dropped the letter onto my bed and left.

I picked the envelope up. *Don't write,* Isaak had said. *A letter could give everything away.*

276

One more week, I bargained with myself. If I'm still here on the first of December, I will risk the letter.

The next day, the twenty-fourth of November, a package arrived. It was flat and rectangular, the size and shape of a packet of papers. I thanked the Sister who handed it to me and hoped she didn't notice my hand shake as I took it. The return address was from an L. Koopmans of Amsterdam — a contact person? My new identity?

I hurried to my room with the package, checked the halls to make sure no one was around, then closed the door and slid down to the floor. I tore it open and didn't even care that I ruined the brown paper — that's how sure I was of what was inside, that I wouldn't need to save any more paper.

The package held an empty notebook, the kind used in the upper grades at school. There was no note, only a line inscribed on the inside cover: *For your poems. Save them.*

I tossed the notebook across the room, and buried my head in my knees in despair.

And then I realized Leona's true gift.

I wrote to her, thanking her, promising to come see her when I could get back to Holland, and then asking her to forward my letter to Isaak. She would do this. She wouldn't ask any questions. I ripped open the letter to Jet, pulled out Isaak's note, and sealed it inside Leona's letter. Then I hurried downstairs to the main desk where outgoing mail was collected. It would make the four o'clock pickup.

Over and over I calculated how long it might take. The postal service in Germany was still good, I'd heard. Still efficient. In the Netherlands, it was not so reliable anymore. Three weeks, perhaps four. By the middle of December — by the end, certainly — Isaak would know I was here. Sometime in the month of January, I would be rescued. Each night, I lay in the dark dreaming of the time I could whisper to Isaak: *We conceived a baby.* The weight of those words. The unspeakable wonder that would bind him to me.

Unless —

No. A baby could not be conceived that way.

The sixth of December was Sinterklaas Day — in Holland, gifts were left the night before. Sinterklaas was the patron saint of children, but also of robbers, perfumers, sailors, travelers, and . . . unmarried girls. There were now eleven other girls from the Netherlands at the home, so on the night of the fifth I cut eleven little wooden shoes from wrapping paper I'd saved, and on the back of each I wrote a poem wishing good luck, then slipped them under the Dutch girls' doors.

I already had my good luck. He would be coming for me soon.

But on the ninth, my birthday, we awoke to a blizzard with half a meter of snow on the ground already. At breakfast, some of the German girls were talking about winter in Bavaria; as soon as I could, I found my way to Sister Ilse in the newborns' nursery.

"We could be snowed in for a week? Is that true?" I asked.

"Sometimes, yes." A baby began to fuss in his bassinet and she went over to pick him up. "This one. A little piglet already, hungry every hour. But look at those dimples!" She handed him to me. "Try to keep him quiet while I go heat a bottle. I've got to go over to the orphanage for more formula."

I pulled the blanket from the baby's face. He frowned deeper and furrowed his soft new brow. Indignant already. I held him against my neck and smelled the faintly sour scent of formula — the scent of abandonment in here. I pressed him closer and he was comforted. It wasn't milk he was hungry for.

When she came back, Sister Ilse took the baby over to a chair by a bank of windows and sat down. I pulled another chair along-side and smiled at the baby, who began to suck at his bottle urgently. Then I leaned back and looked out the window. The fall-ing flakes were thicker now, and I felt suf-focated.

"How long before they clear the roads?"

Sister Ilse looked up at me, puzzled.

"If we get snowed in?"

"Oh. Not too long. This is a large town. Some of the smaller villages higher up can get snowed in for a month at a time. The people there know how to manage."

"But what about here?" I pressed.

"Well, we're not a priority, but we're not last on the list, either. You don't have to worry, Anneke. We have plenty of food and supplies, and there's always heat."

"But what if there's an emergency? What if someone needs to leave?"

She cut her eyes to me sharply. "What are you worried about, Anneke? I've been here through two winters, and it's been fine. There's always a doctor in the home, so it's the safest place to be. And you're not due until May, right?"

"Well, it's just that . . . I guess I'm not used to feeling trapped. It doesn't snow like this in the Netherlands."

Sister Ilse eased the bottle from the baby's

mouth and held him over her shoulder for a burp. She rubbed little circles into his back before answering.

"Trapped." She looked into my eyes for too long. "Well, I guess you're trapped here anyway, snow or no snow. Where would you go, Anneke?"

THIRTY-SEVEN

One day in the middle of December, we were told of a change to the dining schedule for that night: Our main meal would be served at noon, and from five to six we could come down for a light supper of cold meats and salads. The dining room was needed for a Christmas party for the staff. Perhaps Isaak knew this; perhaps it was the opportunity he had been waiting for.

As usual, I went straight to Ilse.

"No new babies today," she said, looking up from her paperwork.

"Are you going tonight? Will everyone be there?"

Ilse made a face of disgust. "You should stay far away, too."

"Why?"

A student nurse stepped out of the labor ward and walked past. Ilse got up from the desk and went over to a stack of boxes beside the doorway. She handed me a box and took one herself. "Come help me mix some formula," she said, a little louder than she needed to.

I followed her into a small supply room, but she didn't make any move toward the rows of bottles or the sink — just stacked our boxes of powdered-milk packets on a shelf with others. She went over to the side door and leaned against the window to the nursery and gazed at the tiny bundles, wrapped tightly like loaves of bread. "It's not their fault."

Then she went back to the hall door and pulled it shut firmly. "Do you know what tonight really is?"

"A Christmas party. They delivered beer and schnapps this morning."

"It's a party, yes. They'll bring in a shipment of SS officers and any of the girls working here who aren't pregnant now probably will be by tomorrow morning. So, more babies like this. That's the big plan. I'm going home to see my father. I have the weekend off. My first in a year."

"Well, so . . . all the rest of the staff will be there, though, right? All the Sisters and nurses?" I tried to keep my voice from sounding too eager. "All the guards?"

"All the staff *except* the guards. In fact, they're doubling up the patrols — they don't want any interruptions tonight. No unwelcome guests."

I tried to seem merely curious. "Who are they worried about?"

"This is Bavaria, Anneke. The villagers around here are mostly Catholic. Very conservative. Just the fact that unmarried girls are welcomed here upsets them. Any hint of what's really going on here tonight, and they might stage a demonstration."

"And what is really going on? How will they —"

"Oh, nothing blatant. Everyone's been fed the propaganda for years — they know what's expected. This party is just an excuse to get the men here, to give everyone the opportunity to meet. Then they'll go off to the Sisters' rooms."

She turned back to gaze through the window. I joined her.

"It's not their fault," she said, "and it breaks my heart to think about what's in store for all these children as they grow up."

"What do you mean?"

"If I tell you something, you have to promise to tell no one."

"Of course." I had become very good at keeping secrets.

Sister Ilse glanced at the door. Her voice was lower when she spoke. "America has entered the war. The Japanese attacked them last week, and then Hitler declared war on them."

I could only stare at her.

"It's true. You won't hear it in here, of course. There hasn't been a newspaper delivered for days, not even *Der Stürmer,* have you noticed that? We've been ordered not to discuss it inside the home. My father says it proves Hitler's insane — we won't be able to withstand the Americans and the British together; we just don't have the strength left. We're going to lose the war."

"Are you sure about this? When, do you think?"

Ilse shrugged. "Soon, I hope. But my father thinks a year at least. And that things will likely get worse here before that happens. The Nazis will step things up. Anyway, I'm glad of it. I'd much rather take my chances with the Americans than with the Nazis. But I'm worried about all these children, what the world will think of them afterward." She leaned against the glass and gazed at the babies again. "They might as well have swastikas tattooed on their foreheads."

I looked at the babies. Six of them, four girls and two boys. Only one, a little girl-child in the nearest crib, was half-awake.

Her eyes fluttered beneath the translucent lids, squinting open now and then to take tiny hesitant peeks at the world. I stroked my belly, taut now, rounding with a life. "No one will hold it against them. Who could do that?"

"You're young, Anneke," she said. We heard a door open and steps in the hall. Ilse looked at her watch. "My replacement. I want to catch the early train. I have the weekend off . . . I'll see you in a few days."

"I'll see you in a few days," I answered. There would be no escape tonight.

But I was cheered by Ilse's news. When Neve came into our room after the meal, I wanted to tell her. If it had been anyone but Ilse who'd asked me, I wouldn't have kept the secret.

Neve pulled something wrapped in a napkin from her pocket and put it into her top drawer. Since the time I'd taken her lighter, she hadn't bothered to hide the fact that she kept a cache of food. I'd never asked her about it.

Now I gestured to the drawer. "Neve . . . the food?"

She shrugged. *"Carpe diem."*

"Carpe diem?"

"In case this ends. We could be thrown out tomorrow. At least I won't starve for a

286

few days."

"Why would we be thrown out?" I wondered if she'd heard the news about the Americans and knew something I didn't.

She threw her hands in the air. "I don't know. That's the point. I don't count on anything. Do you? When was the last time something worked out the way you planned it?"

Her question struck me. I fell back on the bed, laughing, the movement feeling strange in my shoulders. "It's been quite a while, Neve. Maybe never, now that you mention it."

Neve rolled her eyes and began to undress.

Suddenly I had an idea. "Neve, what do you do with it?"

"The food? I flush it away every couple of days. I like thinking that I'm helping some German soldier go hungry."

"On Fridays, can I have anything you're going to flush away instead?"

"On Fridays?" She stood in her slip, a graying hand-me-down, with her bottom lip pushed out, thinking. With her thin legs and her head cocked on her thin neck, she looked like a little wren. Suddenly I realized I liked Neve a lot, in spite of how much she didn't seem to want that. "Oh. The cleaning woman?"

I nodded. "I'll start doing it, too."

"I don't know . . ."

"I'll tell her to be careful. And if someone finds out, I'll take all the blame."

Neve thought for a moment. "I suppose if you go into my top drawer on Fridays, I'm not really involved. And it's better than flushing it away." She gave me a tiny smile, then she pulled the one good dress she owned from the wardrobe and tugged it on over her belly. She looked at me and seemed to notice for the first time that I was already dressed for bed. "Aren't you coming downstairs?"

"No. I'm staying away." I waved at some books on prenatal care I'd brought up from the library. "I'm just going to read."

"You're crazy," she muttered, putting on her shoes. "Music! How long since we've heard music! And dancing . . . I just want to see dancing again."

"They're not going to let you in. Do you know what it really is?"

"I know." She combed her hair behind her ears, then blew a fine strand from her eyes. "A stud party. I don't want to go in. I just want to watch. And listen."

"It doesn't bother you?"

"I feel sorry for them. But they're getting what they deserve. No love, no lust even.

What's the point? The Germans are a nation of rutting goats."

"That's a nice image," I laughed. "I'm not going to be able to keep a straight face when I look at Frau Klaus now."

"I take it back. I've seen goats rutting — the males, at least, are enjoying it. Can you imagine how horrible it would be to have some man pumping away at you, not wanting you at all, only doing his duty? No, thanks, I'll take love or lust."

"Neve," I started, then hesitated. Neve kept a strict fence around certain things. But tonight she seemed to have unlatched the gate. I risked my question. "Which was it for you and the father?"

She gave a wry smile and looked at me as if to say, yes, that's the question, isn't it? "One of each. That was the problem."

I was glad she didn't turn the question on me.

She went downstairs and I closed the door behind her; still, I could hear the phonograph and the laughter. The dark roar of the men's voices seemed dangerous in this place of soft, fleshy girls. As the night went on and the men grew drunker, their cries grew louder. I got out of bed and went to my calendar to mark off another day. Suddenly I thought of something and began to make some calculations. Yes; it was the first night of Hanukkah.

It had been five years. But tonight the idea of a miracle for Jews seemed a good thing to celebrate. I pulled a candle from the drawer and lit it, whispering the blessing.

From downstairs came the sound of glass breaking, followed by a surprised silence, and then more laughter and more glass.

I blew out my candle and put it away.

THIRTY-EIGHT

January first came, the new year. A week passed, and then another. Word spread about the Americans; after a few days of excited whispering among those of us from occupied countries, our hope faded as nothing changed. What had we expected? That the Americans would come roaring up to the homes in their big Cadillacs to escort us back to suddenly rebuilt towns and suddenly welcoming families? Whatever was going to happen would take months or years, and pregnant girls measured time differently. Another week passed and another. Surely, Isaak had gotten my note by now. Still, he didn't come.

One day became another, indistinguishable from all the others, unmarked even by walks out-of-doors. Lunch after breakfast, night after day, sun after snow. I began to nap constantly and when I awoke, at first I could only tell whether it was night or day by the loudness of the clock — at night each tick was a gunshot.

The dull light of boredom had settled over all the rooms in the home with the exception of the labor room — as often as I could I would go there to stand on the waxed floors and look through the sparkling windows just to feel the shimmer of anticipation that hung in the air — and the newborns' nursery. One morning, though, I went to visit the nursery and found it empty; there had been three babies there only a few days before, so I was puzzled.

"The little boy's gone. The two girls have been moved over to the orphanage. They're big enough."

I felt a sudden loneliness and the day stretched out before me, unbearably infinite.

"Ilse, may I go there? To the orphanage?"

Ilse shrugged. "It's not off-limits. But the girls don't. Why do you want to?"

I shrugged back. "The babies. It's something to do."

"It's something to do, all right. And I'm glad to have a few days free of it. But let's go see if you can visit. Why not?" Ilse stopped for her coat and handed me a sweater. "It's fastest this way." We left the east wing and crossed the patio, where curls of swept snow frosted the flagstones, and

Sister Ilse pulled at the oak entry door, which opened immediately onto a heavy set of swinging doors. Even before we entered those, I heard the crying. My womb tensed at the sound, which, once we stepped inside, was so loud it seemed impossible we hadn't heard it in the east wing.

"Why isn't anyone here?"

Sister Ilse gestured to the nurses' station across the hall. A nurse was sitting beside a lamp, scratching the back of her neck, bent over a ledger. "There she is."

"But these babies are crying!"

Ilse looked back toward the cribs, as if she had to see if this was true. "A few are. If anything were wrong, she'd come out."

"They're lying here crying!"

Ilse shrugged. "At night I know they separate them — the crying ones go into another room. Maybe it's time for their feeding now, it's probably not a good time to visit. Sister Solvig is in charge here. She's a friend. We could come back when she's here."

Ilse turned to leave, but I stood rooted, looking over the room. A dozen white cribs, larger than in the newborns' nursery, formed two straight ranks along the windows. Little soldiers already, except for their cries, which sounded especially forlorn in this room of hard sunshine and glass, of hard polished tiles and long steel cabinets. The only soft things were the nine babies in their iron cages.

"Anneke — this is a Lebensborn. You don't have to worry. These are the best-cared-for babies in the country."

"Are they?"

"Of course. That's what they do here. They're fed every four hours. They're clean, they have vitamins, medicine . . . they have the best of whatever they need."

"What happens in between?" I asked.

"In between?"

"What happens to them in between the feedings?"

"I don't know . . . this isn't my wing. They sleep, I imagine. They're babies."

Suddenly I felt Benjamin in my arms. He would fuss if he was awake and alone; my stepmother said I spoiled him, carrying him around all day, but she stroked my hair and smiled at me when she said it. And Benjamin had smiled at me, too, all the time . . . a big, drunken love-smile that only I got as we caressed each other's faces.

My baby, curled and nestled tight against my ribs now, would never lie in a crib crying. Whenever he needed me I would hold him. Or Isaak would . . . well, but I would have to teach him that. I tried to picture Isaak's face and felt a moment of panic when I couldn't. But then I conjured an image of him lying beside me in his narrow cot — his profile, with his eyes closed. And I remembered how his skin tightened as if chilled when my fingertips brushed against it. I would have to teach him.

I bent down to the little girl in the nearest crib and stroked the soft skin of her hand. She didn't move, only stared up at me, wary. When I teased her palm open with a fingertip, she squeezed it, still looking at me cautiously.

In the next crib, another little girl furrowed her face and began to whimper, adding her thin distress to the others', and again I felt it in my womb, as if a wire were drawing it up my spine.

"Some of these babies must be six months old, Ilse," I said, deliberately using only her first name. "Are you telling me no one holds them or plays with them? What are they even doing here? I thought they were all adopted."

"They will be. Some families don't want infants. They'll all have their families soon enough. I think we should leave. It's not good to upset yourself in your condition."

"My condition?" I stretched my open

hands toward the cribs. "I'm carrying a baby, a living baby like the ones in here — it's not a medical condition!" Leona's words. They hadn't worked for her. "Ilse, where is Leona's baby? Was he adopted already? Or is he here?"

"I have no idea."

"Can you find out?"

She shook her head. "Probably not . . . I wouldn't even know how. Let's go back, Anneke."

"Why can't you find out?"

Ilse glanced at the nurses' window again and then leaned over to place her palm on the belly of a stirring boy. "For one thing, the records aren't even kept here." Her voice dropped. "There's a separate registry in Munich. These numbers and names on the cribs . . . they're not going to refer to the birth mothers."

"Please. I want to know if he's here."

Ilse straightened and put her hands on her hips. I mirrored her and held her gaze until she shook her head and sighed. "When was he born?"

THIRTY-NINE

On the last day of January, I lay on my bed in the middle of the morning solving a crossword puzzle and hoping to fall asleep. I rolled onto my side and felt something shift inside — just a little flutter, but separate from me. Alive. I rolled back and forth trying to feel it again, but my baby was hiding. Smiling at me in his secret game. When I went downstairs for lunch, eager to find Neve to tell her, I had another surprise: a small blue card in my mailbox. An appointment notice for my six-month examination, the next afternoon. I stood rooted in the hall and stared at it. A panicked urge to flee ran through me — a feeling I had more and more lately — and I reasoned it down.

I had calculated that Anneke was either six or ten weeks ahead of me. This notice told me it was six — better than ten, but still, a doctor would spot the discrepancy. I went to the newborns' nursery immediately.

"I need something."

Sister Ilse looked up from her report and then stopped writing, looked at me harder. "Are you feeling all right?"

I motioned her over to the bank of windows farthest from the hall and looked out, not daring to meet her eyes. "I need my chart. Please don't ask me why."

Ilse was quiet for a moment, looking out at the frozen mountains in the distance. "The files are locked, Anneke. There are a lot of secrets here."

"Just tell me how to get in, and you don't have to be involved after that."

"It's not that easy. The office is locked, too. And only a few of us have keys."

"I wouldn't ask if I didn't have to. Please trust me."

Ilse put her hands to my shoulders and turned me to face her. She let her eyes tell me what she wanted to say next. I met her gaze without wavering and reached down to stroke my belly, telling her it was for my baby I was asking. A lie I didn't have the courage to commit in words.

She sighed. "There's a staff meeting tonight. I'll slip out at seven forty-five. Be at the main desk. If it feels safe, I'll let you into the office."

I was there exactly at seven forty-five,

sweat prickling and then cooling under my arms. Ilse came down the hall toward me looking grim, as if she regretted her promise. "Five minutes," she said. "The key to the filing cabinet is in the third drawer of the desk under the window. The meeting's almost over. If someone comes, I'll rap if I can, and you'll have to hide. I can't help you more than that."

I found Anneke's file and went through the documents. It was difficult to see her laid out like that — a series of statistics fitted into neat boxes. I had to stop reading the words and only look for a date. There it was, on the top of Anneke's gynecological-exam report. One May. I took the pen from my pocket and was about to cross out the date when I realized how lucky I was. I drew a three in front of the one.

I had just bought myself thirty days.

In the hall, Sister Ilse put her finger to her lips and hurried me away. Suddenly she put her arm around my shoulder. "Don't worry about it. It's completely normal. Let me know if you have any spotting."

There he was rounding a corner in front of us — Dr. Ebner himself, the chief medical officer of all the homes, with his brilliantined hair and his mouth a neat, wide slash across his jaw as if cut with an ax.

"It's nothing," Sister Ilse assured him. "A little cramping. An overanxious mother."

He nodded and smiled down indulgently, his mouth split even wider. "Never hesitate to bring any concerns to us. Better safe than sorry, *Fraülein,* eh?"

I curled my fingers around the pen I still held and gave a weak smile. "Thank you again," I said to Sister Ilse. "I feel much better now."

We parted in the lobby and Ilse took my hand, casually, and pressed a slip of paper into it. In my room, I opened it up. Just a name — Adolf K — with a number after it.

So Leona's baby was here, and tomorrow I would get to see him. I smiled . . . it had not been a bad night. But with my relief came a surge of anger. Where was Isaak? Or my aunt? They'd looked into my eyes and promised they'd come for me, promised I'd be safe here until then. Were they worrying about me today? Did they even remember? I was so tired of everything — so tired of hiding and lying and worrying. My laundry basket sat at the end of my bed, full of the folded left-behind clothes I'd been wearing these days — nothing I had come with fit anymore. I knocked the basket to the floor and threw myself down on the bed.

"What's going on?" Neve asked. I hadn't

heard her come in.

I opened one eye to her. "I'm having a tantrum, I guess."

"Good," she said. "Want some company?"

I waved toward her basket of laundry and she kicked it to the floor. Clothing was strewn from one wall to the other. "I hate all this stuff anyway," Neve said, easing down on her bed with a satisfied smile. "I absolutely hate it."

She leaned over and picked up a blouse and held it out with one finger, grimacing as if it were a dead rat. "Look at this — my grandmother wore a blouse like this. I want to wear something pretty. I want to wear a belt again. I want to go shopping again!" She flung the blouse away.

I laughed. "You remind me of my cousin. She used to say things like that. But she was serious!"

"Used to?"

It was suddenly hard to breathe, as if Anneke's death was in the room, drawing all the air out of it.

"She died?" Neve asked. "The war?"

I waited, calmed my breathing. "Yes," I answered, surprised by the truth of it. "The war."

"I'm sorry. It's what I really hate, of course."

"It can't last much longer," I said.

Neve rolled over to face me, her chin propped up with one hand. "Do you know something? When I try to remember what it was like before, I can't. It hasn't even been two years. And when I try to imagine what it would be like to have the war over, I can't do that, either."

I nodded. "I can't imagine what it would be like not to have to think about it every minute. To have it be part of everything I do or say."

"You know what I want most?" Neve leaned back and stroked little circles into her belly. "I want to wake up and make a decision. I want to say what I want to say or eat what I want to eat or go where I want to go. I swear, when it's over, I will never let another person tell me what to do."

I wondered how it was Neve and I hadn't become friends before this. There was not so much separating us after all. "Me, too," I agreed. "Never again. But what I want most is to wake up and not have to be alert. I'm tired of living like a mouse in a roomful of cats. I want to let my guard down."

"Well, at least we can do that here," Neve said. "It's ironic — how our enemies are going to such lengths to protect us. All because of a random bit of bad luck."

"Bad luck?"

"Well, except for the German girls, it's not as if any of us got pregnant on purpose. Who would do such a thing?"

"Someone very foolish," I said quietly.

Someone who had let her guard down.

The next morning, I arrived early for my appointment. "Excuse me," I asked the nurse at the desk. "But I'm wondering if there's been a mistake. I'm not due until the end of May, so I wasn't expecting my six-month checkup this early."

"I make all the appointments," the nurse said, as if this fact precluded the possibility of error. She looked down at her list and checked me in, then waved for me to take a seat. When I didn't leave, she went through a stack of charts on her desk with a big show of irritation. I watched her read mine, find the date. Her forehead creased and she looked up at me, suspicious.

"They did the initial exam in the Netherlands," I suggested. "You know how they are there. . . ."

She nodded then and dropped my chart. "Incompetents. Well, you can go now. We'll see you in a month."

The close call woke me up. That night, I started to make my plans — I would no longer wait for Isaak to rescue me. The biggest problem was how to make it past the guards, of course. I put that aside, trusting I would come up with that piece soon. Meanwhile, it was the details that consumed me.

First, I would need money. I hadn't touched any of the notes my aunt had packed, so there were still ten guilders. Which I would need when I was back in Holland. To leave Steinhöring, I would need German bills, enough for a train ride to the border. And I would have to steal them.

As soon as I escaped the home, I would find a post office and call Isaak or my aunt. The thought of finally hearing one of their voices gave me strength.

Timing. I went over this a hundred times. The weather was the main factor. As much as I wanted to run right now, I couldn't consider it: Even one night in the bitter cold or snow would be a serious risk. The later I left, the safer traveling would be. But the later I left, the more vulnerable I was. I studied the girls in the home — after eight months, they seemed barely able to lumber along, waddling swaybacked and slow, their faces drained from exertion.

In mid-April I would be seven months pregnant and the winter would have broken. I made a tiny mark on my calendar — April fifteenth.

Would they come after me? Probably, out of worry if nothing else. Should I try to hide for a while somewhere along the border? Disguise myself?

Once I was back in the Netherlands, I would feel much safer. There were German guards everywhere, of course, and I couldn't risk showing them Anneke's papers. But at least I would feel reasonably safe knocking on a farmhouse door. "I've been robbed of my papers," I would say. "I'm afraid to be out without them. Could you please take me in?"

But where would I go then?

FORTY

I found him right away. I hadn't needed Ilse's help. All I had to do was look at his face, imprinted with my friend's, to know beyond doubt.

"May I?" I asked Sister Solvig, the nurse who had met me at the door, a kind-looking woman of about sixty.

"One less baby to worry about while we see to these others, eh? Of course."

"Hello, there," I said as I picked him up. "Look at you." He didn't squirm, only lay in my arms, inspecting me gravely. I held him close, suddenly shaken. "Look at you." I buried my face in his neck, and when I pulled away, it was wet.

I looked up to see Sister Solvig still watching me. She smiled. "It's feeding time. I've got one helper" — she nodded to a Little Brown Sister wheeling a cart into the room — "and seven hungry mouths. Why don't you feed this one for me?"

She brought me a warm bottle and I sat down and fed him. We stared into each other's eyes, reading each other. I couldn't stop smiling — he was so beautiful at four months, fat and sturdy — but he remained serious. "This won't do," I said to him. "I'm going to teach you to smile. Those dimples — I know how they're supposed to look." I smiled more widely at him and he looked back at me, worried, and sucked harder. I laughed and nuzzled him and whispered into his ear. "First of all, you are certainly not Adolf. Who could smile with a name like that?" I thought for a moment, then gave him his name. "Klaas. It will be our secret. It means victory of the people. Your mother would have liked that. You have her curls, exactly. And she loved you, you know. She loved you."

And so those first few weeks in February passed, more quickly than any others in the home. I went to the orphanage almost every day. Sister Solvig welcomed me: As long as I helped with the four o'clock feeding and changing of the babies — tasks as comforting and sustaining as kneading bread — she didn't mind how long I stayed. Sometimes I was there all afternoon: I could hold Klaas, simply hold him tight against the mound of my own child, for hours.

These afternoons lulled me into a false sense of peace. Until the morning an announcement was made at breakfast: Sometime after the meal, we were to stop into the laundry, to pick up new linens.

The tables were covered with whites, folded and stacked high. Heavy sheets, bordered with wide lace and narrow satin piping. Towels with thick loops, bright whites, creams, blue stripes. There was a table full of draperies — velvet, brocade, tulle — and a large pile of table linens. I picked up a tablecloth to feel the starched fabric between my fingertips — for a second I could actually see my mother ironing a tablecloth exactly like it, the fragrant linen steam rising in front of her arm.

I returned to the pile of sheets and chose a new set — crisp white cotton with a crocheted edge along the pillowcase. "What's the occasion?" I asked Inge, who was standing next to me. Inge's room was on the same hall as Neve's and mine, and she was the only German girl who didn't seem to resent those of us from other countries. Instead, she acted as though we were all conspirators in a special club, all as thrilled about being pregnant as she was, which she showed by exaggerating her discomforts — puffing out her cheeks and rolling her eyes to show how fat she felt, or waddling like a duck, even though she was only four or five months along. I liked Inge.

"They've just closed a ghetto, probably," she said.

"What do you mean?"

"Everything here comes from the ghettos. Didn't you know that?"

Another German girl stepped between us to lift a white pillowcase from the pile. She inspected the monogramming, picked at a loose thread. "Those people don't deserve things like these."

"What people?" My voice was as thin as smoke.

The girl tossed the pillowcase aside. "They're Jews. Why do you care?"

I dropped the bedclothes and stared: My mother might have ironed this very tablecloth. My neighbors might have slept on these sheets, wrapped their children in these towels. Where were they now? I ran from the room, a blade through my heart.

As hard as I tried not to hear Isaak's voice, it seemed to echo through the halls as I ran. When they close the ghetto, they're relocated. And that means to the camps. A labor camp . . . my father might be in a labor camp. Because he was a valuable worker. He told me that. But no, there were a lot of ghettos. . . .

Everything I passed accused: the credenza, the Persian rug, the mirrors and paintings. Everything stolen. From people who were . . . where? Even in my room, the bureau seemed to stare at me, the bed-clothes, the bed itself. Only the books beside my bed belonged to me. I lifted *Letters to a Young Poet.* "Let Rilke seep into you," my teacher had said. "Read him over and over. Let him unlock the poet in you."

I thumbed the book open, my hand shaking, to a letter in the middle.

"There is no measuring with time, no year matters, and ten years are nothing. Patience," the paragraph ended, *"is everything!"*

What did Rilke know of patience? Would he tell those people now forced into camps that time had no meaning? I threw the book against the wall. Even Rilke had deserted me. No, that wasn't it. The world had deserted Rilke. Had deserted all of us. And in here, I didn't even have the luxury of imagining myself an artist. In here I was a mother with a child and a secret inside her, both of them pressing every day closer to birth. These days, time had meaning.

FORTY-ONE

"Anneke, the father is here!"

I dropped my sewing to my lap and stared at Inge in the doorway.

"He's in the dayroom. I was sent to tell you."

I felt an instant of irritation that Isaak hadn't warned me that he was coming, but only an instant. I jumped up and opened the wardrobe. Would I need my papers or would he have new documents for me? Should I pack? And what about the bundle beneath the wardrobe?

I felt Neve's eyes on me. "What are you doing?" she asked. "What are you waiting for?"

"I just thought . . . do I look all right?" I grabbed Inge's hands. "He's really here? Did you see him, Inge?"

She smiled. "He's handsome. If I weren't already pregnant . . ."

Isaak's face flashed before me. For a

311

second I panicked — his dark hair, his dark eyes in this place? But no: He could take care of himself. And now he would take care of me. Five months of worry suddenly swelled over in choking laughter. "He is! He is very handsome!" I rushed out of the room — I couldn't get to him fast enough. In a moment I would see him. In another moment we would leave here. It was over.

"Slow down, be careful," Neve grumbled, hurrying to catch up.

But I couldn't. I tore down the stairs and flew through the halls to the dayroom as though I were afraid he would vanish.

When I caught my first sight of him, through the French doors, I gasped: Bent over the piano with his back to me, he seemed broader than I'd remembered, and he was wearing a Wehrmacht officer's uniform. I pulled open the doors and rushed in, my heart nearly bursting with excitement.

He turned at the sound. I froze.

Neve came in and I quickly made my face a mask and forced myself to take a step toward him. "Karl. You've come." With my eyes, I begged him to not ask the questions I saw in his. Then I turned to Neve. "We'd like some privacy."

Neve left, but she trailed her fingers along

the wainscoting and slid me a look as she passed. I closed the glass doors behind her.

"Where's Anneke?"

"She's not here. Thank you for not saying anything just now."

"I need to see her, Cyrla."

"She's not here," I repeated. "You can leave."

Karl pulled an envelope from his breast pocket and held it up. "I know she's here. And that she's pregnant and that she's named me as the father. So I need to see her."

I glared at him for acting as if news of Anneke's pregnancy surprised him.

"Has she left? Is she at home? And what are you doing here?"

The room grew so bright the colors blanched. Tears threatened. "Shhh! She's not here," I managed one more time. I folded my arms over my belly and whispered, "I'm using her name. You can go. She was never here."

Karl came closer, still holding the envelope. "She's not pregnant?"

I shook my head.

"So . . . what? You did this? You named me as the father and sent for me?"

I could only stare back.

"Or was this her idea?"

"No!" I couldn't think quickly enough. I could see him trying to answer the questions for himself, and my heart began to jump. "I mean, yes. She filled out the forms. I didn't know she'd put your name down. Look, I have reasons for using her name. But you can leave. This doesn't concern you."

"It does." He lifted the envelope again and came closer, his voice lower. "These are orders. I'm expected to take responsibility for Anneke's child once he's born, at least financially. I don't care why you're using her name. But this certainly *does* concern me."

"I'll see that that's corrected," I agreed quickly. "I'll change the name on the forms."

Karl stood a moment, looking at me, then the envelope. Then at me again.

"I'll take care of it today." I crossed the room and picked up his overcoat, wet with snowmelt, and handed it to him.

"How is she?"

I set my jaw and looked away.

Karl took his coat and walked to the doorway. He put his hand on the knob and then turned back. "I wrote to her. She didn't answer. Will you tell her something for me? Tell her that I think about her and hope . . . well, I hope she's happy. Just tell her that."

I could only nod, my lips pressed together so they couldn't give anything away. I looked to the door, but he still didn't leave.

"You know, whenever we met it was almost as if you were there, too — she talked about you that much."

I felt the danger rise in the air and my chest tighten. *Please stop. Please leave now. Please.* But he leaned back against the glass doors and looked at me more deeply.

"She showed me some of your poetry. There was one line . . . it was in a poem about wood, about what wood meant to you. I don't remember it now, but when I heard it I thought, Yes. That's exactly how I feel. I wanted to tell you that. And look," Karl smiled, his teeth so white it startled me, his eyes too blue. "Look. Now I have."

For an instant, I actually smiled back. He had touched a place I had forgotten to harden against him. "I'll take your name off the forms today." My voice was cold.

Karl looked as if I had stung him. Good. He pulled the door open and left, his boots clicking down the hall in sharp military steps, and I collapsed onto the sofa, my hands pressed to my racing heart. The blood was pounding in my ears and I didn't hear him return, but suddenly he was back in the room in front of me.

"No." He threw his coat onto the chair. "I remember something."

FORTY-TWO

"What are you doing here?"

The look in his eyes was not unkind, but I recoiled.

He straightened and I followed his glance. Through the other glass doors — the ones leading to the dining room — two of the kitchen staff, setting the table for dinner, had stopped to stare at us. From the hall came a burst of chatter.

"We'll take a walk." He offered his arm to help me up from the sofa.

I pushed his arm away but told him I would get my coat. Upstairs, I crumpled onto the bed. I knew what he had remembered, what Anneke had told him. It was in the way he looked at me. The other night at dinner, one of the girls had whispered about the Jews found hiding in Zaandam. I stood and crossed to the dresser and splashed water onto my face from the basin. Panic was a luxury my baby could not afford. I

317

still had choices — and one chance.

I would pull myself together, take a walk with Karl, and say whatever it took to get him to leave without reporting me until after he returned to his headquarters. Whatever it took. Because in another few hours it would be dark.

Frau Klaus was behind the desk at the main door. Karl identified himself and told her we would be taking a stroll around the grounds.

"The air is good for her," she agreed. "The girls don't go out enough in the cold weather." She looked us over and seemed to approve. I forced myself to smile up at Karl, as if I were happy to see him again. Karl smiled back and I understood what had made Anneke trust him — it was the kind of smile that could make you believe any lie. I wouldn't make that mistake, though.

Outside, the snow had stopped but it was still windy. Karl turned on the step and tugged my coat together. "It doesn't button around your middle. You need a new one." Then he pulled his gloves from his coat pocket and my breath stopped. I tasted leather and motor oil. And blood.

"What's wrong?"

"Nothing." I walked away from him. He was not the *Oberschütze*. He was as danger-

318

ous, though. I began to walk along the path to the back gardens, swept into commas of dry snow, with him following me. "What do you need to know?"

Karl crossed to my other side and walked sideways, his body blocking the cold wind. "Everything. What are you doing here? This isn't a safe place for you."

"I'm pregnant. That's all."

"That's *not* all. Why are you using Anneke's name?"

I looked away.

"Ah. Papers. But what's Anneke doing for papers, then? Where is she?"

I still didn't look at him. "You're right. I needed her papers. She doesn't need them. You can leave now, Karl."

"No. Something doesn't make sense. Why do you want to be here?"

"Why do you care? This doesn't involve you."

"It does. I'm named as the father, remember? I think that gives me the right to know what's going on. What are you doing here?"

You have a right to know nothing, I thought. *You have no rights at all because you didn't ask about Anneke's baby. Your baby. Because you're pretending you didn't know about him.* I bit my lip so the words wouldn't escape.

We turned the corner and a rush of icy air

stung my face. Karl stepped in front of me and walked backward, waiting for my answer. I didn't want his protection. I turned and headed back to the courtyard.

Karl caught up with me. "All right. I can guess. You got pregnant and this place looked good to you, for the food and the doctors. But you didn't think you could get in without the proper papers. So you used Anneke's. Is she gone, Cyrla? Where?"

"She is gone." If Karl heard my voice waver, he didn't show it.

"I still don't understand why she put my name down."

"I told you — I'll take care of that."

We had reached the courtyard. Karl motioned to a bench tucked into a corner out of the wind. "Sit." He took off his overcoat and wrapped it around my shoulders and sat beside me, so close I could smell his scent — almonds and pine. Too close.

"She's angry, and this was a way to hurt me — is that it? No, that's stupid and dangerous. I don't believe she'd do that. And I don't believe you're pregnant by a German soldier. Cyrla, tell me what this is about."

I was so tense my skin felt like a network of fine wires, buzzing with electricity. But I was angry, too. "And if I don't? What? You'll turn me in?"

"No. Of course not. I just want to know what's going on. I'm not leaving until you tell me."

"You can't force me. I'll lie."

"No. You won't do that." Karl said it with so much confidence, as if he knew me.

I looked straight into his face then, thinking how much I hated this man and keeping my feelings masked. He didn't know me at all. But I knew him. This man was so selfish, he had walked away from my cousin after getting her pregnant, after telling her lies about loving her. He had left her so hopeless and alone she had bled to death trying to empty the womb he had filled. He was the worst kind of coward.

I wanted to accuse him of all this, to make him stand trial here in front of me, at least. But I couldn't afford to anger him. The pent-up words were a pressure in my chest, hardening into a diamond and clearing away my fear. Karl was right — I wasn't going to lie. It didn't matter what he knew about me now, anyway.

"Fine. I'm hiding here. Someone turned me in, or threatened to. You, probably."

Karl reached out and I jerked my head away from his gloved hand. But it wasn't my face he wanted: He pushed back my hair and gently lifted one of Anneke's moonstone earrings. Surprise and hurt were in his eyes.

"She doesn't want these?"

I pulled the earrings off and handed them to him.

"My grandmother's," Karl said, looking at them lying on his glove as if he couldn't understand how they could be there. "She doesn't want them anymore?"

He looked into my eyes, but I didn't look away fast enough.

"What? Oh, no. God, no!"

But my silence told him, *Yes.*

"Anneke died, Cyrla? What happened?"

I raised my palms to him and shook my head as I felt my eyes fill. Karl reached as if to put his arms around me, then pulled back.

"Please tell me. No — she can't be dead."

For an instant, I had an urge to comfort him. Then I came to my senses. This man had killed my cousin as surely as if he had fired a bullet through her heart. And he would turn me in without another thought tonight. But he *did* care about Anneke; that part was real. And it suddenly came to me, as if Anneke herself had whispered in my ear, that his need to know what had happened to her would buy me my escape.

"Come back tomorrow," I whispered. "I

322

can't talk now. Come back tomorrow and I
will tell you everything."

Karl hesitated.

"I promise. Tomorrow."

He nodded. "I'll be back in the morning."

"I'll be here," I lied.

FORTY-THREE

Back in my room, I felt weak with relief. Too weak, too loose, as if my muscles and spine had melted to jelly in the steam heat. I opened the wardrobe and began to plan what clothes to layer.

"The bell rang for first sitting ten minutes ago."

I jumped at Neve's voice behind me.

"What?" she asked. "You're so flustered by your tall soldier you forgot to eat?"

"I . . . I did." I laughed, and it sounded high and false even to me. I pushed everything back inside the wardrobe and closed its door.

"What did he want? I thought you said it was over."

"Are you going down? I'll go with you."

She patted her abdomen, rising huge and taut now. "I can't fit much in these days, but I'm always hungry. I just have to change my shoes." She pulled her clogs out from under her bed and stepped into them. "I can't believe I'm wearing *klompen,* like a farmer," she sighed. "But they're the only shoes that don't pinch." Her ankles were swollen and shot with tiny broken veins — her time was near. I looked more closely at her face. It was drawn and waxy with plum-colored shadows beneath her eyes. In the past month her angles had finally softened and she'd begun to look full and lush, but now she had the look of fruit left too long on the tree.

"Are you all right?"

"Fine. Let's go."

"Neve," I said. "You're going to be all right."

I wasn't hungry. But I would be out walking for hours in the cold, and might not come upon food again for a while so I ate. I stuffed a thick piece of ham into a roll, and then, when no one was looking, I slipped it into my pocket. There was a new Dutch girl at our table. I said hello, but her gaze drifted and I was glad. Around me, the other girls were chatting, but their words were like moths, weightless, flitting in and out of my head. My mind was on what I still needed to pack, on which direction I would set out, and how I would know whose house to trust when I had reached it. My eyes went to the windows, watching for signs of more snow. It was dark, but I wanted to wait until after the night shift began at eight o'clock, when there were fewer guards. Eight-thirty; I would go at eight-thirty.

"How about you? Would you go, Anneke?"

I froze, a spoonful of soup halfway to my mouth.

Betje shook her head and rolled her eyes. "Haven't you been listening?"

"Go where?" I put the spoon down carefully. "I'm sorry. The baby was kicking and I wasn't paying attention."

"Here. To Germany. If you lived in Norway." She leaned in to me and lowered her voice, even though now, with so many girls from Belgium and Holland, we filled our own table. "I overheard two of the Sisters talking this morning. In Norway, the Germans have begun to encourage the girls to come here and to stay. Why just get the calf when you can get the breed cow? They're making it very attractive — bribing the girls."

"They're kidnapping them," the new girl interrupted. She set down her glass of milk and looked across the table at us. "Or at least blackmailing them. If they want to take care of their babies after they're born, they'll have to go."

Betje shrugged. "Another year of the war and there won't be anything left of the Netherlands. Or Norway. Those girls should come here and be glad of it. I wish I could stay."

I looked around the table then, waiting for someone to argue. *The war can't last much longer.* I hadn't heard those words since I'd left Schiedam and now they hung like an accusation. I tried to make myself speak them, but couldn't. Betje was right. Still, I felt discouraged when she pressed the point.

She tore a piece off her roll and buttered it. "Our children will all be here. The men who got us all pregnant will all be here. What else do we have?" She leaned in and gestured at the new girl with her knife. "What else do *you* have?"

The new girl straightened. "Nothing. I have nothing left." Something in her voice drew every eye to her. She gestured over her belly without touching it. "I was late coming home. After curfew. Two soldiers did this. My boyfriend won't look at me. My whole town . . . they took everything I had. I won't stay in this country for a second more than I have to."

There was silence at the table then, long

327

and brittle. I reached across the table and touched her hand. "I want to go home, too. I don't care what's left; I just want to go home."

She looked at me gratefully for a moment, then down at her soup. It had been untouched so long the fat had risen to the top in a thin orange sheen. She folded her napkin and stood, and I had the curious impression that she rose tall and weightless, and that her belly floated ponderously up to meet her — a separate thing. She walked to the dining-room doors, but paused there for a moment as if deciding something, then it seemed her shoulders tightened into her spine and she lifted her head. When she walked out, I had a sense of loss.

I pushed my plate aside and followed her and caught up with her at the top landing. "It happened to me, too." I had had no warning I would say those words.

She bit her lips into her mouth for a moment and her eyes hardened. "It's not a club I want to belong to," she spat after a long silence.

"I only thought —"

"Leave me alone!" She turned and walked away down the hall to her room, two down from mine. I waited until she'd closed her door before walking to mine, wishing I had said good-bye to her.

Neve came up and asked if I was going down to watch the film.

"What is it this week?"

"Nutrition. Sanitation. What is it ever? Who cares?"

It was seven-thirty. "I have a headache," I told her, my fingertips to my forehead. "I just need to go to bed early."

Neve studied me for a moment. "Do you want some aspirin?"

I forced a smile. "Really, I'm just going to bed."

"All right then, if you're sure," she said at last. Then she left.

The hour passed more slowly than any other. At last it was time. My hands shook. I pulled a run in my first pair of hose and fumbled with the buttons of my cardigan, then hung the velvet bag around my neck and tucked it inside my sweater. I looked bulkier than usual, but not obviously so. When I picked up my coat I realized the problem: I couldn't go downstairs wearing it, or even carrying it. Most of the girls were settled in the dayroom watching the film, but there could always be staff in the hall-ways.

I folded my coat into the bottom of my laundry basket, then covered it with the slip and shift I'd just taken off. I took a final look at my room, my home for five months, and then I walked out.

I met no one on the stairs, no one in the main hall. Sister Solvig passed in the east corridor and my heart jumped, but she merely nodded. At the end, the corridor split: To the right was the door for deliveries and to the left was the laundry. And if I continued past the laundry . . . I looked down the hall and willed Leona's son to understand somehow. To not feel the poison of abandonment that withers hearts.

I stepped quickly to the right, pulled my coat from the basket, and tucked it under the stairway in the corner. I brought my basket to the laundry room so it wouldn't cause suspicion, then ran back and put on my coat.

The lights in the hall suddenly grew so bright they stung my eyes and left a shower of sparks on my eyelids. I placed my hands on the bolt, but I couldn't make my arms move to slide it open. Once more, I called upon my trick for bravery. All I had to do, I told myself, was walk to the clump of three fir trees about halfway down the walk. The Ladies Tideman, everyone called them. An earlier resident had christened them after her neighbors, three tall elderly spinsters

330

who were always huddled together in their long dark dresses, whispering, sighing. I would just walk to The Ladies Tideman for some air — it wouldn't be so unusual — and then if I wanted, I could return.

But the trick didn't work. To what could I return? Karl was coming back. I pressed my father's letter to my chest for a second, slid the bolt, and stepped into the night.

The air was frigid and so clear it seemed to have sharpened the stars. A good sign: There'd be no more snow tonight. I ran to the stand of firs and angled myself into them. Even in the cold, the fragrance of the boughs was strong. It steadied me.

One guard. I could see when he lit his cigarette that he was alone. After a few moments, he lifted his wrist to the glowing butt to check his watch, then stubbed it out and walked. My heart raced, but I didn't move. Not yet. In less than ten minutes, he was back at his post.

My calves began to ache from my new weight; still I didn't move, only breathed the cold air in and out of my lungs steadily. Becoming part of the night. The guard left his post again, and still I didn't move — only shifted my position a little. He returned. If this was his routine, he was gone no more than six minutes, maybe seven. He was probably walking the length of the east boundary and back.

He was at his post longer this time — fifteen minutes passed at least. I felt myself coiling. He lit another cigarette, and when he bent into its glow I gasped, he seemed so close. He looked up sharply then, as if he had heard me, and stared into the trees for so long the match singed his fingers. He shook it away and then raised his head slightly, studying the building, smoking. At last he tossed his cigarette into the snow and walked back through the gate.

I took a deep breath and followed, staying on the snow for silence. I pressed myself into the wall, into the cold stones, to slow my heart. Beyond the entrance, the road lay in near-darkness except for two pools of thin yellow light below the main tower, forty meters away. I would run in the opposite direction, shadowing the wall, until I could cross to the other side where a hedge of evergreens offered some protection. The guard was nowhere in sight and I could hear nothing. I stepped out.

"Where do you think you're going?" He grabbed my forearm and spun me around. I tried to struggle out of his grasp, but his fingers were like steel. "Your soldier, the one you were out here with earlier? He's still in town?" The guard's laugh was knowing. "One visit from her tom, and the little cat needs to go find him at night. I've heard that about girls in your condition."

"No!" I spat. But then I shrugged and acted chastened.

He opened his coat and slid his gun back into his holster, the leather and steel creaking loudly in the frigid air. "What are you thinking? It's freezing out here."

"Please let me go," I tried. "I'll be careful. I'm warm enough."

"You're not allowed off the premises alone — you know that. Besides, he can come to your room. The father has privileges. Talk to Frau Klaus, she'll arrange it. Now let's get you back inside."

"I can make it myself," I assured him, cold.

But he walked me back — to the main gate this time — where he handed me off to the guard inside, a sergeant, and shared his insulting joke with him.

"This little cat's in heat. Thought she'd take a stroll into town to visit her soldier. Maybe I'll have to help her out when my shift is over." He thrust his hips back and forth at me, as if I might not have known what he meant.

The sergeant laughed and pushed away a

plate of chicken legs and red cabbage salad to stand. In the bright lights of the entry hall, his lips gleamed with chicken fat. He reached for my chin, trying to lift my face to his; his greasy finger pressed into the triangle of flesh bruised by the *Oberschütze* and found the mark which would always wait there.

I turned on my heel without looking at them and stormed up to my room.

FORTY-FOUR

I peeled off the layers of clothing and dressed for bed, swamped with despair — I had gotten nowhere. Worse, I had alerted people, made them wary. From this moment on, I would make no mistakes. I would be the protection my baby needed — the wall, the fire, the bones. I owed him that.

When Neve came in, I lay still in the dark, pretending to be asleep. She was up all night — using the bathroom, tossing in her bed trying to get comfortable, groaning. I was up all night, too — my throat tight, my body rigid to the roots of my hair trying to hold back sobs.

In the morning, Neve looked bad, with old-woman eyes. She groaned when she got up, and balled her fists into her back.

I rolled over to watch her. She dressed in silence, as if speaking were too great an effort. Then she turned, waiting for me. I told her I didn't feel well and didn't want breakfast. As soon as I was sure she was gone, I buried my face in my pillow and let out the wail that had been building all night. Only one — even muffled, the sound frightened me too much. I got up then and rolled up the blinds. Things always seemed worse at night.

The day was clear, and whorls of fine frozen snow glittered in the air where gusts of wind blew through the fir boughs. But it didn't help. I had told Karl to come back today, and now I would have to face him, and worse, to face whatever he was going to do. I was still at the window when Neve came back. She handed me a napkin: Wrapped inside was a piece of bread folded over thick red jam.

"I couldn't eat," she said, as if she had to excuse her thoughtfulness.

"Leona couldn't eat the day hers was born," I reminded her.

She nodded, then stepped beside me to look out the window. "I'm afraid."

I hugged her. "I'm afraid, too."

When she left, I washed up and dressed, but didn't leave the room. It was too late for both Neve and me. Now all we could do was open our eyes and cope with what we had set in motion when we were blind. I sat down on the bed again with Rilke's *Letters*.

The book fell open to a passage on fate, on the joy of understanding that all incidents are woven together with a tender hand. How dare he advise anyone to be hopeful and trusting? But of course how could he have predicted this world? I closed the book and picked up Neve's biography of Amelia Earhart and began to read — soon enough there would come a knock at the door with the message that I was to go downstairs, that I had a visitor.

Soon enough, the knock came.

"Ja," I replied, not looking up. Stealing the last second.

Suddenly I was aware of a presence — too large, too male. I jumped up. "What are you doing here? Get out!"

Karl looked bewildered. "They told me you'd asked for me to visit here. As a privilege."

The guard. "Well, I didn't." I put on my shoes. "You have no business coming into my room."

"Fine," he said. "Let's go down to the parlor." He picked up Neve's book. "Amelia Earhart . . ."

I grabbed the book from him. "She flew!" I said. I took my cardigan from the end of the bed and started toward the door, but then I dropped it again. "Never mind. We might as well talk here. It's private."

He unbuttoned his coat and looked at me as if I should offer to take it. I shook my head. "This won't take long."

He nodded and hung the coat over his arm. "What happened to her?"

And so I told him. What did it matter now? I stood and I made him stand; I hadn't earned any comfort yet, and Karl would never deserve it.

"All right. My uncle arranged for this, for her to come here. She couldn't face it, though. She —"

"Wait. She was pregnant?"

I glared my scorn at him. "You know she was. And she was devastated when you wouldn't stand by her. She lost everything, all her spirit, all her —"

"Mine? It was mine?"

"Stop it!" I hissed. "She told me everything. That she went to see you and you said you were engaged to someone else."

Part of me wanted him to tell the truth then. If he had just said, *Yes, I let her down, I was a coward and I left her alone with this,* I might have lowered my guard a little. It surprised me that I wanted to. But he didn't.

"I don't know what you're talking about; I'm not engaged to anyone!"

"I know that, too, now. I went to see you,

but you'd left. Your friends told me the truth. Look, do you want to hear this or not?"

"Yes. Yes. But I swear I didn't know. She never told me that."

I waved my hand, cutting him off. "You lied to her. But she never knew it, and I'm glad for that. She died thinking you loved her, but just weren't free."

Karl turned away to look out the window, resting his forehead on the glass. At last he asked the hardest question. "Cyrla, tell me. How did she die?"

Suddenly there were rocks in my lungs and I couldn't catch any air. It was hearing my name the way Anneke had always said it — with the hint of a third syllable in the middle, as if it were lingering on her tongue, safe and loved. My name, sounding safe and loved in this man's mouth, was too much.

"How did she die? You killed her, Karl. You murdered her. You broke her heart and left her alone, so she tried to carve your baby from her body and she bled to death. That's how you murdered her."

"Cyrla!" He took a step toward me.

"Don't call me that," I warned him, backing away. "Call me Anneke."

Don't call me that, Isaak. Don't call me Anneke.

339

"She gave herself an abortion? She died from it? I don't understand this. Why didn't she tell me?"

I almost believed him, he looked so sincere. I could imagine him telling Anneke he loved her, his lie about a fiancée.

"Are you sure she even knew before I left? Because the last time we met, we talked about . . . other things."

"You got her pregnant! She needed you! What other things could there possibly have been to talk about?"

Karl was silent a moment and I could see him thinking. Trying to come up with a lie I would believe.

At last he said, "If she didn't tell you, then she didn't want you to know. If she didn't tell you, then I won't, either."

The most cowardly lie. I reminded myself I already knew this, that he had no courage.

He came closer. "Cyrla. When did it happen? Were you with her? I'm so sorry — I know how much you loved her." He reached out, but I stepped away before he could touch me.

I shook my head at him, unable to speak for a moment. I could not reopen this wound, not in front of the man who had caused it.

I turned to my dresser and removed the

layette my aunt had packed from the bottom drawer. Tucked into the yellow outfit that Anneke herself had worn, rolled into the tiny mittens, were my mother's ruby earrings, her barrette, her wedding band, which I had put there in the morning. I held them out to Karl.

He looked at the jewelry but made no move.

"Take it. It's all I have right now, but if you don't turn me in, I can get you more. I can get money."

He pushed my hand away. "You think you need to bribe me?"

I let my silence tell him what I thought of him.

He glanced back at the closed door, then spoke quietly. "This is not my war. Didn't Anneke tell you that? You can trust me."

I couldn't help myself. "Anneke trusted you."

His face closed. "That's enough. I don't know what would have happened if Anneke had told me. But I wouldn't have walked away."

"It is enough. I told you how she died. Now all I want to know is what it will take to get you to leave here. Not turn me in." I wrapped my arms around my belly, my child. So little protection. "If you cared

341

about Anneke at all, please leave me alone. She would ask you to leave me alone."

"Cyrla, I have no intention of hurting you."

"You won't tell anyone?"

"Of course not."

"And you'll leave now?"

"Yes, all right. But wait — did you change the forms?"

"What? No, I'm sorry, not yet. I will. Today."

"Don't," Karl said. "Don't do it yet."

I waited. There was a new danger here; I could sense it, but I couldn't see its shape.

"I thought about it. If you do it now, you'll draw attention to yourself. And this way I can come to see you. I can make sure you're all right. I can bring you things."

I had to look away — suddenly Karl's face was too hopeful. I remembered the last time I had worn an expression like that — *Isaak, when the war is over, we'll be a family, won't we?* It was the expression of someone waiting to be wounded.

"We could talk," he said.

"I don't want you to come here. We have nothing to talk about."

He recoiled. But I needed to hurt him more. I folded my arms across my chest.

"Anneke isn't something we share."

342

"Look. I'm just trying to help. If you change the father's name, there'll be questions. Just don't do it yet. Let me find out some things."

"If I promise to leave your name on the forms, you won't tell anyone who I am?"

"I wouldn't, anyway. I only want —"

"Fine, I won't. So you can leave now. We're finished here."

He made no move, so I went to the door and opened it.

He spread his hands as if he were going to ask something of me, then dropped them and put on his coat. He didn't speak as he left, and when I closed the door the silence grew even deeper.

FORTY-FIVE

After Karl left, I went downstairs to retrieve the basket I'd left by the laundry door. A Sister caught me by surprise, leaving with a stack of linens; I stumbled over a clumsy excuse about how forgetful I was. She stared at me as if she could see into all of my lies, so I grabbed my basket and fled back to my room before I could give myself away to anyone else.

In the afternoon, I would go to the orphanage and press Klaas to my chest and hold him tight. Until then . . . I was too restless to sew or read, so although it was only Wednesday, I began to clean; dusting and polishing the dressers, the desk, the wardrobe. What I longed to do was take the rugs outside and beat them over a bar until there wasn't a puff of dust left in them. Hiding in plain sight seemed the hardest way of all.

Neve came back. She looked worse than

when she'd left; her skin pale, almost gray. I dropped my rag. "Is it time?"

She shook her head. "I just want to lie down."

"No contractions?"

"No. My back hurts, that's all."

"Maybe Dr. Ebner should look at you. Or we should let Frau Klaus know. Sometimes labor begins in the back."

"No!"

"All right," I soothed. "It's all right. What can I get you? A hot-water bottle? For your back?"

Neve caught her breath and reached out for the dresser to steady herself, wincing.

"Neve, are you sure you're not —"

"I think I can sleep." She straightened a little. "Will you get my nightdress?"

When I helped her pull off her slip, I saw new stretch marks streaking over her hips like purple lightning. Even the nightdress, loose and smocked, stretched tight over her swollen belly. Her hips, though — her hips were so frail and narrow. *"Her pelvis cracked,"* I heard Sister Ilse say again. I eased Neve down onto the bed, where she curled up on her side. I sat beside her and rubbed her shoulders; as soon as she fell asleep, I would alert the staff.

"All this time," she said, so softly I had to

lean over to hear, "all this time I've just been waiting to be done with it. But now —"

"Now what?"

She looked down at herself, huge under the thin blanket. "He hasn't moved for two days. All this time, he's been my . . . my reason. I can't lose him."

"Hush. You're not going to lose him. You're going to *meet* him!" I tried to get up to get her a glass of water but she pulled me back, gripping my hand so hard I could feel her panic seep into my skin. "What's wrong?"

Tears brimmed. I had never seen Neve cry. "I'm so afraid," she said. "Of everything. Of having him. Of losing him. I signed papers. Where will they take him? How will I know he's all right? In a good home?"

I stroked her forehead with my free hand. "Shhh. There's plenty of time for this. You're going to stay a long time, remember? First you have to have him. I think it's soon."

She drew a sharp breath and hissed as she curled tighter.

"A contraction? Neve, you're in labor, aren't you?"

She gave a short nod, her eyes still squeezed shut. Then she seemed to melt, but she still didn't release my hand. She took a short breath through clenched teeth. "What if no one takes him? Some babies end up in the orphanage for . . . for years. You said they just lie there. What if —"

"Neve, you can't pretend this away. It's time to have this baby. I'm going down to get a nurse. I'll just be a minute. You're going to be all right."

Neve let me get up. "You'll come right back, though?"

"Of course," I promised at the door.

"And then you'll stay with me? Until he's born? You won't leave?"

"I won't leave." *People can die if you leave them.* Neve knew this, too.

I hurried to the nurses' station. Frau Klaus was on duty, and for once I was glad of her coolness — she just grabbed her black leather case and followed me up to the room.

Ten minutes passed. Then she called me into the room. "She has a way to go yet, but you can help me bring her down now."

We waited through another contraction, then helped her downstairs and to the labor ward. One of the Little Brown Sisters met us at the door and led Neve to a bed.

Frau Klaus turned to dismiss me.

"I'm going to stay with her." I stepped into the ward and gave Neve a little wave.

"You'll only be in the way. She needs to concentrate on her labor."

I stood my ground, folding my arms across my chest. Frau Klaus looked at me as if she didn't recognize me. Then she shrugged. "Suit yourself. She'll go into the delivery room when she's at nine centimeters. As long as there are no problems, you can stay with her."

I made a face of mock amazement behind her back as she left, and Neve actually laughed out loud. I pulled a chair over to her bedside and took her hand.

The ward overlooked the back courtyard. Fresh snow covered the grounds and the afternoon sky was cloudless, so blue it stung my eyes. The firs bowed under their drapings of snow and it seemed it couldn't have been only last night that I was hiding beneath them. Inside, the room was spotless, with rectangles of bright sunlight spilling to the waxed floors from the huge windows, and smelled comfortingly of bleach and soap. For a moment I had such a feeling of safety, of well-being, it jarred me.

"This is it," I said.

"This is it," Neve agreed. Her eyes, so wide they always looked surprised to me, looked shocked.

Sister Ilse came in and fussed with Neve's pillows. "The first baby all week. It's about time we had some activity in here."

Neve looked relaxed for just a moment, then a new contraction seized her and she cried out. Now that she wasn't trying to hide them, I could see how bad they were.

"Is she all right?" I asked. "Can you give her something for the pain?"

But Ilse only looked at her watch and smiled encouragingly at Neve when it was over, as if Neve had done a good job. "She's fine," Ilse answered then, completely calm. "It's hard work, is all. We'll give her something at the end, don't worry." Then she took off her watch and put it on my wrist. "Time them. If they get to be five minutes apart and I haven't come back yet, or if the doctor hasn't come to examine her, come and get me."

"Wait," I called, standing up. "Are you leaving?"

Ilse laughed. "I'll still be in the ward. I have work to do — babies and new mothers to take care of. First babies take their time. It'll be hours before anything happens. Maybe not until tomorrow. She's doing fine. Don't worry!"

And then she was gone.

"Don't worry!" I repeated to Neve, and

she laughed a little. "Do you want me to get the backgammon set? Or something to read?"

Neve shook her head. "Just sit with me."

We talked about little things, gossip about the other girls, our conversation punctuated by her contractions. But soon she said again how worried she was.

"What if I've made a mistake?" She worked the edge of the sheet between her fingers, rubbing and twisting it. The sheet was thin, as if it had been through a lot of rubbing and twisting. "When Franz refused to have anything to do with this, I was happy to sign away the baby. Why would I want a reminder of him, of how stupid I was? But now . . . no one ever needed me before. I want to take him home."

"Neve, I was wrong." I stopped her. "If I ever made you feel . . . well, it wasn't any of my business. Look at me; who am I to judge anyone?"

"Well, I think I *was* wrong. Or at least I've changed my mind. I don't know. That's the thing — I don't know, and now it's too late."

Another labor pain seized her and she clutched her belly, grunting through clenched teeth. This one was much stronger than the others: The effort brought a sheen of perspiration to her face and the fine hairs framing her forehead curled up against her damp skin, as if every part of her body were coiling in tension. When it was over, she relaxed, but she looked exhausted. I checked the watch — still eight minutes apart. How would she ever make it through if it really took until the next day?

"Look," I said. I pulled the sheet from her hand gently and flattened it out. "I don't think you should be worrying about all this now. There's time. You've got fourteen months to figure it out. To get help, perhaps a lawyer. To talk to Franz. Who knows? In another year the war may be over; then the Germans won't have the power to enforce anything on us. Let's not worry about this now, all right?"

She let it go then, but no matter what I distracted her with, she came back to it always. How could she not? With each contraction, the reality of her baby's presence became harder to ignore.

Every hour the doctor came and examined her, drawing the curtain around her, checking her dilation. Each time we held our breath, but the doctor would just shake his head when he came out. Not yet.

I had an inspiration. I went back up to our room and found the bottle of nail polish I had taken from Anneke's bureau, then came back to the ward. "Let's get you all beautiful before you meet your baby!" I suggested.

Neve took the bottle of nail polish and stared at it in wonder. "How did you get this? It's forbidden, you know."

"Nail polish is forbidden?"

"You don't go to the lectures, Anneke. 'No good German girl would spoil her natural beauty by using lipstick or dyeing her hair or polishing her fingernails.' They're not even supposed to pluck their eyebrows."

"Well, I guess we're not good German girls. How sad." I shrugged with regret and Neve laughed. We painted each other's nails and compared our favorite films, pausing whenever Neve had a contraction. Neve liked American westerns. "I'm going to ride a horse out there, one day," she confided. "One of those places where you can see forever like that. And I'm going to ride like the men do, with one leg on either side, and I'm going to gallop! I'm going to be Barbara Stanwyck in *Annie Oakley*!"

"You want to go to America?"

"Of course. You can take care of yourself there. You don't have to wait for some man to give you a life."

"Well, I'd like to see New York," I conceded. "And maybe Hollywood. I could be a famous movie star." I fluttered my scarlet nails and — for an instant — saw Anneke's hands. "I'm terribly glamorous already."

It felt good for a while. Still, I was relieved when Sister Ilse came back; Neve seemed to feel more relaxed when she was around, but not so relaxed she would talk about what she was worried about in front of her.

"No food for this one," Ilse told me. "But you need to eat, Anneke. Go to dinner. I'm on a break. I'll stay with her."

Neve nodded, so I left. But I ate quickly and hurried back. Ilse stayed with us, playing cards and sharing stories about her sister. Around nine there was a small commotion. Frau Klaus led two girls through the room, explaining things as if they were on a tour.

She lifted Neve's chart from the foot of her bed. "This mother will be delivered tonight or early morning," she said. "Her contractions are four minutes apart and she's six centimeters dilated."

"Will we get to see the delivery?" one of the girls asked.

"No, not until you've been through your training. For now you'll be cleaning and tending to the mothers."

"Training!" Ilse huffed when they left. "What a joke. This is a busy home. They need real nurses here, like me. Not 'Little Blond Sisters.' "

"Little *Blond* Sisters?" Neve and I asked together, alert to the tease of gossip.

"They're here only as a reward for doing their duty."

"Wait!" Neve demanded. She rolled to her side and clutched her belly, hissing through another contraction. "All right," she gasped when it was over, then took a few breaths. "Now, what do you mean?"

"They're all blond and blue-eyed and they're here only because they're sleeping with SS men in order to present the state with a new citizen. They're an insult to *real* nurses."

Ilse told us stories that made us laugh: about a Little Brown Sister running to heat blankets in the big kitchen ovens instead of the warming ovens in the ward — "Roasted them to a crisp with the potatoes!" — or mistaking a placenta for a twin. Neve cried out again and rolled over in pain. Ilse rubbed the small of her back and I squeezed her shoulder gently until it was over. Rounds of sweat had bloomed on her back, her chest, under her arms, darkening the little roses of her nightgown.

I looked at my watch. "Less than three minutes. Should we get someone?"

"Not yet. Soon though." But the next contraction came even faster and was clearly worse. "Now," Sister Ilse said. She patted Neve's hand and then left and returned a moment later with Frau Klaus and a doctor. They pushed me aside and drew the curtain around Neve's bed. Then they helped Neve onto a gurney, moaning, and wheeled her away.

"Good luck!" I called to the double doors as they swung shut behind Neve.

Too late.

FORTY-SIX

"No visitors allowed."

It was the same story when I had tried before lunch, and when I sat down for the meal, the empty seat beside me made me uneasy. I was glad when I felt someone move to sit in it, surprised to look up and see the new girl. Her name, I'd heard, was Corrie. She didn't say anything to me, but her presence felt like a gesture of forgiveness for the other night. I turned to her and smiled. She nodded and looked down at her plate — that was all, one nod. It made me feel absurdly joyful.

"Neve's having hers," I said. Again Corrie nodded, and again I felt a surge of irrational happiness.

Was that all we really wanted? I thought. To spin even single threads of connection between ourselves and other human beings? And if it was, why was that such a hard thing to do? Or was I the only one who failed at it over and over again?

By tiny, shared gestures — a disgusted twitch of the lip at beet soup for the third straight day; an arched eyebrow at a raucous peal of laughter from the German girls — Corrie and I spun our threads. We still didn't speak, but every time I slid a sideways glance at her, I thought I saw the faintest smile. I felt she saw the same thing.

I saw something else I recognized: the startled look down at her belly that meant her baby had kicked. Then what I saw on her face shocked me — a burst of fury and terror, like an animal caught in a trap. Corrie would have cut her pregnancy from her body if she could have.

She looked up and saw me reading her expression. She lifted her shoulder and turned away — only the slightest degree, but there may as well have been a wall of iron between us for the rest of the meal.

After lunch I tried to see Neve again. "No visitors," I was told again. Finally, late in the afternoon, I saw an opportunity to slip into the ward when the nurses' station was empty.

I found Neve in a room by herself, awake, although groggy.

"My baby," she asked, reaching for me,

357

missing my arm. "Where is he?"

"I don't know," I told her, sitting at the edge of the bed and smiling. I tucked her hand back onto the bed as you would with a sleeping child. "It was a boy?"

"Where is he? They took him away."

"You must have needed your rest. I'll go tell them you're ready for him."

Neve struggled to drag her legs over the side of the bed. Ugly bruises seeped over her ankles and knees. "They took him away —"

"I'll take care of it," I promised, pushing her back gently. "You lie down now. I'm sure it's fine."

I hurried back into the hall and pulled at the sleeve of the first nurse I saw. "Where is Neve De Vries's baby? Why hasn't he been brought to her for feeding?"

She turned and I saw she was one of the new student nurses. I let go of her sleeve and went to the nurses' station. Frau Klaus was there, sitting at her desk with a file open in front of her, but not really working.

"Where is Neve De Vries's baby?"

Frau Klaus turned away and raised her shoulder to me, pretending to search for something in the file. When I didn't leave, she looked up with a warning scowl. "Get back to your wing. You don't belong here."

I knew then that they had taken him. Someone had heard Neve questioning her decision, or had heard me advising her. How could I have been so stupid?

"She needs to nurse him," I tried anyway. "She hasn't seen him. She was planning on taking care of him."

Frau Klaus dropped the file onto the desk and looked up toward the door — a gesture that every girl in the home knew was a threat to call a guard. I would have stood my ground even then, but from the corner of my eye I saw Sister Ilse, standing out of view of Frau Klaus, glance at me and tip her head.

I turned and walked down the corridor as if to leave, but once I'd passed through the big swinging doors, I stepped back into the labor room, flooded with harsh sunlight this morning. Sister Ilse opened the door a moment later, but shook her head. She was carrying a basket of linens; as I passed by her in the doorway she whispered, "The laundry room."

There was no one in the laundry room, but she handed me a pile of towels to fold and didn't speak right away. With every moment I felt dread build.

"He was born wrong. Harelipped" was all she said when she spoke at last. "You must not ask about him."

"But why haven't they let her see him? They've taken him to correct it already?"

Sister Ilse stared at the pillowcase in her hands for a moment, folded it neatly, then looked up at me. "Here, a child is either perfect or he's not. There's no correcting. It's best if you leave this alone."

"But where is he?"

"He wasn't *Edelprodukt,* Anneke — top-quality goods for adoption. Do you understand?" She pulled a sheet from the basket and shook it out. She wouldn't meet my eyes.

For an instant, I had hope. "So he won't be adopted? Can she take him home?"

Ilse dropped the sheet back into the basket and turned to me, looked straight at me. "He's not here. He's gone. You must stop asking questions."

"He's gone? Someone's got to ask questions! Someone knows where he is, someone took him, and I'm going to find out." I turned for the door but Sister Ilse gripped my arm.

"You really don't want to do that."

I struggled away. "Yes, I really do." I pulled the door open.

"Wait." She placed her hand over mine on the doorknob. "All right." She pulled a key ring from her pocket, slid a key off and handed it to me. "I have a room here," she whispered. "You know where the nurses' quarters are? It's an outside door. The number's on the key. Wait there."

I left, went outside, and let myself into Ilse's room. I paced.

At last she came.

"Where is he?"

"Sit down." She motioned to a cot. We sat.

"Where is he?"

"He was taken to the institute at Gorden."

"When will they bring him back?"

"They don't come back."

I lost control. "What are you telling me? Where do they go, Ilse? Babies don't just disappear . . . are you telling me . . . are you telling me that they could . . . *mordują a niemowlęta?*"

Sister Ilse's face snapped to me in shock. It took me a moment to realize what I had just done.

"You're Polish!" she said, as if this was of any importance right now.

I could only stare back.

"That's your big secret?"

I wrapped my arms tight around my belly. "You think they might *kill* babies if they're born with a defect? Answer me!"

" 'Disinfected' is the word here. No, not usually. Neve's soldier denied paternity at the end, did you know that? He said he couldn't be sure the baby was his. If that hadn't happened, they'd be doing everything they could to repair the defect."

"Why not just send him home with Neve?"

"Babies aren't babies here — haven't you noticed? They're potential soldiers. If Neve took her son back to Holland, he might grow up to be an enemy soldier."

"So if something's wrong . . . Wait . . . What about Marta's little girl? Was she really stillborn?"

"Deaf."

"But she was a girl!"

"She might have borne a soldier to fight against Germany."

"They actually say this?"

"Of course not."

"Then how do you know?"

"I don't. That's the whole point. I don't know what's happened to your friend's baby. And I can't ask. But even if I could . . . who could live through knowing something like that?" She patted the air at her heart — as if that place was too sensitive to bear touch — her face wrenched in agony. " 'Disinfected' means whatever you can bear it to mean." She sighed and lowered her head.

"So you're telling me you just close your eyes to it? Pretend it's not happening? As if Neve's baby isn't real?"

Until this moment I hadn't allowed myself to picture him. But now I had a sudden image — a little red face, heart-shaped like Neve's, and two tiny hands reaching — and it split my heart open. Sobs overtook me. Ilse moved to put her arms around me; her eyes were filled with tears also, but I pushed her away. I slumped against the door, one hand over my face and the other tight over my belly, and I cried.

After a few moments, Ilse touched my shoulder.

I wiped my face with my palms and looked up. "How can you work here? How can you be part of this?"

Ilse's face told me she struggled with these questions daily, and what the struggle cost her. "Choice is a thing of the past."

"But how can you bear it?"

Ilse stepped to her dresser and picked up a photograph in an oval frame, gazed at it. "I'm a coward. Yes. I look away. I don't allow myself to think about certain things. I can't. It would kill me. So this is how I survive. This is how everyone I know survives, except we can't even talk about it.

We're all cowards." Ilse placed the photograph back on the lace runner and turned
back to face me, slumped against the dresser
as if she hadn't the strength to stand on her
own. "I know it must be difficult to understand. But surely you know that I can't just
stand up and say, 'This thing you're doing
is horrific. Stop it at once!' I'd be arrested
within hours, for one thing. Probably killed.
And then what good would I be? I've found
a way to make a difference here in my work,
but to do it, I have to block out certain
things. Everything is a compromise these
days. Especially for women. You know this,
Anneke, you know this! Terrible compromises."

My anger melted. She was not the enemy.
I'd known this all along — otherwise I'd
have been too afraid to rage against her like
this. I had my own terrible compromises.
"You *do* make a difference here."

"Well, it's true, I like being around the
babies and some of the mothers. They aren't
to blame, and you can almost forget about
the war in a delivery room. But that's not
what I mean."

"What then?"

Ilse lowered her voice to a whisper. "I talk
to the girls. Not the fanatics — that would
be too big a risk, and besides, they're lost

anyway. But some of the girls just need someone to remind them of things. Like that they have other options than to become broodmares. I talk about the future their babies might have if the war were over. I talk to them about what it really means to be a mother. Hitler and Himmler probably played at war games. Maybe their mothers could have stopped that."

"That sounds dangerous."

"I'm careful. But I have to do this. Men start wars. But women might end them." She put her hand to the doorknob.

"Wait. Who will tell Neve?"

"Whoever's on duty."

"Let me. Please. She's been through so much."

"It's not allowed."

"Would you do it then? Please?"

She sighed. "I'll see that she has plenty of morphine."

"And you'll tell her he was stillborn?"

She nodded. "That's what they're all told."

"I'll go with you."

She waved me back. This had been enough. And to my shame, I was relieved not to have to be there when Neve was told.

It didn't matter, though. All evening, through the chattering of the other girls and through the silence of my own room, I could hear her screams.

And that night I dreamed of my own child. Of his dark, dark curls.

The next morning, Sister Ilse pulled me aside as I was leaving breakfast. "They're sending her home today. You can see her now; there's a staff meeting until ten, so it's safe."

"Today?"

Ilse spread her hands. There was no baby for her to care for.

When I opened the door to Neve's room, I reminded myself to wear a face that showed only sadness, not horror. She was drugged, but the drugs hadn't touched her pain. She clawed clumsily at my arm and pulled me to the bed.

"I know," I told her, stroking the back of her hand. It was cold and dry, like fine kid leather. "I heard. I'm so sorry. The nurses said he was beautiful."

"He was? They said that?"

"They said he was perfect. They said they'd never seen such a beautiful child." Lies made in kindness were easier to tell. It was fear that gave most lies away.

Ilse came into the room. "He was an angel."

Neve's eyes filled with new tears, but she

lay back on her pillow, comforted. Then she moaned and cupped her breasts.

Ilse frowned. "Your milk's come in early. They should have helped you with that! Here, I'll show you what to do so it won't hurt so much."

I helped Ilse strip off Neve's nightgown. Her belly was soft and empty, but her breasts were hard and full, laced with veins. Then we wrapped her chest in bandages, tightly. "Keep these on as long as you can," Ilse told her. "For a week, if you have to."

Then she bent and opened a suitcase that was standing at the foot of the bed. I hadn't noticed it before. I wondered who had been in our room packing up her things, and my heart jumped. Ilse began to dress Neve, who seemed to have no will or strength of her own. I picked out a sweater and tried to help, but Ilse shook her head. "They'll be coming for her soon. You should leave now."

I leaned over and kissed Neve's wet cheek. "We'll see each other again. When this is all over." One last lie. None of us would ever look each other up. We were going to spend the rest of our lives trying to erase this time.

FORTY-SEVEN

After all that had happened with Neve, I spent even more time in the orphanage — sometimes four hours a day — pressing Klaas close, whispering to him lies about how safe he was, how loved. I began to keep a journal for Leona in the back of the notebook she had sent me:

He has three cowlicks, three! And what a sense of humor . . . as soon as I pick him up, he grabs at my sleeve, asking me to hide behind it and then peek out so he can laugh. He has your laugh and the same dimples . . .

Small comfort, but then these were days of small comforts, and it pleased me to think of how Leona might like to know I was finding parts of her in her son. I found myself wondering which parts of him were his father's. Could I sieve out Leona's traits and find anything of the man she had loved, for that night at least? The way he slept with his fists under his chin? His big ears? What kind of a man had he been, that slow kisser with the cinema passes?

Caring for Klaas filled my days; and during the nights I thought only about how it would be when Isaak came for me, which I decided would be when the weather broke. Nothing else at the home seemed real, and I had forgotten completely about Karl when he suddenly reappeared. Not being prepared made me anxious. He got up when I entered the parlor and walked to me, smiling. I looked through his smile, trying to predict what threat he would reveal. Blackmail, I hoped. Maybe he'd thought about it and decided to profit from what he knew.

"Are you feeling all right?" he asked. "How is the baby?"

"What do you want?"

"I've learned some things. We should talk, Cyrla."

My eyes darted to the door.

"I know," Karl said. "I won't call you that if anyone's around. Can we talk?"

I took a deep breath and spread my hands to him. "Fine."

"Well, let's sit down. You look tired."

I sat in the armchair so he wouldn't have

a chance to sit beside me. So I wouldn't have to be touched by that uniform. He pulled the matching armchair up to mine. Then he jumped up again, went to a side chair at the door, and drew a large box from underneath his coat. He brought it to me, smiling. But trying not to. "Open it."

Again I searched his face for the danger.

"Open it," he said again. But he didn't wait; he knelt beside me and pulled the silver ribbon from the box, then lifted the top. He lifted a coat and draped it over my lap — cobalt-blue wool, thick and soft, with wide lapels of curly black lamb.

"Do you like it? It will fit, I know. My sister helped me pick it out — she's been, well, she's had a baby. See, it wraps around, so you can wear it after, too."

"What is this?" I interrupted him. I pushed the coat back into the box. "What are you thinking?"

"You need a new coat. Your old one won't button around you."

"But I don't need one from you. I don't need anything from you."

Karl put the cover back on the box and set it on the floor. "I think you do." He went to the door, pulled it shut, and sat beside me again. "I think you don't have anyone else. If you did, they'd at least make sure you had a coat that fit."

I looked out the window beside me. The ragged fog which now clung to the mountaintops every day was thicker and darker today, crawling lower.

"Snow," Karl said, reading my thoughts. This angered me and I hardened my shoulders to him and didn't answer.

"Look, I've been talking to some people. First, you haven't taken my name off those forms, have you?"

I shook my head. After the guard had caught me trying to run away, I'd been trying not to attract any more attention. And then, after Neve, it felt even less safe.

"Good. Don't. That's the most important thing. When the baby comes, he'll be much better off if there's a father's name on that certificate. And so will you. It gives you options. Did they tell you that?"

I shrugged, not implying yes or no.

"And if I'm on the forms, I can make some choices that you can't."

I folded my arms across my chest and still didn't turn from the window.

"Like where he goes afterward. You're going to try to take him with you, of course. How do you think you can do that?"

I looked down at my hands. I'd painted my nails again and the bright scarlet sur-

prised me as it had each time I'd seen it.
My hands looked so much like Anneke's
now. I curled my fingertips into my palms,
pushed my hands down to the sides of my
lap, buried them in the stiff horsehair of the
cushion.

"Oh, God. You're going to leave before
he's born? You're in Germany, Cyrla. How
are you going to manage? Do you have
someone on the outside helping you?"

I seized that to end his questioning. "All
right," I whispered, facing him. "Yes, I'm
going home soon. So none of this matters.
You don't have to be involved."

"What do you mean, you're going home?"

"Shhh . . . home! Schiedam. It's all arranged. Now you see there's really nothing
for us to talk about. You can leave."

Karl didn't, though. He looked at me in a
way I didn't like and leaned in. His soap —
almonds and pine again.

"Cyrla, when was the last time you spoke
to your aunt and uncle?"

"Oh, a day or two ago."

I made a dismissive gesture with my hand
and he reached to take it, but I pulled it
back.

"Do you even know where they are?" he
asked softly.

A scorched scent entered the room, as if

the draperies were beginning to burn.

Karl slumped back, the fingertips of one hand pressed to his forehead, studying me. "I have to tell you something. After you told me about Anneke, I wanted to write to your aunt and uncle. But I knew they'd probably throw away a letter, so I called a friend who's still stationed in Schiedam and asked him to stop in, in person, to convey my condolences. I just heard from him yesterday."

"What?" The blood rushed in my head so loudly I could hardly hear my word.

"They're gone." Karl saw my face collapsc and then hurried to explain. "No. I mean they've left. The house has been requisitioned as an officers' headquarters."

"Where?"

"I don't know. He didn't learn anything except that the house had been taken several months before. And by the way, I never told him your name, so I didn't put you at any risk. You don't have to worry about that."

As if that was my worry. *If you leave people, they can die.*

"So why don't you tell me what you're really planning? If you had a way out — a way to leave — I think you would have taken it by now. I can help you."

I studied the man in front of me, stared

373

into his eyes for the first time. He was a liar. But he was not lying now.

"Can you find out where they are? If they're safe?" I asked.

"I can try. But what I meant was —"

"That's what you can do to help me."

"All right. Do you have any idea where they might have gone?"

"Tell your friend to ask the Schaaps next door — the house to the right, with the green door and the iron fencing along the walk. They probably won't trust him, but he can try. And see if my uncle's shop is open."

Karl nodded and stood to leave. I felt a surge of hope — this man was allowed to simply walk out of here and, once outside, he could make telephone calls.

And then I suddenly thought of Neve. *Carpe diem.*

"Wait," I said. "Do you really want to do something for me?"

FORTY-EIGHT

"Take me to dinner. You're allowed to take me out of here, you know."

"I know. 'Outings of no more than four hours, to be completed before eight in the evening, subject to permission from the chief of staff on duty.' "

"That's exactly right," I answered, surprised.

"The rules came with the notification," Karl explained. "I just never expected —" He broke into a smile. "Where would you like to go?"

In the months she was seeing Karl, Anneke used to drift off in the middle of a conversation, her face soft and dreamy. I reminded myself to be careful around this man. Around that smile. "Anywhere," I answered. "But let's go now. I'll just change my clothes."

"Now?"

I tried a helpless shrug and patted my rising waist. "We're hungry now."

"All right, I'll make you a deal. I'll take you anywhere you want to go right now. And you'll wear this coat."

Before he could ask any more questions, I went upstairs. I changed into different clothes so he wouldn't be suspicious, and then I dug to the bottom of my drawer for the money my aunt had packed. I pulled out a few useless guilders and stuffed them into my purse.

Karl was at the front desk, signing a form. I heard him tell Frau Klaus that we would be driving, and this gave me a new hope: If it turned out that I had to leave on my own in the spring, running away from one man on an outing would be a hundred times simpler than running away from an armed Nazi institution. I would make this afternoon enjoyable.

He stopped on the steps and lifted my collar to button it around my neck.

"Thank you for the coat, Karl. Truly. It's very kind of you."

"Are you warm? And see — it's cut so it will still wrap around, all the way through." Karl was still beaming when we got into the car, as if he had made the coat himself. As if he had invented coats. I couldn't help smiling.

"Yes, it's warm. And it fits. You're very thoughtful."

"Well, my sister helped. Actually, she picked it out."

"She's here? I thought Anneke had said your family was from Hamburg."

"Outside Hamburg. But no, she's here now." Karl's face clouded and warned me not to ask anything more. It had begun to snow — fat, soft flakes that glowed against the darkening afternoon sky — and we talked about the weather in the mountains as we drove toward the town. Then he asked where I wanted to eat.

"I don't care. No — I do. Someplace small. For the past five months I've eaten every meal in a big dining hall."

"Someplace small, then."

"And someplace where they have soft white bread!" I laughed. "And food that's been cooked for hours! Nothing raw!"

"I noticed a guesthouse at the edge of the main village. Let's try that."

I suddenly felt disoriented. Of course — I hadn't been in an automobile for five months, or been alone with a man, or even left the grounds of the home. Still, it wasn't the unfamiliarity of these things that made me anxious — it was their very normalcy. It was the freedom after so long; I remembered reading about animals in the zoo who tried to run back into their cages when they were released. The baby moved, swimming like a little otter — he, at least, was nothing but happy about it all.

At the guesthouse, the manager greeted us as if we were only a young couple who had come in for a meal. When he saw I was pregnant, he made a fuss about seating us near the fire — asking me if I were warm enough or too warm, pointing out the antique beer steins on a shelf above us, the paintings of the Alps lining the dark-beamed walls. We ordered *Jägerschnitzel* and salad, and while we were waiting, we each had a beer, dark and cool. I told Karl more about my days at the home. I began to relax. Perhaps the beer and the fire relaxed Karl, too, because he told me more about his sister.

"Her name is Erika. We're twins."

"Are you close?"

Karl nodded. He had lit a cigarette, but he now put it out, picking shreds of tobacco from his tongue and then leaning back before he answered me. "We were the only ones, so we were always together. She was a lot smaller, so people thought I was the older brother, and that infuriated her. She insisted on doing everything I did, which was fine until we were eight and I started spending time in the boatyard."

"She didn't want to do that?"

"Oh, no. She did." He smiled to himself at the memory. "But my grandfather and my uncles were old-fashioned. They didn't want a girl there. I took her side and made a big show of letting her come with me, as if I were the indulgent brother. But the truth was I wanted her there. She's funny and smart, and when she was young she was absolutely fearless. It's hard to explain, but when she wasn't with me, I never felt completely whole. Because we were twins, I guess."

"Anneke told me you had a niece. Erika's daughter?"

Karl smiled. "Lina."

"So she's married."

His smile disappeared. "Was." He looked away and studied a hunting trophy on the wall beside us, then turned back. "Six weeks after their wedding, Bengt was sent to the Russian front. Erika was pregnant. Two weeks before Lina was born, he was killed."

"I'm sorry. How awful — to be alone. And with a new baby." Karl looked up at me and I raised my chin — I was not alone. Or I wouldn't be, soon.

"It is awful. The worst thing for Erika is

that Bengt never saw the baby. He never knew it was a girl. He wanted a little girl. Erika manages, but just barely."

"And she's here in Munich now? So you see her?"

"She took a flat here when I was transferred. My mother came to live with her. She helps take care of the baby — she's a year old. Oh . . . I have a picture."

The baby sat on Karl's sister's lap, smiling up coyly at the photographer from behind her mother's protective arm, one hand thrown back for a reassuring touch to her mother's neck. Erika was looking away from the camera slightly, as if searching for someone behind the photographer. I wondered — if I didn't know what she had lost, would this woman still look so sad to me? I thought so.

"They're beautiful." I passed the photograph back. "They both look like you."

Karl nodded, pleased. He studied the photo for a moment before sliding it back into his wallet. "She was studying to be a teacher, but now she works in a butcher shop. And that's good, because at least they have meat. Milk is always a problem, though. I send them my paycheck — without that . . ."

Karl looked around the dining room as if

he were suddenly worried about being overheard. It was too early for dinner, and only one elderly couple sat drinking tea in little glass cups across the room.

"I've been watching them," I said, knowing he wanted to change the subject. "See how he nods all the time, how he's agreeing with everything, yet it seems he's trying to calm her. She keeps getting agitated and picking at the buttons of her sweater. It's nice to see — just an ordinary couple. I haven't seen an ordinary couple in five months."

The meal came, and while we ate we talked of nothing dangerous. Every few moments, my fingers found my purse, squeezed the clasp.

"What are you smiling about?" Karl asked.

"Oh, nothing." I placed my hands on the table, like a schoolgirl caught passing a note. "It's just so nice to be out. I haven't been off the grounds since I came."

"Why not?"

I explained about the regulations. "They don't feel we're safe outside alone. We have to be accompanied by a guard. Or . . . the father of the baby."

Karl took my bait. "Well, I can take you out whenever you want."

"How is that possible? All the German

girls are complaining — some of their boyfriends haven't had leave in a year or more!"

Karl nodded. "I've been promoted." He tapped the insignia on his arm. "I have duties, but I'm not restricted."

"What do you do?"

He hesitated. "I build things."

I waited for him to explain, but he didn't. Suddenly I wanted to know something. "Do you think Germany will win the war?"

No one else had come in and the elderly couple couldn't possibly hear us, but Karl leaned in and spoke in a low voice, curt. "This isn't the place." He picked up his fork, but he only pushed his salad around his plate, then looked out at the falling snow and drank some beer. "Yes. I think so," he said quietly. It was impossible to tell what was in his voice, but it was not happiness. We had come to the end of another conversation, and we finished our meal in quiet.

I forced myself to wait a little longer.

"Karl," I said, as if it had just occurred to me. "I saw a bakery around the corner when we drove in. I'd like to get some rolls like these for my friends — we don't get anything like them in the home." I opened my purse, withdrew my Dutch money, and frowned. "But all I have is this. Could you exchange it?"

Karl seemed pleased. "We'll stop on our way out. But I'll buy them. I want to." He pushed my hand back across the table. "Let's order dessert first. They have a Linzer torte. Then we'll get the bill and go to the bakery."

"No, really," I insisted. "You have dessert — I'm too full. I'll run over and take care of it now."

Karl studied me for a moment but then he pulled out a five-mark note. "Fine. But keep your money. I insist on that."

I took the money and stood up from the table, trying not to seem too eager. I smiled at him brightly and told him again I'd be right back, then walked away without turning around, afraid that if he saw my guilty face he would leap up and follow me. I left the guesthouse and headed to the right, away from the windows, until I was certain there was no way Karl could still see me.

A minute later, I doubled back and slipped behind the inn and walked to the post office I had seen. Long columns of swastika bunting hung beside the entrance — red and black snakes rustling patiently.

"I'd like to make a telephone call, long distance," I told the clerk at the desk. More bunting was draped across the windows.

"The Netherlands. Schiedam."

She took out a booklet and calculated the charge. I paid her and she counted out my change; then I hurried into the booth to wait for the connection to go through. It took forever. A man came in and stood a polite distance behind me, waiting for his turn.

Finally I heard the ringing at the other end. The meter above the telephone began to tick as a woman's voice picked up.

"Isaak Meier," I said. "Please hurry."

"What is your business?"

"I need to speak to him right now. It's an emergency."

There was silence for a moment.

"Please get him!"

"I'm sorry, he's no longer here. Is this Council business? Because the Amsterdam Council —"

"What do you mean, he's no longer there? Where is he?"

"I'm really not allowed —"

"Never mind!" I forced my voice to be calm, but thirty seconds had gone by. "Please let me speak to Rabbi Geron. Now."

The woman left. A full minute passed. I turned my back to the meter. In front of me now was a portrait of Adolf Hitler, his arm raised toward my face. I closed my eyes.

Finally, finally, Rabbi Geron picked up the telephone.

"This is Cyrla Van der Berg, Isaak's friend. I need to speak to him."

"Cyrla? But —"

"Please. Where is he?"

"He's . . . you don't know this? He's at Westerbork."

For a second, I couldn't remember how to breathe. "Westerbork?" I managed.

"The roundup in October, of all non-Dutch Jews. You must have heard."

"No . . . that's impossible. Isaak's Dutch, and —"

"He volunteered to accompany them — he thought he could help, as a lawyer."

"No!"

"I couldn't keep him here." Rabbi Geron had read my mind. "I didn't agree with his decision, but it was his decision. We pray every day that he will return to us soon. That all of them —"

"Is he all right? What have you heard?"

"We think —"

And then the meter rang and the line went dead.

"No, no . . . wait! Connect me again! It's an emergency!" I stood holding the telephone because if I put it down, Isaak would fall even further away. The man behind me shifted and coughed. The black receiver suddenly weighed a hundred kilos — I dropped it into the cradle and stumbled out onto the street. The bunting tongues flapped beside me in a rising gust.

Isaak was gone.

I walked across the street to the bakery; I didn't feel my steps or the snow on my face. Isaak was gone. Karl was already there, talking to the girl behind the counter. He spun around at the sound of the door's bell, and suddenly I was reminded of the first time we'd met, in Anneke's bakery — the same scents of warm sugar and vanilla. But this time Karl's eyes didn't slip over me. He ran to me and took hold of my shoulders. I saw his hands, but I didn't feel them.

"Where were you? I was worried!"

"I was . . . I had to use the washroom. What's wrong?"

Karl looked around the shop, then put his hand to the small of my back and guided me out the door. "Cyrla, I thought you had run away. I just had a feeling in the guest-house, and when I got to the bakery and you weren't there . . . I was worried." His face grew angry, but it was the anger mothers allow themselves at their children after they've given them a fright. "Don't do that again. It's dangerous."

"Karl." I laughed, trying to sound light. "I just went to the washroom, that's all."

He studied me and I had to look away. "All right. But tell me where you're going next time. I'm responsible for you. Now let's go in and buy those rolls."

Stupidly, I agreed. We went back inside and I chose a dozen little seeded rolls and watched the *Fräulein* tie them up in a paper box. All the while my mind raced — was he all right? What did that mean, he had volunteered? Why?

"Sixty pfennigs," the young woman said, and without thinking I reached into my pocket and pulled out some coins.

Coins. Karl looked at them in my hand and then looked at my face. I felt it drain of blood.

FORTY-NINE

Karl paid for the rolls, his face a gathering storm. Then he grabbed my arm and pulled me out onto the street.

"You're hurting me!"

He pushed me into the car and then got in. "Do you need money, Cyrla?" He shifted in his seat and pulled his wallet from a pocket, yanked the bills out, and threw them onto my lap. "Here. You can have money. Just ask!"

I scowled and pushed the bills off my lap, but I was more afraid than angry.

"You've been lying to me since I met you. Here and now, tell me the truth."

Karl leaned across me and locked the door and suddenly I was in the alley beside my uncle's shop, my head scraping the gravel and there was no air anymore. I cried out and struggled to unlock the door.

Karl pulled back and let me, staring. "What's wrong? I'm not going to hurt you,

Cyrla. But I want you to tell me what's going on."

I kept a grip on the door handle. "And I'm your prisoner now? Are you going to turn me in if I don't answer?"

Karl spread his hands. "If that's what you need to believe, then yes."

"Yes?"

"Yes. I will turn you in. I'll drive you right now to my headquarters in Munich. If you try to run, I'll issue a warrant for you."

"You wouldn't do that."

"You're right, I wouldn't. Cyrla, I am not a Nazi. I will never raise my right hand in their salute. But if you need to feel that threat, I'll play the game. Now tell me what just happened."

"Why? Why do you care?"

Karl threw his hands up and then slammed them down on the steering wheel. "Right now, I'm not sure I do." He glared his anger at me for a moment, then let it go. I'd never seen a man do this. My uncle cherished his anger, fed it. Isaak smoldered. My father never got angry, he grew morose. Only Anneke's anger had burst and cleared like this.

"You worry me, I guess," he said. "And I don't think you have anyone else."

We sat in silence for a minute. Then Karl

reached over and touched my chin, carefully turned my face to him. "I think you're
in trouble. And I think you're alone."

It was the truth of the words that undid
me. All the sorrow I'd held back for so long
was about this — I was alone. I curled over,
my face in my hands, and began to cry.

Karl pulled me to him and held me. "Start
at the beginning."

And so I told him. I told him what had
happened the night of Anneke's death and
what my aunt had done about it. I didn't
tell him I hadn't already been pregnant — I
was ashamed of that now. I told him the
plan, and that Isaak hadn't come for me
and that I had just learned why. "He's at
Westerbork. He's strong," I said, as if Karl
needed the reassurance. "And he volunteered, so maybe he can leave . . ."

Karl let me go then. "Do you love him?"

I was surprised by his question, but I nodded.

"Does he love you?"

I wiped my eyes and looked out the
window at the snow before answering. It
was falling in heavy swirls now and glowing
in the warm light that spilled from the inn's
windows. "It's getting deep," I said. "Maybe
we should get back."

But Karl just watched me.

"Isaak won't allow it. He says caring about someone is a liability with the world the way it is — that he might make mistakes if he loved someone."

"He's right." Karl surprised me again. "I feel that way about my sister and my niece. I probably *do* make mistakes because I love them, because I'm afraid of what might happen to them. But they give me something to hold on to. I don't know what would happen if I didn't have that. I don't know if I would survive."

I looked into his eyes and saw that he was serious. Sister Ilse had used that word, too. Then I saw his next thought. "Isaak won't do anything stupid. He'll be fine!"

Karl spread his hands. "I only mean . . . he's not coming for you. That's the point. What are you going to do now?" He didn't wait for an answer. "Look, I can help you."

"How? Can you find out if he's all right? Can you get a message to him?"

"Well, maybe. I still have that friend stationed in Schiedam. But what I was thinking of was . . . I don't think your plan was very good in the first place. I think that a Jew coming to rescue you in Germany would be incredibly difficult and dangerous. I could help you with that. You really just need to get out of here safely before your baby is born — is that right?"

I nodded. He might get a message to Isaak.

"I'll ask some questions. When I learn something, I'll let you know." He pulled out a pen and wrote down some numbers on the bakery box between us on the seat. "Meanwhile, if you need anything, call me. The first number will reach me during the day. Use the second number at night."

Relief and gratitude melted through me. I smiled at him and for the first time, it wasn't a lie. "Look. I've soaked your coat." I pulled out a handkerchief and began to dab at the stains I'd left on his chest — so many tears. There would be no more. "Do you really think it's possible to get a message to him?"

"I'll try. Tell me his last name."

I wiped off a button and I saw it — the German eagle pressed into the brass. I recoiled as if I'd been clawed by those talons.

"Cyrla?"

"Take me back."

FIFTY

Corrie was sitting on my bed when I got back. "Does he know?"

I hung up my new coat slowly, then took off my wet shoes.

"I saw him with you today. Doesn't he know?"

"No, he doesn't."

Corrie nodded as if she'd expected this. She got up. "You're lucky. My whole town knew. I didn't have the choice of telling my boyfriend or not. He wouldn't speak to me after. As if *I'm* the one who's dirty." She went to the door and stopped. "Whose is it?"

"I don't know. I think it's . . . Karl's. But I don't know."

"You're lucky, then," she said again. She opened the door and then stopped one more time. "How was it afterward? How is it now, when he sleeps with you?"

I shook my head. "We haven't . . . it happened right after he left."

"Well, I'll tell you how it will be. You will never be free of it. When any man touches you, you will feel the other one's hands. He'll always be with you. The two who did it to me will always be there. Forever." Then she left.

I worried after that day. About everything, all the time. About Isaak, how being raped would change how he felt about me. But mostly about how I was going to get out of this place and what I would do after. About all the things I had told Karl. My hands no longer looked like Anneke's, I had bitten the nails so ragged. The baby seemed to sense my agitation — he moved restlessly now, as if pacing the dark waters of my womb. When I held Klaas, he fussed and squirmed in my unquiet arms. I lost weight at both of the next two weigh-ins and spent all my time sitting on my bed and staring out at the cold mountains.

I got a second blue notice in my mailbox and of course I worried about that: Two weeks would be obvious to an obstetrician — how could I have been so foolish? I practiced looking surprised, perplexed, then shrugging it off. Mistakes happen, I might say. Then I worried my practiced response would give me away.

But nothing did. The exam was unpleasant — in a cold room with harsh lights, and even there, photographs of Hitler frowned down from the walls. But the doctor didn't act as if he were surprised at anything he found, and soon enough it was over. I could dress.

"All is fine, young lady," the doctor said when he came back. "The heartbeat is strong, and I don't see any signs that the birth will be difficult. You seem a little small for twenty-six weeks, but it's nothing to be alarmed about. I don't want to see another weight loss, though. You're taking the vitamins, of course?"

I assured him I was and got up to leave.

"Babies grow at their own rate," he said. "There's nothing any of us can do to change that."

The next morning, I was told I had a visitor.

"We're going to take a walk. I've already signed you out."

I didn't bother arguing. In the car, I asked Karl what he had come for.

"I have some things to talk over with you."

I turned to face him, waiting.

"Not yet. I know a good place for a walk. It's like spring today."

We drove in silence for about fifteen minutes, then turned off to a narrow rutted road. We stopped in front of a barn beside a broad meadow.

"A friend of mine grew up here," Karl said. "His family used to raise sheep. Until the sheep were 'liberated.' "

He opened my door to help me out and I stepped away from his hand. "All right," I said. "What do you want to talk about?"

"Not yet. Let's walk a while first."

I shrugged and started down the path along the edge of the meadow. Karl walked beside me, matching my slow pace — at six months, the baby nudged my lungs, making me short of breath easily. After a while he broke the quiet. "It's nice out. Warm for March."

It was more than nice out — it was glorious, with the mist rising from the fields carrying the scent of softening earth, and spring chasing winter away with such confidence — but I didn't answer him. The eagerness in his voice, the whole business of taking me away on an outing as if we were friends, angered me. I had spent the past two weeks arming myself — reminding myself of all the things I'd almost forgotten about Karl. About what he had done to my cousin. And what his uniform had done to people I loved. About what someone in his uniform had done to me. I didn't want to allow him to give me the smallest of plea-sures, even a walk on a warm, sunny day. If I enjoyed it, I would enjoy it in secret.

We stopped by a tree, still winter-bare but somehow the first haze of bloom shimmered in the air around it. "That's an apple; a Bie-tigheimer, I think," Karl said. "They don't keep well, but they make good wine. Do you have them in Holland, or is the ground too low? They like their roots dry." He snapped off a twig, the tiniest pale green buds bursting miraculously from the gray wood, and handed it to me. "The wood is wonderful to carve. You can smell the apple in it."

I nodded and put the twig into my pocket, fingering the satin buds slyly. "It looks like a regular apple tree. We have apple trees in Holland."

Karl kicked at some weeds by the side of the path. "Lamb's-quarter? Goldenrod? You have those in Holland, too?"

I narrowed my eyes and looked straight ahead.

"Come on. I only want to talk. Why won't you talk with me?"

"We're talking."

"You know what I mean. I want to help

you. Anneke would have asked me to do that. But the truth is, I want to, anyway. So you might as well get used to me. I can be extremely charming, you know. You haven't seen anything yet."

For a second I almost smiled in spite of myself. But I walked away from him.

Karl sighed and followed. The crunch of the winter grasses beneath our steps grew louder in the quiet. Then he stopped and turned me to him with a hand on my shoulder. I looked at his hand and thought unexpectedly, *Bullets to the back of the neck.*

"Cyrla, listen to me. I didn't walk out on Anneke. I swear to you I didn't know she was going to have a baby. Until you believe me, things are going to stay like this. And I don't want them to."

Two hawks circled over the far end of the meadow, near the tree line. I watched them, waiting.

"I didn't want to tell you this if Anneke hadn't. But now I think I should. That last night we met, Anneke didn't tell me she was pregnant. She didn't get a chance to. I knew she had news, but I couldn't wait for it. I'd been working up the courage to tell her something all week, and I had to do it while I could. Cyrla, I told her I was leaving for Germany and that I wanted to end things because I wasn't in love with her. It just didn't feel right anymore, not to tell her the truth."

My cheeks flushed at this blow to Anneke's pride, at how unfair it felt with her not here. Well, what if what Karl was saying was true? But it wasn't. How could any man not have loved Anneke? No, he was just trying to shift the blame.

"Cyrla, did you hear me? I'm ashamed of myself for that night because when I saw how much I had hurt her, how devastated she was, I thought it was just because she couldn't bear to lose me. I was so stupid and so arrogant."

"You were worse than that, Karl. Look what happened."

"A hundred times since you told me what happened, I've wished things had been different. If only I'd let her speak first. I don't know for sure what I would have done if I'd known about the baby, but I know I wouldn't have left her alone with it. I might have married her. Or maybe she would have ended up here, where you are. But she wouldn't have been alone."

I let my expression tell him — *That's easy to say now.*

"In any case, I think she would be alive now. So you're right: I'm to blame for her death. But not the way you think. And it's important to me that you know this."

I studied his face, trying to find where he was hiding his lie. I couldn't. But still . . .

"Cyrla, do you believe me?"

I looked away. In the distance were deep forests, the kind of forests that sheltered wolves. Holland had no such forests. No wolves. "Anneke wouldn't lie." But I wondered. I started to walk again, but Karl caught my hand.

"Cyrla, is this always going to be between us?"

I pulled my hand away.

"Fine, then. I give up. But whatever you feel about me, I'm going to try to help you." He motioned to a sunny spot on the stone wall along the path. "Let's sit down. I'll tell you what I've learned."

I sat and when he sat beside me, I almost shifted away. But I didn't — I realized with surprise that my irritation with him was spent the instant he had said he had given up. And now it seemed childish.

"I did some research. I've thought about everything. I'd really like you to listen."

"Go ahead."

Karl took a deep breath and began. "Here's how I see it. You have three choices. First, you could run away before the baby is born and try to make it back to Holland. I guess that's what you're planning to do?"

I hesitated, but then I said yes.

"Well, I think that's a pretty bad idea — your worst choice, in fact — but if that's what you end up deciding to do, at least I can help."

I edged forward and stared back at him. "How?"

"Well, I could get you out of the home, of course. That part would be easy. But then I could take you closer to the border. We have four hours on an outing, so I could drive you four hours closer before anyone would count you missing."

He had my full attention now. "You would really do that?"

"Yes. And then I'd say we'd gone in the opposite direction, though — to Salzburg, for example — and you'd run away from me there. That would buy you a little time."

"That's good," I agreed carefully. It was better than good, though. If I could trust him to do all that.

"No, it's really not," Karl said. "You still have all the problems. Once you're declared missing, Anneke's papers will be useless. A four-hour drive might get you halfway. That leaves a lot of distance to cover with people looking for you. You couldn't get through a checkpoint, and you certainly wouldn't be able to cross the border."

"Do you have a better idea?"

"I do. Much better. You stay here until the baby is born —"

My hands flew up. "No!"

"Just hear me out."

I pressed my lips together and then nodded.

"All right. Don't say anything until I'm finished. Here's what I've learned: I am the first choice for the adoptive father of your baby. I wanted to find out if I could take the baby without being married if my sister agreed to raise him. The main offices are right in Munich, in the Herzog-Max-Strasse, so instead of writing the petition, I made an appointment to see Dr. Ebner."

"You didn't! He's going to be watching me now."

Karl put his hand over mine and squeezed it. "I did you a favor. He's met me and I've claimed paternity in person. Now listen to me. You need to hear this, Cyrla. What you do is your choice, but you need to know the options."

"Fine, Karl. I'll hear you out. But I'm not going to stay here."

"Dr. Ebner gave permission. And Erika agreed. So that's where it stands now —

I'm going to adopt him officially."

"What? You had no right. I would never allow that!"

"Well, remember — you don't have any say in it. If your baby is born here, he will be adopted. And if I want him, I can have him."

"But he won't be born here. That's why I'm leaving."

"If you're leaving, what difference does it make what the adoption papers say? Now calm down. I'm almost finished. Let's just say you *did* stay and have your baby here and I've arranged to take him. You could go home safely the next day if you want. Have you thought about that?"

"No. Because I'm not going to be here."

"Well, think about that part. You'd be escorted back to Holland. Because you wouldn't have run away, Anneke's papers would be fine, and there would be no reason you couldn't keep using them. You could live anywhere."

For a moment, I tried to imagine so many of my problems simply disappearing. I couldn't take it in, except piece by piece. I could leave Steinhöring. They would drive me to the border. I could walk down the clean, wide streets of Holland again, without fear. I'd look up Leona, maybe share a flat with her. Or Neve. I could search for my family, find out about Isaak. Each one of these would be a miracle.

Karl watched me patiently until I came back to the most important thing.

"It would only be temporary," he rushed to assure me. "We'd care for the baby only until you were settled and we could find a way to get him to you. He'd be safe with us, Cyrla."

I just sat there for a few moments, completely overwhelmed. The very appeal of the idea felt dangerous.

"I promise you he'd be safe."

I thought about what Karl was promising; then I thought about what he couldn't. I shook my head.

"Why? Do you really think I'm going to steal your child?"

"No, it's not that." I ran my fingers over the edge of the stone I was sitting on, picked at a patch of lichen, then patted it back in place. Lichen could grow for a hundred years, I'd once read, before a human being would notice the growth. "Isaak is Jewish. He has black hair. All the babies born at the home are blond, Karl. What if —"

"We'll plan to take him away immediately, then. I don't think that's anything to worry about. Erika can say that Lina had black

404

hair when she was born, too. I could arrange to be there and say it's a family trait."

"You don't understand. You don't know what the Lebensborns are really about."

He also didn't know what my family was about — its history of abandoning children under the pretense of keeping them safe running like poison through its veins.

"I *do* know. This baby you're carrying is supposed to grow up in a German home. They're pleased I'm going to take him. And Cyrla, you're talking about a day-old baby."

I thought about what had happened to Neve's day-old baby and shuddered. "I won't take that chance. I don't even want to talk about it anymore."

Karl raised his hands in surrender. "Fine. You don't have to decide today. But think about it."

"I don't have to think about it. I've made my decision, and it's final."

"You want to try running?"

"If you'll help me, I could do it. But Karl . . . how fast are the trains? If you put me on a train in Munich instead, could I reach the border in four hours?"

Karl snapped off a switch of dried weed; last year's shriveled seed pods still clung to the tips. He stripped them and tossed them away, frowning. "Maybe. Probably five or six. But it's a help. I could still say you got away from me in Salzburg, and then they shouldn't be looking for you anywhere else. That's better. But you'd still be alone, and your papers would be no good. I don't like it, Cyrla."

"What if someone were waiting for me at the border. My aunt?"

"Well . . ."

"That's it, then. I have to find her. And then I can go! When, do you think?"

"I suppose as soon as you're sure you've got someone waiting for you. With new papers."

"And if I don't have that? If I don't reach her?"

"Then you can't go until the weather breaks. I won't even consider you out there, pregnant, at night when it's still like this."

"Next month?"

Karl shook his head. "May."

"May first, then." I couldn't keep the smile from my face.

"Mid-May." Karl was not smiling.

"Two months." We both said the words at once, but from Karl's lips they were a dirge, from mine they were a hymn of hope. We heard that and we laughed, and a small brick fell away from the wall between us.

"Karl, why do you want to do all this? Why

406

do you even want to be involved?"

"I have a lot of reasons."

"Anneke?"

He nodded slowly. "Anneke, of course." He looked across the fields for a moment. "There's a symmetry that makes it feel right. I build boats. That appeals to me."

"What do you mean?"

"Anneke and her baby — my baby — are gone, and I'm here. Isaak is gone and you and your baby are here. The pieces fit. There's a balance when you align all the pieces." He held his hands up, the fingertips touching but at right angles to each other. Then he rotated them and laced them together. "Do you know what I mean?"

I raised my hands, turned them and laced them together like his, and smiled. Yes.

"And do you remember what I told you about my sister and my niece? About how caring for them gives me something to hold on to? I think there's some of that, too."

"I understand."

"But that's not the main reason." Karl looked into my eyes for a long moment, as if he thought the words he needed were there. Then he turned away, as if they weren't. He stood up. "Never mind. We should go. It looks like it might rain."

We walked back without talking any more,

but now the quiet was peaceful. As he put the key to the ignition, I stopped him. "Wait. You said there were three choices. What's the third one?"

He pulled the key out and looked down at it in his palm. "You could marry me."

His response stunned me so much that I laughed. Karl tightened his eyes and stared straight ahead, his forearms resting on the steering wheel.

"Karl — you're not serious."

"Actually, I am. It's one of your options. I asked Dr. Ebner about that, too."

Now I was too shocked to form words.

Karl turned to face me. He flushed. "Here it is: If you and I got married, I could take you out right now. It would be optional for you to stay. You'd have to become a German citizen, but they've set up paperwork to do that easily for these situations." I could tell he had practiced this speech, and I was surprised to find that it touched me.

"Karl." I laid my hand on his arm. "Karl, no. That's really not one of my options."

"Because of Isaak?"

"Isaak, Anneke, me, you. Everything."

He nodded as if he'd expected this.

"I want you to know how much I appreciate everything. But you have to understand — I loved Anneke."

"Cyrla. I really didn't know she was pregnant."

I looked into his eyes and saw that he was telling the truth. Or maybe it was just what I wanted to see. "It's still hard. But I really am grateful for all the trouble you went to and for what you're going to do for me. Just the fact that you want to help means a lot. In the six months I've been here, I've had no one. I've been completely alone."

"I think you're very brave. To come here in order to make your baby safe. Well, you aren't alone now." He put the key back into the ignition and started the engine.

I wasn't alone now. All my life, I'd done nothing but lose people. My mother and father, my brothers. My aunt and uncle, Anneke, Isaak. All ghosts. Now, for the first time in six years, someone was asking to come into my life. I suddenly knew that no matter the barriers which would always remain between Karl and me, I wanted to try. No matter the cost.

"Karl, when will you see your sister?"

"Tomorrow. Why?"

"Could you come here first, for just a few minutes?"

"I could. But why?"

"Trust me. Tomorrow morning, all right?"

We had reached the home and I had

reached another decision.

"Karl. Isaak's last name is Meier."

FIFTY-ONE

When I got back, I found a surprise. "I'm Anneke," I introduced myself to the girl unpacking her suitcase.

"Eva."

By now, I had become used to living among a sea of girls with rising bellies. Our shared situation was obvious to all, which made for a strangely immediate intimacy. Yet there was a strict code about the boundaries of privacy. The first questions were always *Where are you from? How far along are you?* and *How long will you stay?* It was only after a certain level of familiarity had been achieved — impossible to predict when it would happen, but unmistakable once it had — that one could ask about the father.

I sat on my bed as Eva unpacked. She was petite — possibly the smallest girl in this place which seemed to revere tall women — and very pretty, although her face looked tight and newly formed, as if it had never contorted in grief or expanded in joy. When she moved, it was with the twitchy grace of a cat.

I asked the questions.

Eva was from Haarlem and she was exactly five months pregnant — for the first time, I had the seniority that came with being further along than one's roommate. This brought a slight sense of urgency — for the first time, my baby's birth felt imminent. But it was her answer to the third question that brought me to panic.

"Jurn's put in for leave to marry me. I'll stay until that happens."

I put down my book. The German girls often married their boyfriends, of course, but I hadn't heard of any girls from other countries doing it. It was one thing to sleep with the enemy. Quite another to marry him and move to the Fatherland.

"And afterward," I asked, trying to keep my voice neutral, "you'll stay here, in Germany?"

"No. Jurn is from Haarlem, too. We'll stay there."

Eva watched me as understanding dawned, her small face a mask. Her boyfriend was in the Waffen SS. I was the one who was sleeping with the enemy. For only two months more, I reminded myself, blessing Karl again for what he had promised.

That night in the dining hall, Eva established her status. At five months, she was still sinuous and sexy. Even the German girls seemed to sense a danger behind her pretty face and they shrank away, leaving a space around her. I'd seen this space before: Sometimes when Anneke had entered a room, the women had stepped back and eyed her, feeling threatened. Anneke never allowed this — she went out of her way to put other women at ease, even going so far as to act less graceful than she was, less feminine. A few minutes of her charm would melt all jealousy.

But Eva did nothing to encourage any approach, let alone any friendship.

Well, if it was distance she wanted, I'd be happy to give it to her.

In the morning, I headed straight to the newborns' nursery before breakfast. "I need a favor."

Ilse shook her head. "No. Last time was too close." She turned away as if she didn't trust herself to stay firm if she looked at me.

I laughed and tugged at her sleeve. "No, this one is easy. Really."

Ilse put down the stack of folded diapers she'd been carrying. "What is it?" she groaned.

"I need some formula." I held out my coat. "Whatever will fit in the pockets."

"Why on earth —"

"Don't ask. It's for a baby — that's all I'm going to tell you. She doesn't have milk. And all you have to do is let me into the supply room and then turn your back."

"And let you steal it? I don't know. That's a pretty big favor." But she threw up her hands and led me down the hall.

"There's no one around this morning. I'll help you." We pulled down a case of cans of concentrated formula — my pockets were large and held two cans each. I opened the coat and showed her two smaller pockets inside.

"How about powdered milk?" she suggested. "If we folded a packet, it might fit." We tried, but the packet wouldn't bend enough to slip inside. "This baby is really hungry?" she asked.

I nodded. Ilse checked the hall, then took a pair of surgical scissors from a drawer. She opened my coat and slit the silk lining from the wool at the neck. She dropped several packets of dried milk into the space and shook them down to the hem, then several more. "This is how we do it."

"We?"

"A lot of the nurses have families. Hungry families."

Then she opened a cabinet and took a handful of small dropper-bottles. "Vitamins. Three drops a day in any liquid." She filled the two inside pockets. "If the mother's been nursing, she ought to take the vitamins, too. Six drops." She patted my pockets. "There you go, you little thief. If you get caught, I never saw you this morning."

I hugged her. "You are so good, Ilse. I'm so glad you're here."

I waited downstairs for Karl, sitting still as a stone — if I shifted at all, the treacherous clink of the vials sent my heart thudding. But I was happy — it had been so long since I'd had people to care for. As soon as he pulled into the driveway, I ran out to meet him.

"What are you doing? Put your coat on." But I just waved him back to the car.

Inside, I spilled the treasures onto the seat between us. It took only a second for his face to light up. "For Lina? All this?"

"For Lina, yes. But Erika and your mother should take some vitamins, too."

"They gave you all this?"

"Well, they don't exactly *know* they've

given it to me."

"Cyrla! You stole it?"

I clapped my hands to my face.

"This isn't funny. You've just stolen supplies from a Nazi institution. You could be thrown in prison for doing that."

"Oh, I doubt that." I patted my stomach. "We're too valuable, remember?"

"They shoot people for less than that. Don't you ever do anything so stupid again."

Karl must have caught my hurt look because he softened. "I'm sorry. It's just that sometimes I don't think you understand how dangerous things are." He gathered the stolen supplies and began to hide them beneath the seat. "I'm really grateful. You have no idea how much this will mean to them." Karl made a move toward me, and I flinched without thinking. But immediately I was ashamed — he had simply tried to hug me.

"*I'm* the one who's grateful, Karl. I know I haven't made it easy for you, and I'm sorry for that. What you're doing, helping me get home, helping find my family —"

"Cyrla, I have some news about that."

His look melted my teasing mood like cold rain. "What is it?"

"Don't be upset. It's not bad news, exactly."

416

"Karl, tell me now."

"All right. I had an inspiration after I left you yesterday. I saw an easy way for me to ask about your aunt and uncle without arousing any suspicion."

"Tell me."

"I will; be patient. I told my commander that I wanted to marry you, but that you insisted I speak to your parents. He patched me through to the commander in charge of the unit using your old home."

"Where are they?"

"They're gone. Apparently, there was a warrant for your uncle. He came home one night, late, and they kept him locked up there. Sometime in the middle of the night, your aunt set fire to the house."

"Fire?"

"Calm down. Of course it was extinguished right away. But in the confusion, your aunt and uncle slipped away. They're still missing."

"She set fire to the house?"

"It's not exactly something to be celebrating, Cyrla. But it means they're all right. I would have been told if they'd been arrested."

"Wait. Why was there a warrant for him? The blanket order?"

"No, not that. But what matters is that

you're not going to reach your aunt now. I'm sorry."

"Not the blankets? But then —"

Karl looked away and then I knew.

"But how did they know?"

"It doesn't matter. They escaped. What matters is —"

My father's Sabbath candlesticks. The stack of his letters.

"Cyrla, did you hear me? I think you should reconsider now. I really think you should stay and let me take the baby. Or you should marry me."

I raised my palms to him. "I've decided."

"You'll only make it worse for them if you go home. You see that, don't you?"

"I won't go near them," I said. "I'll find Leona. But I have to go back now. Do you understand?"

Karl sighed as if he had been dreading this. "No. But we'll talk about this later. And remember, we agreed: You can't leave until May." I nodded and he looked away. "My sister will be wondering. And I can't wait to bring this to her — she's going to be so happy." Karl got out, opened my door and helped me out. At the entrance, he stopped and turned to me. "Thank you."

I reached up and put my arms around him to make up for my foolish rudeness before.

My belly was hard between us, but I squeezed him, and when I pulled away, he held me fast for a second. Later, I wondered if it was just the wind in the trees or the rustle of our clothes I heard, or if he had whispered my name.

And all that day I caught the scent of almonds and pine in my hair.

FIFTY-TWO

For the first time since I'd arrived here, I had something I could close my eyes and picture that wasn't a nightmare. Seeing the photograph of Erika and Lina had made them real for me, and I loved imagining how my gift might have made Erika's face lose its sadness for a bit or fattened Lina's cheeks. I thought of that photo many times: how Erika's face, and even Karl's, shone in Lina's, and I wondered who her father had been, where he lived in that child. I wondered about the child I was carrying, where its father would present himself.

One afternoon I stopped at Corrie's room and told her to come with me. She'd looked at me for a long moment without speaking, without even asking me where. "Come with me," I insisted. She hesitated as we entered the orphanage, but she followed me in.

"What do you think you're doing?" she hissed under her breath. "Do you think I'm suddenly going to feel fine about this baby I'm carrying? Do you think I'm going to forgive those men?"

"But it's not their fault," I said, gesturing to the babies — Ilse's words.

"I know that. I don't care. I'm fine. You don't have to rescue me."

"Just sit with me." I drew two chairs to the windows and went to get Klaas. I held him on my lap and Corrie sat beside me, looking out over the mountains, not speaking. But not leaving, either.

And she came the next day. And the next. She never held a baby, just sat beside me while I fed Klaas and played with him. And sometimes she would talk.

"Do you dream of him?" she asked me once. "The one who did it?"

"A few times."

"Just a few? You're lucky." And then she left.

A few days later, I tried to hand her a little girl — about two months old, with a mouth like a tiny strawberry — while I went for a diaper. She wrapped her arms tighter to her chest and shook her head, her face squeezed.

"They used their rifles."

I wasn't sure I'd heard her, but then she repeated it, louder.

"To strip me. Their rifles with the bayonets. They stripped me with their bayonets.
It was a game. They laughed. They took
turns. My clothes were shredded, in the
mud."

Another time she asked, "Don't you care
that you might be carrying his baby?
Doesn't it remind you all the time?"

I looked down at Klaas, smiling up at me
— he smiled all the time now — and then
back at Corrie. "I don't care," I said, the
words a shock to me. "I don't care who the
father is."

"Because we're leaving them here. We're
getting rid of them." Corrie held me in her
stare, waiting for my agreement.

"No," I said. "That's not why."

For an instant she looked furious, then
betrayed. She didn't come to the orphanage
again.

When Karl came again, I was happy to see
him. We could never really be friends, but it
was good that we were no longer enemies.

"Erika sends her thanks. You can't imagine
how much it meant to them." He raised a
garment bag. "She wants you to have these."

We went into the parlor and sat and I
opened the bag. Maternity clothing. Beautiful things. Three blouses, all of them nicer

than anything I'd been wearing — crepe de chine, rayon, silk. A skirt and a dress. A flared black velvet jacket with frog closures and a scarlet lining. A pair of chocolate wool pants, cleverly made with a gathered panel in front and a row of buttons along the waistband to accommodate my growing size. Anneke's trousers hadn't fit me for a month now, even though I'd opened up the darts and the seams and moved the button. Prettiest of all was a wraparound slip, robin's-egg-blue satin with heavy cream lace. For the six weeks I had left, it would be a pleasure to get dressed.

"These are wonderful. Thank her for me. But I don't know how to return them. I won't be able to pack when we leave."

"She doesn't want them back. They remind her of too much."

I held the slip to my cheek. "Everything's so beautiful." So expensive.

Karl read my mind. "We had money then. It was . . . before."

"Before what?"

Two new Belgian girls came in. They came over at once, drawn like moths to the finery on my lap. And drawn to Karl, I saw by their exaggerated gestures and flirty giggles. Well, he was handsome; I had to give him that. Karl stood back and watched, smiling, until everything had been admired. Then he offered me his hand. "Let's take a walk."

I kept Karl's hand as we walked across the room, and I turned back at the door and nodded to the girls to make sure they saw. Because Anneke would have done that.

I brought the clothes to my room and hung everything in the wardrobe, then buttoned the velvet jacket over my dress and went down to join Karl. I did a little twirl to show him how pretty the jacket was, but he only gave me a half-smile.

We walked to a patio at the back of the property and sat on a stone bench overlooking the lake. It was mild and sunny, but we were the only ones out. Karl took a lighter from his pocket and looked down at it for a moment, flipping it over and over, before lighting his cigarette.

"You know I'm a boatbuilder."

I nodded.

"Fourth generation. We always had four or five people working for us. Bengt designed our engines. We were known for our cabinetry — we made the finest sailboats and yachts on the Baltic. We had our own timberland — over three hundred acres of white oak for framing. Well, we still own that."

"You don't still own the boatyard?"

"No, not for a year and a half now. Until then, the navy sent us work. That's why I was able to avoid service for so long — I was 'essential labor.' But then in September of '40, they took the boatyard. It included my parents' home."

"Where did they go?"

"They moved in with Erika; she and Bengt had a house in town. He was in Russia already, and Erika was pregnant. They kept my father on to oversee things, but everyone else was conscripted. That's when I was sent to Holland."

"Well, when the war is over, you'll own the boatyard again, won't you? You have a place to go back to."

Karl shook his head and ran a thumb down his jawbone, over the light stubble of his beard. For a second I thought of the *Oberschütze* with his short bristle. But only for a second.

Karl mashed his cigarette out and watched while the last thread of smoke spiraled away. "It's gone. A bombing raid last summer."

"There's nothing left?"

"There's a lot of fuel stored at a boatyard, and varnish and paint and oil. The buildings went first — it must have been a firestorm. Once the boats started to blow up, there was fuel all over the water. The harbor caught on fire. They said the water itself was burning."

"Your father . . ."

"He went down to the boatyard that night. He didn't come back."

I put my hand over his. "I'm so sorry. They never found him?"

"There were bodies everywhere. Dozens. Charred. The worst thing, though —"

I saw Karl's eyes fill, saw him work his face to stop the tears. The way men do. I waited.

"They said . . . they said some of the people who had burns ran to the river. They jumped in. They caught fire there in the river. When I think of that . . ."

He stopped again and I waited again, my hand stroking his arm.

"I hope my father didn't die that way. But in a way, well . . . he was dead already. When the Nazis took over his boatyard, it ripped his heart out. Both of his brothers had joined the Party, so it wasn't anything that was ever spoken about, but the business was his entire life; it was what he had to give to me. He felt he failed because he let it go."

"He didn't have any choice."

"I know. But he felt it was his responsibility to pass it on, the way his father had and his grandfather."

"What about you?" I asked Karl. "Do you still want to build boats?"

"Yes. I guess it's in my blood. I was apprenticed there when I was fifteen. I had only one more year left before I'd have been a full master."

"Karl." I stopped him. "How old are you?"

"Twenty-seven. Maybe I'm too old to learn something new. But I'm suited to boatbuilding. I like everything about it: the feel of the wood as I shape it, the quiet of the work, even the tools. I have my grandfather's chisels — you should see them, how beautiful they are. And I love the ocean."

I knew what he meant. I loved everything about poetry. I had a fountain pen once — it was tortoiseshell and silver, and it was balanced perfectly. It felt serious in my hand. I'd sold it last year to make a contribution when money got tight, and I'd cried in secret for a week. I loved the feel of good paper, the smell of new books, and the look of a desk cleared for writing. I had never told anyone this, and I didn't tell Karl now. But I wanted to.

"What I love most of all, though," he went on, "is the feeling that I'm creating something so beautiful from these simple raw materials. There's a balance: I take things from the earth — wood, cotton, metal —

and craft them into something that works with the air and the sea so perfectly it's almost magic. That pleases me."

"With poetry, it's like that, too. All the words are there, the simple raw materials. It's the poet's job to string them together, to shape them, to produce the most powerful combinations of pain and joy, understanding and mystery. That's like being an alchemist."

Karl shifted to look at me more squarely. He laid his arm along the back of the bench. If I leaned back just the slightest bit, my shoulder would graze his fingertips. I thought about how that might feel — those fingers that understood wood and beauty, touching me. How it might feel to him, my raw materials under his hand. What magic might happen? My gaze fell to his lips and my treacherous heart began to thud against my ribs. I straightened up and looked away quickly.

"Vertel me wat je denkt," he said.

I felt the heat rise in my cheeks. "Only that — Wait! You know Dutch?"

"Not really. I asked Anneke to teach me a few phrases."

"And 'Tell me what you're thinking' was one of the things you wanted to know how to say?"

He reddened and I immediately regretted my teasing tone. "What else?" I asked, more gently.

Karl looked away. "Nothing important. I've forgotten anyway."

"Really. I want to know."

Karl pulled his arm back and turned to face the lake. The ice had been thawing for weeks, and in places dark water, deep and alive, reflected the mountains above. A flock of geese skidded in and even from this distance we could see the spray. I waited.

Finally he turned back to me.

"I have to tell you something."

There was such sadness in his face that I smiled at him encouragingly. I didn't sense the danger.

"Do you remember the day we met? In the bakery?"

I nodded. The smile faded from my lips as I remembered: He'd betrayed his true self that day, that first moment.

"I couldn't look at you," he said. "Anneke said, 'This is Cyrla,' and I thought, *Please let her not be like her poems. Please let her be plain, and silly, and shallow.* I shook your hand and I had to look away."

I felt a clutch of panic and stood.

Karl followed and took my arm. "I had to look away so I wouldn't fall in love with

429

you right there, in front of Anneke. I looked all around the bakery, I looked out the door, anywhere but at your face."

"No," I whispered.

"But it was too late. I knew. When you were standing there, I saw a fine light glowing around you, outlining you. Not the light from the window, because Anneke was right next to you and it wasn't around her. It was setting you apart for me."

"Stop it. How could you?"

"I have to tell you this — there's nothing more I can say to you until I've said this."

"I don't want to hear anything else you have to say."

"I knew more about you already, from your poems, than I knew about Anneke. But after I met you, I realized something: There was simply more to know about you than there was about Anneke. And that's when I decided it was wrong to go on seeing her. We had nothing in common, and in fact I had more in common with you — someone I'd known for only one minute —"

"How dare you!" I spat, stepping away. "We have nothing in common. Except that for a little while you were lucky enough to know her. But you let her go."

I left the courtyard then, left him standing there with his betrayal. Of course, I had let her go as well. And that night, in my bed, I wondered what I would look like with a fine edge of light choosing me.

Betraying Anneke again.

FIFTY-THREE

"You have a telephone call."

I left the lunch table and followed the Sister, thinking: Isaak, or my aunt. At last.

"Where are you?" Karl's voice asked. It had been over a week since our argument.

"In the hall by the dayroom."

"Is there anyone around who can hear?"

"No. Why?"

"Good. Just listen, and don't repeat anything I say. Don't ask any questions. It's important."

"All right," I promised, wary.

"Tomorrow after lunch, find a way to get into the gardeners' supply building, at the west end of the property, beyond the garages. You know the one?"

"Yes."

"Take a walk, pretend you're interested in the new plantings. When no one is looking, slip inside. Find a place inside to hide where you won't be seen, but you can see. I don't think any guards patrol there, but just in case someone finds you, make up a story about looking for a trowel, about wanting to plant some flower seeds. Something like that."

"Why?"

"Don't ask questions! Just be there tomorrow afternoon. I can't phone you again about this. Trust me."

All that day I tried to work out what Karl was up to. I couldn't, but I was surprised to find that it helped the day pass more quickly than most — to have a small, harmless mystery to solve.

The next morning, at breakfast, I kept glancing toward the western part of the grounds, where the gardens lay behind the tall lilac hedges, already bunched with cones of tight purple buds. A transport truck rumbled down the gravel drive — the kind that often brought details from the camps to work here — and then came back through a few moments later. This worried me.

I asked the girl sitting beside me if she knew what was going on today, but she just shrugged and spread apple syrup over a piece of bread. "There's a naming ceremony at the end of the week. Maybe they'll hold it outdoors."

I grew more nervous. I never liked surprises.

By lunch, I couldn't eat. I sat facing the windows that overlooked the west gardens, watching, watching. Nothing happened. Several times, workers in prison uniforms came through the hedge carrying hods of bricks, but that was all.

As soon as I could leave the table without causing notice, I did. I went to my room and put on a cardigan, my belly bulging out below the three buttons which could still meet. It felt unprotected, so I switched it for the big canvas coat Leona had left. I hurried down the stairs and out the front way, nodding to the guards as usual. I was going for a walk in the spring air. That was all.

Turning the corner to the patio, visible to anyone in the dayroom, I began to have doubts. Often, we would see Dr. Ebner standing at the windows there or in the dining room, binoculars raised, watching what the workers were doing.

I walked down the path toward the lilac hedge, but then suddenly felt conspicuous. I stopped at the arched arbor and pretended to stretch, then pulled my arms in, knowing I looked guilty. This was foolish. Probably the whole thing was just another of Karl's ploys to get me to lower my guard to him, to win favor after our argument. Maybe he had arranged for a gift to be there, something he knew I'd enjoy seeing. Some potted flowers, maybe. No, that didn't make sense; why wouldn't he just bring the gift himself? I gave up. Really, why was I even considering following instructions from this man? Hadn't Neve and I sworn we would never again let someone else tell us what to do?

I turned, walked back to the front door, and went inside. In the dayroom, some girls were playing cards. I took off my coat and joined them. Later, when I was sitting with Klaas, I found myself still thinking about it. "Never mind," I whispered to the baby. "If he didn't want to tell me what he was up to, what do I care?"

A week later, Karl appeared. He had me sent for, and when I walked into the parlor, he was standing in the middle of the room, his coat over his arm. He closed the door behind me. "Well?" he asked.

"Well, what?"

"Did it go all right last week? You didn't get caught?"

It took me a minute to remember. "The garden shed?"

"Of course!" He stared at me, waiting.

"Oh, I didn't go," I said, as coolly as I could. To take some pleasure from him.

He stared at me. "You didn't go? You didn't go?"

"No. Maybe if you'd told me what was going on —"

"You never went to the shed at all?"

"No, Karl, I didn't. Is it really such a big thing?"

"Oh, my God!" Karl sank to the sofa and dropped his head into his hands. I felt my lips curl into a small smile I was helpless to hide. Another casualty of war: my kind nature.

Karl looked up as though he was about to say something, but he caught sight of my face and scowled. Then he stood, picked up his coat and strode to the door. He turned.

"I took such a risk for you. I asked other people to take terrible risks. And you weren't worth it."

His look was furious now, but full of despair, too. It made me uneasy. "Wait! Before you go, tell me what it was, at least," I said, trying to be light.

"I shouldn't. It will kill you to know. But I'm sick of trying to protect you and getting slapped in the face. I'm sick of your feeling righteous about not trusting me." He stared a moment, deciding something. The small muscles of his cheek knotted over his clenched jaw.

"What was in the shed, Karl? Please tell me."

"Fine." he said, his voice was low and icy. "You deserve this. *He* was in the shed. I arranged it. Your Isaak."

FIFTY-FOUR

Karl caught me before I fell and helped me
to the couch. But he was still furious.

"Tell me," I whispered, my mouth full of
ashes.

Standing in front of me, Karl seemed very
tall. I reached up to pull at the buttons on
his tunic, but he pushed me away, and every
time he looked at me he winced and recoiled, his eyes cutting away as if the sight
of me scorched them.

"Here? Isaak was here that day?"

"For several days, probably." Karl's voice
was so cold and hard — a low hiss — I
almost didn't recognize it. "My friend —
the one who's stationed near Schiedam — I
went to school with him and I trust him. I
asked a favor from him, an enormous favor.
You have no idea the risk we both took. . . .
Never mind that. His sister is married to a
clerk at Westerbork. She knows I come here
to see you. She told Werner that you'd be

getting a new playground — her husband mentioned he'd seen a work order for this Lebensborn. When I heard that, I had Werner pressure his brother-in-law to alter the work-crew list, to add Isaak's name to it. And to get a message to Isaak, to tell him to find a way to get into the shed. I told Werner that Isaak had been helpful to me when I was in Schiedam, and I wanted to see that he was all right. Do you have any idea how dangerous all of that was? And you didn't go."

I was crying now. "I thought . . . I thought. . . ."

"You thought . . . what? What *did* you think? That I have nothing better to do than set up traps for you? God! The people who risked so much for this."

"I'm sorry," I sobbed. "I didn't know."

"All the times I've come here, have I ever hurt you? Have I ever lied to you, put you at risk?"

"Did he know I was here? Did he expect me?"

"I assume he figured that out, yes. Cyrla, have I ever once done anything except help you?"

"Please stop," I begged. "Please just tell me where he is now. Please bring him here again."

Karl stared at me in disbelief. "Never. Even if I wanted to. For one thing, Werner's brother-in-law was transferred. Three days ago, he suddenly was sent to Amsterdam. There's no way to know if it's just a co-incidence or whether someone got suspicious, and it's too dangerous to try to find out. No matter, there's no way I can have any contact at Westerbork ever again. I wouldn't bother, anyway. You had your chance. You got what you deserve."

Karl turned from me and was at the door before I could get up.

"Wait."

He stood with his hand on the knob. But he waited. I hurried to his side and touched his arm.

"One thing. Please."

He hesitated, opening a small door to me. His arm relaxed under my hand.

"Isaak. Is he all right?"

Karl's face darkened and he bit back whatever he had been about to say. Then he stormed out, slamming the door, leaving me alone with a monstrous guilt.

FIFTY-FIVE

Day after day, my remorse grew, as if it were a living thing. I imagined Isaak in the shed, waiting for me, waiting. Learning I would not come. I had been so close to him; to touching him. Where was he now? But I was stunned to find that when I closed my eyes, it was Karl's face that haunted me — the look he wore when he'd said, "And you weren't worth it."

Finally, after a week, I called him. "I need to talk with you." I held my breath and pictured him standing there with the receiver pressed to his ear, his head bent, rubbing the space between his eyebrows with his middle finger.

After a minute, he said, "All right. Go ahead," and I breathed again.

"No, I need to *see* you. Can you get away?"

Silence.

"Please."

It felt like an hour before he answered. "All right, tonight. Eight o'clock."

"Good. Karl, I'm sorry —"

But he had hung up.

I waited for him in the front hall. When he walked in, I searched his face but couldn't tell anything. "Do you want to take a drive?" he asked. There was nothing in his voice, either. The guard at the front desk looked up.

"I can't leave. It's too late."

Karl looked down the hall toward the parlor.

"No," I said. "It's Tuesday." Before he could ask what that meant, I walked over to the desk. "This is the father. We have some things to talk about, but all the rooms are being used. Could I bring him upstairs?"

The guard looked at his watch and nodded. "Be out by nine," he warned Karl.

In my room, the air tightened to glass. When I spoke, I almost expected it to shatter. "On Tuesday nights, the League of German Maidens holds a session in the dayroom." I was stalling. "Homemaking and patriotism. All the German girls have to attend. The rest of us spend the evening in the parlor — it's our favorite night of the week, so peaceful without them. Except when they're singing."

"I can imagine," Karl said.

I wondered if he could. If he could know how chilling it was to hear those voices singing songs about their superiority, their destiny. But I let it go. I shut the door and leaned back against it. "Karl, I need to apologize. I didn't trust you and I should have. I'm ashamed of myself."

Karl's face still didn't show anything. But he listened.

"You've been nothing but honest and generous to me. More than that — what you did last week, bringing Isaak here . . . oh, God. And such a risk! I ruined it — I don't blame you if you can't forgive me. I just needed to try to apologize."

Karl crossed to the window and lifted the wooden slats. "I was angry," he said after a moment. "But if you're telling me that you trust me now, maybe we can put everything behind us." He turned from the window to look at me, and his face was warmer. "I'd really like it if we could start over. If we could be friends."

I smiled back and took a step toward him, then opened my mouth to say something. But the words didn't come.

"What is it?"

"There's something . . . I've been thinking —" I hesitated. Some things were still difficult to express in German. This would be difficult to express in any lauguage. "Anneke lives inside me, Karl. I've stolen her life. I can't change that, and it affects how things are between us."

"You didn't steal her life. She lost it. And you're only using her name."

I walked over and stood beside him. "No, it's more than her name. I was always so jealous of her, of how easy everything was for her. And now in this place, I'm trying to be her. She was supposed to be here. I didn't come here to keep my baby safe — nothing as heroic as that. I got pregnant so I could step into her life, to keep myself safe. No, to do something even more selfish. And I really am using more than her name."

"How do you mean?"

"Well, in here, I try to become her. I'm quiet. Anneke was chatty. In here, I let her speak for me. And even in that, I'm a fraud. Anneke never had to choose her words carefully, the way I do — she was so pure, she could just say whatever she was thinking. She never had anything to hide. And she was carrying a German baby. I'm not, and that feels too dangerous to even let myself remember. I act like her and I try to think like her. So it feels like she's still here. Like there are two of us living in my skin."

Just then the baby bumped me, as if he'd been listening and didn't like the slight. I laughed, relieved, and pressed my hand over his heel. "All right, there are *three* of us in here."

Karl looked down. His eyes asked if he could touch me. I took his hand and placed it over the baby's foot, still kicking.

"So . . . do you think of him as mine?" Karl asked softly.

"Well, in theory, yes. When I'm downstairs or talking to the other girls, I try to think of myself as carrying a German soldier's baby. But when I'm alone, no. It's so complicated. And when you ask if we can be friends, well, that's *really* complicated with her here with me so strongly. Do you understand?"

Karl took his hand off my belly — reluctantly, I thought. His face looked pained, but for me or for him, I didn't know. "We had a dog at the boatyard once, when I was young. She had puppies and when one of them died, I took it out of the litter. I thought that was a good thing to do. But the dog got upset — she circled the nest, she was frantic, looking for that puppy. My father told me to bring the puppy's body back, so she could understand. I did and she picked it up, carried it outside, and left it under some bushes. Then she came back and she was calm. So he was right."

"I didn't see her buried, Karl, that's true. But I saw her dead." I pressed my hands over my heart and waited while the image washed over me. Karl put his arm around me and pulled me to his side. "I know she's dead," I told him. "I can say it; I cry over it. But still, I keep her alive."

"Maybe you need to bury her."

"Maybe I do. But I don't know how."

"Cyrla, don't you think she'd want us to be friends?"

"Yes, I do. You're right. I know that. She told me that once, in fact — she said I'd like you and trust you. But when I'm trying so hard to be Anneke here, and I see you, sometimes I'm so angry at you. You hurt her, and if she . . ."

Karl released me and I felt strangely shapeless all of a sudden. As if my own skin was no longer enough to hold me together.

"I think about that all the time," he said. "The thing is, I told her what I did to save her from hurt. We weren't suited for each other. Given some time, I think she would have seen that."

"So do I. I think I just needed to tell you all this. I need you to understand what it feels like to me."

"I'm glad you did. And I'm sorry for how hard it must be for you here." He hugged me again and kept his arm around me. In the quiet we heard singing from below. *"Deutschland über Alles."* "This all must be so hard."

"That's the song they end on," I said. "You should go now."

He nodded and picked up his coat from the bed. He didn't leave, though. "You know, I think we should celebrate. We've just declared peace, and that's always something to celebrate."

"It is," I agreed. A knot that had been tightening in my chest for a long time was finally loosening. "It certainly is."

"I can come this weekend. They're setting up some new equipment so I only have paperwork to do. Let me take you out, maybe a film or a meal."

Karl was right — it was peace we had made. But it was more: I had been granted forgiveness. I felt washed in grace. By Saturday morning, when I got ready, it really did feel as though I was getting ready for a celebration. I bathed and dressed in the prettiest things from Erika's gifts. I checked the clock constantly. Finally it was time. I went downstairs and found Karl already there, leaning over the front desk, saying something to the nurse on duty. She smiled at him, rolled her eyes as though he were an exasperating child, then waved him off.

He came over and helped me put my sweater on. "We have eight hours today. It's eleven now, so I don't have to bring you back until dinnertime."

"How did you do that?"

"I charmed her. I told her I didn't come last weekend, so I want to make up for it. I convinced her to look at it as two outings at once. I told her it was a special occasion and I had a surprise for you."

"And do you?"

"I do. But you'll have to wait until we get there. But before we go, I want you to go get something of Anneke's."

"Why?"

"Trust me. Remember, you're going to trust me now."

I went back to my room and looked around. Almost everything I had here was Anneke's. Suddenly I knew what Karl wanted. I picked up the bottle of nail polish and one of her handkerchiefs and slipped them into my pocket.

In the backseat of the car there was a bouquet of red roses and a spade. I showed Karl what I had brought.

"Are you ready?" he asked.

"I am ready," I answered.

We drove out to the sheep farm again and walked in silence along the path we had taken the last time. When we came to the overlook, we stopped. Karl looked to me and I nodded.

"She's really buried in Apeldoorn," I told him. "I'm going to visit when I can."

"Apeldoorn. I'll go there, too, someday."

He dropped the spade into the earth and dug a small hole. I wrapped the bottle of blood-red polish in its lacy shroud, bent down, and placed it in the hole. Then Karl filled it in and laid the roses on top.

"No." I picked them up. "Not with the thorns." One by one, I plucked the petals off and dropped them over the fresh dirt. They fell like little slices of my heart. *This should hurt more,* I thought. I told Anneke the things I would have said to her if I'd known and squeezed the rose stems until I felt the tiny thorns pierce my palm. Karl looked down and pried the stems from my hand and threw them away.

"I was wrong about something," I said. "When you first came here, I told you Anneke wasn't something we shared. But she is."

He took my hand and pressed our palms

together, our fingers laced. We walked back, quiet, until we reached the car.

"I brought a picnic," Karl said. "It's supposed to be beautiful this afternoon. We can do something else, though, if you want. Go into Munich. . . ."

"No. I haven't been on a picnic for so long. It sounds so normal!"

He tossed the spade into the trunk and pulled out a large basket and a blanket and a bag. We walked to the far end of the field, behind the barn, and set them under a huge elm. Apple trees surrounded the field, their blossoms forming soft pink halos around them.

"I'm starving. I have to eat every ten minutes these days." I bent over the picnic basket. "What did you bring?"

There was a distant rumble and I jumped a little. Even after almost two years, I jumped. Karl read my worry. "It's only thunder."

We looked to the sky. Purple thunderheads were piling up, bruising the sky above the mountains. "It'll pass quickly," Karl said. "But let's bring everything inside."

The barn was dark, even with the door open partway, and sweet with the scent of hay and sheep. I smiled in wonder.

"What?"

"I don't know, exactly. I feel so safe here, hidden. I think it's just been a long time since I stood somewhere and thought: Nobody knows where I am."

"I know where you are." Karl took a step toward me, then stopped and looked down at his hands. "I know what you mean, though."

Then he climbed the ladder to the loft and pushed two bales of hay over the edge. He climbed down, took out his pocketknife, and slit them open. "We can pretend we're outside," he said, spreading the hay. He shook the blanket out.

"You said you had a surprise," I reminded him.

"I do. And now's a good time. Turn around."

"You think I'll turn my back on you?" I was feeling playful — another sensation I hadn't had in a very long time.

"Suit yourself." Karl took off his tie and then began to undo the buttons of his uniform tunic. He tossed it aside and bent over the basket. From it he withdrew a navy sweater, bulky with cable stitches; the muscles of his back bunched as he pulled it over his head. Then he turned and spread his arms, looking pleased with himself.

"What? That's your surprise? A sweater?"

"I could be court-martialed for putting on civilian clothes, and that's the reception I get?" Karl sighed and grew serious. "This is the other thing between us. I've seen how you look at me. Or how you *don't* look at me — how you look at my uniform instead. That's all you see, Cyrla. You never see me."

"I see you, Karl. And you wear that uniform."

"Not by choice. So can't you see past it for one day? That's what I want from you: just one day when you're a woman and I'm a man. When you don't have to worry about what Anneke might feel and you don't have to protect yourself from an enemy. Will you do that for just one day?"

"I don't think I can." My throat tightened with a dangerous ache.

"You're leaving in three weeks. We have three weeks. What could it harm?"

"It's wrong."

"Why?"

"I don't know! Because what if —" I wrapped my arms around my belly and looked up at him — "I can't let *this* go. And I don't want to. This baby is Jewish. His father is Jewish, and I owe him something. And you're German."

"Do you really think I'd harm a baby?"

I clasped my hands more firmly around

the baby. "This is all I have now. It's everything. I've done a terrible job of it so far — look at where I am, Karl! I'm trying to make it up to him, to do the best I can right now."

I turned away then. There was another clap of thunder, closer. After a minute I felt him come up behind me, his presence too close to me, and yet I didn't shrink away. The air between us seemed to throb with invisible vibrations. I heard the rain begin, just a hushed rustling.

And then he touched me. Not on the arm, not on the shoulder, not on the back of the neck as I had been expecting. Wanting. Instead he eased his body against my back and placed his hands on my waist. I didn't turn toward him, but I didn't pull away, either. I waited, my breath caught in my throat.

Very slowly, as if giving me time to understand his motions, he stroked his hands down the sides of my hipbones, his fingers following the arc where my body met the rising moon of my child. He bent forward, his face beside mine now, his cheek to my cheek. Gently, he laced his fingers beneath my baby's swell and he lifted. He lifted my burden from me and took it for himself.

I came undone. Sobs of relief shook me.

Karl moved to pull his arms away, as if he was afraid he had upset me, but I held them firm. We stood like that for a long time — me crying and him cradling my burden — and then I turned inside the circle of his arms and found his mouth.

FIFTY-SIX

We kissed. I could not get enough of his hot mouth, his hot tongue. Our mouths were sealed together, sealed, and I had only one clear thought: *If this were a choice, it would be wrong. But this is not a choice.* It was a need, as undeniable as breath, and it grew until I was nothing more than hollowness and shivers, and Karl only muscle and heat.

"Lie down," he said.

And I lay down.

Karl curled himself behind me and leaned over my shoulder to find my hungry mouth. We kissed and he pressed into me and we kissed and he pulled off our clothes and we kissed. He stopped to ask if it was all right to do this — all right for the baby — and I pulled his mouth back to mine and arched back until I found what I needed. We kissed and when he came into me, I cried tears of joy into our completed circle.

And Corrie was wrong: The other one was

not there. Not then.

Afterward, I lay still in the curve of Karl's arm, so still I could feel his pulse against my cheek, listening to the perfect rain. Karl stroked my skin and I felt I had never known touch before, the exquisite miracle of it. He ran his hand down my spine and then over my belly. He found a bump and cupped it, propped himself up to examine it. "An elbow."

"Or a knee. Or a heel. My little gymnast."

"Are you sure that was all right to do? Not dangerous?"

"It's fine. Right up until the last month."

"How do you know?"

"We have a whole library full of books. Prenatal care, birth, child raising. And I have a lot of time on my hands."

He leaned over and kissed my belly. "All right, then. All right."

When the rain had passed, Karl went to the barn door and pushed it open all the way. Sun shafts streamed in; beyond, the meadow gleamed green, washed. Birds had begun to sing again, pouring out their joy after the rain, as if the afternoon was a miracle. I lay back, smiling, and thought they were right.

Karl turned back to me. "Are you hungry?"

"No."

"Do you want to leave? Go somewhere else?"

"No."

"Do you want to take a walk?"

"All right."

We walked slowly and only Karl talked, pointing out trees and wildflowers along the way. I held his hand. It was solid, warm, and sure, and it felt like my only connection to the world. When he dropped it to shake the rain off a branch of apple blossoms for me to smell, I felt suddenly anxious, as though I might burn away like the mist. When we walked back, I held it even tighter.

The ground was still wet, so Karl went back to the car for a canvas to spread under the blanket. Then he set out the picnic: cheese and bread and a tin of anchovies, green olives, dried apricots, walnuts, and something that rattled in a box, which he wouldn't let me open.

"Where did you get all this?"

"I have connections."

He took out two glasses and uncorked a bottle of red wine.

I looked at the label in wonder. "Chianti?"

"I told you — I have connections. And I'm half Italian, you know — what good is a meal without wine?"

"You're half Italian? I didn't know that."

Karl shrugged as if it hadn't been worth mentioning. As if having parents from two different worlds didn't leave a person split down the middle, through the heart. "My mother was from Tuscany. My father met her on a trip to buy olive wood — a special order for a customer. Love at first sight."

"Karl, doesn't it make you feel torn in half? As if you don't belong anywhere?"

He poured the wine. "No. Not at all. Except for being grateful because it means I could never be recruited by the Nazis — I've never even thought about it. Is that how *you* feel?"

I nodded and sipped my wine, feeling its comforting heat rise through me like a blush. "It's different. Imagine if your mother died and your father sent you to Italy to live with her relatives."

"I'd feel terrible. He would never have done that."

I turned away, drank more wine. "Some people are easier to send away, I guess."

Karl put down his glass and took my face in his hands. "That's not what happened. Anneke said you came in '36. When did your mother die?"

"In 1930."

"Well, see? It wasn't because of that. Pilsudski had just died, and there was the new regime. The Nuremberg Laws here . . . well, obviously your father was worried about what was coming. He was right. But think of how hard it must have been."

"Maybe not. Maybe it made things easier for him."

"Easier? To lose his daughter?"

"He never spoke of my mother after she died. He got rid of everything that reminded him of her. Maybe . . . well, I'll never know."

Karl leaned back on his elbows and smiled as if he held a secret. "I think you will know. I think when the baby's born, you'll understand a lot. That's how it's been with my sister and me, after Lina was born. I feel a little like her father, you know. Having Lina has made Erika and me understand our parents."

I looked at him doubtfully, but wanting to believe.

"Really. Wait until the baby is born; think about it then. Right now, you should eat." He rose to his knees and began to set food out for us. He had forgotten silverware, so he tore off chunks of bread and used his pocketknife to open the tins and slice cheese.

"This is one place I *did* feel it, having an Italian mother," Karl said. He shook out olives, glistening in their oil, onto a piece of bread and handed it to me. "When I was young, all my friends wanted to eat with us. Once a year — the last week in August — she made a trip to Italy to the markets. Erika and I always begged to go with her — it was our favorite week of the year. We'd help her buy sardines and great tins of olive oil, braids of garlic, boxes of pine nuts, big jugs of wine. Pancetta — do you know what that is? A cured meat, smoky. Figs and prunes; cheeses. There was a certain flour she needed to make her pasta and an almond paste for her baking. Erika and I would wander through the stalls sampling everything, then my mother would let us get gelato. On the last day, she'd buy four or five crates of plum tomatoes — she couldn't get those at home — and one of lemons, and a huge sack of coffee beans. Then we'd ride home with everything on the train. I can still remember how wonderful our compartment smelled — she insisted that everything had to ride with us."

I eased down on my side, my head propped up by one elbow to eat and listen to Karl. Sometimes when people talked about their mothers, I felt pinched with jealousy, as if they'd stolen their memories at my expense. But not now.

"I think the last time she went was six or seven years ago. You'd be surprised, though, at what she still manages to cook. Like these" — he reached for the box he'd kept away from me and opened it — "amaretti. Almond macaroons."

I took one. It was small and pale gold, like Anneke's favorite *spekulaas*. I put it back in the box. "Maybe later," I said.

I helped Karl put away the food. We broke the rest of the loaf of bread into crumbs and sprinkled them along the stone wall for the birds, then cleaned our fingers in the little pools of rainwater that had collected in the cupped stones. We wandered back to the blanket, drowsy with food and wine and the sudden warmth of the afternoon.

Karl poured the last of the wine into our glasses, then peeled off his sweater and undershirt and stretched out on his stomach. I lay back with my wine, looking up at the drifting clouds. The sun felt wonderful on my face and arms, prickling my skin at first and then melting into the wine's warm flush. I sat up and took off my stockings and then unbuttoned my blouse and untied the little satin ribbons wrapping my slip around me to let the sun fall on the top of my belly. It glowed, the heat of the sun reaching down to meet my baby's heat, the hot engine of his growth. I slid the elastic of my skirt down a little. A little more.

Karl rolled over and looked at me. He smiled and eased the elastic down until my whole belly was basking in the sunshine.

"Do you think she can feel the sun?" he asked.

I lay back with my eyes closed, his fingers caressing my belly lightly. I laid my hand over his, sealing it to me. The sunlight glowed through my lids, dappled red and yellow. "Yes," I decided. "Yes, *he* can."

Karl laid his head lightly over my belly, pretended to listen to something. Then he raised his head to look at me, his face grave. "She says to tell you she's a girl. And you'd better get used to that."

Then he placed his hand back on the top of my belly, warm from the sun, warmer under his hand. He traced the tautness of my swell with gentle fingers, and I kept my eyes closed to feel it better, the loveliness of it. "You look like you've swallowed the moon," he said. "And it's rising inside you."

"I'm as big as the moon." I wove my fingers into his hair. Mine to touch.

"You're as beautiful as the moon." Karl leaned in to me and began to kiss me, his fingertips drifting lower. I felt myself flooded with something hot and bright, like a tide of molten gold. I melted into it. Then he rose and I felt his lips on my skin — he kissed my belly, kissed my baby. I stretched back and offered him more. I was ripe.

He rose to his knees and stroked me with both hands now, slowly and grave with concentration, and my skin was newly born. For the first time I understood that touch was a language, too, and that the things he was saying I had been waiting all my life to hear. He freed my breasts from the satin slip and in the cool air I felt a heat rise between my legs. When he lowered himself to lie over me, his mouth on my mouth, his hands caressing my breasts so softly, I was lost in yearning, I thought I could never want more than this.

And then I did want even more. I began to moan. He lifted my skirt and moved to kneel between my legs. I kept my eyes closed, but I could feel him watching me as he caressed me, asking me something. "Yes," I breathed — whatever it was, the answer was yes. He bent over to lift me and put his lips to me, and I told him things with my secret mouth that I had not known I knew. Then he eased my hips up his thighs until our bodies met, and this time I was softened and I took his hardness like a kiss. *I know you, I know you,* we said with every movement, and the joy of that shook us at the same time.

Karl fell gently beside me, our limbs tangled and loose. He smiled into my dazed eyes. "It's supposed to be like that." He reached over me to brush the torn grass from my fingers and kiss my dry lips closed. "It's supposed to be like that." Then he closed his eyes and rested his head on my shoulder, his hand cupped over my breast in a way that brought me excitement and peace at once.

I turned my head to look through the apple blossoms at the clouds swimming through the impossibly blue sky. I could almost see the green leaves unfurling, they were so eager to burst. And bees! Drifting lines of them, clustering and breaking apart in the pink shell blossoms; drunk on pollen, mad with abundance. My eyes closed and just before I fell asleep, I saw the image of the beekeeper again, covered in bees. How could I ever have thought them dangerous?

I woke up with a dream crouching over me, a cold shadow just out of sight. In the dream there was something I had forgotten, and Isaak had been angry with me about that. As my mind cleared, I recognized his face as the one he'd worn that last night. When he'd found out what had happened to me.

I looked at the man beside me, suddenly a stranger. I pulled away from him and tied my slip around me. Karl woke. He remembered and smiled. I looked away.

"What's wrong?" he asked. He put his hand on my knee, stroking softly. I pushed it away.

He sat up, awake now. "What's wrong, Cyrla?" he asked again.

"I don't know what this is," I whispered at last. "What do we call this?"

"Why do we have to call it anything?"

"I need to know what it is."

Karl nodded as if he had expected this answer. "You and your words. You have to label everything, dissect it into words. I build boats. For me, something just has to work. If it's beautiful and it works, that's more than enough."

"I just want to know — what is it we're doing?"

"I think some things are better unlabeled." He pulled his clothes on as though they were armor against me and we were about to go into battle. "And I wish you'd stop labeling me. When you label me Anneke's boyfriend, you feel you're betraying Anneke. And when you label me a German, you feel you're betraying your family. So you're

465

judging me by *what* I am to you, Cyrla. Not *who* I am."

I couldn't deny it.

"Look, I don't know what this is, either. There are no words for some things. So could we just not ask the question for now?"

"But it happened. I can't ignore it."

Karl looked at me as understanding dawned. When I saw my thoughts reflected in his face, I realized too late how hurtful they were. "Ignore it? Why would you want to ignore it?" He studied me and I wanted to take everything back, start over. But I couldn't. "You're trying to excuse it. As if it's something you feel guilty about. You want me to help you say it was a mistake. It was the wine, it was the day? Well, I don't feel guilty about it. And I don't want to be some mistake you have to rationalize."

"Karl, I just asked what this was."

"Well, then, fine. We can call it love."

"No. It can't be love."

"What do you mean, it can't be? There are rules? Do rules make you feel safe, Cyrla? Because I don't think that's the point."

I gathered my skirt and shoes and dressed also. Somehow, we were indeed in battle. "You have no right. What have you ever lost?"

"Enough, Cyrla. Maybe not as much as you. But enough. I think the question is what have you ever gained? Do your rules keep you safe?" He stood. "It's late," he said, without looking at his watch. "I'll take you back."

I glanced at the sky. It couldn't be much past five. But I didn't argue.

Karl gathered the things we had brought and packed them in the car. I sat beneath the elm and watched him erase all traces of what had happened from the barn and the meadow. I locked my arms around my knees.

We rode the whole way in cold silence. Still when the home came into view, I didn't want to be there. It seemed wrong that the tall granite wall looked the same, now that the world it was keeping out was so different.

Karl pulled the car to the curb across from the gates and turned the engine off. He took the keys out of the ignition and sat without moving in the new quiet, staring down at them in his palm. Not looking at me. "I lost a child. Do you ever think about that?"

I couldn't answer, but I felt shame rise in my cheeks.

"I won't come anymore. Until it's time to take you out. If that's what you want."

I looked away then, too. "Fine," I lied.

I didn't wait for him to open my door — I just got out and crossed the street without looking back. I heard the car engine start.

And then I ran back to him.

FIFTY-SEVEN

That last week of April and the first week of May, Karl came every time he could steal away for a few hours. I didn't know what I needed so much — that with him I didn't have to pretend to be someone else, that it was the only time I felt safe, or that only when his fingers touched my skin was it alive — but I needed it fiercely. I needed *him* fiercely and I didn't care how naked my desire was: His shoulders were raked raw with my nail marks, and once I drew blood from his lip when I kissed him. Each time, we drove to the abandoned farm and wrapped ourselves in the hay and blankets and came together. Only after that would Karl talk about what was to happen in mid-May, as if he could only think about my absence after he'd reassured himself of my presence.

Each time, the conversation began the same way: "Cyrla, have you given any thought to —"

Each time, I told him I wasn't going to change my mind. Karl would sigh and then go over whatever new piece of information he had brought — a map, a list of the border stations, train schedules. His hands never left my body while we talked. He made me practice the things I might say if I were questioned. Over and over he made me promise that if I were caught, I would reach him, even if it meant naming him as my accomplice. We worked out a code for the letter I would write to Erika once I reached Leona in Amsterdam. Each time we talked about the plan, I became more uneasy.

We met for the last time on the second Saturday in May — eight days later, on the seventeenth, we would leave. We lay down on the blanket and held each other — we didn't make love and we didn't talk. I understood he was saying good-bye. After a long while, he began the ritual: "Cyrla, I still think you should —"

I put my finger to his lips. "No more. Tell me something unrelated. Tell me something wonderful."

Karl hesitated, looking worried. Then he nodded and lay back and I curled myself over his chest. With his free hand, he worked his wallet out and pulled a photo from it.

470

"My boat."

"The one you built? It's beautiful."

"*She's* beautiful," he corrected me. He took the photograph back and gazed at it, and his look was in fact that of a man gazing at a woman. "A channel cutter, ten meters. And she's as beautiful to sail as she is to look at."

"You sound like you're in love with her."

Karl smiled. "I guess I am. When you're sailing the perfect boat on the perfect sea, it's like making love. All the pieces fit, and you can't tell where the boat ends and the water begins."

"Where do you keep her?"

"The Elbe. There's a place where the river makes a hairpin turn. Hills sliding down from the east and flatlands on the west shore. The current's so strong at the corner, it's scoured a pool at least five fathoms deep. She's there at the bottom of that pool."

"What? It sank?"

Karl grinned. "Like a rock. Imagine that: I opened the seacock and she went down."

I raised myself up to look at him. "You sank your boat on purpose?"

" 'Scuttled' is the term. Lie back down with me."

I eased myself back into the curve of his

arm, my head over his heart. "But you love that boat."

"Exactly. I love that boat. More than I love having her. So I couldn't risk the Nazis finding her. Taking her, using her. Ruining her."

"You sank it yourself."

"Yes. The day before, I stripped her. I'd already taken the rig down — that's the mast and the boom and the running rigging — and buried it. Then I timed the slack tide and rowed out with a pair of sweeps. I made everything ready, opened the seacock, and swam in to shore. I sat there on the bank in the dark with a bottle of wine and watched her go down. It took an hour."

"That must have been awful."

"Yes and no. It felt like I was cutting off my own leg. But there was a sense of satisfaction about what I'd prevented. And it was beautiful in its way. I know that sounds strange, but I sat there watching and it was beautiful. So dark — there was no moon — and so quiet. She went down silently, until the very end."

"And then?"

"And then she just sighed and went under. There was no trace. I love that about water — it's so mysterious. It's transparent, but all we can see is the surface. The Nazis could cruise over that pool a thousand times and never suspect."

"It must have just about killed you to lose her."

"But I haven't lost her. Just hidden her for a while."

I sat up again. "What do you mean?"

"When it's over, I'll raise her."

"You can do that?"

Karl pulled me back down and wrapped both his arms around me. Motes of dust drifted in the bars of sunlight slanting down through the barn siding. I listened to the beat of his heart, thinking, *I am happy.* Thinking how unusual that felt. How good. Thinking that it was the last time.

"Someday this will be over. No matter how it ends, it will end. As soon as it's safe, I'll get a couple of friends to help me. We'll use a barge with a crane. I'll dive down and find her — I know exactly where. Exactly. I'll hook two sets of straps around her hull, fore and aft, and then we'll raise her."

I found Karl's hand and wove my fingers through his. "And then what? Tell me everything." Don't let this time end.

"Well, dirt will be the main problem. Everything will be covered in sediment. But I dogged the hatches and screwed the companionway shut, so the interior won't be too bad. She'll need a complete scrubbing after we haul her out, but that's just cosmetic. After the cleaning, I'll open everything up. She'll have to dry for a while — under a tarp or indoors, no direct sunlight. It might take six months to do it right, so there isn't too much warping. Then I'll refinish her: sand her down, varnish and repaint."

"And then you can sail her again?" I squeezed Karl's hand and rubbed my thumb down the warm, smooth shaft of his wrist.

"Well, I'll need to replace the fastenings, rebuild the engine, and put it back in. I soaked it in oil and wrapped it in canvas before I buried it, so it should be all right. Then I'll have to put up the rig again. The whole thing could take a year. But yes, then I'll sail her again."

I pulled my head back so I could see his face. "And where will you go? When the war is over, where will you go in this boat?"

"Oh, away from here. Away from anyplace gray and from any mark of war. To an island, maybe. Someplace warm and green. Where will *you* go, Cyrla?"

"Home," I said immediately.

"Where's that?" Karl asked it gently, as if he knew what wounds his question would tear open.

"I don't know," I whispered. "I don't

know. I don't know!" I began to cry.

Karl pulled me to him and held me tight while my grief flooded through. Then he raised himself up to wipe the tears from my face and stroke my hair.

"Sometimes I dream I'm walking through a field of sunflowers," I told him. "And they are always all facing away from me."

"You'll find a home. You'll make a home with your baby," he said. "It's going to be all right."

But it wasn't going to be all right. And I knew why. I had known it all along, but I hadn't been able to face it. And now I needed to tell Karl, but I couldn't make the words come out. Instead, I told him it was time to leave.

We drove in silence, Karl sliding sideways glances at me as if he knew I was struggling. The words built up. We turned a corner and the tower to the home came into view. I pointed to the side of the road — my eyes filling up and my throat sore. Karl pulled over.

"Why did you tell me about your boat?" I asked him.

"Why? What do you mean?"

"Never mind." I pressed my fists to my eyes and steadied my breathing. Then I looked back at him. "I've changed my mind."

Karl looked at his watch and then tipped his wrist to me. "We can't stay out much longer."

"No. I mean" — it became hard to take a breath, as if something had been cut from my heart and the pain left no room for air — "Karl, promise you'll take care of him for me! You'll be there when he's born — I'll need to be able to reach you when it's time — and if anything's wrong, or if . . . you'll take him, you'll keep him safe. Promise me."

"Cyrla, are you saying —"

"And I have to meet your sister. Can you take me to her? Please, I need to talk to her."

"Of course, of course. And you can see Lina, too. This is the right thing. You know I'll make sure nothing happens. And we'll get him back to you soon. You just find a safe place."

"And you'll hold him. And Erika will hold him. And when he cries —"

"Cyrla, calm down. It'll be all right." Karl pried my hand from his sleeve and held it. "We'll take care of him for you."

But I couldn't calm down. I cried harder, as if I could feel it already, my baby being pulled from my arms. "And photographs.

You have to take photographs for me. And you have to show him pictures of me so he knows I'm his mother."

Karl squeezed my hand. "Shhhh. It's going to be fine. We'll send pictures — we can do that, you know, because now you won't need to hide. Have you thought about that? You'll be safe in Holland now, with good papers."

"And his name. I'll tell you what to name him —"

"Cyrla, stop." Karl's voice was firm, but he was smiling. He wiped the tears from my face. "We have a month now. No, you're staying. So five weeks, right? Maybe six."

At first I was puzzled. Then I understood. And finally I relaxed. "We have time."

"But not now," Karl said. "I'll come back as soon as I can and we'll talk about all of it. But you have to go in now." He started the engine and we drove up to the entrance. On the front steps, I kissed him. For a long time.

And I was struck with something: Isaak had never kissed me. I had kissed him once, on my back step, and then again that first time, on the roof. But in all the times we'd lain together, he had never found my lips and opened himself to me.

Inside, everything looked different to me.

The walls, the guards, even Frau Klaus looked protective, not threatening. Walking down the hallway, I had a sudden urge to see Neve or Leona. But not Eva.

I stopped a few steps from our room. I didn't trust Eva and since she'd come, I'd trained myself to pull Anneke's skin more firmly around me before entering her presence. It was easier now — this afternoon I really *was* a girl with a German lover fathering my child. Then I walked to the doorway, quietly as we all did — pregnant girls needed to nap.

The door was open. Inside, I saw Eva asleep, one arm flung out, the other draped over a breast. Her swelling belly was turned to the door, pulling at her nightgown, and one leg, naked almost to the hip, curled up to meet it. Provocative even in sleep.

I crept through the door without a sound, but inside I nearly screamed: In the shadows at the foot of Eva's bed stood a Little Brown Sister. She jumped and ran from the room, but not before I'd seen the ache in her glazed eyes, devouring Eva, drowning with longing.

I passed her in the hall a few days later. I wanted to tell her I knew better than anyone that we want whom we want and it's not a choice. I wanted to tell her I was the last person who would judge her. But she turned her head in shame and hurried away.

I should have stopped her. I should have told her what a waste shame was.

FIFTY-EIGHT

Klaas was gone one day, just like that. I went down to the orphanage and he wasn't there. I grabbed a Little Brown Sister hard, and she looked at me alarmed. "He was adopted. Yesterday," she said and shook me away. As if that were all, as if the person in this place I had loved the most hadn't just been torn from safety into a world where anything could happen to him. There was nothing I could do about it, though. I went to my room and made my last entry into the journal I'd begun to keep for Leona:

Everything is funny to him: He had the hiccups yesterday and he laughed all the way through! When I put a bootie over my hand and wave it at him, he becomes hysterical. He makes me do this a hundred times, and each time he finds it funnier. And his face, when he sleeps . . . he is more beautiful than I can describe.

They will love him. It would be impossible not to *love* him.

With my afternoons now empty, I began to think about my baby's birth in earnest. It was as if before, when I hadn't known where I would give birth, I hadn't been able to imagine it. Now it was all I was able to see when I closed my eyes.

I read everything I could get my hands on and bothered Sister Ilse incessantly. She never grew impatient, only answered my fears with reassuring information: Only a few times since she'd come here had a mother died, and in most of those cases the mother's health had been complicated by previous illness. No, a forceps delivery wasn't likely to do permanent damage. Yes, if it was necessary, the doctors were prepared to perform a cesarean delivery.

"What about Sofie?" I asked her. I hadn't seen it, but the girls on the first floor had come upon Sofie wedged in her doorway, screaming into a towel she'd stuffed between her jaws. They'd pulled her out and found the head of her baby mashed between her thighs.

"She waited too long. She was afraid of the doctors. You won't be afraid of the doctors, will you?"

"What about Sigi?"

"A breech at the end. We usually catch that. And they're both fine!"

What about . . . ? What if . . . ?

"Women have been doing this for thousands of years, Anneke," she would always comfort me. "You're strong. You'll do fine."

One day while I was visiting with Ilse in the nursery, rolling booties into pairs while she measured out doses of medicine, she asked me if I'd thought about staying for a while after the birth. "It's so good for the baby. Even a few weeks of nursing is such a benefit."

The idea made me anxious, but I'd been wondering about it myself. Allowing it to seep in. Maybe. I would talk to Karl about it.

"And forgive me if this is none of my business, Anneke," she said. "But I've seen you with the father . . . why are you in such a hurry to leave? Is he married?"

Before I could come up with an answer, Ilse dropped the measuring spoon and jumped up from the table. She flew to the window.

"What is it?"

Ilse dug her fingertips into the mullions. An official wagon, a guard in a black uniform standing by its open rear door, was parked in the delivery ward's entrance.

"The soldiers? What's wrong, Ilse?"

"That's not the Wehrmacht, Anneke, that's the Gestapo," she whispered, her voice tense. "They've come for someone." She ran to the next window and twisted her head to see more. Her face drained. "They're inside. They're here."

"Are you . . . what should we do?"

She went back to the table and gripped the edge, her head down. Then she looked up at me. "You should go. You're not really supposed to be here." She shook her head and fell into the chair. "No, stay. They don't know those rules. Just go back to what we were doing."

I sat across from her and picked up a pair of booties. If they've come to this wing, I told myself, they're not looking for me. I wondered what Ilse was telling herself. I'd never seen her so disturbed.

She sat rigid, her back to the door, clenching a beaker so hard I worried it might shatter. "Can you see them?" she asked.

I risked a quick glance through the door to the nurses' station. "Yes. They're at the desk. No, they're moving away. Frau Klaus is getting up."

"Are they coming this way?"

"I can't tell. They're talking. No, they're

483

leaving. They're heading down the west corridor."

"The west corridor? To the nurses' quarters?"

She didn't wait for my answer, but jumped up and ran back to the windows.

They were out in a minute. Two men, dragging a small older woman. A third followed with Frau Klaus.

Ilse's face crumpled. "No," she breathed. "Solvig. No!"

The men pulled the little nurse along roughly as though she were fighting them. She wasn't — Sister Solvig was probably sixty years old, and often I'd heard her talk about the arthritis in her hips — she was only crying hard and trying to clutch a sweater around her shoulders.

"What's she done, Ilse?"

Ilse's eyes never left the woman, and she cringed every time the men jerked her along. "Nothing. She did nothing. What have any of us done?"

"But why are they taking her?"

"Her husband's Jewish," she whispered. "They've been hiding it." Ilse's eyes filled with tears, but then suddenly widened in terror. "No!" she cried. Her hands pressed against the windowpane as if she could stop what was happening.

We watched in horror as Sister Solvig slipped free from one policeman's grip and strained to pull away. The officer on her other side yanked the arm he held and spun her back. At the same instant, the guard at the wagon's door raised the dark wooden butt of his rifle and drove it into her temple. She dropped and my heart pitched down with her. Just before her head hit the gravel, the first policeman reared back and kicked her with his hobnailed boot, splitting her face open from eye to jaw in a shower of blood. Ilse and I gasped at the same time, our hands flying to our cheeks as if we felt the sickening blow outselves.

The men picked up Sister Solvig's limp body as if it were a bag of onions, carried it to the wagon with one foot dragging along the walk, and then heaved it into the back. And then they were gone — taking with them the hope that my baby and I would be safe in this place.

Ilse stiffened. I grabbed her arm, but she wrenched away from me. All I could do was watch from the window as she stormed down the walk to the spot where the men had attacked the little nurse. She bent and picked up a shoe, pressed it to her chest. I could see the hatred in her eyes.

Still at the entryway, Frau Klaus was

watching her, too.

The next time Karl came, he had only an hour. We went outside to the gardens, which had burst into purple bloom with tulips, lavender, and lilacs. The patios were full — dozens of girls chatted or read on lounge chairs, babies napped in prams lined up against the wall, heedless of the swastika banners ruffling in the breeze above them. In the east garden, Dr. Ebner was leading a tour of uniformed men.

Karl and I chose a bench as far away from the others as possible. I ached to lie skin to skin with him — how greedy I'd become. Instead, I had to content myself with the press of his knee against mine, the warm strength of his hand on my back, as I began to tell him the things I'd been worrying about.

"You must take him the first day. The day he's born, do you hear me?"

"I know. We've already discussed this."

"It's important. Get him out of here and don't bring him back. Not for more formula, not for a checkup."

"What's wrong?"

I started to tell him, but I couldn't put the image of what had happened to Sister Solvig near any thought of my baby. "It's

486

just not a safe place for him," I said.

"It will be fine, I promise. Nobody will be suspicious — there's no reason. You can stop worrying, all right?"

I relaxed a little then. "All right. But there's more. I have so much to tell you. In the beginning, babies shouldn't be in the sun. Your mother can take him outside when she brings Lina out — is there a park they go to? — but keep him covered in a pram. Later in the summer, she can put a hat on him."

"On her."

"What? Oh, all right. She can put a hat on *her.* Just no direct sun. And where will he sleep at night? Will Erika be able to hear him? Her? And remember, he'll be able to roll over by three months, so she should never leave him alone —"

"Maybe you should write all this down. I'll give the list to Erika."

Something in his voice alerted me. "What is it?"

Karl looked sad, but relieved also, as though he'd been anxious to tell me something but hadn't known how to begin. "It won't change anything, and I don't want you to worry," he started. Immediately I pulled back and braced for the blow.

"I'm being transferred." He took my

hands. "It's all right. It won't be until after the baby is here, I promise. Not until August or maybe September."

"Where?" My voice was hard and tight. I pulled my hands from his and held them in a fist on my lap.

"Peenemunde. It's on the coast."

"How far away is it?"

"Five hours."

"But —"

"No, don't worry. Erika and I have already talked about it. If it seems I'll be there for a while, and if it feels right, they'll move closer. We'll do what's best."

"And if they don't move? Will you be able to visit?"

"I'm sorry, I don't know any more than that. I'll know more when I get back. I'm going there Monday."

"But you said —"

"It's just for a week. Just to prepare. You're not due for a month."

"But —"

Karl stood up. "I have to go. Walk me to the car."

At the car, he kissed me then pulled me close. "Don't worry about this. It won't change anything."

"Karl, what is it you do?"

He opened the car door and got in. "I'll

be back at the end of the week. I'll see you then. Don't worry about this."

But of course I did. And my heart plunged when he came back at the end of the week — something about him reminded me of Anneke when she'd returned from her examination. "What's wrong?" I asked.

"How have you been? The baby?"

He sounded unconcerned, but he wouldn't look at me.

"We're fine. Look at me — I'm an elephant. But we're fine. Is something wrong?"

"I don't have much time today. I've borrowed a camera."

"A camera?"

"You said you wanted a photograph for the baby to see. You're due in three weeks. We should take one now. It's in the car, I'll go get it."

"No, no pictures. It's a rule — no pictures of the mothers in here. But Karl, tell me what happened when you went away. What's going on?"

"Fine. Let's take a drive. We'll stop somewhere and take a photograph."

For a second, I wondered if he'd been drinking. But then I dismissed it — his eyes were old, but not dull, and he hesitated before he spoke, but his words weren't slurred.

We left, and in the car I was quiet and a little afraid. He took the road to our farm and I felt relieved — we would talk in the barn. He always relaxed in there. But when we got there, he didn't want to go inside.

"It's so hot. I know a stream," he said. He took the camera from the backseat and set off. I followed him, watching carefully. He stopped after a few paces to unbutton his tunic, and then he threw it to the ground. I grew very worried then.

Karl spoke only once as we walked. "It wasn't always this quiet," he said, almost apologetically.

"What do you mean?"

"Even the birds know to be quiet."

I slipped my hand into his and that seemed to calm him.

"No one talks anymore," he said. "In the whole country, no one can talk. We're too afraid."

"*We're* talking," I said gently.

"Yes. I can talk to you. But you're the only one."

"What about Erika?"

"I could, but we don't. For one thing, it's safe only if we know her neighbors in the next flat are all at work. But even then we don't, because it upsets my mother."

"Why don't you talk to me now, then?" I said. "Tell me what happened last week. You're starting to scare me."

Karl shook his head. He pointed. "The stream's just ahead. Listen, you can hear it. It's still talking, anyway."

The stream rushed swollen and fast over rocks and the roots of the pines and birches that overhung its banks. Almost singing. Karl took off his boots and his socks and rolled up his trousers. He stepped in and held his hand out for me. I took off my shoes and stockings and joined him. He climbed onto a wide, flat rock and I sat down on one a few meters away. Still I waited, observing him, as I dipped my feet into the clear water.

Karl looked over at me and smiled. "You look like a girl," he said. "You look very young. Maybe twelve."

I leaned back and patted my huge belly. "Quite a reputation I'd have."

He took a packet of cigarettes and shook one out, then lit it. He inhaled deeply and then took the cigarette from his mouth and stared at it, as if he couldn't remember how it had come to be there. He tossed it into the bubbling water, and we watched it dance for a moment in an eddy, then disappear.

"I saw things."

I looked up at Karl and saw his face wrenched in despair, his teeth clenched, his palms pressed to his forehead as if trying to crush an image, his arms trembling. I jumped up and splashed across to him, wrapping my arms around him. He buried his face in my chest, then pulled away and clawed at the buttons of my blouse, ripped aside my slip, and pressed his head between my breasts, shaking.

"I saw things."

FIFTY-NINE

I stood there in the stream with Karl's head on my chest, the cold snowmelt rushing around my shins and his hot tears soaking my skin. Finally, he pushed me away and turned to look across to the meadow, to where the yellow wildflowers were spattered like gold coins. I tried to put my arm around his shoulder but he shook his head. He wiped his eyes and swallowed, then he began to talk.

"Prisoners. From the camp there. Hundreds. They all looked the same, with their gray skin, their shaved skulls, their gray uniforms. I couldn't tell one from another; I didn't even know if they were men or women. They were skeletons."

He took another moment. "I was walking along an assembly line, being given the tour. A corporal was telling me about a new paint they were trying that would resist higher temperatures. Then he shot a man."

Karl folded over, his fists pressed to the sides of his head, as if he heard the gunshot again. I waited, my dread building.

At last he straightened.

"He hardly even looked. The man was so close, he didn't have to aim. He was talking to me, he was explaining about the paint — how it had to be applied — and then he glanced over at this skeleton working beside us and a look came over his face. It said, *oh, what an irritation,* and then he pulled out a pistol and —"

"Don't," I whispered.

Karl raised his hands as if to keep me back. They were shaking. "No. I have to tell this." He drew a ragged breath and this time the words poured out. "He pulled out a pistol and he didn't look, he just shot a hole through this man's head. Then he turned. He looked at the man next to the fallen one — he had stopped working. He was covered in blood. Brains, bone. And he shot him, too. Through the chest. Then he went on talking to me as if nothing had happened. 'Of course, it's a lot more expensive than the old paint.' That's what he said."

"What did you do?" I asked, even as I felt my heart shrink back, numb, as if my ribs were sticks of ice.

"Nothing. I did nothing. A cart drew up

with bodies piled on it. They heaved the two dead men onto it and took them away. The corporal raised his hand and stuck two fingers into the air. He was calling for two replacements. I looked away. The corporal handed me off to the man at the next station. I let him shake my hand." Karl raised his hand and looked at it as if it had betrayed him.

I saw Isaak's face. I saw him standing in a prisoner's uniform. I saw him fall. "Where were they from? The prisoners?"

Karl ignored me. But then I realized I hadn't asked it aloud.

"There must have been a hundred people who saw what happened. None of them raised an eyebrow. So now I know it's all true. All of it."

There was so much despair in his eyes. My arms tried to reach for him again, but it was only half a gesture; I couldn't touch him. He pushed them down anyway, as if he didn't deserve the comfort I couldn't give him. He began to talk again, his voice flat.

"When I was still at the boatyard, in '39, there were rumors. About the camps, about things that might happen there. But nothing . . . well, it was difficult to get information, and no one knew anything. Then in

'40, when I went into the service, it all stopped."

"What?"

"Everything. Rumors, information, talking. We had war news, but it was only what they wanted us to know. I was relieved. It was so much easier. I had nothing to struggle with except the ship I was repairing — broken metal and wood. We had no consciences to struggle with. We all felt that way, I think. Do you understand that? How it could be easier to not see?"

I knew that too well. *You can't walk around blind just because you don't want to see.*

"And do you know how much of a coward that makes me? All of us? We were all like that — cowards." He swallowed and looked at me, asking me for something. But I had nothing to give him.

"It was uncomfortable being in another country, seeing the people's faces when I'd walk around in my uniform. I knew they hated us for being there. But that was all. And with Anneke — well, if she could see past my uniform, then I could pretend it wasn't very important. And you know how Anneke was."

I knew that, too — how Anneke's brightness could burn away any clouds. How appealing that was.

"And then when I came to Munich — the new job — it was even easier. I hardly ever have to face anything here."

"Karl, what is it you do?"

"Mostly I build models. Of rockets. I'm part of a team: We're given designs and we make models of rockets out of wood. You should hear us talk: about how it will revolutionize travel someday, the good we're doing. But I can't pretend anymore. We're helping to build weapons that will kill thousands of people. And I knew it all along. The only thing I didn't know was how we're murdering people just to make those weapons."

Karl stopped and looked at me for the first time. And he saw. "Oh, God. Cyrla, I'm sorry. Isaak . . . I'm sorry, I didn't think."

As soon as I saw it written on his face, I couldn't bear it. "No. No. He's at Westerbork. Remember? That's where he is now. He's all right. And my father is in Lodz. My family is safe in Lodz."

Karl took me and held me hard to him against the rough rock. I let him. I needed him to. We clung together in the sound and the cold of the water.

At last he pulled away. "I don't know what to do." His face was filled with anguish. "If I ever speak about this, I'll be shot immediately. But we are making God angry. We are making God so angry, Cyrla. What's the point in staying alive?"

"They won't shoot you. You're valuable."

"Everyone's more valuable as a warning. They'd gladly shoot me to keep a hundred others in line. All the time now, I think: I should refuse to serve. At least my conscience would be clear. But even if I were heroic enough, I couldn't risk what they'd do to Erika and the baby, and my mother. For something like that, they'd be sent to a camp. Maybe worse. And I can't desert for the same reason."

Karl read my mind. "No. I gave Erika my word, and now I'm giving it to you."

"There's a woman who works at the home," I said. And then I told Karl about Sister Ilse, how she'd found something she could do, a way to live with her compromise.

"Does she think it makes everything all right? Does she sleep at night?"

"It's the best she can do."

Karl leaned over and cupped a hand in the stream and watched the water flow around his fingers. "She's lying to herself. She's telling herself it's some sort of atonement . . . well, I wish I could do that. It won't work, though. At night, in the dark, it doesn't work."

I thought of Ilse running out to the walk, her hatred so naked, and I realized something terrible. At night, in the dark, it didn't work for her. And she didn't care anymore what happened to her.

"Karl, promise me," I said. I pulled him around to face me. And then I didn't know what I could ask him to promise. "What you're doing, taking my baby . . . it's such a good thing."

Karl looked out over the clearing beside us. He didn't believe me.

"*I'm* the coward, Karl — running home to be safe. Leaving him."

"No. What you're doing takes courage."

I sat on the mossy rock beside him and pulled my feet up. But I leaned back, away from him. It was my turn to avoid the mirror of his face. "Maybe not. Maybe it's a family trait — abandoning children."

I needed to tell him then. The list of people who had sent me away under the ruse of keeping me safe: my mother, when she knew she was dying . . . "Go to school! Go now." My father, my aunt and uncle. Anneke and Isaak. Everyone I'd ever tried to love. "And it's further back than that. It's all through my family, on both sides."

I told him about my grandmother, how she cut my mother out of her life for marrying my father, how she pretended I didn't exist. "And my father's family, too. They were polite to me, but I didn't pass through the birth canal of a Jewish woman. I wasn't part of their family." A memory of walking to school. My grandparents lived on the way; I'd imagine them behind the windows, watching me walk by, scowling at my blond hair, angry at my father for having chosen wrong.

I sat up again and rested my head against Karl's shoulder, and pulled his arm around my belly. "This isn't what I want. I want to give my baby a big family that welcomes him from all sides. I want him to feel that they'll never let him go. But I can't even give him a mother."

"You could," Karl said.

I pulled back to search his face.

"Marry me. I can keep you safe, too, then."

I looked away. It took an eternity to form the right word. It was an anvil, the heaviest I'd ever pulled from my throat. "No," I finally said. *Because I can't keep you safe. And because I can't bear to imagine your skull smashed by the dark wood of a rifle butt. I can't bear to imagine Erika's face split open from jaw to mouth in a spray of blood. Or your mother's body dragged and tossed into the*

500

back of a wagon.

"Don't ask me why," I told him. "Just keep him safe for me. Give him a family until I can."

Karl sighed and looked out over the stream. Then he pulled me to him and kissed the top of my head. "All right. *You're* his family, though. We'll keep him for a little while, but you'll raise him."

I tried to picture it — raising a child. Not just caring for him, but making decisions about his upbringing.

Karl must have been reading my thoughts. "Would you raise him as a Jew?"

"Yes. If I could. I'd like to study, too. That seems right."

"Because it would balance things out?"

"Yes. I've been hiding and lying too long. But also because . . . Karl, Isaak will want that. You know he will want to raise this child, too."

Karl straightened and pulled his arm from me. He lit a cigarette and leaned forward, kicking at the water. "You're right," he said, after a moment. "Isaak. Of course." His face was wreathed in smoke so I couldn't see his expression. "I don't want to talk anymore." He slid off the rock and offered his hand to me. "What I want to do is take your picture. I want something good to remember."

I didn't want to talk anymore, either. Karl took pictures of me — sitting in the meadow, standing beside a tree, and back by the river. He seemed better, but the haunted look never left his face completely. I wondered if it ever would.

"Karl," I reminded him at last. "You said you didn't have much time today."

He looked at his watch. "I was due back an hour ago."

"Then let's go."

"Let's not. Maybe this is my solution. Maybe being late is exactly the right infraction — not so bad they'll hang me, but serious enough that they'll throw me in prison for the rest of the war."

"I don't think that's funny. Let's go back."

"In a while. I'm not in a hurry."

He packed up the camera, and we began to walk back. We stopped several times — to investigate a fox den, to look for some peach trees his friend had told him about, to listen to some blackbirds. To kiss. It seemed he wanted to forget the things we had talked about.

"Will you recite one of your poems to me?" Karl asked as we were walking by the barn to the car.

I suddenly wanted to. But not here, not now. "Not today," I said at last.

"All right. But will you at least tell me how you write them?"

I thought for a moment. I had never asked myself that question. "Sometimes the first line just comes to me. It's such a wild thing — almost dangerous — that I need to write the rest of it to control it. It feels like something's running away from me, and I have to write it down to corral it. That probably sounds crazy."

"No. Wanting to control something sounds like the most sensible thing in the world." He stepped off the path to pick up his tunic. He threw it over his shoulder without even brushing it off — this new carelessness frightened me. We walked to the car, to the end of our time together, and I realized something else. I loved him. That frightened me more.

At the car, we held each other tight. Then he pulled away. I was afraid he was going to say it was our last time. I didn't want to hear that again. But he surprised me. "I hate that face you make."

"What face?"

"The one you always make after I kiss you or hold you. As if you regret it. As if you feel guilty about it."

I touched Karl's cheek. "I can't help it. Sometimes I feel as if I'm stealing something from Anneke."

"What . . . me? You can't steal something she never had."

"No, but she wanted you. I guess that's what makes me feel bad. If she were alive, we wouldn't be here. And besides, she'd never have done anything like this to me."

"What do you mean?"

"Well, if she were alive, I don't think she'd ever have been with Isaak. Even if Isaak and I weren't together."

Something flickered across Karl's face for an instant. He covered it, but I'd seen surprise, worry. Something.

"What is it?" I asked him. "What's the matter?"

"Nothing. We should go."

And then I knew. "Anneke and Isaak?" I fell back against the car. Every fiber of my body resisted the thought, and yet everything I knew about Anneke and Isaak told me it was true. It explained so much. "Karl, look at me. Anneke and Isaak?"

Karl winced as if it caused him physical pain to answer.

"And you knew?"

"She told me. When it happened, she started to tell you about it. She said you were so close, she thought you'd be happy. She started to tell you she was seeing Isaak, but something you said made her realize you had a crush on him."

"A crush?"

"I think you were about sixteen. They were young, too. She said it had been silly and hadn't meant anything, and she ended it."

It had meant something to Isaak, though.

"Are you all right, Cyrla?"

I felt as if I'd been kicked. But also somehow as if I'd been waiting to know this. I couldn't find the words. I held up my hands the way Karl had done once, turning them to interlock my fingers.

"The pieces fit?"

I nodded again. There was a symmetry to it that felt right. Cruel but right.

"Anneke loved you so much. She said she always felt terrible about it."

An ache to see her closed like a fist around my chest. I'd tell her not to feel terrible. She didn't take anything from me, and she was right about Isaak. He always reminded me of my father, and I saw now that I'd gotten that confused with love. I felt a lump constrict my throat. I raised my palms to Karl and then got into the car. I needed to go back. To be alone.

When we pulled into the drive, Karl put his hand over mine. "I'm sorry."

"No. I just don't want to talk about it now. Maybe next time."

"Cyrla, things are different now. I might not be able to get away again." He saw the panic rise in my face, and he squeezed my hand. "No, whatever happens, I'll be there when the baby's born. Everything's going to be all right."

I suddenly didn't want to get out of the car. Or couldn't. "Everything's not going to be all right. I'm so afraid. I'm afraid for you now, I'm afraid for the baby —"

"Nothing's going to change. I promise you that. I'm not going to do anything. And you're not going to worry about any of this."

"I'm going to worry about all of it!"

"No, you won't. You're braver than that. I know you."

I wasn't brave. I didn't even have the courage to tell Karl what I was really afraid of. And Karl couldn't know me — I didn't even know myself anymore. Where was the person who swore she'd never ask love to follow rules? Who called Isaak a coward for not daring to love anyone? Who told her uncle love is the opposite of shame?

I knew a trick for when I was afraid. But I didn't need it anymore.

"Karl." My voice was steady. "I love you."

Sixty

On the first of June, I awoke late — Eva had already gone down to breakfast — and I lay in bed feeling a growing sense of restlessness. I hurried out of bed, seized by a sudden urge to clean everything, pack, prepare. I dragged my suitcase from under the bed and flung open the doors of the wardrobe. The old maternity clothes could stay, and Erika didn't want hers back. But I'd need clothes for after — I dug out the things of Anneke's that my aunt had packed so long ago. I held up the pearl-gray trousers — even with the seams let out, the waist seemed impossibly small. The thought of fitting into normal clothes again made me grin. I dumped all of Anneke's clothes onto the bed beside the suitcase and then looked in my bureau: In the bottom drawer were a few things from before. Everything on top of the bureau I would leave until the last . . . but the velvet bag! I couldn't risk anyone finding it after I'd gone into labor.

I eased myself to the floor and reached under the wardrobe — it was difficult with my huge belly in the way. I found the bag and tore the tape off, grunting. I tossed it onto the bed with my clothes, hauled myself up, and then had another sudden thought — the baby's clothes.

Erika had sent over a few things to add to Anneke's layette. Suddenly I needed to wash everything: to feel the soft fabrics and care for the tiny clothes my baby would soon wear against his skin. It wasn't one of my scheduled laundry days, but after breakfast I'd rinse them out.

Breakfast! I dressed in a hurry, grabbed the baby clothes, and went downstairs. In the dining room, the air was soft with the rich scent of lilacs and the hushed chatter of round-bellied girls. I said hello to Eva, who was leaving, ate some bread with honey, talked with the girls who sat next to me — all without really paying any attention. There was still so much to do. I reminded myself to pack Neve's books with mine — maybe I could find a way to get her address. First, though, I had to find Sister Ilse. I didn't want anyone else in charge. I hadn't seen her for a few days, so maybe she was away — I'd go down to her station as soon as I finished the laundry.

In the laundry, I washed the baby things in the special mild soap used for newborns' clothing. The tiny sleeves, the little necks and fastenings, the embroidered hems, all gave me such pleasure. It dawned on me — I was nesting! It was one of the signs Leona had read to me from her booklet: *A sudden energy; a compulsion to clean and prepare things.* I hung up the little clothes and went back to my room, smiling to myself at this miracle . . . *birth was imminent.*

When I opened the door, I was still smiling. I'd be leaving this room soon. I would see my baby's face soon!

That was my last clear thought.

There — on my bed next to the jumble of clothes to pack — was the blue velvet bag.

Empty.

I stared at it, unable to understand. Then I fell on it and turned it over and over, turned it inside out, tore through the clothes on the bed, unable to believe. I hurried to the door and shut it. Then threw it open again. The hall was empty — a tunnel stretching away forever. At the end, impossibly far away, was the telephone.

I made myself walk out. Step after step, without feeling the floor, I hurried toward the telephone. When I got there, my hand shook so hard, I dropped the receiver. The crash echoed down the hall as I realized I didn't have Karl's number. My head cleared. Karl and Ilse. I could trust them both. I was not alone.

I went back to my room, steadying myself with these thoughts, and found Karl's number. On the way back to the phone, I passed Inge and her roommate. They nodded at me and Inge pressed on her back and groaned. They didn't know. Yet.

I dialed and it took forever for someone to answer. A man's voice, not Karl's.

But Karl came to the phone.

"Come *now.* They know!"

"Cyrla?"

"Come now! *Come now!*"

I dropped the phone. Even with my huge bulk, I ran down the stairs, ran to the delivery wing. At the main desk sat a nurse I had never seen. I asked for Sister Ilse.

"She's not here."

"Where is she?"

"She's gone. What do you need?"

My hands flew to my forehead — a sudden searing pain.

The nurse dipped her head to peer over her glasses. "What's wrong with you?"

I took a breath, forced my hands to my sides. No panic. "Nothing. I just want to ask her something. Could you tell me where she is?"

The nurse put down her paperwork and pushed herself back from the desk to inspect me. She crossed her arms over her chest; a silver mother's cross rode on her lapel, the swastika glaring at me from the center. "Sister Ilse's services were no longer needed. What did you want with her?"

"She had tea, she gave me tea," I mumbled, backing away.

"Come back."

I turned and kept walking.

"Come back here." The scrape of a chair. "What's your name?"

I was at the door, but I turned back. "Eva De Groot, 12B."

In the hallway, I realized I was out of ideas. I pushed through the door of the laundry room, hoping to steal a minute of quiet so I could think.

And in the laundry room was my salvation.

She was bent over the open washing machine, pulling clothes out, her back to me: the Little Brown Sister whose longing for Eva I'd interrupted. She was pregnant, her apron tied above her rounding waist. I did the unconscious calculation that came with living here: five or six months. The

Christmas party? How terrible, to have to give yourself to loud, rough men if what you craved was soft and quiet. Or had that made it easier?

She turned, her arms full of wet clothes, and caught her breath when she saw me. The wet laundry dropped to the floor.

I stood as tall as I could and faced her coldly. "Give me your cap."

Her eyes darted to the door. I stepped to block it. Her mouth worked as if she wanted to say something. I stuck my hand out, my eyes a dare.

She faltered and bit her lip. Then she unpinned her cap and gave it to me.

"And your apron."

I put on her things, never taking my eyes from her, keeping them hard. "I'm leaving here. You could sound an alert. But you won't. You do not want me back." Then I grabbed a basket and walked out. Out of the laundry room, down the hallway to the delivery door and out. Out onto the shadowless walk, down the walk straight out to the side entrance, where one guard stood, facing the street.

He heard my steps and turned. I nodded and lifted the basket, made a face as if to say, *Look what they've got me doing, and at my stage.* I flashed him a smile bright with sheer desperation.

And he smiled back.

He raised his hand — half wave, half salute. And he smiled. *People see what they expect to see. You just have to allow them to see it.*

I passed him — so close I was sure he could smell the sweat coursing down my back.

On the street, I headed away from the main gate. The instant my back was to the guard, my bravado vanished. The pavement shimmered dangerously, my legs threatened to buckle, the blood in my veins felt papery as though I were going to faint. With each step I imagined the guard's hands on my neck. I wanted to run but I forced myself to walk. To saunter. The sidewalk ran the length of the property — three hundred meters from the gate at least — until finally I could turn the corner onto the main street. There I dropped the basket and fell against the trunk of an elm, shaking hard.

I heard the sound of an engine; something rough — a jeep. I crossed the road and pressed myself into the privet hedge there. The branches tore at the skin of my arms and legs and the back of my neck — but they gave way. The shrubs were so dense they held me up — otherwise I might have collapsed. The jeep passed, four soldiers in it. It didn't slow down.

I wedged myself farther into the shrubbery. Of course they would find me, but if Karl came first . . . He would come. He had heard me and he would come.

I snapped off branches until I'd made a tunnel through the hedge to watch for him. The trip took forty minutes; if he had left immediately, he might be here soon. Before the dogs.

A truck passed. Two cars — not military. I watched, tense, my legs aching. There were no cars for a long while. Then the dairy cart, with its big metal cans of milk clanging. I eased myself down, felt the sharp branches scrape my legs. And then I heard it: the heavy, gliding purr of a Mercedes. The car was dark and sleek, but from this distance, through the branches, I couldn't tell anything else. I clawed closer to the pavement. No — it was two-toned gray, not black. The car roared by. Another jeep passed — this one braked as it turned the corner, as if it might be entering the home.

And then I heard it again — like an oiled growl, coming fast. I peered at the car — dark, dark enough to be black. It came closer and I saw the grille that always seemed to be leering. I scrambled out.

It was Karl.

SIXTY-ONE

"Drive!"

Karl drove. "What happened?"

"Drive!" I pitched myself over, my head almost on Karl's lap, out of sight, but I imagined the hot breath of wolves on my neck. *"Drive!"*

He drove, but it didn't feel fast enough. And then I felt him brake. I raised my head. We were turning onto the road to the sheep farm. "No. Keep driving!"

"Look behind us — do you see anyone coming? No one can see us."

"But —"

"Cyrla, you're nine months pregnant. We have to stop and think. Make a plan."

He parked behind the barn. "You're bleeding. What happened?" He began to dab at my face, but I brushed him off and got out and hurried inside. I made Karl close the barn door and slide the bolt. Then I made him open it again so I could keep watch.

"Cyrla, try to be calm. Did you ever tell anyone about this place?"

"No, but —"

"Neither did I. So it's safe. Sit down and tell me what happened."

He led me to the pile of feed bags he had stuffed with straw for us long ago and eased me down and held me. I told him everything that had happened, and he only nodded and asked questions and held me tighter. My eyes never left the barn door.

"All right," Karl said. He took out his handkerchief and began to clean my face gently, as if my scrapes were the worst thing that had happened and we had all the time in the world. He tipped my face back and began to dab at my neck.

I grabbed his hand. "Karl, they know. What am I going to do?"

"I don't know yet. For now, you're going to stay here and rest. I'll go find out what I can."

"Wait. You're leaving?"

"I have to. You'll be safe here. Get some water from the stream —"

"When can you come back?"

"There's a big cocktail party tonight. I'll have to make an appearance and be intro-duced around. It would be noticed if I weren't there. Afterward, they'll all be drinking and playing skat — I won't be missed then."

"Not until then?"

"No one will look for you here. Try to sleep. I'll find out what's going on. I'll come up with a plan."

He tried to rise, but I held his arm. "Karl, Eva found out. I have to leave."

"Maybe. Yes, probably. But not in broad daylight. I'll be back by eight. Go to the stream and get water. There might be strawberries by now — do you remember where we saw the plants? I have to go now."

He kissed me twice. Then he left.

When he was gone, a strange calm settled over me. Every hour or so I walked to the stream, drank cold water, found tiny wild strawberries, and ate them. But mostly I lay on the straw in the barn, thinking of all the other times I'd lain here, thinking of how this place more than any other was my home. Thinking of how I would never see it again. I plucked a tuft of wool from a post beside me and inhaled the scent of lanolin, knowing I would never wear a sweater again without thinking of Karl. Above me, swallows cut endless arcs to their nests in the eaves, leaving trails of dust motes swirling in their wake, witness to the exquisite grace of free things.

The baby kicked hard, demanding my attention. I lifted my blouse and followed the liquid wriggle of his course. Impatient. A foot appeared for an instant at the top of my swell — a perfect foot pressed against my skin, complete with the curve of five toes, like coffee beans under my skin. And then it was gone and he was still. After a while, I fell asleep. But I awoke to screaming, and it took a long time to realize the screams were mine. I didn't lie down again, I just sat with my arms wrapped around my belly, watching the sky change over the mountains.

Finally he was back.

He'd brought food — a loaf of bread and a can of peaches. "I'm sorry — it's all I could get at the commissary." I ate and Karl told me what he had learned. I listened calmly, as if he were talking about someone else.

"They came this afternoon. Had I known you were Jewish? Did I know you'd run away? I said no, acted shocked and betrayed. They watched me all day."

"Did they know I had called you?"

"I took care of it. I told the secretary that if my sister called again, to say I was too busy to come to the phone."

I put the can of peaches down. "What am

I going to do now?"

"You're going home to Holland. I'm taking you to the border."

I threw my arms around him. He held me tight while shudders of relief racked my body. I pulled back to look at him. "What about you?"

"I'll say I went looking for you. I'll play the betrayed lover. Beside myself with anger. I've thought it out."

"But —"

"No. You worry about yourself. Not about me." He passed me a thermos of tea. I drank a mouthful then handed it back. "If I drink it, we'll be stopping every twenty minutes. The baby's so big now. . . ."

"Will you be all right? You'll have to walk for a while."

I nodded. I had to be all right. "Are they looking for me?"

"No. They figure they'll get you when you try to cross the border. Even so, I don't want to leave until it's dark."

"How will I get across?"

Karl hesitated for just a second. "I'll explain when it's time."

"How close do you think you can get me?"

"Close. Don't worry about that part right now." He glanced at the sky. The clouds in the west were beginning to turn gold. "It'll be dark in half an hour. Cyrla . . . come and lie down with me. Tonight is the last time —"

"Don't." I pressed my fingertips to his lips. "Don't."

And we lay down and held each other one last time on our bed of straw. We kissed and caressed each other slowly, imprinting the memory of our bodies on our mouths and hands. As if we had all the time in the world. As if we would never see each other again.

Then we lay quietly, stealing the last moments, watching the heedless sky turn red and then deep violet. Karl raised himself beside me. He touched my cheek, then trailed his fingertips down my jaw, my neck, across my collarbone to my shoulder and then slowly down the length of my arm and over my hand. He pressed his palm to mine. "It's time," he said. And he broke our touch.

He got up and helped me to my feet. "Wait." He reached into his pocket and pulled out something small and round wrapped in tissue. "I was going to give it to you when the baby was born."

I opened it. Inside was a wooden sunflower head — the spiraling rows of tiny seeds and the curling petals carved in detail.

"Turn it over."

On the other side was another sunflower face.

We drove into the dark. Karl had a map marked with the checkpoints, and we kept to the small roads where the villages were as black as the forests. It seemed we were hurtling through a tunnel; in the green glow of the dashboard lights, the stubble of Karl's beard glinted like gold dust. When a half-moon rose, it lit everything outside with a thin silvery glow. The Rhine came into view — a shining thread leading to my home. All we had to do was follow it, and then . . .

But Karl wouldn't talk about that final piece — the way I would cross — except to tell me where. "We'll cut over at Bruggen. The forest is thick there. You'll end up in a small town south of Nijmegen — Beesel. Do you know it?"

"No."

"It's mostly farms. You'll probably have to stay there a few days before you can get to Leona's. You'll need a story for why you're out on foot, without papers, without luggage or money. I could give you some *Reichsmarks,* but that would be suspicious."

"I could say my house was bombed. That's what I was planning to say when I thought I was going to run in April."

"A bombing raid. That's good. That will explain the cuts. They won't find out if it's true or not for a day or two."

"Where should I say it happened?"

"Maybe Nijmegen. You could say you took a train from there. They'll ask about your family, though — they'll expect you to try to reach a relative. You'll have to say you have no one."

"I have no one," I repeated.

"And your husband —"

"I have a husband?"

"You did. He was a soldier. He was killed months ago."

"You're killing off my husband? Just like that?"

Karl shrugged. "He fought bravely."

"He fought bravely."

"But you never loved him."

"But I never loved him. Wait . . . what?"

"You couldn't love him because you were always in love with a boatbuilder from Germany. A very handsome man."

"I was, was I?"

"Yes. Stop laughing, it was very serious. Very romantic. You met him in a bakery. It was love at first sight. You felt as if there was a fine light around him, setting him apart for you."

"Love at first sight?"

523

"Yes. And lust. It was all you could do not to tear your clothes off and throw yourself at him."

"It's strange," I mused. "I don't remember that part."

Karl nodded sagely. "It probably embarrasses you too much."

"That's probably it."

It was good to laugh. Everything real was so grim. I looked across at Karl. His face was so beautiful to me, so precious. "I love you," I told him.

"I love you," he said.

For the next few hours, we talked of nothing painful or dangerous. We exchanged stories of our childhoods — only the happy memories, as if wrapping ourselves in each other's histories would keep us safe. I asked Karl to tell me more about the trips he and Erika had taken to Italy, and I told him about a vacation my father and mother had taken me on the year before she'd gotten ill.

The hours flew by with the landscape. Not quickly enough. Too quickly.

Around three-thirty, Karl stopped the car by a field; the flat landscape under the moonlight called to me. Familiar. Beyond the field stood a wood of evergreens.

"Karl, look."

Icicles dripped from the branches. Of course it wasn't ice on such a warm night. It looked as if the whole forest had been decorated for Christmas, with millions of silver streamers shimmering in the moonlight. I got out of the car to stare in wonder.

"Tinsel?" I asked, incredulous, as Karl came up beside me. *"Eis-Lametta?"*

"No, it's tinfoil. They drop it from planes to interfere with radio signals."

"Bombing raids?"

"Yes."

"We're close to the border?"

Karl pointed into the forest. My chest tightened. I wasn't prepared. I would never be prepared. "Is it time? Do you want me to go?"

"No. I want you to get into the car."

I reached for the door, relieved.

"No. Get in the back." Karl's voice had changed. I turned to question him. His eyes had changed also. "Get in the backseat and lie down."

"But —"

"Just do it. Trust me."

I lay down on the seat. Karl opened the trunk, pulled out a blanket and threw it over me. Then he got into the car and started the engine and pulled back onto the road.

I sat up and pulled the blanket around

me. Our blanket. It smelled of hay and safety, but I didn't feel safe now. "Trust me," he'd said. I did, but in the dashboard lights I had seen the muscles of his neck and jaw harden. He was driving fast now. We passed a sign for Bruggen. And then the sign for the border checkpoint.

"Karl, stop. Those lights — that's the border."

"Get down!"

He didn't stop. The gears strained as we accelerated. I tried to raise myself up again, but Karl sensed it and threw his arm back over me, hard.

"Stay down."

And still he didn't stop. He picked up speed. Harsh light flashed over us, and I heard the splintering of wood and the scrape of metal, then glass smashing as we crashed through the barrier. Still he didn't stop; I pressed myself into the seat now, frozen, as we hurtled into the darkened countryside. Into Holland.

After a few moments I felt the car brake. I sat up. Before I could ask anything, Karl pulled the car to the side of the road and turned around to face me.

"You must run now. *Now.* You have to trust me." He reached to the floor and pulled out a liquor bottle. He opened it and poured some down his throat then spilled the rest over his uniform and the floor, his eyes to the rearview mirror. "Go! *Go!*" His voice was harsh. But in the mirror, I could see his face was streaming with tears.

Behind us, faintly, the wail of a siren. A second one joined it, as if in sympathy.

Karl got out and pulled open my door, dragged me to my feet on the road. *"Go!"* He held me tight, then pushed me away. "Follow this road until you come to a farmhouse that feels safe. Stay behind the trees. Go. Don't turn around. Go now!"

I stumbled away, splitting in two: my legs carrying my child toward safety, my heart bleeding in the road. I made it to the shoulder, then slipped down the bank to a culvert overhung with pines, scrambling to catch my footing and skidding the rest of the way. I felt a rip as if my womb were wrenching away from my spine, and I curled in a heap under the boughs. I wrapped my arms around my baby, trying to hold on to the world.

A light grew along the road from the distance. Sirens screamed closer. *Run to me,* I begged Karl silently, but he only turned his face to the trees where I was hidden, raised his arms, and locked his fingers together. The pieces fit.

And then they were on him. I lay in the muddy ditch and watched as two cars and a jeep skidded to circle him. Soldiers ran from each, shouting, guns and lights drawn. Karl stood calmly at the center of the chaos. He held his arms out straight, giving his wrists up to them. For the briefest second as they bound his hands behind him, in the arcing beam of a flashlight, I thought I saw the faint curve of a smile on his lips. Then they dragged him away, past the headlights, and I couldn't see his face anymore, only his silhouette. With a fine light edging him.

Setting him apart for me.

SIXTY-TWO

September 1947

I am standing at the doorstep, my knuckles raised, my arm suddenly weak, after circling the block three times trying to prepare myself. So much is at stake. I knock.

It's Erika. I know this at once. Her face is older than I would have thought and more broken, but in it I see his. For a split second, the shadow of fear races across her eyes — it's the same fear I feel every time there's an unexpected knock at my door. Then it passes — *No, it's over.* She stares at me. Behind her, a little girl runs past and then, seeing the open door and the strangers on the step, comes to hide behind her mother's knees.

"Cyrla?" the woman asks. We have never met. But she knows.

Our hands fly to our mouths like twin birds, our eyes fill with tears, and we both stand there, overwhelmed. It's the girls who

529

break the frozen tableau. Lina twists her head around her mother's hip and smiles shyly, flirting with Anneke — the very image of the baby in the photograph I saw five years ago. Anneke holds her arm out straight, offering the stuffed rabbit she always carries. I have never seen her offer it before.

Erika and I gasp at the same time, and she steps out to embrace me. We can't form words and for a moment we don't need to. But only for a moment.

"Is he here?"

She pulls back and shakes her head. "No."

Before the word is out of her mouth, I am trying to divine its meaning.

"Come in, Cyrla," she says. "Come in." She smiles and my heart beats again.

We embrace once more in the hallway and then we say all the usual things . . . the words that try to express what words can't express. She leads me to a small parlor and tells me to sit down while she makes tea. As I look around the room, I regret my decision to dress up. My feathered hat, Anneke's big lemon-colored bow, make the flat look shabbier. Things have been harder for them here. I stand again and cross to a wall of framed photographs. There he is as a baby, there he is as a boy with a new bicycle, as a young man beside the ribs of a boat. In each — even the baby picture — his twin sister is beside him, looking up at him adoringly. There are none of him in uniform.

All the while I am drinking in his face, I am able to concentrate on only one thing. He's not here . . . But she'd smiled.

When she comes back into the room, she apologizes for not having anything to offer me with the tea.

I can't wait. Civility was lost years ago. "Where is he?"

She puts the tray down on the side table and picks up a letter beside it. She hands it to me. I look at the return address, my knees so weak now I wish I were sitting.

And then I smile, too. "So he's all right?"

"Yes, he's all right." Erika's expression changes, becomes unreadable. "No, of course he's not all right. He spent three years in Dachau."

She hands me my tea and we sit together on the single sofa. "No one is all right now," she says. "How could we be?"

We sit for a moment with that unanswerable question. I wait. She sees from my face that I must hear everything.

"They broke his hands so he couldn't build things anymore. Then they worked him nearly to death. I didn't recognize him when he got off the train, he was so thin. I walked right past him, searching the platform, and he had to call out to me. For a long time after, he barely spoke. Our mother died, and I think it was from a broken heart."

Through it all, the girls play at our feet. I hear Lina tell about a dog she had, a very heroic dog. I can tell she never had such a dog, never had a pet. She brings out a box of paper dolls and explains to my daughter the strict rules about how each must be dressed. Somehow Anneke understands, although she doesn't know German, and she allows this bossiness, something she wouldn't do at home. Every now and then, Lina reaches to touch her mother's knee, and once she climbs up onto the sofa, sits for a moment with her head in her mother's lap. It was much worse for them here.

"Does he blame me?"

"Blame you? Oh, no. That's not how he sees it. Karl thinks you saved his life. Without you, his life wouldn't have been worth saving. That's how he puts it."

"And now? What is his life now?"

She tells me and I close my eyes, picturing it. "Is he —"

She glances at my left hand. "Married? No."

I feel my relief burn a blush across my face.

Erika reaches down and strokes Anneke's blond curls. "Karl always worried about her. He's going to be so happy to hear. Where did you have her?"

"I went into labor the next day. The farmhouse I went to that night — it was a good choice, thank God. They took me in without asking any questions. I stayed six months."

"Karl searched for you. He tried everything to find you."

I almost break down at this. "I've been searching, too."

"How did you find us?"

"I looked in Munich first. No Karl Getz. Well, there were — but none were him." I pause, overwhelmed by the inadequacy of these words. So many street corners. So many registries and so many clerks. *Look again. Please. Look again.*

"*Ja,*" she said. "It's still so hard to find people."

"After that, I came to Hamburg. All I knew was that he had grown up outside of Hamburg somewhere on the Elbe. I searched every village on the river — I've been here almost a month. I asked about Karl. I asked about you. And then I asked about Lina."

The little girl's head turns at the mention of her name. She studies her mother and then me, decides there's no risk, then goes back to her dolls.

"I went to every school in every town along the river. I didn't know your last name, but I asked for a little girl of six named Lina, with a mother named Erika. And an uncle. No luck. Until today. Lina's teacher didn't want to give me your address at first, but I convinced her. I told her the girls were related."

"They almost were. No, they *are,*" Erika says. "Karl searched for months. He wrote to every town in the Netherlands. He didn't think to look in England."

I look up, surprised, until I remember that my daughter has spoken a few words. "Yes, England. I've been working in an orphanage there."

"How did you get there?" she asks.

"I went to Isaak's synagogue as soon as I could. I had to find out."

Erika leans over and covers my hand with hers. "Isaak? The father? Is he. . . ."

I shake my head and look away, waiting for the tears to fill my eyes and then retreat. "Buchenwald."

"I'm sorry."

I wait until the tightness in my throat eases. I didn't go to the shed. I will be haunted by that forever. "He had taken care of things for me before he . . . new papers, complete identification. I was a woman with connections in England. With those, I was able to get passage. Isaak hadn't counted on the baby — he thought I would be leaving months before she was born — so that was difficult, but I managed. Well, it doesn't matter now."

Only one thing matters now. In this room, I'm so close to him, at last. But not close enough.

I lift a letter. "May I?" I take a pen and a little notebook from my purse and copy down the return address.

"He'll be so happy. You'll write at once?"

"No. I'm not going to write."

She looks at me, puzzled. "But he should know. He deserves to know."

"I need to see his face. I need to see what's in his eyes that first moment." Because I've remembered the last thing Anneke told me — what I would find in them if he were the one. Erika is a woman. She understands. Anneke and I make our good-byes and then get back on a tram for Hamburg. It's still early enough. We ask directions to the nearest travel agency.

■ ■ ■ ■

"I can get you berths on a steamer on the nineteenth."

"No," I decide suddenly. "We must leave tomorrow."

The woman checks a schedule, a register. "It will cost a lot more, such short notice."

The tickets cost almost all the money I have left.

My first view of him, after all this time: at the keel of a sailboat, his skin the same color as the sleek wood gleaming in the hot sun. He bends to dip a brush into a pail of varnish. I remember him bent over exactly like this, in the parlor in Steinhöring. I know his back now. And even at this distance, I can see what they did to his hands. I walk closer, the sand silencing my steps. I can barely breathe, but I hold Anneke and wait, whispering to her to be still.

She can't. Where I see only one thing, she sees water in a color she's never known before, black and white birds tumbling in a line along the shore, palm trees — which must look like giant green umbrellas waving to her — spilling from the cliffs.

I drop her to the sand and she runs.

He straightens, watches her. I imagine he's

smiling faintly, as people do. I imagine he's picturing Lina there at the shore, picking up shells. Then, as people do when they see a child alone, he scans the beach for a caretaker. Children can't be left alone.

He turns.

I have a sudden instant of panic: We have been apart so long! People can be lost to each other in so many ways . . .

The brush drops from his hand.

And in his eyes I see my home.

AUTHOR'S NOTE

THE LEBENSBORN ORGANIZATION

The birthrate in Germany had plummeted after the First World War — the male population had been decimated, the country was in financial ruin, and abortion was available, although illegal. In 1935 Heinrich Himmler set up the Lebensborn (Wellspring or Fountain of Life) Organization, under the umbrella of the Nazi SS Race and Resettlement Office, whose goal was to increase the population of the "Master Race."

The program consisted of three phases. First was a massive public-relations campaign to encourage all "racially valuable" women and girls to have as many children as possible, with or without the benefit of marriage. It was not uncommon for fanaticized German girls as young as fifteen to have relations with SS men in order to present their country with new citizens and future soldiers. Maternity homes were set up throughout Germany, mostly in confiscated Jewish spas, resorts, and villas, where girls and women could go through their pregnancies and give birth in comfort, secrecy, and safety.

The second phase was an expansion of the program to occupied countries. Maternity homes were set up where "suitably Aryan" girls pregnant by occupying forces could have their babies. These children were considered German citizens at birth and were taken to be raised in Nazi homes or institutions. In all, homes were set up in seven countries, but girls from virtually every Western European country, including the British Channel Islands, were involved and lost their children.

The third phase consisted of the wholesale kidnapping of children from eastern occupied countries — over 200,000 children from Poland alone. The vast majority were never returned to their families after the war.

Mothers who had given birth in Lebensborn homes who tried to find their children after the war were unable to; records were deliberately kept secret and, in many cases, destroyed. Babies and children still in the Lebensborn homes or in orphanages or institutions were often abandoned. In the occupied countries, these children bore the stigma of their conception and suffered from neglect and abuse. Disproportionate numbers of them grew up autistic or were incorrectly labeled as mentally deficient and institutionalized. Even today, as older adults, they suffer elevated rates of depression, alcoholism, and suicide.

The tragedy of the Lebensborn experience is incalculable and affected women and children across Europe. Yet it remains one of the least-known aspects of World War II history.

ACKNOWLEDGMENTS

A book is never written alone. For six years, whenever I mentioned the project I was working on, people invariably responded, "I might be able to help you" — during the writing of this book, I discovered as much about human generosity as I did about the history I was researching. Because I had so much to learn before I could tell the story, I am indebted to literally hundreds of people; it would be impossible to thank them all, but I would be remiss not to try.

First, I wish to thank the Virginia Center for the Creative Arts. For three years, they have granted me fellowships during which I worked on major parts of this book. By providing space, freedom from responsibilities, and a supportive environment, they created for me a heaven — the safe place from which I could write along the borders of hell. For the same reason, I wish also to thank the Ragdale Foundation and the

Vermont Studio Center, each of which granted me a residency during which I worked on this book.

Tom Gallen. We took a walk, you mentioned the Lebensborns and then patiently answered my questions about them . . . seven years later, look what's come of that. My writing group . . . words fail. Maureen Hourihan, Rose Connors, Pauline Grocki, Penny Haughwaut . . . smart, talented, bighearted women who nourish and inspire and inform me week after week, and then do me the enormous favor of cutting the crap out of my pages.

Shana Deets, poetess and force of nature, who generously provided the poetry and the poet's soul of my character. In the same manner, Brad Pease, of Pease Boat Works in Chatham, MA — who answered my many questions about boatbuilding and, more important, gave me an insight into the passionate heart of someone who loves the art. Thank you to Harm de Blij, the renowned geographer and historian, who sat in my living room and painted pictures of Occupied Holland for me. Thank you to so many people who — in person, in their books and diaries and online journals — shared their memories when that was difficult. Pauline and Siggi, especially . . . I hope you smile when you see the details you contributed. And thank you to the Netherlands Institute for War Documentation for their careful read and their insightful feedback.

In my research I drew on a great deal of resources and historical matter; these are a few of those which I found most helpful: "Hitler's Perfect Children," a video from the History Channel, transcript: 20/20, air date: 00/04/26; *Wartime Encounter with Geography* by Harm de Blij, The Book Guild Ltd, 2000; *Of Pure Blood,* by Marc Hillel and Clarissa Henry, Pocket Books, 1978; *The Holocaust Chronicle,* various contributing authors, Publications International, Ltd., 2000; *Master Race* by Catrine Clay and Michael Leapman, Hodder & Stoughton, Ltd.; *WWII — Time-Life Books History of the Second World War,* Prentice Hall Trade, 1989.

So many readers to thank: the wonderful writers Anne LeClaire, who looked at the rough pieces I had in the beginning and told me she believed I could do this thing, and Jackie Mitchard, who took a look at the end and told me she believed that I had. The Tideline Writers for weighing in with wisdom on many of the chapters; Jebba, Ginny, and Ann for doing the same for the book as a whole.

And then it was a manuscript . . . which it would be still if it weren't for my agent, Steven Malk. As always, I am so grateful for your belief in me and for your integrity, and for what a relief it is to be able to hand over a stack of pages and know that you will see it as a book. Thank you next to Jenna Johnson, my editor at Harcourt, who took a chance on the possibility and then wisely showed me the final form this novel should take . . . it's been a pleasure.

And finally, my love and gratitude to my children, Caleb and Hillary — for all the times I was writing this book instead of being with them. And for everything else.

We hope you have enjoyed this Large Print book. Other Thorndike, Wheeler, and Chivers Press Large Print books are available at your library or directly from the publishers.

For information about current and upcoming titles, please call or write, without obligation, to:

Publisher
Thorndike Press
295 Kennedy Memorial Drive
Waterville, ME 04901
Tel. (800) 223-1244

or visit our Web site at:

http://gale.cengage.com/thorndike

OR

Chivers Large Print
published by BBC Audiobooks Ltd
St James House, The Square
Lower Bristol Road
Bath BA2 3SB
England
Tel. +44(0) 800 136919
email: bbcaudiobooks@bbc.co.uk
www.bbcaudiobooks.co.uk

All our Large Print titles are designed for easy reading, and all our books are made to last.